MW00896302

# THE MAD PROFESSOR

Also by Rupert Schmitt

The Interview and Other Poems by Rupert Schmitt
Published by iUniverse 2008

# THE MAD PROFESSOR

*A novel by*
## RUPERT SCHMITT

iUniverse, Inc.
Bloomington

The Mad Professor
A Novel

Copyright © 2011 by Rupert Schmitt

All rights reserved. No part of this book may be used or reproduced by any means, graphic, electronic, or mechanical, including photocopying, recording, taping or by any information storage retrieval system without the written permission of the publisher except in the case of brief quotations embodied in critical articles and reviews.

This is a work of fiction. All of the characters, names, incidents, organizations, and dialogue in this novel are either the products of the author's imagination or are used fictitiously.

iUniverse books may be ordered through booksellers or by contacting:

iUniverse
1663 Liberty Drive
Bloomington, IN 47403
www.iuniverse.com
1-800-Authors (1-800-288-4677)

Because of the dynamic nature of the Internet, any web addresses or links contained in this book may have changed since publication and may no longer be valid. The views expressed in this work are solely those of the author and do not necessarily reflect the views of the publisher, and the publisher hereby disclaims any responsibility for them.

Cover by Erik Schmitt Studio 1500sf
Back cover by Studio 1500sf

ISBN: 978-1-4502-8840-8 (sc)
ISBN: 978-1-4502-8841-5 (ebk)

Printed in the United States of America

iUniverse rev. date: 02/04/2011

## To Jean Gant

And in memory of Otto Greubel who lost his job teaching German at the University of Wisconsin during World War I

Special Thanks to Claire Phillips, Pat Johnson, Wendee Cloutier, Lois Linblad, Marjorie Hillson, Susan Watkins, Luther Nichols, Ina Smith, Rita Kepner & John Matthesson & the editorial Staff of iUniverse. Curriculum advisors Jim Pierce, Bonnie Robinett, and Rick Emry.

# TABLE OF CONTENTS

# PREFACE

This is my story. My name is Leo Bauer. As a boy my parents told me my ankles were too weak to skate Wisconsin's ice. Now these ankles are mountain trail stalkers. Oh I love when my hair catches wind as if pulled by electricity from the clouds. There is tangled wire over my wind cave chest. I admit it. I howl on the trail, in the canoe, in the water, in coition. Like all men my voice is resonant when confident, when in active exhalation. When mind lashed, crushed and mocked my voice is a thin sad echo. Poor baby. Don't you feel sorry for me? Just because I mentioned coition, don't get your hopes up. This book is not about sex. If you want to read about sex go somewhere else.

I weigh one fourteenth of a ton no matter what the season. It's been the same since puberty. Now you have to go to your dictionary and calculator. You might ask. A British or American ton? What do you think?

My brain projects storms, eddies, and tranquil ponds. Occasional electron blips fall up. I have otterflash eyes. I like to think I crack taboos like eggs. Sometimes needing resuscitation I seek an alchemic team to gather a reverse storm of earth, fire, water and air. Friendly ladies, men and children chanting and dancing cause flowers to bloom and I rise up, spin, twirl and fly.

Throughout my life unbelievers have threatened my existence. Bits

1

and pieces of me have died and will continue to die until just before I die, there may be nothing left except a shell. How can you have a hero in a shell? Turtles have carapaces and snails spirals. Take your pick. Grab a baker's dozen and I'll slap your hand.

# CHAPTER 1.

# BIRTH AND EARLY LIFE

I was born in the shadow of a burnished copper beer cooker while Aries watched and Orion laughed. I lived in a big new Tudor style orange brick house on a maple shaded quiet street. Thirteen million people were out of work. It was 1932. Life was a bowl of cherries.

In the second grade a nun trapped me for the crime of daydreaming. My mind was outside. I was playing with Scallopini. Running through the forest. Giggling when my face was licked by my wet nosed curly haired black cocker spaniel. I was sitting in my seat giggling when my hand, my arm were grabbed, yanked, I was dragged to that closet, the door flung open, I was tossed inside to be locked in grey fuzz. Furious I kicked, smashed the door with my fist, yelled, then quieted. Catlike I reached along a smooth shelf and swept onto the floor poster paper, drawing paper, lined paper, paper clips, file cards, ink, glue, scissors, knives, chalk, crayons, poster paint, string, twine, tacks, pins, rulers, and pictures of the Virgin Mary and Jesus. Unscrewed the glue. Made my first collage on the floor of Jesus, the Virgin Mary, and pages from the Baltimore Catechism, the main textbook for the teaching of Catholic doctrine.

Suddenly there was light. The door opened. I looked into the nun's blackness. Afraid to look up, I waited staring into the darkness of my religion.

Sister Cecilia glared at crumpled torn papers, wet ink and paint drying over Jesus.

Terrified I was grabbed, squeezed against starched whiteness, shivering dragged kicking, scratching and swearing to the office. The mother superior called my father. "We can't handle the boy."

Immediately after my expulsion I was sent to public school. I felt as if I was submerged in a haze of gnats. I tried to do what I was supposed to do. Often reproached, rarely praised, I dreaded school, classmates and my father. Time was spent in fields and woods with my black cocker spaniel Scallopini. I petted him, he was my salvation. I looked at leaves and was aware that my God was sky, grass, trees and Scallopini.

The other God was false. Church on Sundays: Talcumed ladies made me sneeze. I hated that perfumed powder. Father Kelly preached love. I remembered God's bride, Cecilia and Mother Superior Greta. While the priest gave his sermon, under my breath I said, "Father Kelly, you aren't talking to me. You tell the parishioners, 'Attend mass every Sunday. Be good Catholics. Confess your sins. Don't worship false gods. Honor your father and mother. Give money to the church.' "Father Kelly, What is God's Message for me?"

After the service people gathered on the wide concrete patio. I joined the other boys and listened to the altar boys telling dirty jokes. I tried to grin. Tried to grin.

I did not tell my parents or the priest my God was nature. I was not like other boys who discovered great truths. Unlike Joseph Smith I never found plates of gold carved by the tongue of God. Angels never spoke to me, not even once. I didn't know how to translate foreign tongues. I was not a boy priest. Just a kid trying to survive: After the trouble I began to speak to Scallopini. I talked to the trees, sky, rivers, spiders and moss. Fortunately I lived near forests. In a big city I may have been unable to speak.

If I had been caught talking to rivers, lakes, bushes, and assorted weeds, the act would have been interpreted as an indication of derangement and they might have sent me to a psychiatrist.

My logorrhea spouted forth as poetry, speeches, monologues, and dialogues. I said, "Tree, I love you. Sky, in you the birds fly. That is why you are. I love the dirt. I love beetles crawling in the soil. I love rain falling on my head."

My words were recorded on atoms of the air, in the movement of the wind, on falling raindrops, and on forest mold. Words written in such a fashion may have been the words of madness. The sane reader is advised to read no further.

Those afflicted with insanity may find meaning in this book, but this is doubtful. It is impossible to imagine words written on the wind to have meaning for anyone other than the wind.

When the moon was full my dog and I looked at the glowing sphere and howled, "OOOOOOOOOOOOOOOOOOOOOOOOOOOOOOOWWW."

I tried to talk to my classmates. They were too busy to listen to my crazy rambling. Sometimes they would encircle me and spit in my face and hair. They would laugh when I cried. When in retaliation I threw rocks at them they said, "You're really going to get it now." They piled on me and pushed my face in the gritty soil, or turned me over and rapidly patted my belly until it was pink and sore, or twisted my thin arms, one fist clamped rotating one way, another fist clamped rotating the other way. After they walked away in a group laughing, I would wipe my face, get up, and stumble crying into the woods. The boys never mocked me when Scallopini was by my side. I guess they didn't want to get bitten.

I learned that if I wanted to talk to other children I had to find one boy alone. Then there could be conversation and sometimes we would play. But if another boy would come over and join us I lost out. They would go off and play and I would be excluded. I could never understand why this happened. I tried to be included, I even showed off by climbing trees and swinging from branches; risking my life for attention.

A few people, especially my sister, listened and praised me for having a fantastic imagination. My mother said, "Leo, you're a good boy." She enjoyed gardening with me. We especially liked to see green shoots exposed and fragile in the bright spring light and to smell lilies of the valley.

My father liked having me by his side when he cleared land of brush. Face sweating, smeared with dirt, he watched me clipping small bushes near the roots, sticking with the job until it got dark. Then, hands sore, we went inside and ate dinner. Sometimes I went fishing with my dad and berry picking with my mother My oldest sister taught me a wild dance and my brother taught me to swim the breast stroke and the crawl. I would have liked to learn the butterfly, but only my brother could do that. On holidays our family got together with relatives and my aunts fawned over me. Worried because I was thin; they tried to feed me more than anyone else. I devoured homemade rolls smelling of yeast, rare roast beef, turkey, and thick sweet pecan pie. And my relatives said lots of nice things about me. So childhood was not all grim and bad. And when I played one to one with other children, I often laughed and had much fun. As I got older I became more clever and learned to conceal my imagination, unless I found myself with someone who also had crazy ideas. Perhaps this is why I went to college.

# CHAPTER 2.

## COLLEGE AND A FENDER BENDER

Utah State University sits expansively on a bench of the eroded rough Wasatch Mountains. Adjacent to and yet below the campus is the small town of Logan. To the West is the duck marshed cow pastured Cache Valley. Against the horizon lies the low gentle Wellsville Mountain Range. It is 1956.

Pungent scents rise from the yellow sunflowers, bushy junipers and sagebrush in the warming May sun. Horned larks sing, undulating the balsam sweet air.

A blurred spinning shape rolls along the Wellsville Mountains. One of my hobbies is cartwheeling. Let us go back in time and watch as I, young Leo, spin through flower fields, stirring up dust on the drying trail. Reaching the crest, I seem to hover in the air, the warm shimmering air, watching a spiraling red tailed hawk. I cannot talk when I am cartwheeling. I am not a multi-tasker. It is therefore up to you, the reader, to describe what is happening. Listen. Dogs are barking in the valley. Can you hear, listen to those far off cars. Look at the canals. Long lines of Lombardy poplars like torches mark the clear water canals flowing to rich Mormon fields.

That night in my Quonset hut student housing I wrote in my journal:

I am not part of the Mormon culture. In Wisconsin I cartwheeled a canoe. I cartwheeled a motor scooter as a soldier in France. I cartwheeled Montana along the Continental Divide past marmots, glacier lilies and elephant flowers without taking the time to stop and say hello to the flower field root rooting snooting grizzly bears.

I discover another way to cartwheel in June. On the way to school I collide with another Chevrolet. Furious I stomp my way to the other car's driver yelling, "Look what you've done to my car."

She cries, says "I'm sorry." Tears fall. Her hair becomes ripe wheat in the sunlight.

Repentant monster, I say, "I'm so sorry. Can we meet tonight to discuss our minor problem? Perhaps we can have a beer and decide what to do. Oh what should we do?"

She brightens. Gives me her name, Cleo, and phone number. Unable to withstand beauty, I fall in love. At our meeting, we dance, kiss, forget about the damaged fender.

In the beginning we date every night. I praise her looks, saying, "You are beautiful." She says, "you are a smart man."

On weekends and on other days, after classes are over, we take a jug of wine, cheese, French bread, and a blanket up one of the forested canyons near Logan. Somewhere in literature was written something like a glass of wine, bread and thou. Perhaps that is in the bible. Surrounded by flowers, listening to a creek, we kiss; I love seeing her lips glistening from the red wine. I plunge my nose into her clean fresh hair, inhaling deeply, burrowing as if I am a ground squirrel. She gently caresses my back saying, "My strong lion." We visit every place to dance or to sit, talk and drink beer in Northern Utah, Southern Idaho, and Southwestern Wyoming. Of course we marry. It is 1958. Parents and friends congratulate us. Cleo and I are a perfect couple.

We have friends, who like us, live for the mountains, the river and literature. On weekends we all go into the canyon, drink beer, fish and hike. Hemingway is our favorite author. Each of our walls holds a photograph of that virile man with a magnificent white beard.

I talk about snowflakes, moss and water falling from icicles and my listeners give me time and attention. I possess power. My love of nature is infectious. One friend, an art major, and another a literature major, switch to biology because of my influence. And the land, animals and plants are sacred to all of us.

At this time Cleo and I are into astronomy. We are at a star party on Prophet's Table, a mesa in southern Utah. While she is looking through a friend's telescope at the Andromeda Spiral Galaxy, I wander off to pee from the top of a cliff. Looking for shooting stars, I finish my task and listen. There is a grinding sound, as if someone is sharpening an ax on a grindstone. Peering carefully over the cliff I see a flash. Something is grinding the rocks. I notice circular objects heading directly into the face of the cliff, grinding their way through hard rock, producing flurries of bright orange sparks.

Cleo is incredulous when I tell her what I saw. "You saw what? A shower of sparks that illuminated the cliff, illuminated the trees? An animal that cuts through stone? You've got to be kidding. You've got some dope. Come on. Share. What's yours is mine, what's mine is yours."

I say, "No booze, no drugs, I saw little spinning animals cutting through the rocks."

She says, "Did you smell sulfur burning?"

I say, "As a matter of fact there was the smell of sulfur in the air."

Cleo says, "Andromeda is twice the size of the Milky Way. In 3 billion years the galaxies will collide."

My discovery of the rock grinding Swirlopeds gave me a subject to study later one when I went to graduate school.

Before we have a chance to fully mine the mother lode of our romance, in November of 1959 we have a son Karl. Huh. I wonder how that happened? The same thing happens with our friends. Love, marriages, pregnancies, births, all the while we, the husbands, are taking classes: Then we all graduate and rarely see each other again.

I apply to six graduate schools. Intermountain University offers me a teaching assistantship at two thousand dollars a year for half time work. The move to Montana is easy. We have few possessions. We rent a house in Missoula close to the campus. I walk to my classes. Explore Rattlesnake Park, and the wilder snaggly area adjacent to Rattlesnake Creek. We are wildly optimistic.

My graduate school committee asks me, "Leo, what area of science do you dislike the most?" In all honesty I say, "I hate physics."

The zoology professors, with infinite wisdom, determine that I need a year of freshman physics. First term I receive a C, second term a D. Recognizing a trend, at the start of the third quarter I meet with the teacher. My heart speeds up as I tell him (he is younger than I), "I do not like physics. In fact, I hate physics."

Assuming the visage of an elderly wise man he says, "You are older than the other students Leo. You should set an example. You should set a good example."

Looking in his evil athlete's eyes I say, "I do not like the way you teach physics. You are a terrible teacher. All we do is memorize. You should stick to teaching football. That's your real skill, football. I'm dropping this course." My voice is quivering. His huge face reddens. He has an ugly mole on his chin.

He says, "You won't get your degree without physics."

Fortunately the footballer teaching assistant is wrong. The D is not computed with my graduate grades because it is a freshman course. I never tell the so-called teacher my main objection to the course. Some of my students in biology were my classmates in physics. The corrected weekly exams were left on a table in the hallway for the students to pickup. Each week, my students saw my abysmal grades. They must have thought I was a dummy.

Unwilling to complain to Cleo I write in my journal:

I am a rotting tree that can be blown over by any wind. The trap of existence closes. Not even a scream leaves the throat of the condemned. I wait for life to be good. I'd like to go to Mediterranean beaches and meet laughing people. Even Cleo has been frowning. The world is like a rotting orange covered with human aphids. When dry, the seeds will rattle as the shell floats through space (Actually the seeds in dried out oranges and lemons do not rattle).

While Cleo is visiting her brother in San Francisco I write:

Dearest Cleo: I miss you and Karl. Friends are unknown in this arid graduate school where everything is done because I'm supposed to do it, not because I want to do it.

Professors give me a cynical critical eye. Looking for weeds, they think they are gardeners and I am a weed.

It is impossible to lead a normal life. Today at a shopping center, on the parking lot, I saw a bobcat on the end of a rope. The bobcat was spinning in a wild kaleidoscope of claws. I feel like that bobcat.

You are my life. I miss bouncing Karl on my lap. It is neat when he giggles. Hurry back. I need you. I need some giggles. I love you.

Before going to bed I write:

There is a storyteller in space. People cross the starry universe to listen but no one can find him. Because he lives in a vacuum, no one could listen if they would find him. He continues to tell his stories, and people continue to try to hear him.

I conclude: It is all right to talk with myself.

A few more words: GRADUATE SCHOOL

Who goes to graduate school? I ask you. Why are we here?

To prove ourselves, that's why. It is probable that the most insecure are the people who go all the way. Then, cloaked with a Ph.D. they determine the destiny of others who are seeking security and success.

The professors show the world a false face. They wobble through hallways crowded with students seeking and scrabbling for watermelon wisdom.

(Editor's note: This essay shows much irrationality; this was characteristic of Bauer, especially at the end of an evening of beer drinking. The computer indicates that malt beverages produced the essay, which continues):

We have the rights and responsibilities of a chain gang. Our weapon is a stone age skull used to break the rocks of knowledge into bits that we examine like monkeys seeking fleas. If we persist, these particles of knowledge will someday be magnified, described and published in journals read by no one.

One of our fellows, you know who, was told by the elders, "My boy, we have decided you are not graduate school material."

The student got angry, a strange response for someone whose career is over: He slammed the door. The glass broke. I was in the hallway.

Later, over coffee in the faculty lounge, I overheard his teachers say, "Can you imagine. The clod became angry when we told him he didn't have it. He mumbled something about three years of study and research down the drain. He snorted when we offered him a masters degree, and ran out the door."

Actually, the graduate program in zoology is quite progressive. I memorized much significant information.

In Ichthyology I studied fin rays, lateral lines, scales, tails and skulls. After boiling a skull each of us separated and labeled each bone. There were hundreds of bones.

During examinations student eyes and nostrils perceived dozens of bleached formaldehyde perfumed fish swimming in black trays.

For the reader's intellectual edification some of the correct answers follow:

*Rajidae, Raja binoculata*
*Chimaeridae, Hydrolagus collei*
*Salmonidae, Salmo salar, Salmo trutta, Salmo gairdnerii,*

Unfortunately, possessing an atrocious memory, I forgot the scientific names soon after the examination. However, in later years, while trying to remember someone's name, suddenly out of the blue I came up with *Rajo binoculata*.

Years later, on a Cascadian dock, standing next to a fisherman who had just caught a flopping prize, he said to me, "looks like a *Mola mola*." I looked over at him and said, I agree.

A bright spot of graduate school is my research on Swirlopeds. I discover there are aquatic, aerial, and terrestrial Swirlopeds in addition to the rock grinding Swirlopeds. As a reward for learning significant facts, I receive a Master's degree and suddenly am qualified to teach. Within two weeks I apply to twenty-two community colleges in the west and Wisconsin and Michigan. My letters to the Deans are as follows:

Dear Dean:

I enjoy teaching. Many students memorize for a grade. They should learn to think creatively.

I will develop my courses around ecological themes. Camping in Central America I watched monkeys. I've sniffed spices in Zanzibar and led hikes along the Continental Divide. I've fed pelicans in Florida and raccoons in Wisconsin. I also read Walden.

My graduate research has been devoted to the field study, collection, and identification of Swirlopeds. As you know, having legs only on their left side, they whirl like tops through the air, water, rocks and soil.

While waiting for the job offers to flood in, I make a vow which I tape to the refrigerator. Cleo makes me remove it, so I reverently place it on the inside cover of Walden.

A VOW IN INDIA INK

I shall no more go into bondage regarding work. I shall enter into no contracts, legal or psychological, in which I will be under someone's thumb.

Let the winds of creation cleanse this bogged down mind. My research goes too slow.

Part of my trouble is my own fault. I have never been good in my ancestral language, German.

Birds and mammals have been studied since pre historic times. Whole books have been written in English about lions, elephants, porpoises, wolves, octopuses and gorillas. However the only books written on Swirlopeds are in German.

I try to check our *Das Tierbuch*, the major Swirloped encyclopedia. When I tell the librarian, "I need *Das Tierbuch* for my research," I speak with a German accent.

Clamping her lips and flattening her hands on the counter, she says, "I'm sorry. We don't let reserved books out of the library."

I splutter, "I need these books for my research." I admit not what I'd do with the books if they were checked out to me. I think I'll cross that bridge when I come to it. I am too poor to hire a translator.

She again refuses me, saying, "These books are reserved books. It is library policy not to check out reserved books."

Voice rising, working my way up to a heart attack I say, "I want to see your supervisor."

She takes me to see her boss, a thin man in his fifties. Looking down at the man's bald spot, I speak loudly, "These books are in German." Rapidly flipping the pages, I add, "It's obvious, no one has ever read this book." I don't mention that I can't read the book either.

During my outburst the librarian pushes his chair against the wall, squirming like the *Mola Mola* on the dock. Note: the ocean sunfish is the heaviest bony fish in the world. It would collapse some docks.

I continue, "I am the only person in the history of this university who has ever studied or who will ever study Swirlopeds. If I can't check out these books they will never be used."

Smirking, the boss librarian stands up. He says, "I'm sorry. It's against library policy." However Mr. Bauer, you can come to the library and use them." I immediately answer, "Yes. I do enjoy light reading."

The librarian helpfully adds, "You can Xerox them."

I say, "I'm a poor man, not a corporation. I have no staff. No budget. Keep your fucking Das *Tierbuch*." I kick over three chairs on my way out.

After this incident I keep away from the library. I learn about Swirlopeds by studying articles and illustrations I copy while in other university libraries.

You might be interested in my findings. I learned that individual species had ventrally located reproductive organs. In the male they are close to the neck and resemble ice tongs. They are called gonopods. I call them tongs.

The articles don't tell me what Swirlopeds eat, because that hasn't been studied yet. For your information, no researchers have ever studied the tongs in action.


I become a bit obsessive compulsive. I want to know how do they use those damn tongs? To learn this, I become a voyeur of the forest and creek beds. I discover that Swirlopeds tonged together while whirling in the air, in the water, and even spinning through the soil.

Despite my fieldwork, which seems brilliant to me, I get fed up with the laboratory part of research.

I am frustrated with my own ignorance. Half of my creatures are new to science. All are new to me. Because I work alone I have no one to confide in, no one to ask for help. Some of my fellow students are brilliant, admired by their professors. How can I admit my lack of knowledge?

In this way, I continue with my research while waiting for responses to my letters to community colleges.

I often think, what will my professors say about me: Will they blackball me? Will I get any job offers? Most of the people here are friendly. Everyone says hello. It's my fault I've got such a dumb research project. Next time I do research, I'll go to Alaska to study wolves, or I'll go into the ocean and study whales.

# CHAPTER 3.

# FIVE THOUSAND BIRD BEAKS

I n 1965, shortly before spring vacation, I receive an invitation to visit Humaluh Valley College in Cascadia. Our hopes jump when Cleo and I read, "If we decide to hire you there is an excellent chance the position will become permanent."

We celebrate by going out for pizza. Eyes sparkling in the light from plastic Tiffany lampshades, Cleo says, "I'm sure you'll get the job."

Karl's balloon floats to the ceiling. Through fast forming tears he watches the red bubble pop.

The first day of vacation, in the morning, I kiss Cleo and Karl goodbye and head towards Cascadia. The first night, in my sleeping bag, I fall asleep listening to a stream, looking at the diamonds of Orion. The next day, after hours of passage through the huge fields of greening wheat, the car swoops through the Columbia River Canyon. My eyes hungrily devour the views of ridges superimposed upon ridges. As I follow the river my eyes take in the yellow comets, red glow, blue glow, and fire red flowers scattered over the sagebrush slopes from the river to the cliffs.

Piercing the spine of the Cascades the open bright canyon quickly changes as if through witchcraft, into dense forestclutching steep hills and fissures in the cliffs. Attracted by full waterfalls tumbling over the canyon top, I take a break from driving. Parking, I walk up a short trail, feel the spray, am refreshed; hear the rumbling, feel the ground shake and am in awe.

The gorge gives way to a wide river valley and gentle hills. The highway gives way to octopus freeways. Changing direction, I follow another river north past farms and forests until I see in the distance the fabled city of Duwamps, whose description I had read described by the famous anthropologist Jack Gunter who performed research on mastodons and women's nude volley ball that he filmed on snow covered slopes during his research on the past, present and future of Cascadia. I especially liked his paintings of Mastodons trudging across snow bridges while guided by the slanting compass of the Duwamps Needle.

Usually repelled by cities, I am attracted by the hills covered with buildings following the undulations of the land. Bridges connect city islands. Freighters nestle beneath orange Brobdingnagian towers. Large ships are anchored in the harbor, snouts pointed to the wind.

Rushing, pushing northward I go over the words I will tell the dean. Passing through suburbs I see snowy mountains to the west and to the east. To close out stinky outside air, I roll up the windows to keep out the paper mill sulfurous scents of Port Gardner. There are white spots on a bright green background. A minute later the pretty green transforms into a sewage lagoon and the gulls fly away. After crossing the Gardner River, crowded with pilings, the road climbs, enters forests and levels.

A humble sign announces HUMALUH COUNTY LINE. There are more forests, than pastures and barns. The road drops. A mahogany colt runs exultant in the sun's warmth.

Parking briefly on the shoulder I leave the car and inhale the sweet clean air. The soft grass feels good after hours of pressing rubber to steel. The Humaluh River lies on the land like a twisting serpent. The river divides into two forks near the sea, and then divides again and again. Like the branches of a maple meeting the sky the many lines touch the sea. Slowly spinning, I have a panoramic view of the valley ringed by hills and mountains. In the far distance glaciers whiten sleeping volcanoes. Below the cliffs the forested slopes are dark. I have a revelation; my God I can study life in the sea, the river, marshes and forests. This is paradise.

Driving again, ravenously hungry, I spot a super dooper giant hot dog dripping with mustard dangling from a pole like a short dirigible gasping for breath. I am repelled and fascinated by the sign. Of course I pull in. Just inside the front door I scrutinize a glass terrarium containing garter snakes. After listening to the snakes shedding, I read a goofy sign saying: TRAINED FLEAS! Bending to my left, squinting through the glass of a second terrarium I see black shiny gray specks perched on a velvet violet slope. A girl laughs. She has long hair reaching her waist. She stuffs crumbling cheese into her mouth, her lips twist seeking particles like a Panamanian tapir seeking ants.

Scratching her pumpkin pregnant belly, she asks, "Want some? Made from goat's milk."

"No. Just a hot dog," I say.

"OK." She turns and runs from the room, yelling, "I gotta pee," as she disappears behind a purple tie-dye curtain.

I hear a flush. She returns an instant later. Picking up wooden tongs she plucks out a long hot dog, which drops. She says, "Yeek."

Watching it fall, I wonder. Will she pick it up, rinse it and serve it to me?

She exclaims "Yah!" triumphantly catching the wiener in the open bun.

Open-mouthed, I must have looked like an idiot watching her squirt a line of bright yellow mustard along the meaty cylinder. She dumps a dripping bundle of sauerkraut on the brown bun. Bowing before me she announces, "Your hot dog, Sir."

Her masterpiece bulges like Pinocchio's wart.

I worry about choking, done in by sauerkraut. She is poking fun at me. Of course, I quickly gobble the dog, pay and leave. Her smile follows me. I will not soon forget her giggle. Driving again, belching, I taste caraway, catsup and mustard. Not a bad aftertaste.

Minutes later a green sign with white letters says Duhkwuh. I switch lanes, and quickly exit the freeway. Duhkwuh is that small. There are only two exits. The commercial area of stores and a few small factories manufacturing plywood tulips is confined to land within a twist of the Humaluh. The upland holds houses, churches and many trees. A two-lane road passes between cow pastures and then I am at the college.

While parking, the bright white stone buildings glow in the sunshine. I see the top of an ugly tower like structure, perhaps made of metal, planted in the center of the grassy quad between a rectangular classroom building on the left and the administration building in the background and classrooms on the right. Why would they have that thing on campus? It must be made of old rusty iron and is over a hundred feet tall. Must be a great place for pigeons, English sparrows and turkey vultures to nest. I wonder, is it a weird sort of sundial or an avant-garde piece of sculpture made by D students.

After parking, in a few steps I am in the Union. The cafeteria is in front, administrative offices to the right, and the men's room to the left. Shaving kit in hand, I enter the men's room. I didn't shave in the hot dog restaurant because of the dim light, dirty mirror, and cold water. The college restroom is excellent. Shiny Chromium dispensers hold paper towels. Eye blinking lights brighten the white tile floor. A large mirror covers the wall above the sink.

The clean warm water feels good. I whip up a good lather with mug and brush. I know it's old fashioned but it feels great. Gone are two days of whiskers. I'm so glad no one saw me during my first minute at the college. I am pleased with my image. I see a curly brunette haired handsome man in his early thirties. My hair newly cut and shorter than it has been in years. Last week's haircut removed unruly hair. I feel respectable. I shaved off my beard two months earlier, in honor of the job application photos, as part of my courtship of respectability. Today in my brand new tailored gray pin striped Kuppenheimer suit, I look conservative. Well lah te dah.

Stashing the shaving kit in my car I return to the building, walk past the food service and stop at the secretarial desks. "Pardon me, can you tell me, where's the dean's office? I have an appointment." A thin middle-aged woman points me to the office of the Dean, Rodney Mann. I have to stop a second time. A young mini-skirted woman swivels. I cannot help myself when it comes to a woman in a miniskirt. I am compelled to watch those silky legs. "Hello. I'm Leo Bauer."

"We've been expecting you Mr. Bauer. Welcome to Humaluh Valley College," she smiles.

"Thank you. It's good to be here."

"Please sit down. I'll tell the dean you're here."

Upright as a heron, while waiting in an easy chair next to her desk, I watch her legs as she moves about the office watering plants, filing. Intent upon my anatomical studies, I am surprised by the rapid approach of a man over six feet tall, of solid muscle, as if a laborer or a neck-cracking wrestler. His nose is bent. Blue eyes and short blonde hair; is the dean a Scandinavian soccer brawler?

"Hello. Welcome," he says, extending his paw."

My hand shakes, subduing my normal distain for over muscular male bodies I attempt to respond with force. Ha, that's a laugh. I have the handshake of a chess match winner.

The dean says, "Welcome Leo. I'm glad to meet you."

The dean's hand is surprisingly soft. At the minimum I expected to receive a phalangeal fracture in my right hand.

"Certainly, certainly," I say, following the man of steel. We enter the fluorescent-lit office and sit where directed on a blue leather couch. He sits at a neat desk with a baseball, in a mitt and a color photograph of a woman and two young girls. Behind his back on the wall is a map of Scandinavia with a line drawing of Leif Erickson. From behind the desk, the dean says, "Have a good trip?"

"Yes. I'm in love with this land." My voice is quivery loud and confident. I manage to hide my fears. I like the dean's relaxed manner and his black turtle neck sweater.

The dean says, "We have fantastic recreation. We ski Komo Kulshan and fish the Humaluh. Hunting is excellent. Do you hunt?"

"No."

"Too bad. Do you play baseball?"

"No. But I canoe, swim and fish." I rarely fish, but it seems important for me to convince the dean of my all around athletic ability.

"The faculty has a basketball team, and a baseball team. Once each year we play the students. We've only lost twice." The dean smiles.

I say, "Perhaps I can learn to play."

"If we hire you, you'll learn. No need to worry about that," says the dean.

"I like to hike. I'm really into hiking. Are there good trails?"

"You can take a trail at the edge of Duhkwuh and walk a week without crossing a highway."

"You're on the edge of the wilderness."

"You have a son?"

"I'll show you a picture." Bending forward, I extract my wallet and pull forth a color photo of serious towheaded Karl holding hands with Cleo; she is smiling in very short shorts.

The Dean leans over, intently studying the photo. "Your wife is very pretty. Your son is blonde. This will be a good place for them." Returning to his desk, examining his pen, he says, "As I've told you, our faculty is above average. We are very careful who we hire."

Spreading his hands, he adds, "Sometimes we make mistakes. When that happens, they don't stay long."

"That's good," I say. Wondering, will I be one of the mistakes?

"We have close ties to the community. I belong to the Duhkwuh Rotary. We do good works for the community."

"How do you get into the Rotary?"

"Each business or organization can have a member. The weekly meeting is time well spent. We have guest speakers, outstanding people from the community."

I'm glad I don't belong to any Rotary. I'd hate to have to go to weekly meetings. The phone rings. While Mann talks. I read titles on the bookshelves:

*Teaching Fawns and Calves to Walk*
*Ten Steps to Scholarly Achievement*
*The Future Civil War Between Conservatives and Liberals.*

It is obvious-the Dean is quite a scholar.

He cuts his phone call short. Turning to me, he says, "Excuse me. I get one phone call after another."

"You're very busy."

"I'm going eight days a week. A man has to if he wants to succeed."

"I guess so."

"Our faculty is a big happy family. You believe in team work?"

"Absolutely." I answer firmly and honestly. Preferring to work alone, I heartily approve of teamwork for others.

"Leo. Are you aware of the pioneering accomplishments of our biology department?"

"Please tell me."

"When I was the head of the Science Division, biology developed a program so good, it is imitated by other colleges. The University of Cascadia is considering a modified version of our program."

After allowing a moment's silence to honor that great accomplishment, I say, "I didn't think community colleges could lead."

"Ours is the exception. Our core courses emphasize the quintessence of knowledge. Once cored, the students take advanced courses." He laughs.

"Great," I say. I wonder. What is the quintessence?

"Have you taught the DNA Litany?"

My gut tightens. My only contact with the Litany had been as a teaching assistant when I had corrected examinations with the aid of a key prepared by Dr. Bluenstoorf. It had been slow stumbling work. Pulling at the threads of memory I snared knowledge from my past. Squeezing my chin I say, "DNA is the secret of life. I am especially enamored of the way the genetic message, duplicated in the nucleus, ascends through the nuclear membrane, passes to the ribosomes and codes the assembly of amino acids into protein."

Mann says, "Excellent. You seem well prepared."

"Thank you," I say. More confident, leaning forward I ask, "Do you offer natural history?"

"We plan to add a natural history course. In fact Leo, we are considering you to instruct, because of your knowledge of birds, bats, frogs and bogs." The dean chuckles. I nod. My face warms. The dean continues, "If you are hired, we will start you easy. The first year you will teach general biology."

"That's fine with me," I say.

"The biology department is chaired by John Isawaddy. He's been with us for twenty years; almost as long as President Davis. You may be interested in his thesis. *A Molecular Analysis of Bird Beaks.* An arduous project. He had to grind up over five thousand beaks."

"Quite a job." I wonder, can I ever like such a man?

"He teaches vertebrate zoology, human anatomy, physiology and general biology. He also coaches wrestling, goes to church three times a week, and at night teaches auto mechanics."

"Quite a man." Yeeech. I think of the coaches who made fun of me. I got beaten up in wrestling. The other boys laughed at me. Those jerks. I hated someone pushing my butt down when I did push ups.

"You will like Bobby Pompa. Only twentythree. He'll have his Ph.D. soon. His thesis is a classic study: *The Biochemistry of Slug Excrement.* In addition to teaching botany, invertebrate zoology, and general biology, he coaches boxing."

"Impressive," I say, wondering, What can I coach? Tiddlywinks for Dumb bells?

"The last member of our department is Robert Jackson. After spending years studying fern pollen, he sneezed one day and blew away half his collection." This is funny. If they hire me, maybe I won't be the low man on the totem pole.

Mann says, "Leo. As I've said before I'm impressed with your credentials. Oh ... By the way." At this point he focuses on my eyes. I shift. "Why did you refuse to continue with physiology?" The dean's sapphire pupils catch my eyes. Damn I'm a goner.

Palms sweating, rigid, I answer. "That was five years ago." I talk slowly, my future hanging on every word. I can feel my heart. "Loving nature, I have always read anything I could find about animals. While taking physiology, a friend loaned me a copy of *The Animal World of Albert Schweitzer*. Schweitzer said, 'whenever I injure any kind of life, I must be certain it is necessary!'"

"That sounds reasonable." The Dean nods.

Despite the dean's agreeable words I feel as if I am in a terrarium. My right foot seems made of lead. I reply. "At the time I vowed to stop killing animals, I stopped eating meat. You probably think it's silly, I walked carefully so as not to step on ants. In physiology we operated on and killed frogs, turtles, cats and dogs. Before the operation the dogs licked my hands. The cats purred when I petted them. I told my professor, 'it is against my conscience to experiment on living creatures.' He couldn't understand my attitude. He said, 'You can't graduate in zoology without a year of physiology.' My entire future seemed doomed."

"How did you graduate?" asks Mann.

"For a few more weeks I cringed when insects hit my windshield. It may sound silly, but I worried and worried about the harm I was causing the animals. Well my room-mate, this was before I was married, worried about me. Sitting me down, looking me square in the eye, he talked with me all one night. His main point made sense. He said, 'It is impossible to live and not take other life.' Right away I changed my mind. In fact I made peace with my physiology professor, although I took no more physiology. In graduate school they even put me in charge of killing the frogs and turtles. I did the killing out of compassion. I did not want to see those poor injured dying bleeding creatures crawl around the bottom of the trash barrel."

The dean clutches his knees while softly swaying. He speaks. "I also would have opposed the granting of a degree to anyone holding those views. I am glad you came to your senses."

Exhaling, I feel less tense. "Yes. Such views are totally impractical. How can someone go through life with their head wrapped in gauze so as not to breathe in gnats? I don't want to cork my ears to keep out the beetles." We laugh.

Mann says, "Leo, I'm impressed. Students will be fascinated by your experiences. I've always wanted to visit Zanzibar and Panama. You've done it. You've had adventures. You've been to places visited by Darwin on the Beagle. You can bring balance to the department."

My hopes rise. The dean looks at his watch. "Do you have any more questions? Do you still want to teach here?"

I fervently say, "I would rather teach at Humaluh, than at any other college on earth."

"I'll be honest with you. We've had over twenty applicants. We've narrowed the choice to two. You and a man named Bush from Texas. He's a former ballplayer. We'll make our decision after we interview him. I'll let you know within two weeks."

"I have a good chance then?"

"You have an excellent chance. Thanks for coming such a long way."

"Thank you. Thank you," I spout. If I had a tail now it would wiggle. We both get up wearing great smiles and shake hands. Grinning I leave the office. Mann is so unlike the arrogant graduate school professors.

I waltz drive homeward along the Columbia River and across the cold northern desert, which now seems warm and cheerful. When Cleo and Karl hear the good news, they laugh and spin across the living room. Tumbling against an end table they knock over a lamp, which breaks. They whirl away from the broken glass. We all laugh.

# CHAPTER 4.

## LOVE LETTERS

On the second day of April I pick up the phone. It is Dean Mann. "Are you still interested?"

"Yes. Of course."

"Would you like the job?"

"Certainly."

"You don't have to make up your mind today. Take a week and let me know."

"No. I accept now. My mind's made up."

"Don't you want to discuss this with your wife?"

"We've already talked. We accept."

After the call, Cleo races to the store. She quickly returns with chilled champagne. I pop the cork, which smacks the ceiling. Glass raised, eyes sparkling, Cleo burbles, "To the future." Surging bubbles tickle her throat. She laughs and licks glistening open lips.

I reflect upon my mother. When I was a child, when there was good news, did her lips glisten with champagne, reflect the candlelight of my father's love? Why did they always seem so formal?

"Cleo I love you." I say. Kissing her soft lips my hand tilts. A champagne rain falls on Karl. He licks drops from his hand.

Acting refined, Cleo slowly raises her glass. Laughter escapes while she says, "Leo, you are my clown. I love you."

We toast each other and kiss. We toast Karl, "Our handsome son," and fill his glass with seltzer. Raising his small hand, he says, "To daddy's new job." Later that night, when all of us are falling asleep we are secure and confident of the future.

Two days later triplicate contract copies arrive. The document is an agreement between the Board of Directors of Humaluh Valley College, Humaluh County, Cascadia, hereinafter called the District, and Leo Bauer. I have to agree to teach or perform other assigned professional services in the public schools of such district, and perform such duties as are prescribed, none that are proscribed, by the laws of the State of Cascadia, and by rules and regulations (that are ubiquitous) for one year, (which was composed of 187 days of service) and this year, (which was not a year) would begin in September and end the following August.

This contract gives the employee, Leo Bauer, the salary of $6,711, which was to be paid in twelve installments. If said teacher does not promptly return the signed contract, the board reserves the right to withdraw the offer.

In addition, the contract will not become effective until said employee registers a valid teaching certificate and a valid health certificate, and signs the affidavit before an officer duly authorized to administer oaths. Six members of the Board of Directors signed the contract, and a clerk or secretary (who was the Duhkwuh Superintendent of Schools) and a Notary Public named Herbert Truezinski.

A form enclosed with the contract reveals that on the salary schedule I am in the fifth column because I possess an M.A. plus 45 hours of course work. I am also given credit for two years of experience, one year of which was military service. I remembered my readings of the Spanish Civil War. A Fifth Column was supposed to undermine a government or organization from within.

I pop a copy into my strong box on top of a certificate of live birth from Milwaukee County, and two sheepskins (which were not made of sheepskin). I deposit the original signed copy of the contract in the mailbox and then worry. What if the mail is delayed? The plane might crash. There might be a fire in the post office.

Four days later I relax as I read the letter "welcoming Mr. and Mr. Bauer," and promising to do "everything in our power to make your life with us enjoyable and your job as rewarding as possible. Your papers and application indicate that you will be a treasured addition to our staff."

The letter mentions terminal education. I wonder if our students will be the dead and dying. Further on it states, "This letter will serve as official notice of your election. We also need official transcripts." The letter ends with, "Our local board stipulates that an employee must have a satisfactory credit rating. You will receive a final validation upon receiving such a rating from the credit bureau."

Although happy I wonder, was the vote unanimous? What is my credit rating? I have been a student most of my life; have never bought on credit. How in the hell can I have a good credit rating? We have not accumulated furniture, tools, appliances, TV's, and electric *hors d'oeuvres* trays. Will the job fall through my fingers because I have no credit rating?

The next day we receive a letter from President Elmore Davis, which says, "We eagerly await the arrival of you and your family. If you have any questions please communicate directly with Mr. John Isawaddy. I am sure he and Dean Mann will be joyful to assist you and your family.

"The board requires a credit investigation to make this absolutely final. Normally this is a mere formality. Again welcome."

Fortunately, because I have used gasoline credit cards since puberty, I soon receive my credit report. It is good and will continue to get better.

After completing exams I focus on the observation of Swirlopeds. I especially enjoy watching aquatic Swirlopeds, the only gill bearing members of the Cochleopoda. Voracious eaters, like the aerial Swirlopeds, they eat both living and dead plant and animal food.

Flat on my chest, nose just above the water, I watch the rhythmic oscillatory movements of the paddle shaped legs as they propel a Swirloped in fast spirals. They whirl into prey like spinning ricocheting rocks, and spear minnows with the sharp spines of their toxicognaths.

Despite my brilliant fieldwork, at least I think so, I am fed up with the laboratory part of research, and the hundreds of hours I've spent observing the tongs on slides. I often feel like telling my graduate committee to go tong themselves.

I am also frustrated with my ignorance of a subject I'm supposed to be an expert in. Half of my creatures are new to science. All are new to me. I have no one to confide in, no one to ask for help. Because of the tough competition and the brilliance of my fellows, I cannot admit my stupidity.

It is fascinating to observe as the delicate hair like rays form into a funnel and suck fingerling trout into the toxicognath, the glove of death.

I was elated, the day I discovered the swooshing sucking sounds I've often heard at ponds and lakes are made by Swirlopeds attacking prey at or near the surface.

My eyes got injured in a confrontation with a terrestrial Swirloped. I got squirted by tiny jets of noxious oily fluid. When grabbed, beaked, or bitten, these fearsome creatures emit blasts of hydrocyanic acid. I had to stay in bed for three days covering my eyes with a washcloth. On other days, wearing goggles, I often watched them swirl their way through old rotting leaves and duff of the forest floor. I get excited when I see them flatten their bodies and spin through cracks and fissures in cliffs and boulders, and between rocks of the talus slides.

Walking along a trail at the base of a cliff I saw a gray Persian cat walking towards me. I halted. The cat kept coming, and brushed against my leg. I moved. The cat jumped. I petted the cat. The cat rubbed back and forth in a sinuous dance. Suddenly the cat froze and stared at a crack in the cliff. I knelt next to the cat. A small cloud of dust blew out of the crack. A cloud of tiny flies hovered around the cat's head.

I hoped he wouldn't inhale any of them. I heard a quick slurp in the stream in back of him. The cat's ears turned. The cat resisted the urge to investigate. We could see no more movement. My knee hurt where it was pressing into the gravel. The cat jumped back. A flurry of dirt hit my goggles. The cat was biting what looked like a disc of glistening amber. Then the cat spat out a Swirloped the size of a man's palm and dashed through some brambles. Without stopping at the riverbank, while sounding a sad meowww, the cat dove into the river. Wearing gloves, I reached quickly for the Swirloped and dropped it into a jar. Thinking it a new species, I imagined myself as an American Linnaeus who would discover dozens of new species and become famous through my Swirloped studies. My reverie was broken by a rapid succession of horrible yowling choking sounds in back of me. Turning, I saw the cat swimming in wild circles underwater and above water while sucking in and spitting out huge mouthfuls of water. From these observations I determined that hydrocyanic acid did not taste good to cats.

While I was exploring moist river valleys and observing Swirlopeds and cats, Cleo was reading about Cascadia. She learned that the cities are in the valleys. When a valley filled up with houses the city crept up the slopes. If the slopes were too steep the houses fell down during heavy rainfalls. There was warfare in Cascadia. On the East side of the Cascades ponderosa pine battled sagebrush. During dry years the sagebrush won the battle. The trees on the front lines lost needles and often died. During years of above average rainfall, the ponderosa won the battle and grew new bunches of long dark green needles.

# CHAPTER 5.

## THE MOVE TO CASCADIA

Cleo says, "I want to watch the fighting plants." However in the heat of August she has a struggle of her own packing clothes and dishes. Feeling overworked she yells at me, "Damn it. Why can't you help me?"

I yell, "I've got to get my Swirlopeds packed?"

She yells "Well help me when you're done."

As it works out, she spends several days doing the inside packing, and I spend one afternoon doing the outside packing.

I fit the boxes together as if I am completing a jigsaw puzzle. Sipping a whiskey and Seven Up, Cleo covers her grinning mouth when she sees me discovering that the pile is too high: I have to restack all of the boxes.

Cleo and Karl sleep through the wheat country. Half awake and hazy in the heat, she isn't excited by the occasional brown needle clusters that mark the combat zone. She much prefers waterfalls, and is disappointed because I won't stop at waysides and parks. I tell her, I don't want to wake Karl. Don't feel bad. We'll come back soon. OK?"

Karl wakens, sees the ocean for the first time, says, "Is that the ocean? Where are the beaches and the waves? Can we stop? Can we stop? Can I walk along the shore?"

I say, "Do you like those big ships?"

"I want to play in the sand," says Karl.

I say, "Sometime we can come back and visit one of the big ships. There's no sand here. The sand is further west. On the beaches."

"I want to play in the sand," says Karl.

We rent a cheap motel room in Duhkwuh. I write my mom a letter:

Dear Mom:

We got into Duhkwuh late and were lucky to get a motel room. Karl was asleep as I carried him into the room. Cleo undressed him and put him to bed. Even though I've been driving all day, the highway traffic keeps me awake. We can cook in this place, but it is tiny and cramped. In front of the window there is a gravel parking lot. I hope we find a house soon. This is not a good place for Karl. No place to play. I have to get to bed now. I hope I get to sleep soon.

The day after our arrival we go with Mrs. Green to see if we can find a house to rent. The Dean's secretary recommended her. First she takes us to the low lands across the river where it floods. The houses are crumby. Rentals are in short supply, and we are discouraged. Then she says, "I know. You're not planning to buy now, but I know a real good buy."

While we drive up the hill to the house, she happens to mention, the place has been written up in Sunset Magazine. It is different. Standing at the big front windows, we don't stare across the street into other people's living rooms. This house is angled to get the full effect of the sun, especially in winter. We can lie on the carpet and feel toasty. The living room has high ceilings. On a rainy day I can look out on the patio, which will be a great play area for Karl. And the roses are sweet. More like native roses. I smell them as soon as I go into the garden.

They're all over the place. Against the fence are bushes of Portuguese laurel, Rhododendron, forsythia and quince. Bunches of reeds swish against the living room window. It will be a great place for our parents to visit. My mother can set up her easel and paint the flowers.

The inside and outside walls are of split cedar from the upriver valley, and they're stained, not painted. The place reminds me of the Wisconsin cabin, except instead of pines there are Douglas firs, and instead of being in the woods it's in a small town.

It's got the greatest heating system in the world. Hundreds of feet of copper pipe form a maze in the concrete floor. The last owners used to lie on their backs enjoying the warmth. It would feel great on a sore back.

In my second letter to my Mom I write: The Dean told me my job would probably be permanent. He said it would be bad for morale if they brought people here for just one year.

We can get a GI loan for only 5% interest, and the price is only $13,000. Could you loan us enough for the down payment?

My mother gives us the down payment as a gift. The monthly payments are $75.00 a month including taxes and insurance. We sign the documents. It is September 1965. We have to furnish the house. This is easy. We go to the Bon Marche, the best department store in Duwamps, and buy solid handcrafted ranch oak furniture put together with wooden pegs, and made of rough oak, which matches the surface of the walls.

After moving in, a little over a month after sending the first letter to my mother, I sit in our new easy chair, my feet on the concrete ledge of the limestone fireplace. Crystals glisten from the stone face. My hands caress the armrests. I am impatient for cold weather. I want to watch the flames of our hearth. While I contemplate the future, Cleo paints Karl's room buttercup, and selects the best place to hang a mobile of carousel ponies, and two paintings she did of laughing clowns.

We are part of a neighborhood for the first time in our married life. Kathleen Leary, from across the street, invites Cleo over for coffee, and Cleo meets three more neighborhood wives. Later in the week, at a barbecue, I get to meet the neighbors. It is sort of like being back in Milwaukee, for the neighbor men include a physician, a banker, and a CPA. In Milwaukee our neighbors had included a doctor, an attorney, a banker and a butcher. Sounds like a nursery rhyme, doesn't it?

# CHAPTER 6.

## CHROME DOME

Soon my wife and son will meet President Davis. Like many famous people, this man talks continuously. This ability came upon him miraculously, immediately upon assuming the presidency. When only a mere teacher he had been forced to wait for a break in the conversation before attempting to say his piece. As president, he decided when there would be breaks.

He is called Chrome Dome behind his back. From above he looks like Yul Bryner emerging from a tube of toothpaste, although he does not look as youthful as Bryner who delighted audiences by leaping up stairways while belting out triumphant Siamese songs.

No one recalls hearing Davis sing, not even athletic comrade shower mates. However there is much to remember about his physical appearance. Thick lenses, like large drops of oil, magnify eyes that push forward. Below his eyes dark bags perch on either side of a narrow delicate nose. His thin lips look as if they perpetually yearn for a breast or cigar. Although he still smokes cigars, he probably has given up sucking breasts.

He reminds people of a man who while bowling inhaled too deeply and swallowed the ball. This caused a big pull against his backbone creating a sigmoid curve. The depression of his upper chest also seemed to be formed and created by the pull of the ball of his belly. His face leans ahead as if he is eager to be first, and his shoulders hunch forward. His physique leads the viewer to think, the man's off balance. If he doesn't watch his step he'll fall on his nose and put a hole in the floor. In addition, his arms and legs are thin and his feet point to the side when he walks.

A pure man, he never frequents bars or cocktail lounges and never smokes dope or drops acid. Occasionally he takes sleeping pills. In the faculty lounge, when a short-skirted coed prances by on the sidewalk, most of the learned professors swivel their heads like night monkeys. You can hear the clicking of dozens of cervical vertebrae as the necks move. This is real teamwork. By contrast, the president, at times like that comments, "That dress is too short."

Apparently he never lusts or leers at women, girls, men, boys, sheep or red rumped baboons. Instead he often seems to be looking at people as if they are varieties of cabbage or kale. This particular cabbage dresses austerely. Silvery jewelry would have been like soil sullying silk sheets.

Mrs. Davis however, is not a cabbage. She wears things like English woolens from the tourist destination hand fashioned lodge in Watertown Lakes, Canada. Keeping to the background she seems happy to knit in his shade, keeping on the edge of his aura. They married during a wartime furlough in 1944. After the war they abandoned the Baptist Church and become Episcopalians. Their two children were good students, well behaved, a disappointment to Chrome Dome's detractors who would have preferred failure.

At one time Davis was active in sports. Because of his studies, research, teaching, and finally the presidency, he reluctantly gave up athletics. When invited to join the faculty teams he always said, "I'd like to, but I'm too darn busy."

Later that school year, in the warmth of late spring, I shared a motel pool with the president after a seminar *On Meeting Tomorrow's Needs the Day Before Yesterday.* Gazing at the heaving stomach of his recumbency, extending to emaciated looking legs, I was reminded of my father the year before he died.

Davis became a college president in his fortyfifth year. Despite white shoes and bright suits, he was not youthful. He walked with seriousness as if in deep thought. Once curly haired, he had been sought by several Alabama maidens. While barefooted he had watched people frolic from the edges of Big Jim Folsom picnics. Big Jim was proud of being called the Kissing Governor.

When opposed, Davis threw tantrums of heroic proportions accompanied by small releases of urine. This trait won him the nickname of Piss Pants. During the time of quiet following his anger he escaped first to change his BVDs, then to retreat to a quiet nook to read. Like happens with many others who achieve greatness, getting mocked in childhood caused him to develop strong willpower. The boy was driven to show he was better than his classmates. After school and after dinner when the other children were playing or reading Erskine Caldwell trash of ministers seducing girls, he read, took notes, completed assignments, and became the top student in his small high school in Leeds Alabama. The pride of his teachers, and an oddity to his classmates. Later on he served as a tank commander in the Second World War and became a hero. After the war he discovered that the best way to be accepted by other men was to participate in athletics. Therefore in college he took many P.E. classes, and at Humaluh became a coach in his early years in addition to teaching.

While entering the outskirts of Duhkwuh a fly buzzing my ear told me that Davis was meeting with his administrative staff in the faculty lunchroom. At the time we were sniffing pea vine scented air, which smelled sort of like manure. The fly said, The beige walls of the lunchroom are free of paintings, which are liable to distract intellectual perambulators. In one corner a tall chromium coffee maker dwarfs the corded teapot. Another corner gives refuge to a small rattling refrigerator. Coats smother the third corner, and the fourth gave space to a rack with brochures extolling teacher's union benefits and medical insurance.

The Vice President, Gary Pantagruel, was the first to arrive. After opening the high windows he looked past the food service garbage cans over a board fence to the quad empty of students. Turning he inspected the room. Discovering no sugar on the coffee table, he briskly left the room, returning a moment later with a box of packets of Hawaiian sweetness. He scored a cup of coffee, ripped open a sugar packet, sniffed the surface, sipped, licked his lips, walked to a table and sat down. Lighting a cigar he exhaled, sniffed, and said, "Hello Ben," to the new arrival, Ben Coolsen, the Business Manager, who got a cup of coffee and joined him at the table as the fly's twin picked up several grains of sugar with its proboscis.

The room soon contained seven men, two women and the fly waiting and listening to the refrigerator and the coffee machine. Wearing a plaid sports jacket and white patent leather shoes, the president slowly entered the room with great dignity. After getting his own coffee, he sat in an orange plastic chair next to Pantagruel, and with his right index finger traced the palm lines of his left hand while reviewing his speech.

Standing straight, and marine-like Dean Mann braced his hands on the chromium strip edging the table. Looking down on the bright shiny forehead of his boss he asked, "Are you ready chief?"

The president said, "Of course."

J. M. Keene, the Director of Continuing Studies, entered the room as the dean announced, "Gentlemen, our president." The staff laughed at Keene's embarrassment. Without bowing Keene stealthily walked to a chair skipping coffee or tea.

Ignoring Keene, the president made a few preparatory mumbles, "Ahum, hmmn." Hearing their leader, the staff stopped chuckling and looked at Davis who began to speak. "Colleagues be reassured. Each one of you is a valued member of our team. As you know, I am a former military man. The chain of command, is vital to the military and vital to a college. Remember, always follow the chain. During the Second World War, if I had stuck my head through the hatch at the wrong time, I would have lost my head. None of us wants to lose our heads, do we? Therefore, let us all follow our procedures manual."

"What procedures manual?" broke in Keene.

Frowning Davis said, "It's being written. You'll get your copy next week; back to the war. Winning those battles was hard. My tank, in the vanguard, crushed all opposition. Well people, now that war is over, but we are in another struggle. Today we are in the front lines of the battle for academic excellence. In this struggle, it is imperative for us to act decisively." Keene squelched a yawn, sucked on his cigar and watched the smoke.

Davis said, "Gentlemen, ever since my military days I have been a team player. I know how important it is to have a close knit team." Across the table, arms crossed, Coolson rubbed his elbows "Comparing the people and equipment and supplies in your area with those in another area will cause dissension. Those unaware of all the facts will cause trouble. Too much information is bad."

"I don't want to kick a dead horse, but we all know, when Hawthorne was president he fouled up. He had to leave because he relied too much on individuals and not enough on the team."

Abandoning his notes Davis scanned their eyes. "Boat rockers and trouble makers will not be part of our team." Standing, he tightly gripped the table edge. His face reddened. "Some people will have to go. We can't tolerate immoral godless sons of bitches. If any bastards corrupt students and dare to wave the flag of academic freedom under our noses, they will go fast." In his anger, Davis resembled a red cabbage, a talking red cabbage with dry outer leaves and a juicy middle. He said, "I am a liberal. I don't give a damn what your politics are. Nevertheless, freedom is not license.

"Hawthorne left an unfortunate legacy. He hired too many teachers. His support of the arts was commendable. I support the arts myself. My last time in San Francisco I bought a painting. That ought to prove something.

"There are too many teachers in fine arts and humanities. I'm sorry Barnaby, but some of your people will have to go." Barnaby Thomas, Chairman of Fine Arts, stared at the president's right red ear.

" Last year Hawthorne hired nine new teachers. He did not ask me, yet I must live with his choices and priorities. We must find a way to escape this terrible budget crunch.

"Thank you for your overwhelming support."

While the administrators clapped vigorously, Mann reached over and congratulated Davis, "fine presentation. Excellent."

Walter Simons, the voc tech chairman, pounced on Davis's hand. Resembling a buzz saw, his voice said, "Thanks for expanding our program in welding, electronics and auto mechanics."

Barnaby Thomas slipped out the door without congratulating his boss who was saying "Thank you. Thank you. Thank you."

# CHAPTER 7.

## THE COMMUNITY COLLEGE-
## AN AMERICAN PHENOMENON

W e, the faculty, meet in September for preschool instruction. I pass the tall ugly rusty iron sculpture while walking to the meetings. It casts its long shadow over me before I enter the auditorium. I make a mental note to ask someone soon, what in the hell is that thing? I sit next to a short thin balding man, Maurie Girodias, the librarian. After mutual introductions, Girodias says, "Isn't it inspiring. This week in thousands of community colleges, administrators are patiently telling faculties the history of the community college movement, a mighty wave cresting, breaking, and squirting through the college doors and windows, thousands of them tumbling, crashing, thundering, splashing, dripping and oozing into the future. And yet we CC's are just the tip of that mighty churning surging howling frozen iceberg, America, which laden with potential, waits for leaders to thaw things out."

"Be patient Maurie," I whisper, amazed at such erudition in the hinterlands. "Consider the Sequoias tiny seeds, which wait in small cones until the day they fall weppeling to earth, where they must continue to wait on bare earth for rain and snow and warmth until the day of germination, and then they must grow and wait only another 4000 years for greatness."

Our conversation halts as Davis, Mann and Isawaddy walk on stage and sit in an intimate arc. Dean Mann reminds me of an astronaut as he speaks in a clear easy to understand voice. "Friends, we're going to chat with you about our college. In the beginning the faculty was a handful of men. These first teachers became leaders. The first physical science teacher created physical science. The first biology teacher established biology, and so on until all of the divisions were formed. And sports were part of the beginning. Teachers who played a particular sport became coaches. There was a splendid merger of academia and athletics.

"Oh those were good times. Students and faculty were a family. When friends met, that was a faculty meeting."

"Don't get the wrong idea," says Isawaddy. His voice is thinner and requires more listening effort. "The early days were rough. When cupboards and shelves were needed, we built them. If the floor was dirty, we swept it."

President Davis says, "There were times when it seemed as if the college would fold. Enrollments rose in the beginning, but during the Second World War the young men went off to fight, and some of us teachers saw combat. Enrollment plummeted until we won the war. Joyous with victory, Humaluh welcomed the veterans with a parade. They were all good students. New faculty was hired including Rodney and myself. Enrollment climbed. After the boom, when enrollment dropped, we stuck together. Nobody lost their job."

Isawaddy says, "We weren't divided into divisions. The English teacher, the chemist, the historian, we all drank coffee together."

Girodias whispers in my ear, "It was like paradise before the eating of the apple."

"The faculty trounced the student basketball team nine straight times," says Mann, leaning back, hands on his thighs. "We'd let them get ahead in the first quarter, and then we'd kick the living daylights out of them." Mann winks at the faculty and chuckles.

"The college has been good to me," says Isawaddy. "My closest friends are the people I met my first year. And the students like this place. Just talk to the alumni. They wouldn't trade Humaluh for Stanford or Cascadia."

During the break I munch cookies provided by the faculty wives and listen to Girodias. "They forgot to mention poor Hawthorne. Brought in from Columbia, he pushed the arts. The teachers complained, said our president is up in the clouds and away from reality. Too tightly tied to the past, obviously he can't plan for the future."

I ask, "Did he have any supporters?"

"Sure. He strengthened humanities and fine arts by more hiring. They thought he was great. The rest of the faculty resisted his innovations. Disappointed with the lack of support he resigned last year and went to Massachusetts. The Alcott School was delighted to have him."

"Why was Davis acceptable?"

"The faculty wanted a known quantity. They told the board, give us a president who has proven himself with us. We need stability."

"Stability's boring."

"The first of the faculty to acquire a Ph.D. was Davis. Although a lover of ties, he won for us the right of no ties required. A nondrinker, he won for us the right to drink in local bars."

"So everybody loved Davis?"

"No. Not everyone. Some said he was a communist because he refused to support Senator Joseph McCarthy. At that time Davis defended himself by saying, 'Sure my dad was a union man, but I belong to the American Legion'. Under pressure, with misgivings, in a split vote the board selected Davis. And Davis, to demonstrate his changing priorities hired two science and three voc-tech teachers. Listen."

Hearing the sounds of a band we run outside. My eyes blinking in the sun, I see Tom Magnum, handle bar mustache twitching, leading the faculty chorus and band. Magnum's cheeks are round beefsteak tomatoes as he puffs into the shiny brass tube. He reminds me of a friendly fuzzy bear. The words pulsing over the lawn are carried forth on the blast of the tuba. I listen to the words of *Welcome*, sung by the faculty:

Oh ... Oh...
Welcome.
We take you
Into our hearts.
Join with us
Be our friends
You are welcome.

The President says
Welcome.
The Dean says
Welcome.
The flowers bloom
Welcome.
While the coffee perks.

Their song completed, the band disassembles. I walk over to Magnum and say, "Your band is wonderful. So cheerful."

"Life without fun is like a tuba without wind," says Magnum taking my hand and flopping it like a newly caught trout.

Regaining my hand I say, "This is a joyful place."

His gentle eyes on me, Magnum replies, "Sometimes we have fun. We sing about being on the same team, but I'll tell you something. Here or anywhere, it's every man for himself."

"I don't agree. I think men can live in love and friendship. Don't you believe in brotherhood?"

"Sure I believe in brotherhood, apple pie, and Daddy Laddy and the Big Spook. And you Leo, when have you been surrounded with love and brotherhood?"

"Several times,"

"For how long?"

"When I fell in love with Cleo, I was covered with love like a shortcake smothered in strawberries and whipped cream."

"That's smotherhood, not brotherhood."

"When I was a baby my mother sat with me in our lion chair. According to my aunt I was covered with kisses."

"Still smotherhood. Any other times?"

"Oh lots of times"

"For how long?"

"Oh up to an hour or two, depending on the girl," I grin. He has me.

"You see, you agree," says the massive mischievous gnome that is Maqnum. I sense brotherhood as we laugh and chortle.

"We must go," says Magnum, observing the other teachers returning to the auditorium. Excusing himself he goes to sit with the band. Regretting his loss, I rejoin Girodias.


Dean Mann walks like a lion to the podium and watches the teachers. When the room is mostly silent the Dean says, "Today I present a man I greatly admire. He has willingly done whatever the college has required."

Girodias whispers, "Like a good German."

"He has come from a humble beginning. Once a bare footed scholar in Leeds Alabama, then a scaler of Olympian academic heights, and now our president."

"The airs too rarified to breathe," whispers Girodias.

"In 1946, new to Humaluh Valley Junior College, as we were called, he rolled up his sleeves and helped direct the movement of men and materials out of the high school basement and into the Quonset huts." Soft laughter greeted the dean's humor.

"His brilliant Ph.D. thesis is titled *Machiavelli the Humanist*. Machiavelli wrote, 'There is no other way of guarding one's self against flattery than by letting men know they will not offend you by speaking the truth.' Today I speak the truth.

"An inspiring teacher, he has taught *Great Dictators, Isms and Schisms, People as Numbers, Social Control,* and *Cascadian Hagiography.* As chairman of the humanities division he preached what he practiced.

"He has coached winning teams in basketball and baseball, and authored a recent book review for the *Christian Science Monitor.* He is an all around man." Throwing out his right arm, Mann says, "Our esteemed president, Elmore Davis." Mann briskly walks to a front row seat.

The smiling president, wearing an olive green suit with square shoulders, slowly walks to the podium. His alligator shoes and shiny forehead reflect the spotlights. Smiling he says, "Thank you Rodney for that generous introduction that reminds me of another saying by Machiavelli, 'There is nothing more difficult to carry out, nor more doubtful of success than to initiate a new order of things.'

"Machiavelli was not completely correct. My reforms will not create an enemy of anyone who wants our college on top." His voice reaches out like a friendly warm wave as he welcomes the old teachers who have returned and those who are new. When he said, "all of you are aware of our nationwide reputation and the brilliance of our staff," Girodias softly says to me, "Our brilliant staff, Ha. Most of these yokels can't find their way to the library." Trying to listen to the president I close my ears to Girodias.

The president rumbles on, "Community Colleges are an original American phenomenon. The first public community college was in Joliet, Illinois in 1901." Girodias snickers, "Also the home of Statesville Prison." I feel like telling Girodias to shut up.

"In 1647, in the Massachusetts Bay Colony, every township of one hundred or more households was ordered to conduct a grammar school. Public schools grew. Many of the wealthy class said they wouldn't send their children to pauper schools." Girodias says, "If I had big bucks I wouldn't send my kids to public school."

When Davis thumps the lectern he wakes up two dozing professors. "Don't ever forget the landmark Kalamazoo Decision: 'Public high schools are to be supported by public taxation.' And the Morrill Act that provided public land to establish colleges to teach agriculture and the mechanic arts. As some people had sneered at public grammar and high schools, others sneered at the new colleges."

"That's a lot of sneering," says Girodias.

"Many colleges started from high schools. Farmer's High School developed into Pennsylvania State College." I think of the Penn State woodchucks and how much wood could a woodchuck chuck. I hear a gentle mooooooooooo in back of me.

"These colleges were popular for a good reason. Schultz estimated, the lifetime earnings of a man with a college degree will total $151,000. This is double the lifetime earnings of a high school graduate."

"We teach our young people the trades. Our graduates enter the job market as well paid craftsmen." Girodias whispers, "I wouldn't want those lunkheads working on my car."

"It took Zook to say, 'Equal educational abilities for all.' Yes my teachers, we have learned lots of things since Leland Stanford Junior High and the days of George Zook. In fact our college marching band is modeled after Arthur P. Barnes and his skill with silliness."

Girodias softly sings, "My eyes are dim, I have not brought my specs with me."

There is much applause. The dean reappears at the podium. When the room quiets he speaks. "The president has told you of the glowing past, present and future. Unfortunately my task is to talk about some of the problems.

"We have institutional problems and discipline problems, some of which merge and some are separated as discrete entities." Girodias whispers, "What does that mean?"

"To identify each category of problems we must distinguish the principal operational problems in each category. Discipline orientedproblems include articulation, curriculum, and personnel. The principle operative agent to resolve and solve such problems and to actualize their fulfillment and realization must be the department."

The dean continues talking in this lucid manner and when finished is greeted with much applause for his brilliance. Being somewhat ignorant of some of the words, I ask Girodias, "What did he say?"

The universal critic reveals his own stupidity by saying, "Search me?"

During lunch, Girodias says, "I have to listen to the same bullshit each year."

After lunch we hear the director of counseling say, "Thirtythree percent of our students are in the lowest two quintiles of academic ability." I ask Girodias, "What's a quintile?"

Girodias says, "It means they're dumb."

The associate dean of business, Ben Coolsam, describes documents. "All important forms for things such as using the car, must be signed by the president." Chuckling, Gary Pantagruel the next speaker says, "We have an open door policy. First come first served. They have to be able to fill out the application form, give us the five-dollar fee and a copy of their high school records. If they can do these things, with or without help, they're in.

"We award about 250 degrees a year. Half of them are associate of arts degrees, the rest are in nursing and other vocational areas including electronic technology and business mismanagement." The Vice President laughs at the frowns of Ben Coolsam and Henry Rearden, and elaborately corrects himself with a big "Excuse Me. Business Management."

The registrar, John Jennison Drew says, "We use print outs for grading. Please get your grades in on time. You have twentyfour hours after an examination to get your grades in." I think, I'll have trouble meeting that deadline.

Mr. Isawaddy, representing the Humaluh Valley College Teacher's Association says, "We have recently negotiated an employment agreement. Your placement on the salary schedule is determined by your qualifications. Each year, you advance on the schedule."

Girodias whispers, "Until you fall over."

I say, "Please be quiet. I want to hear."

Isawaddy is saying, "Work experience equals one year of teaching experience. Our motto is, the more you learn, the more you earn. To add excitement to our salaries, at the end of each year we have lottery night. The grand sweepstakes winner receives a thirty percent salary increase. As far as I know, we are the only college in the country with this progressive feature. Last years winner was Gary Pantagruel." Pantagruel waves from his seat in the front row. I think, no wonder he's always happy.

During the next two days there are additional speeches including an extensive presentation by the groundskeepers who reveal the history and philosophy of the campus grasses, trees and shrubs.

# CHAPTER 8.

## ARE YOU PENTECOSTAL?

Cleo's heels clack as she climbs the steps to the president's house. Looking things over, I try to think of a compliment, some way to separate it from the neighboring homes at the base of Gazebo Mountain. At the door Florence, the President's wife, is waving to us as if we are best friends. I praise their white shutters.

Davis says, "We're not planning on moving into the clouds with the physicians. We like it lower down with the plumbers and teachers." We laugh.

Davis leads us guys into his library and listens intently to our praise that includes, "I could spend all year in here." "You've got more books than a high school library." "Sir, you must be a real scholar, the books go all the way to the ceiling."

Davis says, "The house I grew up in lacked books. Fortunately, Mr. Maxwell Clark my sixth grade teacher took an interest in me. Once after cleaning his attic he gave me more books than I could carry. That was the start of my collection." He slowly runs his hand over old leather bindings and says, "They used to make books to last. These books from the seventeenth and eighteenth centuries will last hundreds of years more. Yet look at this." He pulls out a copy of *The Hills Beyond*, published during World War II. I see brown pages and think of old newspapers. "Some of the books published today aren't much better," says Davis.

"I'd be afraid to read that book," I say. "The pages might break and crumble."

"Exactly," says Davis.

Leaving the library, we rejoin our wives chirping in the dining room. Mrs. Davis gives each of us a piece of German chocolate cake and a dainty cup of coffee. I am afraid to sit on the furniture, which reminds me of the teacups. I can hardly get my finger through the porcelain handle. I tell the president, "This is a fine get together."

Davis says, "You're a lucky young man."

"How's that?" I say.

"You've been to Zanzibar," says Davis.

"Oh that," I say. "I wandered over there to smell the spices."

After the president wanders off, I return to the library to smell the books. My hands touch *Babbit*, *The Prince*, and *Dead Souls*. I notice stickers on several of the oldest books from the Library of Saint Victor in Paris. The titles are embossed in gold, and a few of the page edges are shiny with gold. A rough translation from the Latin follows of some of the titles:

*A History of Death* by Hermodorus (apparently he was paid 1000 drachmae for the job) revised by Paul La Farge

*Maglogranatum vitorium* or *A Pomegranate of Vice*

*Ars Honeste Petandi in Societate* or *The Art of Public Farting*

*Decrotatorum Scholarium* or *The Rottenness of Scholars*

*De Croquendis Lardonibus Libri* or *Bacon Eating* (Three Volumes)

*De Optimitate Triparum* or *The Super Belly*

*Rostocostojambedanesse de Moustarda Post Prandium Servienda* or *How to Serve Mustard After Dining* (Fourteen Volumes)

*Barbouillamenta Presidenti* or *Presidential Scribbling*

*Callibistratorium Caffardiae par Ehrlichmann Haldemann* or *How to Calibrate Hypocracy*

*Antipericatametanaparbeugedamphicribationes merdicantium de Vita et Honestate Braguardorum par Lourdaudus* or *The Life of Braggarts Beehive by Francis Daniel Pastorius,* Scribe to Pennsylvania County Court

This collection of fine classics makes me realize that the president is definitely a scholar. I take special notice of the care with which he has underlined important passages in scarlet marker ink.

After exploring the library I return to the tour group. Davis is saying, "The year before becoming president we enlarged our home. We removed the wall between the bedrooms. The doubling of the master bedroom allowed us to install health equipment. To stay in shape I do one sit up and two push-ups every late afternoon before dinner. I finish up with three minutes on the Exercycle. It builds circulation and is recommended for astronauts."

Watching the president, who is standing on the exercise mat, I try to imagine him as an astronaut, belly wobbling above the lunar landscape.

He opens the glass doors to the shower and says, "I shower every morning and evening. Keeps me refreshed."

I think of my dad who had gone once a week to the Milwaukee Athletic Club. I hadn't a clue as to what he had done there? I couldn't imagine him lifting weights. Easier to imagine him studying witchcraft. His mind was brilliant and his muscles lethargic. Perhaps he went to the club for companionship. I wonder, did they have a sauna? Did he sweat away belly fat while sitting in a moist overheated room? I only saw him sweat in the summer when he cut weeds and brambles. He would never have pedaled a bicycle to nowhere. I could imagine watching my brother watching him. "Hi Dad. Where ya going?" "Oh three miles out." "What did you see Dad?" "I saw a warn puce carpet and a beige wall." "I have an idea Dad. Let's put up a roll of scenery. If you get bored with the U.S. you can bicycle near Wiesbaden alongside the Rhine."

I rush with Cleo to join everyone else; we are all leaving. My sweetie is glad to see me. Walking to the car she asks, "Where were you?"

"I took the tour to the library and the exercise room. What did you do?"

"We toured the kitchen and pantry. Mrs. Davis is an expert with needlework. I was impressed. I would have liked seeing the exercise equipment."

The next afternoon Cleo, Karl and I go to a salmon barbecue on campus and are introduced to Barnaby Thomas, an artist. During the handshake I silently appreciate his calloused hand, and recall my hands when I had worked in the woods. Thomas said, "Hello. I'm supposed to make you feel welcome." He led us outside to a long narrow concrete pit. We saw 3 to 5 pound salmon halves on an iron rack. "The fish were caught yesterday and today we cook them over an alder fire." Pulled by scents we head for the serving line. A moment later I receive and admire a big chunk of pink fish peeking out from the darkened skin. Karl steals a piece from me and says, "This is good Daddy."

Cleo says, "Be patient Karl."

After we sit down Karl, who has always hated fish, devours his salmon and goes back for seconds. Cleo licks her fingers and says, "This is gourmet dining. We've got to get a barbecue."

Barnaby says, "We make our own sauce."

I say, "Barnaby, I'm surprised. I thought artists wore sandals and had long beards."

"Artists are no different than other people," he says. He is clean-shaven and well groomed. I am angry with myself. I try to stop myself from saying inappropriate things to new acquaintances. The group is quiet. I am grateful when Bobby and Doris Pompa amble over.

Pompa reminds me of a well-fed French shopkeeper. His wife Doris does not look French. She is blonde and lacks curls. She is athletic looking like Cleo. She is about the same height but has larger bones.

"You're the bug man?" Says Pompa. I jump as Pompa's strong short fingers crush my hand. I think, I need revenge.

"Swirlopeds, not bugs," I say. My extreme gravity hides my resentment. Pompa, dark round plastic rims framing each eye, reminds me of an owl with strong talons. His small ears are almost hidden and eyes are partially buried. Beneath a full push broom mustache wanders a flexible mouth with thick sensual lips.

After releasing my crushed fingers, Pompa tenderly cradles Cleo's strong hand as he looks soulfully into her eyes. "You must be Cleo," he says. Cleo smiles. Doris frown smiles. Pompa says, "Mann told me all about you Cleo, and he's right. You are a big improvement over most of the other faculty wives." Still holding her hand he makes a low bow.

Tightening her smile, Doris says, "Hello Cleo. Welcome to Humaluh. Oh, I've lost track of my children. Will you excuse us. We've got to find them."

Pompa, reluctantly releases Cleo's hands, says, "See you later," and follows his wife like a Labrador retriever.

"That was Bobby and Doris Pompa," says Barnaby.

"I guessed that," I say.

A man about fortyfive, thin and tall, comes over with his wife. They remind me of that Norman Rockwell couple standing by the proverbial farmhouse: The man holding a pitchfork, the woman a pitcher, both of them emanating stability and strength of character. Only the man's big ears sticking out like fungi, mar the image. In addition his arms are a trifle long.

"John and Helen Isawaddy," says Barnaby. "I'd like you to meet Leo and Cleo Bauer, and their son Karl."

"Are you settled in yet?" asks Helen.

"We've got a lot to do," says Cleo.

"Can we help?" says Helen.

"No. No. We're almost settled in," she says, her voice dusted with panic.

"We hear your house is very beautiful," says Helen.

"Thank you. We got lucky. Please visit us," says Cleo.

"Feel free to visit us," says Helen. Stepping closer, she looks deeply into Cleo's eyes and says, "Are you Pentecostal?"

"Pentecostal? No," says Cleo.

"You have a radiance about your face. I was sure you were Pentecostal," says Helen. "I was going to invite you to church Sunday."

"We're Unitarians" says Cleo. "Is there a Unitarian church in town?"

"I haven't a clue. What are Unitarians?" says Helen.

"I'm not sure," says Cleo. "We go to church, talk about self fulfillment, freedom of expression, and we form committees."

"Don't you believe in Jesus?"

"That's up to each person. We can either believe Jesus is divine or a myth. No one tells us what to believe." While the women talk, Isawaddy says, "Tomorrow at our department meeting we will discuss classes. Have you read the text?"

"Partly. I'm underlining the important concepts," I tilt my head to maintain eye contact. Isawaddy's eyes are six inches above my eyes."

"Good idea. If you like, you can sit in on our classes. Pompa's section starts before yours. You'll learn some valuable teaching methods from him."

"Thanks for the invitation. My Montana lab held twenty-four students. I've never faced a large class."

"Don't worry. It's natural to be scared. Our students are friendly. They will accept you."

"Good. It's important to be accepted. I hate rejection."

"After our meeting, you can move into your office. Its across the hall from me."

"That's great," I say. "This is so different from grad school. I hated the backbiting. Everyone wanted what somebody else had."

"We work as a team."

"I'm glad to be one with you," I say smiling.

"I'll see you tomorrow," says Isawaddy walking away with Helen.

"Funny the way his chin pokes out," I say to Cleo.

"He has a dimple," She says.

Barnaby rejoins us and takes us over to teachers in art, psychology, music, drama and English. Some of them remind me of the person I used to be. Inwardly I vow to avoid the radical types during my first year at Humaluh. I will work hard and develop a reputation for conservative reliability.

When the barbecue is over, we are among the last to leave. Karl is swinging beneath a tree.

That night, getting ready for bed, Cleo says, "Why did you have to say something stupid to Barnaby?"

"It was a small thing. I didn't know he'd get angry," I say. Often after a disagreement, even over a small thing, we brood for several days. On this evening, I keep silent, the matter is dropped, and soon we make love. What a wonderful way to settle disagreements.

The next morning the sun is shining. White fluffy clouds hang motionless in the sky. I am marching confidently along the campus walk, head back, shoulders square. I robustly sing a song to the robins who in turn are checking for worms in the squishy bright green grass. My silly words, as recalled by the birds, were:

Oh I'm Leo, that's who
I'm proud to be me

I'm a lucky fellow
Even my wife is happy
She sings all day
Hooray, hooray

My little boy plays with his toys
Hums
He's glad
Hooray

Across the quad
Teachers are walking
My colleagues are light footed
Happy and friendly

Wow
I'm a college professor-
My lectures will be great
I won't bore
I'll modulate my voice

My class will discuss controversial issues without rancor
I'll stimulate them with evolutionary tales
I'll turn them on with love for the earth.
We will love everything

Oh sky
Examinations will be enjoyable
My students will learn to think
Meaningless memorization will be forbidden

Now I can do things my way
I'm done with graduate school
Free as an eagle
My limit is the sky
Hooray, Hooray

John Isawaddy, having just left the administration building, stops, watches, and listens. He is particularly intrigued when I complete three cartwheels.

Walking over to me he smiles and says, "Hello Leo. Great cart wheeling."

"I cartwheel when I'm happy," I say.

"That's wonderful," says Isawaddy. At this moment I feel close to Isawaddy.

"We can have our meeting now," says Isawaddy leading the way to his office in the long white rectangular concrete Watson & Crick Building. He adds, "Leo, I'd like you to meet Dr. Robert Jackson."

While shaking hands and examining the big boned, tall, heavily wattled man, I think I have grabbed a fist full of macaroni. "Glad to meet you," he says adding, "You're the Swirloped man?"

Bobby Pompa comes over and thumps Jackson on the back. Jackson's head jerks back, then he smoothes his blonde hair. Pompa says, "Robert, you must feel forever proud to be one of the world's top authorities on fern pollen?"

"It's over. It's finished. I'm almost finished," grins Jackson.

"You'll continue your research?" said Isawaddy, concern in his voice.

"Nope. I'm gonna take all those test tubes and ash can them," says Jackson. I immediately like Jackson.

"We'll be able to use the room again," laughs Pompa.

"You'll be able to use the room again," says Jackson with a sigh.

"You're throwing out your whole collection?" says Isawaddy.

"Not the slides. I'm keeping some and sending the rest to museums."

"I'm glad you're finished," says Pompa. I was always scared to go into that room. One sneeze and my asthma would have done me in."

"You sound glad it's over," I say.

"It's a release. A little revising and it's off to the journal. I can live again." He looked as if he needed a long vacation.

Isawaddy holds the meeting beneath photographs of row upon row of bird beaks and electron microscope photographs of molecular components. The fibrous sub units Number 13 are exquisitely photographed. The main purpose of the meeting is to welcome and invite me into the department. When the meeting is concluded, I accompany Pompa into the next office and wait, as the file drawer is zunked open. Pompa searches through the folders like a hound sniffing rabbits. I examine the wall photographs of Pompa knocking out his opponent while boxing, scoring a touchdown in slushy snow, and scoring a basket. "Here are some cheat sheets," mumbles Pompa, handing me a handful of keys to past tests. The tests were every bit as rigorous and intellectually probing as those at Intermountain University.

I read: *Obelia dichotoma, Anthopleura artemisia, Gonionemus vertens, Metridium marginatum, Metridium senile, Telia lofotensis, Bugula pacifica, Membranipora membranacea, Aphrodite japonica, Smilodon, Balanus nubilus, Limnoria lignorum, Crago Alaskensis, Hippolyte clarki, Cardium corbis, Ostrea lurida, Loligo opalescens, Monoceros, Solester stimpsoni, Dendraster excentricus,* and *Rostanga pulchra.*

After closing the file drawer, while holding a stack of general biology examinations, he says with great solemnity, "Leo Bauer. I hereby present these documents to you in the fervent hope that you may be able to devise, develop, and produce even more fiendish examinations."

Thanking Pompa, I return to Isawaddy's office. He stacks a pile of textbooks in my arms, which reach my nose. I settle them with difficulty on the floor for temporary storage. Next, Isawaddy in the lead, we quickly walk across the quad to the union and pick up my office key from the dean's smiling secretary. During the short transaction I of course admire her legs. A moment later we are across the hall in front of the president's secretary, a motherly woman by the name of Mrs. Johnson. I do not look at her legs. She asks me, "What do you need?"

"I don't know," I say.

"Come with me," she beckons. I follow her to the treasure trove. She loads me up, while she suggests and I point, with file folders, a thick appointment calendar, large stapler, heavy tape dispenser, transparent tape, paper clips, class roll books, ink, glue, carbon paper, typing paper, erasers, ruler, and an official college stamp. Though a treasure-trove, it reminds me of the closet in grade school when I destroyed damn near everything after my incarceration by the nun.

I back away crablike saying "thank you, thank you." And with the aid of a handcart push the stuff back to the Watson and Crick Building.

Back in my office I pile the new stuff on the wide, light colored desk. Isawaddy comes over. "It's hardwood," He knocks on the wood. "Solid," he adds. I examine the room. The bookshelves contain old journals. A black phone is on the desk. Next to the door a large piece of black plastic closes off the backside of a hall display window. A bumper sticker bearing the legend EAT MORE BEEF, seals a rip in the plastic.

"I'd like to have a new exhibit each month. Would you do that job for me?"

"I've always wanted to work in a museum," I say.

Isawaddy gives me a tour of the department.

I open and close drawers. I love to explore drawers. "Tight, fine job," I say.

"We built the shelves and cupboards. They're of solid birch."

"You did a nice job." While examining the collections of grasses, ferns, flowering plants, bones and furs I ask, "Are there collections of insects, Swirlopeds, mammals or birds?"

"No. However, if you wish you can develop additional collections."

I feel a rush of elation. We enter the prep room. Chemicals occupy one long wall. It smells of alcohol, formaldehyde and dust. The powdered and bottled fluids are in alphabetical order. Gallon jugs of formaldehyde are on deep widely spaced shelves just above the floor. In the back of the room five-gallon containers contain sharks, human babies, cats, monkeys, doves, crabs, crayfish, starfish, squid and fetal pigs. Bits of skin and what looks like a white sandy powder has settled to the bottom of many of the jars. The specimens are bleached to gray. I am especially interested in the shark and human fetuses.

The zoology classroom walls contain charts of eyeballs, skulls, tonsils, guts, kidneys and livers. A cross section of a penis resembles a bundle of telephone cables in Ma Bell's underground.

The botany classroom has charts, cross-sections of tree trunks, pinecones, leaves and flowers. Other charts on wooden stands show the life cycle of mosses and liverworts.

After seeing everything I say, "Thank you."

"We're glad to have you with us. Come to me if you need anything or if you have any difficulty," says Isawaddy.

Returning to my office, I put all the new books on shelves. I dump the examinations unsorted in a file drawer, and the supplies in desk drawers. After years of office sharing, it is great to have my own office.

I return home in time to tuck Karl in. Before falling asleep he asks, "Can I join a baseball team?" I say, "We will find you a baseball team." Cleo says, "I want to find a jogging trail." I say, "There's one that goes around the campus. You will find someone to run with." We are all happy. We make love after Karl is abed. It is our traditional way to celebrate. Life is good.

# CHAPTER 9.

# BOBBY POMPA MASTER TEACHER

Mock student, I wait for Bobby Pompa on the first day of class. Three minutes past the hour a sport shirted rosy faced Bobby Pompa hesitantly enters the room. Poking his head just inside the door, He says, "Is this physics?"

A student says "No."

Pompa scratching his short brown hair stops beneath the transom turns and asks, "What class is this if it isn't physics?"

A youth, his face covered with acne, says, "Biology."

As if suddenly bopped by Newton's apple, Pompa brightens, bows and announces, "How wonderful. This is my class. I am your humble teacher, Bobby Pompa." Smoothing his mustache he leans on the green board, and says, "I'd like to tell you about myself. My ancestors, fortunate people, left England. Unfortunate people, they settled in Des Moines. Frightened by a small flood, in 1851 they moved to the tranquil community of Spirit Lake. Barely escaping massacre by the Sioux, they moved to Mitchell, South Dakota and helped construct the Corn Palace. Corn has been in our blood for over one hundred years, some of my relatives still drink the stuff."

A few of the students chuckle. I think, he's a buffoon. After a moment's pause Pompa continues, "I went to Billy Mitchell High School. Hard work produced success. I don't intend to brag however, in addition to a straight A average I was student body president and had the lead in our senior play. I lettered in football, boxing, basketball, baseball and track, playing tennis and golf on the side. As a halfback I made the all-state team in my senior year. Our last game I scored five touchdowns and ran two hundred and thirty yards. We won the League championship. A guard in basketball, I started for three years and led the team in scoring. In boxing I was a light heavyweight. Third in the golden gloves, I realized I hated talking through puffy lips, so I gave up boxing."

I think, how could such a mildly plump man be so athletic? "When I was at Iowa State I escaped the draft because my graduate school grades were sooo high. As you can imagine, this gave my father great pleasure and me no distress."

While Pompa talks I stare at a molecule revolving from the ceiling. If it was bigger I could slide down that Helix. If it was in a lake, I could use it as a slide and splash in the sun. Pompa says, "Challenged by graduate school, I met some fine people including our president and our dean. Rodney Mann inspired me to select an important new area of research: The biochemistry of slug excrement. Why students, I've spent hundreds of days," he threw out his chest, "bravely crawling through dark dangerous forests on the gooey slime trail of the wild wicked western banana slug. Such delightful creatures. Before my very eyes the little buggers with no hope of reward, produced copious quantities of soft, smooth, gray, greasy green poop."

The class hollers with laughter. Pompa bows. I sit up, wobble my head. Looking proud Pompa continues. "On those days, I carefully scooped their little gifts into vials and returned in triumph to the laboratory. Utilizing the tools of modern science including gas chromatography, that poop was shown to contain all sorts of goodies including ketones, aldehydes, amino, and uric acids, phosphates, nitrates, and ammonia. In return for all that hard work, Cascadia State awarded me a Ph.D. at the ripe old age of twentyfive. That was two years ago. Since then I've become a wise old professor."

A boy's hand shoots up. "Do you still study slug poop?"

Pompa's face shows sad. "Unfortunately, my teaching takes so much time that I've had to abandon slug chasing."

He prances across the front of the room, giving a right hook to an imaginary opponent. "Now I'm dedicated to students," He gives another right hook, "the boxing team, my family and the community." He does a final upward jab.

Walking behind the large black front counter, hands flat on the black surface, hunched forward he says, "Students, are we going to learn biology this quarter? You bet your sweet biffy. But we've got to work. You can't be lazy. I didn't win fights and make Phi Beta Kappa by playing cards all day; I had to do that at night. Oh, I didn't get drunk and go off snoozing and boozing. Oh No. I was working out, keeping fit, toeing the line, and "he winks" at a coed," I didn't break training unless I had a good reason."

I think, thank god the man's human.

Pompa says, "As it was with me, so can it be with you. I give a few A's to hard workers and F's to the shirkers." He stares menacingly at the class. I shrink against my chair. Pompa says, "Don't worry. I won't eat you. Class dismissed. Pick up your class outline on the way out."

Still chuckling, Pompa is the first one out. I trail the students through the door thinking, how can I compete with Pompa? Even though I studied hard, I never received accolades. I wonder why they really hired me. I must try to learn from Pompa. Even if he is a hot shot, I'm not inferior to that son of a bitch. I'll show him.

That evening I tell Cleo, "Pompa is a buffoon. A very smart buffoon."

The next morning I wait for my students in the same lecture hall. The place resembles an auditorium. After the students are seated I walk to the center of the room. My legs quiver. The first time I try to speak, I lean forward, open my dry mouth; no words come forth. Forcing myself, I send out some words in an almost firm voice, but then I'm quiet waiting for the students to hush. I think of the time I had confessed inexperience before a group in a national park when I was a park naturalist. The vacationing people accepted my failings because I did not deceive them.

Remembering the forgiving campers, I began my lecture by confessing ineptitude.


"Welcome. I'm Leo Bauer. I've been working hard on my lecture notes. Even though I've labored, they're rough. I hope you understand."

The students must see me as a curly headed young man wearing a gray Kupenheimer suit. The over sixty young people could not have signed up for the class because of my great reputation. Watching me nervously pacing back and forth in front of the green board, they have little idea whether I will be a good or bad teacher. What they do know is that this course is required for graduation. They also may have realized, by taking the early class, they will get out of school early.

I say to them, "When I was a kid I used to wander through the forests. I'd get on my knees to watch caterpillars, and later I'd chase the butterflies with my net. In my teens field glasses were always around my neck. As an undergraduate I tried to learn everything I could about nature. In graduate school I clambered over rocky streambeds and felt the cold mountain stream push on my rubber hip boats. At that time I helped a friend study the water ouzel, a gray bird that sings like tinkling icicles. While the snow falls they swim through icy torrents. Swimming through the clean clear mountain streams, jumping from the whirling water to a rock they perch, knees bobbing like a rock and roller while blinking pearly white flashing nictitating membranes."

The students laugh. Proud of breaking the ice I say, "I've spent lots of time studying Swirlopeds. Does anyone know what Swirlopeds are?" No hands go up.

"What a shame. Swirlopeds are amazing creatures with legs only on the left side of their body. They whirl like tops, revolving in dirt, swirling in water, and spinning through air."

In the last row two students look at each other and at the same instant say, "Is he for real?"

"Let me demonstrate," I drop to the floor and spin before their eyes. They look astounded. After several revolutions I slow, stop, stand, and breathing rapidly return to my notes.

The students are impressed. Now they are hopeful that biology will be an interesting and entertaining course. Their hopes are slightly dashed when I become Bauer the pedagogue. Talking of tests and the laboratory I say, "Laboratory is required. At the conclusion of every laboratory period you must get your lab manual stamped. This will indicate to us that you know the material." As I say these words I think, it is nonsense to waste time stamping books. It indicates nothing. Yet I must do it because it is required.

I say, "The laboratory manual has been written by members of our department and is easy to understand." while thinking, I hope we can rewrite the damn thing. It confuses me, so how in the hell can the students understand?

Students shift and tap toes while I talk about tests and grades. I put on a sad face when I say some students might get F's. The students don't look worried. I say, "I think it is tragic to get an F." My voice lowers like a storm cloud sneaking across the valley. I try to sound fatherly, while remembering the F's of my past. With more math and better grades I might have gotten a Ph.D. "F's are not the result of ignorance but of negligence. If you find yourself going down the road of scholastic suicide, stop. Take control or drop this course. Think of the consequences of failure." I create silence to give them time to contemplate and visualize their future ruined. I add, "You want to emulate Zorba the Greek and work in the mines or become a fisherman."

Changing emphasis I say, "Please come and visit me. I'm a nice person. Don't just work for a grade. Don't become tape recorders. Enjoy biology. Do outside reading." I shrug. "Much of the course is memorizing, but there is more to learning." I then dismiss the class after talking for fifty minutes. Damn. I got through it. I did OK.

Some of the students make comments and observations as they leave including, "His hair is curly." "His pants are pressed and neat." "He's enthusiastic and a little crazy. I like that in a teacher." "Swirlopeds are weird." "I hate it when someone is so nervous." "I think he's cute."

On the way to my office I hum a little tune.

Cleo seeing me skip through the door immediately brightens. I hear the ice clink as she makes me an old fashioned. I love sipping the sweet amber booze and ice and sucking the red juice from the sweet sweet cherry. While she cooks dinner I continue to suck the bright red cherry and admire the leaves on the Japanese maple, which are glowing in the setting sunlight. In the evening Cleo goes out for a jog with a friend while I prepare tomorrow's lecture.

During the coming days I continue to watch and listen to Pompa's lectures. I was in class the day he entered the room dribbling an imaginary basketball. After a fake to the right and a reverse pivot he drove down the middle of the floor, leapt, and stuffed the ball through the hoop. Catching the ball, after a fake to the right, he dribbled between his legs to his left, stopped and made a jump shot from the top of the key. Pompa shyly smiles as the imaginary crowd goes wild. Again with the ball he races to the baseline, comes up beneath the basket, looks at the hoop and makes a reverse lay in. The crowd is roaring. Seconds tick. The score is tied. Pompa dribbles the ball across the second line, glances at the clock. Six seconds. He fakes to his left, the defender takes the fake, tries to recover. By this time Pompa doing a reverse pivot drives down the middle and stuffs it. The crowd is delirious. The cheerleaders leap to Pompa, and throw their arms around his muscular neck. Untangling the girls arms he says, "Now that we've won the game, we can study molecules. A simple sugar is called a monosaccharide. Examples are sucrose, glucose and ribose.

Hook more than two together and you've got a polysaccharide like starch in potatoes or glycogen in bats."

When I awake the classroom is empty. The next morning I manage to stay awake during my talk on molecules. I lose only two students to sleep.

Waiting for Pompa's next lecture I expect another sports event. Pompa waits at the lectern. When the room quiets he says, "Many of you have recently moved into new quarters. My first quarter in college I looked for a place to stay. Visiting a houseboat, I brightly told my prospective landlord, ' There's a slug on your toilet.' Before he could answer we heard small footsteps." Pompa's right hand fingers danced lightly across the counter. "I asked, 'what's that noise? Another slug?' 'Oh no!' replied the landlord. 'Those are rats. It's time for their feeding.'

"Quickly leaving the squeaking scurrying rats I went ashore and investigated fraternities. I like rats like I like opossums. The only natural enemy of the possum is the automobile." Most of the students laugh. I am scowling.

"My fraternity president, Robert T. Armstrong, brought a possum into a night club. Seeing him enter I yelled, POSSUM! People looked. Bob was petting his possum. A giggly lady asked, 'Mister. Can I pet your possum?' 'Of course,' said Bob. Being a gentle man, he let her scratch the rough hide. Suddenly, he threw the possum against the wall. The lady screamed. Why did the lady scream? Imagine that you are Bob Armstrong. It is 3 AM. You hear cans rattling out back. Irate, you get out of bed and go downstairs. There. There in your garbage is a possum. You grab a shovel. Smash, SMASH, SMASH. SMASH!" Pompa's hands crash the lectern. Each time his arms smash down the possum says "Squee." So it is "Squee, Squee, Squee, Squee."

Some of the students are laughing to tears. I am furious. Pompa continues, "The sorority house next door woke up. Floodlights came on. With each new squee, another light came on. Not understanding why

Armstrong was smashing the earth, the girls giggled and called, 'Go to bed Bob,' as Bob smashed away there was one last squee. Then he went to bed. Now you know why the lady screamed." His voice was almost lost by student laughter as most of the class rocked from side to side and forward to back. A few of them, including me, frowned.

Pompa keeps going, "While we're on animal stories, for Easter Robert carried a raw egg in his pocket. He was plastered. I pushed gently on his pocket. Bob's reflexes were so fast that an hour later he peeked into his pocket and observed, 'this little chickies dead.'"

I am furious at his irreverence for life. I notice a coed abruptly get up, leave the room. I heard later, she threw up outside. That same day she went to the office and switched to my class.

Pompa asks the class, "Do you want to see me lick my forehead?"

Several voices called, "Sure."

"From the inside?" says Pompa. While the class laughs he rapidly covers the green board with chemical equations. The students quickly stop laughing and commence copying the data, rushing to keep up. By the end of the period I have four pages of notes. I think as I scribble, how can I match Pompa? I'm not good at telling jokes. I don't have his background or fluency in biochemistry. I can't match his speed. I hate facts. My neck starts to hurt and my forehead tightens. I begin to rationalize. Because I'm slow I will cover less material. This will give the students time to learn, to write down the facts and ask questions.

There were only a few questions at the end of the lecture. As the class was leaving I heard, "what did he say?" "Did you get it all down?" "Can I borrow your notes?" "Is this biology or chemistry?" "He sure is funny." "His tests aren't supposed to be funny."

After class I stop to talk with Malander. He says, "Yes I delight in simple things. Once I saw Mann get up suddenly, he was blushing. I had put a wet napkin on his seat, slipping it beneath his butt just as he sat down. Once in a very serious discussion, Just as I was about to make my conclusion and convince the audience of my brilliance, that damn

Pompa put a banana peel on my shoulder. How could anyone continue a rational discussion with a banana peel on his shoulder?"

I grin. "That might be a great thing to do at a presidential news conference. 'I have a banana peel for the president.' or, 'give that reporter a banana.'"

"Bananas aside, he almost finished Phoebe White, she's near enough to the brink as it is."

"What did he do to Phoebe?"

"Something simple. He sneaked a collection of old orange peels, soda cans, and potato chip bags into her purse. Getting up to leave the faculty lounge, she dumped the load, and the place howled. Phoebe was mortified. The man isn't all bad however: He was the first one to call Davis Chrome Dome. That's not all. He has bestowed other honorific titles including pin head, wedge nose and snort."

"Can he do anything else?"

"Yes. He can repeatedly pick off glowing cigarette ends with crumpled lunch bags."

"From how far?"

"From across the room. Say twenty feet."

"I'm glad we've got such an outstanding faculty. I'll see you later Joseph. I must get home to Cleo and Karl."

I drive home. Later over chicken I say, "Cleo. Pompa tells horrible sick perverted animal jokes."

Karl says, "Daddy. Tell me some sick jokes about animals."

"Later Karl. Later," I say, not meaning it.

"You can't expect everybody to love animals," says Cleo.

"But the man's a biology teacher," I say.

When we are falling asleep, Cleo says, "Maybe he'll change."

"Maybe," I say, rolling over; moving into sleep mode.

# CHAPTER 10.

# THE CRUNCH AND MUNCH SOCIETY

Being male, I automatically belong to the Crunch and Munch Society, which meets once each month on a Friday afternoon. Walter Simons, the Voc Tech Chairman, welcomes me to the September meeting by pouring me a beer and directing me to a porch overlooking a ravine. While I listen to the creek, the president, beer in hand, comes over. "I'm impressed with your teaching. Yes, I've heard good accounts of you," says Davis.

"Thanks. Thank you very much," I say thinking, what a nice guy.

"You may not think I've noticed you. I'll tell you something though. I keep an eye on things." Beer dribbles down the president's chin due to a slight miscalculation. After wiping himself he continues, "I wish we had more eager ambitious teachers. I like that in you Leo. Of course, most of our people are above average, yet once in a while someone gets under my skin like a sliver."

"That's too bad," I say. The president's pupils, magnified by lenses look huge.

"You're a good observer Leo. I'm known for being broad minded. Sometimes however, I must draw the line. For example, Take Mary Jamison in philosophy. She's a good friend of mine but she just doesn't have it. She'd be okay teaching high school. Hawthorne hired her. Her grades were good. Her thesis on epistemological intuition must have impressed him. Hell, she can't even pronounce epistemological intuition. I doubt if she knows what it means. Have you ever read a history of philosophy?"

"I've read some Durant." I say, wondering what in the hell is epistemological intuition?

"There's never been an outstanding woman philosopher. It isn't her fault, but the students lose."

"Maybe women will be like the Jews. They have to get out of the ghetto first. The Jews gave us Marx, Freud and Einstein."

"That took several generations. As of now, women aren't ready for greatness."

"I'm willing to wait," I say, grinning.

"So am I," says the president chuckling. We quaff our beers. "Its too soon for the queers. Francis Butler. Did you know he's queer?" The president tilts his fulsome chin up.

"No. I didn't realize she was gay." I grin at my sick joke. Then I feel bad for taking a cheap shot. The president chuckles.

"I like your sense of humor. Some day you're going to amount to something."

"Thank you."

"Did you know, in Leeds Alabama I didn't own shoes? People never thought I'd amount to much. My own mother thought I was worthless."

"Is she alive?"

"In her eighties. I haven't seen her for oh, about nine years."

"Don't you want to see her?" My voice softened, as I empathize.

"We never could talk. When I spoke to her she acted like she didn't hear me. Looked straight through me."

"You poor guy."

"She didn't want me around. When I went into the kitchen to watch her cook, she shooed me right out. Said, 'Go, Go, Go bother your father.'"

"What did you do then? Bother your father?" I was sorry the instant I asked such an impudent question.

"Dad was critical too. Its a wonder I ever got away."

"You're fortunate you weren't harmed by them," I say, wondering if the president had been harmed. I gulp my beer, wipe foam from my lips. Our heads tip forward to about a foot apart.

"I had inner strength. One of my teachers, Maxwell E. Clarke, saw something in me. He gave me praise and encouragement. Even after I left Leeds he helped guide me. He was the only one in town who wasn't surprised when I went to college."

"Do you still write to Clarke?"

"He moved to New York City and became principal of Calvin Coolidge High School. He died in harness."

"I'm sorry."

"I'm the only one from Leeds with a Ph. D."

"You must feel proud." Davis's face, especially his eyes, seemed to pulsate. I resolve to move on.

"I've got to get some food. Thanks for the conversation," A bit woozy I wander to the table, grab a handful of corrugated chips and dig out gobs of garlic and cheese dip from a blue plastic bowl. Astutely I notice someone is pounding me on the back. It is Walter Simons munching a pretzel. "Have another beer Leo." His voice seems straight out of a concrete mixer. He unscrews the top off a brown quart beer bottle and spins it like a Frisbee out the door, over the railing and into the ravine. "The barrels empty so we've got to drink this garbage." He pours a glass for himself and one for me.

The foam tickles my nose. "Are you guys busy?" I ask.

"We'll be busy as long as there are automobiles. If you've got anything wrong with your car, bring it in."

"What will you charge me?"

"You pay us for parts and contribute to the doughnut fund. That's it."

"When I have car trouble I'll bring it in."

Simons wanders off to fill plastic red cups. I join Mann and Pompa on the balcony. It is good to again hear the stream. Mann is talking. "The line. The offensive line makes the backfield go. When I played we had the worst backfield in the league. But what a line. We'd blow holes. Fantastic. I was a guard and the fastest guy on the team. All you needed was the hole. James McCabe and I used to trap one guy all the damn time. I used to be 165 pounds. I've never been scared on a football field." Mann turns to me. "Did you play football?"

"No. I didn't weigh enough," I say, not adding that I wouldn't have played football if I weighed a ton.

"Its a great game to watch. Even if you don't play you can watch. You can learn a lot from football. There's an advantage in each position. The ball is hiked. You have the advantage. You go on the ball, go on the count. Move when the ball does and you get out there. Your ability counts, not your size. Take a big man. He can't move fast. As soon as that ball moves I move faster than hell. You know Leo, I'm a glutton for punishment. I like getting hit." Mann smashes his fist into his palm.

"Leo, you could wrestle," says Pompa. "You don't have to be big. The little guy has the advantage. He can wrestle in any weight class. A light guy like yourself could fight anybody."

"I don't want to fight people."

"Hear me out. I've got an example. The state champion from the year before stepped out on the mat. He was a heavyweight. The coach had me back off, so the heavyweight won by forfeit. I wrestled the unlimited and won. We won the match by one point. Our coach was smart. Their coach chewed his ass out. We all grinned when he said, 'Sure its legal, but it isn't right.'"

I imagine myself wrestling a heavyweight. Feel as if I am getting choked. Remember high school. The sweaty stink of the mats. Getting beaten. Hearing the guys laugh at my ineptitude.

Mann talks about Rugby. "We moved the ball. Bam. Bam. Bam. Jesus Christ. How long is an hour? You know how long half time is?" He looks at me. I'm not sure what rugby is.

"Fifteen minutes?"

"Two minutes. That's all. Just two minutes."

"Two minutes."

"Yes two minutes."

"That takes guts."

"You're right. Do you know how long a play lasts?"

"Fifteen seconds," says Pompa.

"In rugby you're constantly going. You've got to concentrate on all the plays. You're going all the time, and you play without pads," says Mann.

"Don't you get hurt?"

"Sure." says Mann. "I like getting hurt. Makes you know you're alive."

"Which do you like most?" I ask Mann.

"Football. Its one blast. I like to hit and be hit. The harder I hit the better I feel."

"Don't you hurt the next day?"

"Sure. I hurt all over and it's great."

Alfo who overhears the president say, "My tank could go anywhere," distracts us. The president says, "Hell their bullets bounced off like they were made of rubber."

Clearing his throat, Alfo produces a powerful motor, treads rumbling and clanking around steel wheels, "Barummmmm, Barummmmm, Barummmmm." We hear the anti-tank shells being fired, "Poom, Poom, Poom."

I half expect the president to return fire. Davis however keeps his pooms within. Smacking Alfo on the back, he laughs. I think, Davis has a remarkable sense of humor. I walk over to Simons and say, "Are these things always this loose?"

"It's good for us. Everyone has to be told he's full of shit at least once a month."

"Maybe we could train the students. 'Hey teach. You're full of shit,'" I say.

"Might be good for bank presidents and financiers."

"Who plans these parties?" I say.

"Anyone, just get two or three friends to share the cost. Run off invitations on the ditto, buy the beer and snacks, hustle your wife off, and you're in business."

Alfo pokes his head into the discussion as if he were a giraffe; "Its a good way to relieve pressurrrrr," he says.

I imagine myself as a Bauer cooker all set to explode, saved in the nick of time by an infusion of beer. Then and there I resolve to come to all Crunch and Munch meetings.

"It's a question of the movement of gassss," says Alfo.

"We have lots of gas but no ass," says Simons. Voc tech must be known for intellectualism.

"We can't have an explosion," I say. Enjoying my new friends, I remember I had promised to take Cleo out for dinner and a movie. I had forgotten to telephone. I look at my watch. It is nine. I shake my head, say, "Oh shit," and get one last beer. Later that evening, undressing quietly in the dark, I reach for Cleo; I must smell of beer, peanuts, pretzels, and chip dip. I feel her back and legs. Her arms are tightly wrapped over her chest. My attempts at cuddling end when Cleo mumbles, "Go screw yourself."

It takes a week for her to forgive me.

At the C and M Meeting I had talked with Joseph Malander again. Sipping wine from cupped hands, Malander an artist with almond eyes had said, "Form is function."

I examine my palms when I see him a week later. "Hello."

Malander, about my height scratches his goatee and says "Hello. "His breath a little rank I step back a foot. Malander says, "Some of us are going for beer. Care to join us?"

"Where?" I say acting as if I know all about Duhkwuh watering holes. I am playing for time, thinking about the wisdom of going out for beer. I remember Cleo's rejection of me the last time I drank with the guys.

Malander grins as if he is the devil. His dark curly hair seems to have tufted horns. He says, "The Schnitzel Haus. Do you know where it is?"

"No. Can I follow you?"

"Ride with me," offers Malander.

While we drive I furtively look at my companion. The Grecian complexion, goatee and mustache seem in conflict with the woven tweed suit and gleaming shoes. He seems unfriendly. I wonder why he asked me?

Entering the bar I open my eyes wide. In the dimness I perceive dozens of tall white beer steins hanging from pegs on low beams above the bar. We walk over to some men sitting at a table by the bathtub fireplace. Malander interrupts the conversation. "Gentlemen. I'd like you to meet Leo Bauer biologist. He knows the identity and secrets of many mysterious creatures." Turning to me he says, "I'd like you to meet these world famous scholars. Tom Magnum, band leader; Maurie Girodias, bookworm; Joseph Apfelboeck, theologian; Paul Dallapicolla, piper; Nolan Volens, friend of the working girl; and Thomas Seabeck, the wizard of electrons."

Each head nods when named, while I gently bow in acknowledgement. To Magnum and Girodias I say, "Good to see you again." To the others I say, "Glad to meet you." Malander and I sit down. Volens hands full steins to us. We drink the cool fluid.

"What do you think of Tweedle Dum and Tweedle Dee?" Says Seabeck to me.

"Who are they?" I say.

"The president is Tweedle Dee," says Seabeck.

"Or Tweedle Dum," says Malander with authority.

"Dean Mann is Tweedle Dum," says Seabeck.

"Or Tweedle Dee," says Malander conclusively.

Trying to stop grinning I say, "They seem most capable."

"How deluded are the new arrivals in heaven," sings Dallapicolla.

With brilliant insight, I perceive I am among dissidents. They might cause me harm. Yet what can I do? I handle the situation by raising my stein. "Gentlemen, a toast." The company lifts their mugs. "To Humaluh. The most wonderful community college in the world."

Malander splutters in his foam. The rest drink. Malander says to Girodias, "Maurie, we've got a job ahead of us. This boy needs educating." He affected a hillbilly accent.

I receive the low down during the next few hours. Fortunately I remember and telephone Cleo. She says, "Thanks for calling me, Fuckhead."

I spend most of my free weekend time studying DNA and look forward to sitting in on the DNA Litany. I want to learn about the Litany from my brilliiant colleagues. Damn I am ignorant about biochemistry. It reminds me of Physics.

On Sunday, after a dinner of potato salad and hamburgers, Cleo says, "What are you going to teach next week?"

"The DNA Litany."

"Why is it called that? Are you guys into religion or something?"

"No. It's just a name. They probably wanted to make it sound important." I have no more idea than she, although soon I will teach the Litany. I wish I could forget about DNA and watch spiders. I have always wanted to learn about spiders. Some day I want to watch a spider start and finish a web, no matter how long it takes. Why can't I teach about spiders? I bet the Litany is like a biochemical catechism. What is the key of life? DNA is the key of life. Just like being back in Catholic grade school. I hope I don't have to lead the class in a song to the molecule.

When I go to sleep, in my dream, a molecule is twisting around me, constricting me like a boa constrictor. Stretching to get free I wake Cleo who shakes me and says, "Leo. Go to sleep. Stop having those wild dreams." I hug her and rub my face in her silky negligee. She feels nice, clean and warm. She smells of citrus. I am lucky to have such a great wife. Maybe I'll do well in the Litany.

WARNING TO READER-THE FOLLOWING EMPHASIZES SCIENCE

THE DNA LITANY-

The DNA Litany, which includes Chapters 11,12,13 and 14, is required reading for people in theology, chemistry, biology, history and masochism. Other readers are urged to lightly browse. If the going gets rough readers may skip to chapter 15 for a more direct route to the completion of the saga of Leo Bauer.

# CHAPTER 11.

## KUNDALINI-IN THE BEGINNING THERE WAS NOTHING, NOT EVEN AN OIL SLICK

Leaving the sun mole eyed I enter a classroom lit by faint images of the sun and moon. I wear black clothes as required by departmental regulation. "Christ, why don't they turn on some lights," I mumble waiting just inside the doorway for my eyes to adjust before walking to an aisle seat where I merge with a mass of barely visible students.

Wrapped in a black cape Pompa strides majestically into the room. Crimson bubbles, wavy water waves and heat waves are embroidered on his blue back robe. He reminds me of Dr. Frankenstein. Pompa speaks. "Oh my students. Aesculapius, the son of Apollo, symbolized DNA in mythology. Poor top God, he was destroyed by lightning hurtled by Jupiter who was goaded by Pluto angry because Aesculapius brought the dead to life."

Pompa pins a painting of a figure in a brilliant red toga on the wall. "This is Aesculapius. As you can see, he holds the DNA Helix in his right hand."

I whisper to myself, "I see my beloved through the scales of a recently shed gossamer snake skin."

Pompa says, "Before knowing DNA people worried about immortality. They were frightened of gods. Now they know that their atoms will go from organism to organism. One life is gloriously consumed by another. DNA is our past. It is our future." He raises a beaker. "We give thanks for this DNA." He shakes a white powder into his hands, sifts it from hand to hand. "This is the molecule created for life." He inhales the dust.

I think, My god, is he snorting cocaine?
Pompa sings:

Molecule *fidelis*
The one molecule above all
No molecule is the like of this
In atoms, in acid
In form, in function.
Rejoice.
Praise DNA with the sounds of trombones.

I whisper lowly, "Boooaa, Boooaa, Boooaa."
"How many of you believe in DNA?" Pompa's voice echoes.

I think of the revivals I had attended in Naples, Florida. The preacher had asked, "do you believe?" And the crowd had screamed back, "Yes we believe."

"Ah, that is good. You believe." Observing the upraised hands Pompa nods. "My class, something good has happened." His head jerks in confirmation. "Talk about miracles. There's no miracle like DNA. Class, in my travels I've met many people who said the greatest thing that's ever happened to them was DNA. They knew that within them every millisecond thousands of tiny helixes are spiraling, unwinding, duplicating. New life is created from old in an eternal recycling."

My mind calls, "recycle your rags. If you have no daughters give them to your sons."

Unaware of my input to the room's mass consciousness Pompa says, "My class, you'd be surprised how many former students have come to me and thanked me for showing them the way. Oh my students. Today we celebrate." His voice becomes a resonating bell, "Oh Helixis, Helixis, Helixis." Pompa smiles. He picks up a flask in each hand and carefully places them on the white cloth covering the front table. Embroidered into the fabric are golden bolts of lightning, the sun and rain. A black beaker glistens on the table near the flasks. He pours white powder into the fluid and swirls the mixture. He brings it to his lips. Sipping the fluid he says, "This is the life fluid." He drinks more, licks his lips and sets the flask on the table. Pompa sings,

This is the salty water
Source of first life.
Atoms
Never die forever atoms

Salty water, the perfect fluid, allowed
Molecular mixing

The culminating combination
The transmogrification
DNA

Wherefore I thank thee oh water
Separated from dry air
Separated from dry earth.

Pompa in the darkness gently walks the aisles sprinkling water on the uplifted faces of the students. I lick my lips and am refreshed. Cape undulating, Pompa turns, flows up the steps. Twisting my neck I see him reach the West wall. Pompa says, "Oh my class. Can you imagine days when there were no living things?"

"No life?" whispers the class.

"No life." Pompa sadly shakes his head. "The earth revolved around the sun. Although the molten sphere cooled and hardened, the atmosphere was deadly."

"Deadly," says the class.

"Why don't these parrots shut up?" I whisper wondering how long it will take me to robotize my students.

Pompa says, "And because there was no life, the chemicals accumulated. The seas thickened and the soupy sea waited beneath swirling clouds of sulfurous vapors, methane and ammonia."

I imagine myself in a soup factory. Conveyor belts noisily carry cans beneath spigots, which pour in broth, noodles, carrots, and occasional fragments of meat.

"They waited for the key, that miracle that given eternity had to happen. Oh that glorious molecule that had to..."

While Pompa glories, I listen to the soup enter each can with a sloop, sloop, sloopity sloop, and hear thipatta, thipatta, groffit as the red and white labels are stuck onto the metal. I imagine myself selecting and opening a can of hearty beef soup, and spooning the congealed stuff into a pot. After heating the mixture to boiling I add wine, thin slices of celery, garlic powder, salt and pepper.

As I devour the last mouthful of soup Pompa concludes the last of eight *DNA Vobiscums*. He then sings the Song of Kundalini.

THE SONG OF KUNDALINI

*Prima materia* became parched ground.
I think, I'm also dry. Hey Bobby, can I have a beer?

Drop of dew.
Streams from the desert. The lifeless ocean rejoices.
Cybil waited.
Before the time of Cybil, Isis waited.
I whisper to myself, "I wait for beer."

Before the time of Isis, when the world was lifeless, there was no
mediatrix.
"Not even card tricks?" whisper I.
Only the sun.
Only the moon.
"No loon or baboon?" say I.

Pompa quiets. I see what resembles a large black vulture. Wavy
hair almost touching the ceiling, Pompa raises, then lowers a bucket of
burning embers onto a small table. He sprinkles water from a perforated
bronze ball. The embers hiss. Steam rises. Pompa plucks forth and kisses
a cinder. He comes down the steps with great gravity and speaks to us
from the front of the room.

I have a message.
Before life the earth longed, as a hiker longs for water.
So longed the earth for DNA.
I whisper, "so longs a guzzler for beer."

There were no voices
Day and night to ask,
Where is your life?
I hear a voice. Listen. This is your life. We now take you back to
your earliest beginnings. To the muck of your genesis.

When I am low
I think of the time of no life.

My students why downcast?
I think, because I wanta go home.
Do not sigh.
Say I, "But I am weary."
Put your hope in science.
Say I, "For boredom."
Believe.
Let us give praise.
Say I, "To Bobby Pompa?"

In the beginning there was space
Without form.
Say I, "No cupped hands, no wine?"
From the beginning before time
There were electrons.
When there were no seas
There were electrons.
When there were no mountains
There were electrons.
Say I, "When there were no electric toothbrushes, there were electrons."

The earth prepared
Like a maiden for a lover.
Think I, Lecherous lady.

The earth trembled
Lightning flashed
Rain fell
Waves tossed
Atoms played
Molecules danced
The earth waited for life.
Say I, "Only a few more millennia. Be patient."

Upwards, downwards, backwards, forwards
To the right and to the left.
Say I, "In and out. In and out. Nothing beats sex."
There was no life.

Water flowed from the mountains.
Four rivers to the plains,
Flowing to the ocean.
No branches floated there.
There was nothing bobbing in the waves.
Say I, "Not even an oil slick."

Kundalini the serpent waited.
Think I, Pity the poor serpent.
For sugar Kundalini waited.
Say I, "One lump or two?"
For Nitrogen bases and phosphates.

Lightning flashed.
The chemicals combined in sun baked seashore pools.
Kundalini caught her coils,
Crawled spirally
From out to in
To the right, to the left
Backwards, forwards
Downwards, upwards
DNA floated in the sunshine.

Oh people
DNA is where the secret of life is.
This molecule is a real place.

It is that busy place directing chemical transmutations
In the cells
In the body.

No doubt about it
DNA is a wonderful molecule.

Why this silence about DNA?
I think you could tell me why people are slow to believe
Slow to take up new ideas.
It is both describable and indescribable
DNA never comes to an end
It is forever
For ever and ever
For eternity.

Pompa sings melodiously, his voice loud and clear echoes in the still room.

Helixis. Helixis. Helixis.
Eternal life, Helixis.
The secret of life,
Helixis
As long as life,
Helixis
Forever
Until, unless consumed with fire.

Is there anything better to see then a helix unwinding?
I whisper, "Yes. A woman undressing. A green plant unfolding. A wolf running"
Pompa's face is cherubic.
Let us now go forth with DNA

And gather knowledge and spread the word.
Reverse your capes.

The student darkness transforms to white. Faces are orange from the flickering tapers. The walls glow. The Helix seems to be a soft flame. A bell chimes. I think, Pompa would have made a superb altar boy. His voice is so clear. The student voices are also fine, like the third string of the Vatican choir. Pompa concludes with,

Helixis. Helixis. Helixis.
Forever unwinding, forever duplicating
Duplicating...

Duplicating hangs in the air like a golden thread until the room is like a church the moment after the organ and choir stop. The departing students gently shake their heads, like people emerging from a dream.

# CHAPTER 12.

## ON THAT DAY EACH ONE GOBBLED UP HIS BROTHER

I am more contented the next afternoon. Pompa had asked everyone to wear old clothes and not to eat, so they would know what it felt like to be a hungry molecule. I enjoy wearing rags. Knees poke through holes and threads hang from my pant bottoms. I think of the molecule floating in the rain, remember Wisconsin where I floated in the sunshine, floated in the rain. Thinking of Kundalini taking in electrons, atoms, molecules I recall my wife taking me to her breast, Wonder, will my sons have children. For some strange reason I am hungry for pea soup. Looking around the room I see the image of a bright sun. The Brobdinagian Helix rotates slowly between two massive mahogany colored Rood beams. As I watch the molecule I wonder, Will Pompa also wear ragged clothes? At precisely one o'clock Pompa resplendent in a damask Laboratory coat whooshes into the room. On his back as he spins I see three ciliated *Paramecia*, a trumpet like *Stentor*, and a false footed *Amoeba*. Turning to the class he says, "Thank you for wearing such elegant attire." Facing the crowd he extends his arms palms facing up. I think of Father O'Brien at Saint Catherine's. Pompa sings,

DNA androgyne
Faithful molecule
One molecule above all
No molecule the equal
In seed, eye of mouse, wing of bat.
Sweet the atoms
Sweet DNA.
I think, Sweet violets.
Pompa winces. Despite the molecular miracle, there was a threat.

"A threat?" Call the students.
I wince mumble, "True believers are the threat."

The chemicals would soon be gone, says Pompa.

"Gone. All gone?" The class sounds like children told no more ice cream.

To continue to survive, to flourish, the molecule had to be able to change. And the first change was the first mutation.
He extends his right hand towards the class.
This mutation enabled those cells to gobble more chemicals. His hands quickly gobble up imaginary molecules.
But even so my class, the food again ran out.
"The food gone?" The class sounds heartbroken.

I whisper to myself, "Daddy the cupboard is bare. Daddy says, brat shut up and eat your bones." The coed in the next seat turns and gives me an icicle stare. I respond by looking at her breasts. She blushes and looks at Pompa who is saying, There was no more food, so the next food had to be one another. Pompa villainously laughs.
And on that day, each one gobbled up his brother.

"Gobbled up his brother." The class laughing evilly repeats the professor's words.

And his mother. Pompa laughs

I wonder, Are brothers better roasted, fried or shish kabobed? Would candlelight and wine be appropriate?

But alas, says a sad Pompa.

I think, alas poor little cells. Nobody feeds them. They ain't got no one to love, and they're gonna get all eaten up.

Pompa says, Alas, soon they were out of even each other. However, all was not lost. There was still a source of energy, and that was...

"The sun, shouted the class. The sun, the sun, the sun, the sun."

I quietly sing, "Da dum, Da dum, Da dum, dum, dum," skillfully merging my voice with the others.

Pompa beams, That's right. The suns energy was tapped. and plants floated the seas. Pompa's hands in triumph float on the seas of the ancient earth. His crimson finely crafted lab coat is glowing. I rub my eyes, squint in the brilliance of the sun, which appears to have gotten brighter. Pompa presses a hidden button. The room suddenly goes black. I hear his footsteps in the dark. Someone sniffs. A pencil drops. Pompa clears his throat. He sings in a sonorous baritone.

And it came to pass
In the monotonous nocturnity of no life
Lightning flashed.
I think, where did that come from? I see lightning
Volcanoes rumbled
The earth cracked open.

The room shakes. The girl next to me screams, clamps her hand on mine.
In the darkness of midnight DNA came into being.
A stiff Helix comes into being.
I feel a stiffness come into being from her hand on my lap.

And it came to pass
A great killing.
A blood red harvest moon appears. I wonder, where are the
pumpkins, scarecrows, witches and goblins?
Organism devoured organism.

The girl's hand pulls away. Damn. Here comes softness.

Energy was absorbed
Beneath the waning moon.

I whisper, "the moon slivered while I salivate"
Students, come for your ashes.

I think, Pompas gonna qet his ashes hauled. In the faint light I
watch the students as one by one they walk to the front of the room and
stop in front of Pompa. His fingers push spirals of ash into each brow, as
he says, From minerals thou art and into minerals thou shalt return.

I join the line, shiver as I feel Pompa's thumb pushing gritty powder
into my forehead, thinking, Does he press this hard on everyone? Is he
attempting to push through to my brain? The sun is rising in the East.
While seeking my seat a green glow perfuses the room. I whisper, "Sure
faith and begorrah, am I in Ireland?" Is Pompa the reincarnation of
Saint Patrick; he wears a soft emerald cloak. Outlined in black on the
back is a twisting vine. Pompa sings,

And it came to pass
The aurora.
Life took from the sun.
What greater miracle?
Miracle of light
Chlorophyll.

Pompa's hands become germinating, unfolding plants.
Cedar in Lebanon
Cypress in Zion
Palm and rose in Jericho
Olives, Lily, Myrrh.

The girl next to me sings, "Marijuana."

The plants grew in gladness
From Maya matrix,
From os crucis,
Bone of the cross
From the tree of Eden.

Rejoice oh earth
Illumined by this molecule.

The earth is delivered from lifelessness
Brightened by the sunshine
The mystery unfolds.

Lifting a black cloth he reveals a green tropical plant with big leaves.

In that vegetable womb the vines flowered.
Soon the cock would crow.

I softly crow, "Cockle doodle doo. Pompa's lost his shoe."

Glory to nucleic acids. Helixis. Helixis. Helixis.
I softly sing, "glory to beer, and brandy, brandy, brandy."

Let us conclude with the sign of the Helix.
Following Pompa's example the students reach out their arms, bend

low, slowly rise as their arms and hands weave imaginary strands into helixes.

After a few minutes of tranquility with the molecule, the students begin to leave. I notice some of them seem transformed as if they have undergone a peak religious experience. I feel like asking some of those who were glowing the most, are you Pentecostal? Instead I walk near Pompa and hear, "It took all of us to make this morning so very, very, meaningful."

I go to Pompa and slowly shake his hand while effusing, "Congratulations. A tremendous show. Tremendous."

"I was good, wasn't I?" says Pompa winking his right eye.

"Yes, I say." As I walk from the room I hear a recorded choir sing, "DNA shall reign for ever and ever. For nucleic acids are the power and the glory. Rejoice. Rejoice. Rejoice."

Walking into the nearby woods I spend an hour watching a wren bouncing about and scratching the forest floor. I join the wren in song and then drive home for dinner with Cleo and Karl.

WARNING-TOTALLY INTO CHEMISTRY

# CHAPTER 13.

# YOU GOTTA GET FRUCTOSED

After having watched Pompa's masterly production of the Litany, I was tremulously reluctantly ready to present my version, which lacked the intellectual depths of Pompa's. I planned to expand my coverage of biochemistry in the future. It was scary facing ninety students. I read an extract from the notes of George Guirch. A theology professor; his critics had called him George Guirchwind.

As God sent his only son to earth to die, DNA was sent by Lucifer as a molecular antichrist. Christ was a sacrifice. DNA was the opposite. If DNA were sacrificed there would no longer be life.

On the sixth day, God created man in the image of himself. This man and woman, in the image of God, have been devoted to the destruction of life. When all life is gone God's creatures will have been successful. Life will be gone. DNA will be gone. Satan will have lost. Satan will no longer matter. God will no longer have reason to exist, and can and will die, and no logician will worry about whether or not it is logical because it will have happened and no one will even know that it has happened and the last second will be eternity and nothing will matter not even matter."

The following are excerpts from my lecture.

Gregor Mendel was a difficult monk for the abbot because he was cantankerous and intelligent. The abbot finally discovered what to do with the difficult monk. He said, 'Gregor, go out and take care of the garden.' In the garden he was supposed to water the peas. Instead, troublemaker that he was, he performed hybridization experiments. Perhaps he was tanked up on monkly liquor. Who knows? At any rate he discovered how parents pass on genetic traits. His data backed him up so conclusively he probably fudged his data.

Class, look at DNA. I press a switch. The room lights darken. A spotlight illuminates a molecular model I have constructed out of old soup cans that I stuck together with coat hangers. Unfortunately, in the rush of creation, I had not taken time to remove the labels.

Look. Pointing to a small Cream of Mushroom nucleotide I get too close and cut my finger on the can top. Damn, I say, pulling out a handkerchief.

The class, startled by the accident is unwilling to laugh so soon after the beginning of the quarter. They look sorry for me. I say, Oh its nothing. Just a scratch, as I lick the DNA laden blood away and say, Sing after me, Oh the pyramidine it is small and the purine it is large. The class sounds like a gang of dying dyspeptic monkeys. It is as if a cabbage can eating Billy goat is leading them.

> The zipper unzips
> From the molecular soup come nucleotides. New strands form, how zingy.
> The zipper zip zips
> Zip, zips.

The message travels. My students. What controls the synthesis of protein, controls the cell. What controls the cell determines the destiny of the body.

A voice heavily accented in German mutters, "Today der cell. Tomorrow der body."

Forging ahead despite this setback my confidence is bolstered by student attentiveness. I talk of respiration. I manage to make the process, which is quite simple, complicated. To help the students learn I teach a strange little song. It goes to the tune of a blueswail.

YOU GOTTA GET FRUCTOSED

Oh the glucose gets phosphate
And the phosphate gets fructosed
And that's the beginning of the song.

Not content with this trash, I change it into a warped kind of torch song.

Oh PGAL twins from a fructosed mother
Lost poor phosphorous,
Ran away with ATP.

And Diphosphoglyceric acid became pyruvic.
With no oxygen it produces alcohol for boozers
And lactic acid for runners.

Give it a shot of oxygen
Goodby hydrogen and CO2.

Hello Coenzyme A
Quiver the A
Hook it to oxaloacetic acid
Complete our song with citric acid.

My voice very low I hold the acid for a long time.

When I hear some Coeds laugh I change my voice to resemble Pompa's Litany voice.

Now my students
Along the way there were hydrogen atoms
Bubbling with energized electrons they joined the magic fountain.
The electron transport system sucked energy.
The end result was water,
Valuable for men, rutabagas and oysters,
Especially oysters.

When my class ended there were no coeds stopping to tell me how inspiring I had been. In fact I think I bombed. What do you think?

## CHAPTER 14.

# IN MEMORY OF ROSY FRANKLIN AND THE CANTICLE OF PATRISTICS

On the morning of the second day of my DNA Litany I am beat. I prepared most of the night. I feel like a trial lawyer. The walls of my classroom hold glowing images of Darwin, Watson and Crick. On the front table a pair of wooden hands clutch a small oak chest. The unusual container attracts students entering the room. They explore the chest with their hands. Failing to open the chest, they go to their seats.

Wearing purple I rush into the room. I have dyed my lab coat with a combination of blue berries and beets and am proud of the result. After straightening my papers I begin speaking with great exhalation.

Class, something good has happened. This afternoon we're going to talk about great people. We will talk of men and women from the present and the past. Oh my students how grateful we are to two men. God-like in their wisdom, foremost among all scientists, these two men discovered the significance, and the power and the glory of DNA.

Oh Helixis to Watson and Crick, for they shall be remembered for ever and ever.

Hands outstretched, I must have resembled the statue in Salt Lake City of the Angel Moroni.

And their names shall be engraved on the heights of the Pantheon of Science. May they be remembered. In gratitude to them, let us all look to the Helix. Stretch forth your arms. Please make the sign of the Helix.

I sweep my hands out from my sternum arms out, fingers wide apart, like a bird scratching its chest with wing tips. After touching the floor I make two imaginary ribbons, lifting, spiraling, on toes reaching, extending, gazing upwards, fingers shaking, vibrating, hands almost touching, my fingers close, arms shaking, I approach ecstasy.

Emulating me the students make the sign of the Helix, stand extended, shaking, quivering as if naked in an autumn wind. Chimes sound.

I say, "I want to tell you about research and Rosy Franklin.

*IN MEMORY OF A DEAD SCIENTIST.*

Students work hard
You can be great.
Be outstanding for science.
Forget about humility.
Remember Watson and Crick.
They had potential.
They worked for the prize.
They beat out Linus Pauling, who was political anyway.
Joseph McCarthy despised Pauling. Think about that.

They beat out Maurice Wilkins
And Rosalind Franklin, a woman now dead.
Wilkins and Franklin separately worked alone
In the same lab.
In science you don't have to be brothers.
Competition is good.

To win the prize
That's important.
As it is in business
As it is in sports
So is it in science
For ever and ever.

Rosy saw the black cross.
The meridional reflection
XRay diffraction, reflections
Strongest at 3.4 Angstroms.
Think of that.
The diameter of the Helix was 20 Angstroms.

Wilson knew
His mind perceived
The double Helix
With the backbone outside
And the outside inside
And he wasn't at the Kings
But at Cavendish
In Cambridge, not Pasadena
Away from America his home
Away from Jesus
In the Cavendish.

Watson and Crick and Wilkins got the prize
The Noble prize.
When Watson was twenty-five
He perceived the double Helix
With the backbone outside
And the outside inside.

Students work hard
Be great
Be outstanding.
Forget about humility.
Work for the prize.
Time is sacred.
Facts our currency.
Brains our catalyst.
The laboratory our universe.
Our life the sacrifice.

Join with me.
Let us deny
Let us deny
Let us deny
Those who deny
Our Litany.

We will dedicate ourselves to science.
Technology means progress.
Let us go forward
Let us go forward
Let us go forward.

Perceptive Goethe wrote something like this, "the future question for naturalists will be how cattle got their horns, and not what they are used for."

Darwin said, "Natural selection will not produce absolute perfection." The master truly spoke the truth. He also said, "The tail of the giraffe looks like an artificially constructed fly-flapper."

The late professor Claparede knew parasitic mites had hair claspers. Enough of these interesting comments from the history of biology. Let us travel back through time to the continent of Europe. Deep-set windows looked out from a castle on the Neckar River. Day after day His's nephew Miescher received supplies of fresh pus. (For some strange reason, at this time, I scratched a pimple on my throat before continuing). Poor Meischer, a martyr, worked long hours in unheated rooms. His chest thickened. He died hard of hearing, a victim of science.

Read the great books. March in the footsteps of those who stepped in great footsteps. Imagine a long Moebius strip with the images of great scientists who were following in the footsteps of those who were following in the footsteps of those who were following in the footsteps and who therefore would never run out of footsteps.

I will now light the candles for the *Canticle of Patristics*.

I turn down the rheostat and darken the room. I read the canticle with the aid of the ruby flame. I light a new candle when I say each new name; it gets easier for me to see as I go along.

## THE CANTICLE OF PATRISTICS

The mighty Greeks knew
Thales knew
Life originated in the water.

Anisimander knew
Mankind came from fish

Xenophanes knew
Fossils came from life.

Concerning nature
Empedocles knew
From chaos came plants, came animals
From hate came monsters.
The poor man fell into a volcano.

In his sandals on the beach
Leucippus felt sand,
Divided drops of water into drops of water into drops of water
Into indivisible atoms.

Aristotle knew
Life came from slime
Many fish lie motionless in the earth.

Saint Augustine knew
The bible was allegory.

Linnaeus gave names to the plants and animals.
Buffon a politician
Knew of a young man from Chartres
Deaf and dumb from birth
Who began to speak all of a sudden
To the entire astonishment of the whole town.

Lamarck with a sore neck and four wives created biology.
Thought of giraffes.
Reasoned, species were not permanent,
Exercise develops organs

Malthus was aware of the struggle for existence.
It was natural to starve
If you didn't have enough to eat.

Charles Darwin
Born on the day Lincoln was born
Prepared to appreciate the struggle.
In a nutshell, he said,
"Favorable variations tend to be preserved

Unfavorable to be destroyed"
Who among you will disagree?

His father wanted him to be a theologian.
To abandon rat catching
To abandon beer drinking
To spit out the beetles.
No wonder he went to sea.

My students
At sea and on land
He sacrificed his stomach
For the Doctrine of evolution
Written while Wallace sailed.

Consider the mechanism:
Variation, Isolation, Selection

For forty years thereafter
Biologists studied comparative anatomy;
The horse walks on middle toes.

Darwin's cousin Francis Galton, looked
At the balls of his fingers.
Man is a statistic.
Good breeding is good for everyone.

Poor weak eyed Weismann could see
From germ plasm flows the stream of life.

De Vries knew mutation's lehre

Mendel bred peas
Yellow and round with green and wrinkled.
And the new peas were all yellow and round.
Not content Mendel crossed yellow and round
With one another: the result a perfect ratio
Nine to three to three to one.

Hook discovered the cell.

Schleiden and Schwann said,
All living things are made of cells.

Strasburger described cell division
The rite of mitosis.

Acolytes Flemming, Bovari, Waldeyer, Golgi
Bodies marching
An unbroken line.
No wonder we know so much.

I am done. I can tell by the expressions on my student's faces as they push and shove in an unbroken line hurrying to leave that I have not inspired everyone.

While driving home I say, "I'm glad that's over." The rest of the quarter I enjoy teaching.

Cleo and I suddenly get along. It is like having a badly needed second honeymoon. After Karl is asleep we nightly drink beneath the twinkling clear lights of the living room and frolic beneath the covers.

# CHAPTER 15.

# CHORAL FLOWERS

During Christmas vacation we erect a Douglas fir tree decorated with ornaments painted, glittered and fashioned from label less tin cans and old egg cartons. Drinking hot buttered rums we sit by the tree listening to the Stones sing, *We Can't get no Satisfaction* while Karl slurps hot buttered brown sugar water. Our family is happy.

Three weeks into winter quarter the college choir sings in the cafeteria. Magnum, Seabeck, Reardon, Apfelboeck and I drink coffee while listening. The choir girls wear carmine corduroy mini skirts. Magnum licks his lips. The red haired choir master, Francis Butler, wearing flowered pants, talks to the choir with his hands, his fingers softly exploring invisible waves. Knees bending his long red hair moves like seaweed in a cross current. The drummer beats. The guitarist plucks above the rosewood stem of a thin electric sandwich. A serious page flapper accompanies the short-skirted pianist. Fingers pecking on the keys she reaches to her right. Rearden says, "I see a beaver."

Ignoring his brilliant insight I see a dress covered with undulating fields of bright red and yellow flowers.

Listening to the jazzy rocky rolly music, Rearden says, "they ought to be recorded. They might make a pile of money."

I listen to the flutist solo. Watch her flower fields. Butler's hands at forehead level are pushing and pulling the music. I worry lest his thumbs poke out his eyes, then lean forward to better hear one of the students, George Parker, sing while Butler's hands dive from upper chest to the front. "Hang in there baby." says Rearden.

Examining teeth while the choir sings, Rearden says, "Think how much money is tied up in orthodonture." Localized laughter hacks into Heydn's hallelujah as the curving lines of singers sing Ave Maria.

Rearden says, "I want to go see go go dancers."

Seabeck answers through his gravelly throat, "You'll have to wait until the president completes the auditions."

"Maybe he's getting it on," Apfelboeck laughs.

"Doubtful," says Seabeck, adding, "Notice that tall guy? He just got taller."

"Been goosed," flatly comments Magnum. Trying not to, I laugh.

A quartet sings, leaning forward, veins bulging, hands at their sides. Their song ending they merge with the other singers.

I write on the edge of the college newspaper: The girl's mouths are open tooth caves. Those glowing white teeth are covered with soft lips. They sing about love and lost love. Lucky girls. May romance play with each of them.

The music quickens. Singers rock and bob. A few are rigid except for oval mouths. The male voices deepen. The band is exploding. Larynxes pop forward sending vibrations above the tables. Flapping lips send sound swimming past my ears like a school of nautilus. The singers seem to pogo. Some bounce almost to the ceiling. Great energy. Flowers surround me. Hands clap. A girl sings, "working for the man every night and day." Parker sings "Rolling on the river." His deep bass holds the river until all are silent. Good old Rearden. He's congratulating Butler. Probably trying to figure a way to make a buck off of the singing.

The next day I hunt for Butler. I want to tell him how much I enjoyed the flower fields. Entering the unlit corridor leading to the stage I see two people embracing. Not wanting to intrude, I halt, watch Butler play with George Parker's hair, see their lips touch. Flushing, shocked, I retreat, walk rapidly to my office. I am not used to seeing guys kiss.

Removing my journal where it is hidden in my desk drawer I write: I saw professor Butler kiss a young man. Intellectually I can comprehend such an act. Yet while watching them enjoying that kiss, my liberalism jumped through the window. I stared at them as if they were another species. Nevertheless I still want to be friends with Butler. I want to know more about how homosexuals think. I will not reject Francis. On the other hand, if he tries anything with me I'll kick him in the balls.

Friday afternoon I join Apfelboeck in the Schnitzel Haus. I say, "I dug the choir."

The sociologist says, "You like short skirts?"

"Of course," I add, "I also enjoyed the singing."

"The choir is O.K., but Butler is losing oomph."

"His oompa and oomph seemed good enough to me."

"You should have seen him three years ago. Just hired, he was the glorious aftermath of a child prodigy."

"Was he a singer in his days of glory?"

"He sang until the proverbial voice change. If they had made him a eunuch his voice would still be lovely. Perhaps if he gargled?"

"Not hardly. I heard he had an ace in the hole. A surgical kit for home use: Suture self."

"Bauer, I ought to suture you. He was also a good pianist. Studied at Julliard before breaking away from his parents when he flew to India and studied the sitar."

"That's rough to learn, isn't it?"

"Some say the hardest in the world. Butler says he's not very good with it, but the students appreciate all those weird sounds. Probably because of the *Yellow Submarine.*"

"So what's wrong?"

"Well music enrollment climbed, He was a whiz the first year. However, the president didn't like him because he attracted a clique of long hairs. His students walked barefoot through the student lounge."

"Oh my God, how terrible. Were they taken out and shot? Made an example of?"

"Damn near. They got the president's goat. Davis told the chorus, going barefoot spreads disease."

"That's funny. So the president is also a physician?"

"He ought to know. He grew up barefoot and hungry. He knows all about naked feet. There are greater crimes."

"I'm all ears," I say as he hunches closer.

"Students visit Butler in his home. I've heard tales. They are supposed to drink beer and wine and smoke marijuana."

"Sounds like a good combination."

"Consider what happens when townspeople find out."

"I remember vampire movies. The Humaluh farmers will form a mob with pitchforks and torches." I draw my hand slowly across my throat.

"Exactly. Mixing with the students is bad for a teacher's career," says Apfelboeck.

Rearden joins us. The conversation shifts. "In college I was getting more ass than a toilet seat," says Rearden.

Apfelboeck says, "I like Butler like I like a pimple on my pecker,"

"Where'd that come from?" I say.

Apfelboeck says, "Find a sheep. Grab the wool. Hold on. Pull. Listen, Baaaaaaaaaaaaaaaaa...Ahhhhhhhhhhhhhhhhhh." says Rearden.

Not wanting to call Butler queer, I keep silent about my discovery of the kissing men.

# CHAPTER 16.

# AN UNFORTUNATE ACCIDENT

In the middle of February the police raid George Parker's apartment. Francis Butler is arrested and charged with contributing to the delinquency of minors. He had been to a student party. Butler told the police, "I stopped to borrow a cup of sugar."

The next day, after being released on bail, Butler visited Elmore Davis at the President's request. Davis motioned him to a chair, his teeth clacking in nervous agitation. Other faculty heard Davis say: "Ordinarily I pay no attention to the personal life of our teachers. Now however I must poke my nose into your business. There was marijuana at that party. I have already received several phone calls from angry parents. They demand that you be fired."

Butler looked surprised. He stood up, gestured in futility, and said, "Dammit I just stopped to borrow some sugar. I couldn't help it if they were having a party."

"It was more than a party. I heard there was whiskey, beer, wine, and marijuana. You were caught with a joint."

"Look Elmore. When the cops came in I was pouring sugar into a cup. A joint, not mine, was in the sink. I saw it. It was soggy and useless. Does that make me a criminal?"

"No. It doesn't make you a criminal. You're only charged, not convicted. Your story sounds plausible. Nevertheless, until it goes to court, watch your step if you value your job." The room was quiet except for the sound of the shuffling of presidential papers. Butler quietly left the room.

When he entered the faculty lounge for a cup of coffee with sugar, some of the other teachers avoided him. The grapevine oozed like sap from an infected purple plum branch. Butler and Parker had been seen holding hands. There had been opium at the party. Some of the students had been snorting cocaine.

Board members, in august conversation, worried about the image of the college. Davis reassured them by saying, "Don't worry, I'll find a way to get rid of him."

I don't understand the president's anger. Today in the faculty lounge Davis screamed, "Effeminate bastard. Either he goes or I go." His face was red. I hope no one gives him horns. He'd probably rush Butler and impale him. I wonder where my red cape is? I can play bullfighter with the Pres. What triggers my greatest rage? Is it betrayal? Or someone being mean to a child or an injured bird? While I gulped my coffee he said, "I run a tight ship. There's no room for queers." His loathing made me shiver. I believe the president may not be a total liberal.

The next day when I see Butler in the corridor I say, "Hello Francis. How're things?"

Butler answers. "You better not talk to me. They might not renew your contract."

"What's happening to your case?"

"It won't stand up. They won't bring me to trial. They want to see me squirm."

"Davis is furious."

Francis snort laughed. "That fascist is a blue dog liberal. Oh wouldn't he love it if I resigned."

"It's stupid. You weren't doing anything."

"Leo, my students dig my class. Before I came to Humaluh music for them was joyless. They had an artsy fartsy choir, which slobber sang at the old folks home. Now the young dig our music."

"You could try sucking on prunes to improve your image," I laugh.

"They expected a tight assed concert pianist and they got me," says Butler.

I say, "Your choir is great. Enthusiastic students."

"They dig it." Butler walks away waving a subtle goodbye.

During additional corridor chats with Butler I hear diversified expletives. The president was referred to as a "dumb shit. A dildo with no appreciation for music or art. The man's brains are up his ass." He cautions me. "You better keep quiet or they'll be after your ass."

"Not a chance. I'm their golden boy."

"Board members are idiots appointed as a reward for mendacious mediocrity. Having gouged us in business, medicine and law they now want to ruin the kids. They try to control us with benign manipulance."

Butler's house sat in the midst of 120 acres of second growth Douglas fir in association with alder, live maple, cedar, and occasional dogwood. His landlord was the Chairman of the Board, Bob Pyle, the President of Valley Manufacturing. In return for a rent reduction the choirmaster helped Pyle prune the orchard and clear trails through the nettles and blackberries. As they worked he had told Pyle of the president's idiosyncrasies, of how demoralizing were the inspirational talks. Pyle would nod his head, as if he agreed. Sometimes he told Butler, "Our board is new. I'm learning. As yet I'm unable to pass judgment."

Pyle, selected by the previous president, seemed to be a capable objective administrator. The board's intent was to follow the mandate of the legislature to offer college courses to every mature citizen.

After the arrest Pyle advised his tenant, "watch your step" as he clipped a thick rose branch with a snap. Butler gingerly tiptoed through the thorns.

Instead of simmering down the antagonism grew. The board, other than Pyle, became more hostile. When Butler ignored Pyle's advice, he did it in spades participating in a rock concert in the soggy woods at the home of the student body president. The police received dozens of complaints. Parked cars were narrowing the highway, amplifiers were high enough to shatter glass. The air was filled with the sounds of youth. As the band boomed the nearby hills, youthful dancing figures carried frothing cups of beer to the dismay of county sheriffs who were too few to make a raid. Within two days mutual assistance pacts linked the police of all counties contiguous to Humaluh County excepting those on the other side of the mountains. Never had there been such cooperation.

I wondered, why had Butler done such a stupid thing?

Some said he held the party to create support among the student body, imagining mobs circling the president's office yelling, we want-Butler.

Ignoring the possibility of massive student opposition, the president and the board in an emergency meeting voted to terminate Butler's contract due to unprofessional conduct. The Humaluh Valley College Teaching Association (HVCTA) asked Butler, who was not a member, if he wanted the assistance of their organization.

Butler flippantly told their emissary, "No thanks. I've got other plans." Eighteen teachers, I among them, signed a petition requesting a hearing or an investigation. We were dismayed that Butler would be fired without being heard. We said, "We want due process. This man's rights are being ignored. If he can be summarily discharged, so can any of us."

Our petition made the president furious. Years later he still remembered the name of every signee.

There is no hearing. Butler acts as if little has happened. When I ask him, "Why don't you ask for a hearing? It is your right. Challenge them." He replies. "Screw them." Then he adds, "You better not talk to me Leo. You have a family. Don't ruin your career."

Now I write beneath my arched bronze goose neck lamp: What will he do? Will he give up teaching? Will his student supporters battle for their professor? Will there be protest demonstrations?

He is not as bad as the president says. Young people corrupt themselves. They are not innocent babies. He is not a fiend. He has weaknesses. It was dumb of him to insult the board. He's immature. It was stupid of him to throw the rock concert. Dumb dumb dumb to be at the parties.

So he's queer. Other faculty are queer. Closet fairies and drinking, morality. It's OK to get drunk with other teachers yet immoral to get drunk with students. Bullshit. We live in hypocrisy. We survive in hypocrisy. We teach in hypocrisy. DAMN HYPOCRISY!

The next day I talk to Magnum in the cafeteria. "Too bad about Butler."

Magnum glares. "I signed the petition because he should be heard, but that dumb bastard dug his own grave."

Walking by the president's office I hear Davis scream at the choirmaster who in return hurtles curses at Davis. They are having a meeting.

I slink past. Glad I'm not the target.

Butler stops meeting students in the classroom. Favorite students visit him in his home where apparently they smoke dope, talk, and listen to music. When Davis hears about this, he becomes more incensed, though that hardly seems possible. Having already fired the man he must be miserable because he can't fire him again. He probably would have enjoyed a public stoning but lives in the wrong culture. It is hard for Davis to acknowledge that in seven days the Butler thorn will be out of his side. Except for the Butler problem, things have gone smoothly. The faculty are happier than they had been under Hawthorne. The faculty is not overly upset about Butler getting it; he is not a faculty favorite.

The penultimate day of classes prior to exam week I pop into the faculty lounge. Tom Magnum twisting his mustache frowns. "Have you heard about Butler?" he asks me.

"Sure. He's going to Mexico. He wants to live in a shack on the beach and watch the waves."

Pushing hard on his mustache Magnum says, "He isn't going to Mexico. He shot himself."

"The hell you say?"

"I am not kidding. He did it in Davis's house, in the library."

"God, he must have hated him. That's some revenge."

"The dumb bastard. He used an old navy fortyfive."

"Is he dead?"

"He'd be better off dead. He's in a coma. Part of him got splattered all over those old books."

"Was Davis there?"

"No. He and his wife were out. Butler broke in. Davis says it's a tragedy."

"Jesus. Was Butler drunk , was he high on acid?"

"I don't know. They'll do toxicological tests. That takes weeks."

"They'll have to tell his family."

"Poor guy."

"The whole thing is so stupid."

Ignoring the suicide angle, the newspapers mentioned that Butler had been seriously wounded with his own gun.

The Humaluh Valley College Teacher's Association sent a bouquet of yellow mums to the hospital. Butler, in a coma, did not appreciate the gesture. George Parker delivered a red tulip.

During exam week I ask Apfelboeck, "do you think he'll live?"

Apfelboeck answers, "He'd be better off dead. His mind will never be the same." Apfelboeck, a man of great compassion adds, "He's lucky about one thing."

"What's that?"

"He's got Blue Cross." Apfelboeck grins.

# CHAPTER 17.

## SKUBA BUBBLES AND DREAMS

Grades in, we are going to Wisconsin. Cleo packs the clothes, books and toys while I pack the Swirlopeds, gently wrapping each small jar in crinkled paper. Other carefully packed containers hold microscopes, lights, forceps, a camera, drawing board on a swiveled shower head, documents describing previously described Swirlopeds, and books describing how to describe undescribed animals. On the road the station wagon contains a man, a boy, a woman, a dog, and a cat.

At the Cascade pass Karl yells, "Daddy, Daddy, Can we stop?" Scooping white crystals in our warm hands, he and I smear our faces, feel the melt streaming down our cheeks, as our feet crunch the spruce needled sweet snow. We inhale the pungent clean fresh smells.

We stop at a sparkly waterfall. While we watch calming energized waters our black cat goes insane in the car, scratching, pooping, yowling. When I open the car the cat shoots out. We conduct a cat search. Set out dishes of tuna. The cat has run off. We are cat less as we leave Idaho and enter Montana.

After many switchbacks, I park on the shoulder above the tree line. We watch marmots slide down a snow bank. At the edge of the snow, eyes shining, a big marmot chomps newly emerging yellow lilies. While

I watch the marmot, Karl carefully molds a snowball, which he tosses, hitting my neck. Wiping the cold away I am pissed. "Damn it Karl. I'm trying to watch these marmots." Seeing Cleo grinning, I scoop up snow, and rapidly running give her and Karl facefulls. I grin, until I notice Karl crying and Cleo stalking to the car. While she sulks I walk to my son, pat his shoulder and say, "I'm sorry. I'm really sorry. I didn't mean to hurt you or your mother. I just got pissed, that's all." Next I walk to the car and tell Cleo, "I'm sorry." Then I walk back and watch the marmots eat more lilies.

We leave the bright green tremulous aspens. The land flattens. We hurry drive until reaching the undulating thickly forested land of Wisconsin. At Oscar the Plumbers we leave the highway on a county road. Crossing Wild Rice River, flowing under the bridge through corrugated steel tubes, I remember the resonance when clacking the corrugations with my paddle I had shot hunched over beneath the road. We watch a heron fly a leisurely line, give a last flap, and settle behind stumps among the green reeds and wild rice. We pass cranberry barns and bogs. Slowing we cross the narrow canal used in the twenties by partygoers traveling to the big house in the bogs. Were they criminals? The banks have caved in. The waterway is hidden to most people.

Leaving the blacktop, we follow the dirt road once bulldozed by order of my father. I feel resentment seeing two new dirt roads with pushed over trees, ripped brush and piles of dirt. The raw trails lead to new cabins shining among the surviving trees. Ironwood lake is visible as if it was winter. My spirits fall. A moment later joy: the cabin. After we park on a patch of fresh green grass we get out. Feel the soft loose sandy soil beneath our feet, hear waves tickling the hard polished shore rocks, and sniff the algae, iron rich water warming, pinesap, fir sap and sweet fern. Cleo runs to the three holed privy on the hill. Karl runs to the swing yelling, "It's still here Daddy. It's still here." He swings while I walk to the cabin that had been built in 1923 for the staff of Camp Ironwood, a place where girls developed confidence in sports and learned crafts. My brother had built an addition in 1946. The low roofed building of dark stained vertical logs is a few feet above the lake. Craning my neck I look at the dark straight trunk of our sacred tall white pine that extends above the forest canopy. I think of my mother bravely watching me when as a boy I climbed to the top of the sacred white pine. While there I looked at nearby lakes in the bogs, in the forest. If the tree is ever hit by lightning it could fall and crush the cabin while we sleep.

Walking a few feet I pat the trunks of a cluster of maples that bump the roof in storms. Moving on, I scratch my fingers over the parchment peeling birch. The aspen like leaves touch the screen on the kitchen window. Crossing the parking area, near the woodshed I had built as a teen-ager, I feel the rough bark of an oak, which had been stunted until my pruning. The tree now is fifteen inches in diameter, healthy and well formed. Sometimes I think I am better hanging out with trees than with my wife and son.

After inserting the shiny spiral key into the brass padlock, entering the cabin is not easy. I push hard to open the door; constructed of solid planks it is suspended on wrought iron hinges. Leaving the door ajar I stop and sniff the air, enjoying the smell of the creosoted logs and the oakum stuffed in the cracks by my mother and me to keep out the wind and cold. I watch the lake reflections flash and dance on the boards of the sloping ceiling, and enter the fireplace bedroom, the original cabin. Red and blue light colors the logs, sweeps across the bed slept in by my parents. Birch leaves tremble against the windows. I turn around and walk out the door we had entered to unlock and enter another building, the tool shed, a major room attached to the cabin by a wooden walkway, cross the room past the electrical switch. A vise is on a stout wooden bench built against the wall by my brother. Flipping a switch I hear the pump attempt to suck water through deep sand. Returning to the cabin I plug in the open refrigerator, which trembles and mumbles as if unhappy with its load of stale air. Next I turn on the kitchen faucet and watch the thin yellow stream, waiting until it clears. I cup my hands and drink. The water is sweet.

Cleo returns. I give her a drink as if it is champagne. We unload the car. I carry the Swirloped research materials to the tiny adjacent cabin called the hospital. It had been the dispensary for the girl's camp. The rest of the luggage goes into the main cabin. While Cleo washes dishes I stand at the front window and watch a breeze cross the bay. We need food. Breaking my reverie I gather my family and drive back over the low bridge five miles to the grocery store. The youthful owner, Tony Wakowski, grins, "Well I'll be," as he watches us troop in.

"Your store is larger. Just like the big city." Picking up a garlic salami I inhale the perfume. We tumble salami, cheddar and pungeant Wisconsin brick cheese, milk, rye bread, eggs, butter and beer into a shopping cart.

At the meat counter Wakowski says, "Try some sirloin. Six pounds ought to be about enough for you guys." He puts twelve steaks on the scale. Sticks his thumb firmly on the stainless steel.

Laughing, I give a thumb down motion. "Not today. Tomorrow I'm coming back to get eight pounds of filet mignon."

That night we fall asleep listening to the trees and the lake. Fireplace flames flicker the ceiling.

The end of June and the beginning of July are rainy. On the warm days we swim, canoe or take the Thompson lap streak motor boat out for a spin. In the evenings we drink beer with cranberry grower friends and recall, with much laughter, former fun and ancient scandals. Cleo plays the guitar and sings *Kum Bay Ya*. Karl plays with the cranberry children.

Each day, I examine and study my Swirloped collection. By the middle of the summer I have managed to identify only five specimens and have grown tired of spending my days castrating the dead. How monotonous to cut and slash with my micro tools, and why? Just to remove and lift up the strange gonopods. How much better to watch them couple, tonging, whirling like dervishes. Yahoo. Alive they are neat. Dead they stink of formaldehyde and alcohol.

On some days, delinquent in my responsibilities, I watch clouds and write in my journal of the playful dragons in the sky and of oak leaf jig saw puzzles. On a cool windy day I describe the sunshine on cream puff clouds, and ask, did any of the French impressionists ever see and paint an aspen or a birch? Can an artist paint movement? In this forest wildly oscillating leaves of hazel nut beg for recognition. Below a brown pine needle, suspended by a spider's thread, twirls; ignores the outburst.

In midsummer the air warms and becomes humid. I acquire a cough from mould, pollen, or the stress of research or from some errant bacteria or virus.

On a clear morning in late July I dive with scuba gear and investigate the green mottled egg strung lily pad cables, feel the goo of rotting leaves in the depths of the iron tinted plankton loaded water. Blurred images swim past. Small perch and walleyes appear through the partially misted faceplate. Letting in water by lifting the edge of the mask, I clear the misted glass, hold off coughing while I blow fluid through the valve. While suspended I see the pinkness of perch gills as water squirts over gill covers. A heavy muskellunge resembles a mysterious antediluvian creature sneaking through the vegetation. Listening to my deep sucking inhalation, I watch silvery darting globules blobulating to the white silvery surface. The big musky, victor of several tackle tussels swims away.

In the early afternoon of the same day, we visit the McTaggerts down the road and sit in the sun guzzling beer on the bright green grass of their treeless front yard. For a change of pace, we get in their boat. Cleo is a master with water skiis. It is beautiful to watch her gracefully skim from side to side. It is my turn. Gene steers while drinking a beer feet tucked firmly into rubber saddles. I hold on while we dart side to side over the motored waves. I try not to tumble. Feel listless. We have almost circled the lake when I think; this little trip would have taken thirty minutes by canoe. On skis it takes a couple of minutes. What is the purpose?

After water skiing we drink beer and watch the children splash along the shore. Looking at her watch Cleo jumps up. "It's late. We've got to go." She grabs my hand, Hustles Karl into the car, "yelling thanks, thanks a lot." We drive to town. Cleo shops while I visit Doctor Johanson. Tethered to his stethoscope he listens intently through the front and back of my rib cage. I say, "I've had this cough for over a week."

The physician looks me in the eye, says, "Leo you've got pneumonia. We'll take Xrays for confirmation."

I think, oh shit. I shouldn't have gone water skiing and scuba diving. The physician prescribes antibiotics and bed rest.

I go to bed, wait prone for the pneumonia to go away. Doctor Johansson said maybe it viral or walking pneumonia; if so he said it would be slower to respond. He was right. The virus laughs at the medicine. For some inexplicable reason, the evening of the visit to the doctor the illness worsens. The next day my eyes hurt.

I write: Surprise. I'm still alive. It is hard to write when overcome by spasms of coughing. Usually there are only occasional coughs. It is almost as if someone were tickling my lungs. This sensation comes from air passing through masses of mucoidal bubbles in my bronchi. Sometimes as an experiment, I inhale deeply and hold my breath. The air seems dammed. Because of the suction in my trachea I can feel and hear the air as it trickles and bubbles.

A few days later I write up a storm: A great tenderness is within me. During a rapid series of coughs it seems as if my guts and stomach will suddenly pour out of my mouth like an eviscerating sea cucumber.

This analogy is all wrong. The trouble is in my lungs. My back also pains. Since this illness started time has little meaning or value. I want the present to quickly pass so that I can get out of bed and cartwheel. Maybe I'll never cartwheel again. Sometimes I play games. I imagine that if I take a couple of deep breaths without coughing, or drink a hot toddy and become soothed that the trouble has left. As if the ailment were only a nervous spasm.

Perhaps I am hallucinating. Much of what I write makes no sense: Once there was a parent so strong that he hugged his child and the child broke like an egg shell and we all stood around and sang *Ave, Ave Maria*.

Another parent yelled at his son and suddenly the boy's brains flowed out through his nose and mouth and the boy was only a hairy skull with brown eyebrows and dirty ears.

Another child was so sad that he controlled his parents as if they were robots, and no one knew the child was...

Angry springs pulled roughly at the tarnished brass gears and the levers tocked.

The well-dressed man walked up to me and said, there is no more time. He quickly walked away and I wondered and waited and thought, there must be more time. If there is no more this is not. If there is just a little, if I can make it go slowly it will always last and last. I'll stop all the clocks. That will show them.

I dream: A South American city clings to the side of an arid canyon. Four and five story buildings imitate the cliffs in back of them. Below the city is the river and across the river on a high plateau a newer city. The old city with the high buildings and narrow streets attracts crowds of tourists who like to wander through the streets admiring, touching and purchasing silver jewelry, ceramic ware and capes and rugs woven with llama and alpaca wool. After a visit of two days in the old city, I cross the bridge connecting the two sides of the canyon. Soon I am sipping wine while seated in the garden of an outside cafe.

An earthquake splashes my port wine upon the white tablecloth. Before my eyes the cliffs of the old city are breaking and cascading down upon the buildings. The tall buildings are breaking and crumbling. Walls slowly lean, floating into the canyon. Fragments splash into the tan green river. There must be great panic in the streets of the old city. And it seems strange: the new town with its broad streets is scarcely affected. I listen to the roaring noise of cliffs falling and buildings collapsing. The noise can not be separated into screams and other evidence of individual tragedies. Then there is quiet.

Finishing my wine I leave the cafe. The waiter is disturbed because I have ruined the tablecloth. I run to the bridge. The dust makes me sneeze. I smell the powdered decay of centuries. Walking carefully I reach the town. There is no fire because the buildings are of stone. Climbing over rubble in the narrow streets I make my way to a church tower. As I am taking photographs four boys grab the shoulder strap, attempting to steal the case. I tell them: look on the outside. They read: This camera is the property of the United States government. Reading the engraving, although they can't read English, they are impressed and let me keep the camera. I continue taking pictures until I run out of film. Because there are no places open where I can buy new film I have to be content with merely looking while dodging an occasional falling stone. I interpret the dream: My body is the old city. The camera is my spirit. I will survive because I still have much to accomplish. Besides as a U.S. citizen I belong to Uncle Sam and it is illegal to destroy government property.

After the dream Cleo brings me the camera. There is film in it. I wonder if there are any photos of the earthquake. I take few pictures during the rest of the summer. After they are developed I am disappointed. There are no photos of the earthquake.

People think I am perverse because I am reading the Magic Mountain by Thomas Mann. The book is about a man in a TB. sanitarium. At the sanitarium a woman breathes through a hole in her chest after a pneumothorax operation. Reading I listen to my breath, hear the whistles, the gurgles. Same as those described by Mann. My father had been in a Swiss sanitarium. I wonder what for? Did he have pneumonia? He sure had a weird looking sort of collapsed appearing rib cage. Obviously he survived. I almost finish volume one. I read until the language turns into French. I keep coughing. I think I have gotten compulsive about it. Taking new prescriptions I feel like a guinea pig. It seems as if the doctors don't have a clue. There is a virus caused so called Walking pneumonia and a bacteria caused pneumonia. What difference does it make if it is Streptococcus or Pneumococcus? Perhaps it is a combination of medically proven killers.

Still feverish, coughing, amidst wadded up Kleenex, spitting up yellow gray green goo, reaching for cough drop after cough drop I write: While sleeping at night the bright moon wakes me. I get out of bed and putting on a robe walk outside and discover that the grass is soft and wet with dew. Walking along a winding path through openings in the forest I see in the moonlight many bushes covered with flowers. The air is perfumed and the white flowers look like popcorn balls. A moth drinks nectar hovering above the flowers. I inhale. Soon the sun comes up and the high clouds are like furrows in a farmer's field, they are orange and fine. Buttercups and green flow over the earth. I smell sweet fern, pine sap and honeysuckle. After a moment I realize I am no longer on the ground. My feet move through the air. Grinning I float and watch the far away flowers, and wonder how the dream can be made to last because there is nothing more important nor will there ever be anything more important.

My interpretation: It is OK to die. I have the permission of the universe. However, much as glaciers slide slowly down valleys, my health improves. We talk of returning to Cascadia.

Though weak and weary, I again go on walks and canoe. I do not return to scuba diving, and stay away from beer until the night before our departure when the McTaggerts give us a going away party. I wish they had respected sickness. Foolish me, I drink too much. Our departure is hangover delayed. Cleo and I have fuzz ball brains. We load the car like worn out puppets. Cleo does most of the work. She has been in the dumps during my sickness. I haven't been much fun. Our home life has been as cheerful as a cancer ward. We all want a quick return to Cascadia.

Cleo drives the entire return. We pass drying cornfields and brown prairies. In Wyoming my cough worsens. Stopping along the way in the waiting room of a private clinic I read a sign on the wall: WE ARE OPPOSED TO SOCIALISM AND TO GOVERNMENT MEDICAL PROGRAMS. The doctor prescribes a new antibiotic. I think, yes, I am a human guinea pig; on the road again, surrounded by fascists. My coughing rips away aesthetics. I fail to appreciate driving through the mountains where the maples are turning red and the aspens yellow. Cleo is delighted with the fall colors.

Reaching Cascadia and our home, I go to bed still coughing.

# CHAPTER 18.

## PROFESSOR I'M IN TROUBLE

No longer a ball of fire I return to the campus the day before the start of classes. Magnum looks at my face, pats my shoulder with his bear paw hand and says, "How are you feeling?"

Popping a cough drop into my mouth I say "Like a jelly fish out of water. Enough said about me. How's Butler?"

Magnum scratching his chest says, "He woke up after an eightythree day sleep. Instead of being happy with survival, feeling the plate in his skull, he yelled, 'the wrath of God. My brain is gone I am alive dead and dead alive.'"

I say, "I'm too weary to visit Butler"

Magnum says, "I am too leery." Magnum relates how Davis had visited briefly, about as long as it takes to walk forward, stop, and immediately turn about and run when Butler screamed "You rotten fucker. Give me back my brain!" Followed immediately by the tossing of his meat loaf, mashed potatoes and gravy dinner in the president's face. The president was dripping gravy as he ran out the door. Plans were immediately made to have Butler transferred to Southern Cascadia Hospital.

Too tired to give a lecture the first day, I hand out class outlines and advice:

## ADVICE TO MY STUDENTS

I will become a close friend to some of you. Don't be deceived. I can flunk a lazy friend as easily as give an eager beaver an A. When studying for a test, if a problem threatens your equanimity, tell me. I can be won over by a young girl's tears, as long as she doesn't drip on my blue suede shoes.

I have had great sympathy for a young man's anguish over the death of his pet caiman and have been known to patiently listen to tales of woe. Don't be afraid of me. If you want an A or B you must work hard. If you have a low C going into the final and bomb, you can easily get a D. If you want a C you may have to study.

If at any time during the quarter you don't know what is expected of you or you have a problem, come in and see me. I want my students to do well. No one has to get an F.

If you imitate a classmate who refuses to study or take notes, consider, he may be a genius. Then again he may be an imbecile. Often it is hard to tell them apart.

Most of us get what we work for. Would you want a dentist to inject you with Novocain who was ignorant of which nerve to jab? How about a surgeon cutting out the wrong kidney? If all your courses are boring to you, look within. Don't remain bored. Change your major or go peel potatoes. If everything's wrong go back to the first square and make your move. Remember, There's nothing wrong with getting the hell out.

If you become disillusioned don't wreck the joint. Have a cup of coffee with me. I will gladly commiserate with you and together we can say, *C'est le Vie.*

If you get in trouble, come and see me.

Leo Bauer


After the class I return to my office to rest and cough. There is a knock on the door. I say, come in. It opens revealing a pretty auburn haired coed. She says, "I'm in trouble."

I look into her face, "We haven't had our first test?"

"It's not biology, I'm pregnant."

"That is biology. Consider your options. Have you talked to the guy?"

"I'm not sure who he is."

"Have you talked to your folks?"

"I'm scared."

"Damn. I'm out of my depth. Talk to the experts. Go to Planned Parenthood or the college nurses."

The next day I lecture from my notes of the previous spring. I do not change a dot or iota whatever iotas are. After the last class listless I go to my doctor. He prescribes pep pills. For several days I become my old self. I must seem confident to my students. I remember to vary my voice, flop my arms, do all those things done by popular professors. I think I am again effective until again my energy runs out and I feel terrible. Stopping the pills I spend two days in bed. I am unmotivated to read any of the books offered free to biology teachers. The best sellers included: *Dynamic Aspects of Biochemistry*; and *The Anatomy of the Sheep.*

I set aside a package stamped MIXED SCI, Bulk Rate, U.S. Postage Paid New York, N.Y. Permit No. 18181818 that contained a free stack of paperbacks. I look at a flyer from Digital which showed big white letters on a black background stating: Join the plot to blow up the PDP-8L. Opening the folder I see a picture of an old fashioned round bomb, fuse burning, with words saying: It's an ingenious plan and you can be part of it. Just take a look inside.

Inside there is a picture of electronic computer guts and the words; now for the first time it's actually possible to expand your PDP-8L to a full unprecedented 32K words of core memory. Just plug a memory into the logic rack any time you desire to add another 4K of memory. I think, how wonderful if I could just plug in another 4Ks of energy. Maybe I'll never be like I was. My teaching is rotten. Praised the first year, will I be fired this year?

# CHAPTER 19.

## THE DEATH OF PHOEBE

My mood is not helped by the sad case of Phoebe White. A friend, she died during the winter. She had been in trouble with the administration. I wrote in her honor:

Phoebe, once you were a little girl
Skipping through daisies
Amber hair sparkling.
Your hands swung in the breeze.
You went to school,
Tasted Chaucer and Byron,
Became a community college teacher.
You were alive Phoebe
Students said, "Take Miss White."

The students listened until they said you wouldn't listen. What happened Phoebe?
Did you walk in place while the students galloped into the future?

One day the dean said
(He had called you into his office. His voice was sympathetic),"Sorry.
We're so sorry
But the students don't like your classes."
The students came in a delegation to protest. They told me, 'She
won't listen,
She gets angry with us. Expects us to read Shakespeare and Chaucer.
Gives mostly D's.
She has turned us off to literature."

The dean said, "Phoebe
I'm sorry.
We have designed new courses for you."
Suspicious, you listened, thought, Oh, oh. This is it.
The dean spoke,
"Next term you are scheduled to teach Business English
And English for welders and auto mechanics."

You asked, "What about literature?"
The dean said, "I'm sorry. No more literature."
At 54 you walked away with clunky steps.
Later that night, while literary owls called,
You popped pills, clenched your fists and clamped your teeth.

The next day the president's secretary said,
"She died in her sleep. The lord is merciful.
We'll miss Miss White."

At your funeral the administration sent a bouquet
And a card saying OUR DEEPEST SYMPATHY.
I saw the dean and president shedding tears.
Your students said, "Too bad about Miss White."

# CHAPTER 20.

# THE WASTE BASKET PAPERS

After Phoebe White is buried, the attention of the faculty is directed towards another English teacher, Silas Thrigwhistle. A would be novelist Silas wrote on scraps of paper. He wrote random lines during faculty meetings, while listening to students, while reading student papers, while sitting shitting on the pot, after making love, and while sick and throwing up. Some of his best writing had been composed while puking. He said it allowed the real Thrigwhistle to come forth. At the end of each day his pockets were filled with papers, his desk bore a load of paper; the floor resembled a suburban lawn in the autumn. Before going home he emptied his pockets of the stories and poems and carefully lifted them and placed them in the wastebasket while saying *E lascia pur grattar dove la rogna:* that means let them scratch where it itches. Sometimes he said it in Italian, *traduzione lascia pur grattar dove pruriti dall inglese al latino.*

After grabbing his sea lion bellied briefcase, the good man walked home. As he walked he leaned forward, giving the impression he was heading into a strong wind.

Unknown to Thrigwhistle, every evening the janitor, Otus Tyton, carefully removed the stack of papers from the wastebasket. Instead of burning them, he placed them in a pocket of his trash carrier. After the floors were mopped and waxed and carefully polished Tyton went home, ate a late supper, and before going to bed edited and typed the professor's words. After eighteen years of this double life Tyton had compiled eight hundred and twenty two thousand words complete with three hundred and twenty nine illustrations.

Tyton was highly qualified for plagiarism: He had a masters in fine art and a minor in English.

He submitted the book to publishers. It was accepted by the twenty third publisher, and hit the market fourteen months later in eight volumes titled *The Waste Basket Papers*.

Instead of being grateful to Tyton for enabling his work to become published, the suddenly famous Thrigwhistle became incensed. Stomping his feet in anger (he got stuck in the wastebasket), he screamed, "those *Waste Basket Papers* mocked me." Ignoring the raves of critics he sued Tyton for three hundred and eighty three million dollars, which would have shot his budget all to hell.

I observe the trial because I am a friend of both men. I listen as thin frail Thrigwhistle speaks. As I watch his gnarled nose, he quickly gets to the point. He says, "Your honor, members of the jury. My days are spent encouraging students to write creatively. I teach them to appreciate Steinbeck, Faulkner and Hemingway. It is difficult for me to write long paragraphs in my own words immediately after reading *The Old Man and The Sea* or *The Great Gatsby*. Sometimes I've written early in the morning when my mind is uncluttered. Often, later in the day I write on student themes, needs a different ending, rewrite. When I've sent my stuff off to magazines the editor's wrote the same damn thing. It's no wonder I've kept my work hidden." He wipes his sweaty brow. Several jurors look compassionate. This emboldens him to continue with his confession, "I write awkward on student papers. The rejection slips I receive are printed. They don't say awkward. They don't even say awk." The jurors laugh. While Thrigwhistle wisely waits for the laughter to subside, he looks at me. I make a circle with thumb and index finger.

Silas speaks, "Many areas of writing are closed to me. If I wrote science fiction, gothic romance, true confessions or mysteries I would be subjected to professional mockery. I can never be the author of a *Duchess Twinkle Toes*. My early morning writing has impeccable style and perfect grammar. I have been careful when I write stories to base them on safe events such as summer vacations, for example that trip I took to Marin, California. Several colleagues, in praising my stories, have said my stuff was good enough for the New Yorker. They especially appreciate the complex structure, subtlety, and symbology of my stories. If the wastebasket papers get out, I am ruined professionally. Part of this has been my own fault. I have been indiscreet. During the day I have jotted down gossip and observations of my neighbors. Each evening however, regretting my impulsive writing, I've tossed all the bad words in the trash. People don't pay taxes to dirty old men to teach their children. If my private thoughts are made public, my head will go on the chopping block." Thrigwhistle cries, wipes tears off the tip of his distorted nose.

In looking about the courtroom I notice that some people are sympathetic. although I hear one woman say "pervert."

Tyton stands. He is a jolly looking sort of man. Focusing his big brown soulful eyes on the jurors he says, "Your honor, members of the jury. When crewless boats are cast adrift, they belong to whoever first grabs them. Likewise, sunken ships belong to the person salvaging them, unless someone has remained aboard.

"Your honor, members of the jury. The scraps of paper written by my good friend Professor Silas Thrigwhistle had been set adrift in the wastebasket. They rightfully belonged to whoever would take them." He humbly removes his janitor's cap. "I saw and recognized their potential, organized and made them into an epic. Without me they would have been burned to cinders. I was their resurrection and gave them life."

Furious, Thrigwhistle demands to speak. His eyes are fiery pools of lava. He looks at the jurors; some had never been to college. He speaks in a strong voice, after the judge has waved for silence. " Judge, Members of the jury. A long established tradition in academia has been the sanctity of the wastebasket. If our wastebaskets are pillaged by janitors, it is the same as if a thief poked through my drawers."

I chuckle, imagining a thief rambling through the oversized boxer shorts of Thrigwhistle. Thrigwhistle scowls at me, and concludes with, "Please good people. Protect our trash from the prying meddlers of the custodial corps."

Tyton gets up to refute the learned man. His eyes are like gold fishponds in the moonlight. "Ladies and gentlemen. The life of a janitor is a hard life. Teachers, administrators, secretaries and students look down upon collectors of waste. Often we are commanded in harsh tones to empty that wastebasket. Take this box. Sweep that floor. Clean this sink. We are at the bottom of the pecking order." Two jurors dab at tears.

"You may ask, 'what keeps you on the job?' I reply. There is one hope, one possible reward that keeps us going, other than our small salary, which is not much, just a little more than a secretary's. Oh I admit, there are minor incentives. I feel pride when I stand on a gleaming floor. When burning garbage the glow of the furnace warms my body. Think of the comfort I sacrificed by not burning those papers. The last two winters were cold. On our shoulders we carry the responsibility of creating the real image of the college. An outstanding custodial staff makes a college sparkle, a place uplifting to visitors, staff and students. How relaxing it is for them to view white bright tiles and toilets, and see themselves clearly in spotless mirrors. Without janitors taxpayer support would go down the drain, schools would deteriorate, students would become dull. It is not only pride that keeps us on the job. We all hope some day to strike it rich and find treasure in the trash. There are many success stories. Need I remind you of the valorous service given our country by janitors who worked as spies in the headquarters of the Gestapo. Many of our brave people were shot in the back as camera in hand, they hovered over wastebaskets. These unsung warriors were an integral part of the garbage can espionage network. Several sharp-eyed garbage collectors have become millionaires. No wonder favored routes service jewelry stores, dentist's offices and the homes of rock stars. Other trashy people became rich after working for presidents, kings and movie actors. By salvaging priceless letters and notes they have written books of interest to historians, politicians and housewives.

"These then are our incentives. If you take away our opportunity to reach the top much of the glory will go out of trash collecting. A glow will leave our lives. Garbage cans will become unattractive. We will lose pride in our work. Many of us will quit our jobs. As the offices and classrooms get dingier and grimier, the pride of others in their work will also decline. There will be reduced output by students, teachers, secretaries, business men and government officials, our nation will be thrown into a terrible depression, and revolution will sweep the land!"

Tyton's white hair jounces as he expels the last firm clear words. The spectators stand, clap and cheer. The judge gavels for quiet.

Normally Thrigwhistle was greatly admired. This court battle upsets him. After Tyton's speech he bows and becomes mumbly. Softly he says, "I'm sorry your honor. Sorry. Won't let it happen again. Didn't realize the terrible consequences. Sorry. Sorry." Still saying sorry, head still low, he shuffles from the room. A few people hiss as he goes out. A bony little old lady shakes her finger and throws her left white shoe at him saying, "You ought to be ashamed of yourself."

Thrigwhistle enters the men's room, which is not nearly as cheery as the campus facilities. Opening his brief case he removes and puts on an old scotch plaid jacket, and sticks on a beard and a red nose larger than his original nose. Walking back to the courtroom the red nosed man sits next to me. I give him a quick glance and look back at the judge who is throwing the case out of court. I clap vigorously and am almost as loud in my cheering as the man next to me wearing the scotch plaid jacket.

The mighty outburst of good feeling engendered by the trial helps lift away the pain of pneumonia from my rib cage.

# CHAPTER 21.

## STAMP COLLECTING

Cleo and I begin having more arguments. I admit, recovering from pneumonia, I am irritable. We consult a psychiatrist, Doctor Eagleton, well schooled in the mental arts. He discovers that each of us has been repressing feelings. I had been repressing myself at the college in an attempt to be accepted by my colleagues, some of whom refused to accept me. In addition some of my students did not like my teaching. The non-acceptance and bad feelings made me angry.

Cleo, in an attempt to receive attention from me drew pictures of Swirlopeds. She hated drawing pictures of Swirlopeds, and was antagonistic towards me for causing her to spend hours staring through a microscope at smelly dead Swirlopeds. She had tried to be nice to me. I had tried to be nice to the men in my department. Being nice got both of us into trouble. I had to forgive Cleo for being nice to me. Years later I told some friends, "I would have been happier if she would have told me to go fuck myself." Cleo rarely said this because she was afraid of making me angry.

We didn't know how to fight. In counseling we discovered that each of us had been collecting stamps during our marriage. Each stamp was for a wrong that had been done to us by the other person. We had started collecting stamps when we were little children. Our collections contained bad feeling stamps from the actions of mothers, fathers, grandparents, aunts, uncles, boyfriends, and girl friends.

On the day of our marriage I transferred all women done wronged me stamps to Cleo. On the day of our marriage she transferred all of her bad men stamps to me. I was her bastard. She was my bitch. After many years of collecting we wanted to cash in our stamps. I no longer liked Cleo. Cleo no longer liked me. We still loved each other. What a mess.

Dr. Eagleton helped us free our emotions. Cleo learned how to tell me to go fuck myself. When she said this to me, I sulked and wanted to scream and slap her. Despite our excellent counseling we regressed to the behavior of childhood.

At work I became more honest, because I had learned it was wrong to repress feelings. Dr Eagleton had told me, "Leo, you're selling yourself short. You are an excellent teacher." Because of Dr Eagleton's confidence in me, I had more confidence in myself, yet I oscillated. I had more highs, more lows.

Wanting to make up for lost time, in an attempt to quickly communicate my true feelings to my department, I wrote a short paper titled, Goals of General Education in Biology. I gave a copy to my chairman. I watched him read:

## GOALS OF GENERAL EDUCATION IN BIOLOGY

My course was developed for the nonscience student to meet the general education science requirement. It should not duplicate the course required for biology majors unless the course for majors is a general education course, which it isn't. The course for majors is designed to be rigorous, so as to properly train future physicians, nurses, occupational therapists, geneticists and biochemists.

By contrast a general education course is supposed to be enjoyable so as to stimulate and encourage further studies.

The science majors, having ambition, are dedicated. They are ready to tackle difficult unenjoyable material because they want to become great scientists and extremely wealthy physicians. I want to become a great teacher. Great teachers show much enthusiasm, have wide knowledge, and are independent. They also have biases. They may claim objectivity, but they have selected what has gone into their course. Give me tons of independence and allow me my biases, so that I also can become great. Let me be a bubbling stew, for the students to munch on.

Let us avoid dispassionate objectivity that merely pours out a mish mash of knowledge. Who likes cold oatmeal? Because of these reasons, I would like to make a few changes.

Leo

Isawaddy turns to me saying: "I like cold oatmeal, and have for years. You have some interesting ideas. However, the majors, as you know, receive tons of biochemistry, and don't get to study living plants and animals now, because they will get to learn all of that later on. Perhaps you've forgotten. There is a difference. In one stimulating week, the nonmajors do get to learn the major characteristics of all living organisms."

I have always had limited patience. Following the guidance of Dr. Eagleton I say, "It is ridiculous to teach students about animals and plants by the memorization of scientific names without observing life. I don't want my students galloping headless and heedless down the evolutionary highway without pausing to look at butterflies and snakes, listening to crickets and meadow larks, or smelling stink bugs."

I do not catch Isawaddy's answer. It sounds like humph.

# CHAPTER 22.

---

# THE MISSING REPRODUCTIVE ORGANS

I sawaddy's end of the year evaluation of my second year teaching is non-committal. Absent are the praises bestowed during the first year, even though I had followed departmental outlines, and patterned my lectures after my colleagues and had used recommended textbooks. During the year I made several proposals during departmental meetings.

I pleaded, "More time should be allowed for preparation. We should revise the lab exercises. The students seem confused.

My colleagues, the coauthors of the manual said, our manual has been praised by the students for its lucidity."

During the year, it seems to me, other teachers are less supportive of my work. The country seems headed for turmoil. A couple of months ago 400,000 marched to the UN protesting the Vietnam War.

The year has also been bad for Cleo. Her optimism and support of me of the previous year has left. She is glad when summer vacation comes. She often claims, she never sees me. I am always working on my lectures. She says, "You don't do things with Karl. You're always burrowing into text books, writing lectures, or drinking beer with your buddies." She spends her time planting azaleas and rhododendrums and does lots of jogging. She has a huge amount of excess energy she has to burn off. It is not a question of fat. She is muscular and in great shape. She watches sports on television. The sound of cheering crowds drives me crazy. I have zero interest in football, baseball and basketball.

Two weeks into the summer she is in the garden weeding. The radio plays, "*If you're going to San Francisco, be sure to wear some flowers in your hair,*" by The Mamas & the Papas. I would like to go to Haight Ashbury to share the energy. Thousands of hippies are there.

I get excitement from a new direction. I say, "Cleo. I've got a collaborator. Dr Verhoeff, the grand old man of Swirlopeds has agreed to help me. He is an icon. Isn't that great?"

Cleo says, "Verhoeff. Never heard of him. Don't they have icons in church? Does he spend most of his time in church?"

"He lives part of the year on Zanzibar. In his early twenties he watched Spiroswirlobolids slashing their way through the forest. He had to cover his head so he didn't get smashed by pieces of broken frangipani and cardamon branches."

"Were they dangerous? Did they attack him?"

"No. They were after cloves. Cloves affect Swirlopeds the way catnip goofs up cats. He wrote me, 'sometimes they become bad pests. The aggravation of these whirling buzz saws is lessened by their economic advantage. The Zanzibar Swirlopeds have red and white circles on their ventral surface. The Zanzibarians, in addition to using them for archery targets bring down the still rotating corpses, which they dry and use as hot plates for stew pots. The legs are used as back scratchers. Unfortunately the Swirloped population became endangered when an overseas market developed.'

"They were used in the United States as targets for bowmen and fringed umbrellas for ladies until the pioneering conservation efforts of Dr Verhoeff caused the International Conservation Foundation to put a ban on the trade."

"Why did you pick him?"

"Anyone who has saved an endangered species must be a good person."

I showed Cleo the letter's ending:

Ja. I would like to examine your specimens. Send them to me. Macht Schnell. Bitte.

VERHOEFF

She says, "He sounds German. Is he German?"

"Search me."

It cost me thirty-eight dollars and seventy-six cents to air mail half my collection to Verhoeff. Weeks passed until I receive a telegram saying: SEND ME MORE SPECIMENS. MACHT SCHNELL. BITTE. VERHOEFF.

I send the rest of the collection and go out to collect more. Another telegram arrives. It says: I CANNOT READ THE LABELS! YOU USED INFERIOR INK! IN THE FUTURE USE INDIA INK OR PENCIL. VERHOEFF.

I feel like a dumb schoolboy. I wonder why Verhoeff has not added Dumm Kopf to his telegram. I draw pictures of the reproductive organs of the Swirlopeds. To help me draw I fashion a device out of a showerhead and a floor mounting from springless pogo sticks. The mounting is screwed on an old bread board with fighting red, yellow and green roosters on one side and USE THIS SIDE N' SAVE MY FACE on the other side. The shower mounting is screwed into the pogo stick holder. A clipboard is bolted onto the shower mounting. I use the clipboard to draw on. It can be turned to any angle. I screw an optical gadget called a camera lucida into the microscope eyepiece. By means of prisms the camera lucida takes the image of the Swirloped from the microscope stage, through the tube, lenses, and prism to project the deflected reflected creature onto my drawing board. If the clipboard is not perfectly parallel with the projected image, the Swirloped drawing looks like two pregnant dachshunds rubbing noses.

One July afternoon I am dissecting a species new to science. Using micro tools (my scalpel blade is one fourth of an inch long; the probes are the diameter of a nose hair from Cleo) in some way I manage to lose a set of gonopods. Although I frantically search the glistening connective tissue I cannot find the missing male organs. Hoping the brilliant Verhoeff will be able to identify the specimen without the missing parts. I send the vial off.

The answer comes back: S-266 APPEARS TO BE A NEW FAMILY. THE REPRODUCTIVE ORGANS ARE MISSING. WITHOUT MALE ORGANS I CAN DO NOTHING. VERHOEFF.

I feel like cabling back: I CAN'T DO ANYTHING WITHOUT MALE ORGANS EITHER. Instead I cable: SORRY. THE ORGANS MUST HAVE SHAKEN LOOSE IN TRANSIT. BAUER.

I worry that Verhoeff will discover my incompetence.

Cleo draws for me. She is an excellent artist and is fast. Perhaps because the research is going well we again become happy. We decide we want a brother or sister for Karl, who seems bored playing alone. In no time at all, Cleo becomes pregnant. We celebrate our success without alcohol. She is nauseated so we don't go out to a restaurant. I imagine Karl playing happily with the baby.

Whenever I am happy, my organizational skills increase. Towards the end of summer I organize my notes and write about my specimens. This is difficult because I don't know their names. I have to refer to them as the big round brown disc one; the speckled one; the fat black one; the curled ringed one; the wide flat concave amber one; or the wrinkled burnt umber one.

Swirloped eyes are arranged in groups of spiraled black dots. After counting dots for several hours I think I have discovered a new way to classify Swirlopeds. I want to abandon the gonopeds and count dots. For a while I write about the fifteen dot one and the fourteen dot one until I discover that the number of eyes is variable. In addition, the older the animal the more eyes. I think, an exceedingly old Swirloped must have eyes all over its body. After that one of ambitions is to collect the oldest Swirloped in the world and get into the Guinness Book of Records. Upon reflection I decide, the last thing I want is to get into the book of records. It would be a shallow honor. At night I see the many-eyed creatures in my dreams. I am tranquil in the presence of the glowing eyes.

# CHAPTER 23.

## STUDENTS, MINORITY AFFAIRS AND THE TWIT

Towards the end of the summer of 1967 I buy a dog. I name her Fang, because she looks like a wolf. She will be a good playmate for the baby, when the baby comes. Her paws are huge. She is a friendly pup. Curious as all get out. When she pees Fang spreads her hind legs, pees on the brown earth, the thick warm pungent urine seeping into the soil. I spend most of my free time for two weeks teaching the pup to come when she is called and to stop when I yell stop. Her big feet make excellent brakes. She is inquisitive, playful and impetuous. In later years I am often glad I had trained her to stop; several times as she bounded toward the highway I yelled STOP; she stopped inches from death.

The theme of the 1967 pre class meetings was the students. President Davis was in Marathon meeting with legislators. We had to miss his speeches. What a shame, what a shame.

Dean Mann introduces the director of counseling, Mr. G. O. Telomyup. Telomyup, a well-groomed brunette overweight male in his early forties smiles and says, "Thank you Dean Mann. I like to listen to people. Students are my main concern. There has been a fantastic increase in research data available on the community college student. In counseling we emphasize the psychological integrity of the individual. We want them to achieve multifaceted self awareness of the inner complexities affecting their interpersonal social contacts."

I wished I was next to Maurice the librarian. I was in need of a translator.

Chewing on the edge of his lower lip Telomyup said, "They come to us with low self esteem. To you they may appear to be snoozing in class, but inwardly they are seething with conflicts. Many feel society has let them down. They have to learn that we teachers didn't become skilled overnight. It took a long, long time."

Next to me Joseph Malander commented, "It took me three weeks."

Telomyup was saying, "Beneath the self evident independence of the student, is what we too easily label as rebellion, most students are scared to go off on their own. They criticized their high school teachers out of low self esteem."

Malander said, "Who wouldn't. Is Low Self Esteem below Upper Low Self Esteem? Is it in Arizona along the Utah border? Perhaps it's a town of polygamists?"

"Some are merely marking time. After graduation, they will gradually fit into society."

In only five to ten years they will become complacent slaves to technology," says Malander.

Valiantly I try to listen as Telomyup says, "Our students are more practical than most college graduates. They don't think they are well prepared for college. They criticize their teachers."

"So what's new," says Malander.

"Unskilled children. They are afraid to admit intellectual urges because of the anti-intellectualism of their past and present," says Telomyup.

"And future," says Malander.

"They are better than university students at cooking, sports, sewing and automobile repairs," says Telomyup.

"Tune that car. Sew that button. Fry that egg. Get it in the basket, sizz boom bah!" says Malander.

"Less intellectually able than their peers in the university," says Telomyup.

"Dum, Dums," says Malander.

"They see college as a way to higher income," says Telomyup.

"That makes cents," says Malander.

"Four year college students are more dedicated to intellectual constructs," says Telomyup.

"Our students are devoted to banging fenders and girls," says Malander.

"Some of our students attend community college year after year and seem afraid to transfer to a larger institution," says Telomyup.

"We could have them committed," says Malander.

"The record attendance of a student at our college is ten years. Jimmy Brinkly, the student body vice president, has been here longer than half the faculty. In his own way he is becoming an expert. So far he has edited the paper, formed a rock band, and rebuilt a nineteen forty-six Hudson," says Telomyup.

"He gets what he wants," says Malander.

Telomyup introduced William Ataruk, the Director of Minority Affairs, by saying, "Mr. Ataruk, a Nupiat, has been exposed to the cold winds of discrimination for a long time. Not letting that stop him, he is our respected expert on minority affairs."

Ataruk, a big man, spoke. "Thank you Mr. Telomyup. Among the innovations we have brought to Humaluh are black studies."

"For our seven basketball players," says Malander.

"Tar Heel studies for the eighteen percent of the students from the Carolinas. Our Chicano Program provides year round work because of the establishment of a tortilla factory on campus."

"On the flats," says Malander.

"We teach the students new dance steps from the Arctic including ice hopping, polar bear leaping, polar bear evasion and coed bouncing," says Ataruk grinning.

"A popular program. If you flunk they bounce you out of sight," says Malander.

"Other college programs cooperate with the ethnic program. White anthropology students made beautiful beaded necklaces and authentic balsa wood carved copies of totem poles that they donate to the Native American Club for their auction," says Ataruk.

"They use the money to buy outboards and motorcycles," says Malander.

"Home economics classes cooked chick peas, pigs feet, hominy grits, sautéed kidney, liver soup, stuffed kufta, badijon moufool, and head cheese."

Malander licks his lips. "I can't wait for the removal of eyes and teeth from a pigs head, the breaking of the bones, and the cooking, and the pouring of the pulp and gravy into molds to cool and jell."

Continuing with his list Ataruk mentions a food for every ethnic group, "sauerkraut, stuffed eggplant, frijoles, okra stew, spinach pie, stuffed shredded wheat, turnip puff, oatmeal bread, prune muffins, cracker pudding, vinegar cake, sour cream cookies and *kaputsa*. President Davis was especially touched when our students gave him some *troubotchki* or cornucopia cookies, and an Okie and Hawaiian delicacy of Spam and pineapple."

Malander says, "Unfortunately the banquet flopped. Some idiot published the menu before they started selling the tickets."

"We only had one major problem, when the Tar Heels fabricated an authentic looking early American still. Unfortunately for them we discovered and destroyed it before they could add their product to the punch." The faculty laughs heartily.

Bringing in Ataruk has been a brilliant move by the administration. Because Ataruk was the only Nupiat in the county they could not be charged with favoring one minority over another. The only negative part of his program had been the Chicano Dance, which had a rock band playing sambas. The dance didn't work out too well because one of the black basketball players had decked a Tar Heel who had called him a nigah. A team mate of his chased the Tar Heel; hitting him as if he were a punching bag. With each punch he said "mother fuckah." In reprisal for this minor disagreement, thirty-four Tar Heels from up river surrounded a car holding the seven blacks. As they were rocking the car preparatory to tipping it over, the ethnic studies director threw up. After the fight there were beads all over the gym floor. The beads scratched the floor and the coaches were furious because of the scratches and the hurt feelings of their star athletes.

At the next Crunch and Munch meeting, after he is mildly snockered, with a quizzical grin, Magnum asks me. "Leo. Do you like our mascot?"

I say, "I've never met our mascot."

"He is most unique," says Malander. Other colleges use macho symbols such as bears, steers, mountain lions and eagles. We use a puce parrot. This magnificent creature, The Twit, has little short legs and takes three hops backward for every three forward. The long hooked beak calls twit with each tiny hop, and it usually goes hop, hop, hop, and therefore says, "twit, twit, twit." However, when it is trying to act like it knows something, it says "progress, curriculum, progress, curriculum, woark, woark." When panicked the Twit loses control and runs zig zagging through classrooms screaming "irrelevant, bad, worse, worst, woark, woark."

"Are you sure The Twit isn't just another administrator?" I say, "Does he scare easily and panic when there is conflict?"

"You get the picture," says Magnum. Raising his glass he says, "To The Twit."

"To The Twit," says I.

Arms interlocked, we sing, "May The Twit cry forever, for you and for meeeeeeeee." Then I go home.

# CHAPTER 24.

## SUSPICION

Being slightly paranoid, I think, my friends drink without me? To investigate this delusion I read the menu inhabiting a disguise of large dark glasses, which makes it almost impossible to see, and a sports jacket I bought at Goodwill. A navy blue beret covers my hair.

The menu reads, THIS RESTAURANT DOES NOT SERVE SCHNITZELS. I think, *Ist das nicht ein Schnitzel Haus? Ja das ist ein Schnitzel Haus. Warom ist der Schnitzel?*

Was it a delusion to expects *schnitzels* at a *Schnitzel Haus*, or are the *schnitzels* lost in translation?

The house specialty is a French dip made of frozen beef and hot rich canned gravy in a paper cup. For my chef's salad I order a blue cheese dressing. The dressing and the dip were made in the kitchens of Linda and Giovanni, in Duwamps. A group of men enter and sit at the next table. I covertly watch Malander, Magnum, Seabeck, and Volens order and drink beer. Magnum speaks. "Where is Leo?"

Malander says, "Is Leo with Cleo? Two lovebirds chirping. Tweet, tweet, tweet." They all laugh.

I mumble, "Bastards."

Volens says, "I forgot to tell him."

Magnum says, "His wife, poor woman. She's lonely."

Seabeck, his voice a sledgehammer says, "She needs a kick in the butt. She ought to work."

Magnum says, "Cleo works in the home, she's a mother and she's pregnant."

Seabeck says, "There are mothers and there are MOTHERS."

Malander says, "I'm tired of listening to Bauer's marital complaints." Malander's eyes are almost closed in the dim light.

Magnum, pressing his thick neck says, "Leo lets events, people, his wife, control him."

Seabeck says, "He could pack up and leave."

Volens says, "That is hard to do. Hard to do."

Malander proclaims, his chest tensing his tweed sports coat, "I've done it several times. Naomi knows the conditions of our relationship."

"You have no children. For you it's easy to proclaim independence," says Magnum.

Malander sneering says, "That's your fault. My wife also wants children but I say, hell no. I'm not about to lose my freedom."

Caressing his beard Magnum says, "I understand marital problems. Cleo should get a job. It's the time of women's liberation. Haven't you guys read *The Feminine Mystique*? My wife works because she wants to. It's her decision. It's good for her. She comes home tired. If she's angry at the boss and not at me I sympathize with her." The entire table laughs heartily. Magnum continues, "She has many good days. She likes the independence from earning her own money. Leo tells me, he can't tell his wife what to do. She wants to be with her child. Won't be able to work until the baby is born. Won't be able to work until the baby's older."

"Cleo feels children need their Mamas."

"Ha. Her hanging around so much doesn't make Karl happy. The poor kid looks like he's lost his best friend."

"That's Leo's fault. He's always working on those damn Swirlopeds or writing lectures. Never takes time to play with the boy."

"The child is in school."

Observing that the beer is all gone, Volens sobs. Compassion filling his soul, Magnum orders another pitcher. Refreshed, Volens complains, "We are gossips and punsters of the worst order. Worse than Mrs. Murphy."

"Who is Mrs. Murphy?" asks Malander.

"She put overalls in the chowder." says Seabeck with indignation. "She was running a bed and breakfast in Chicago."

"Were they her overalls?" says Magnum.

"Where was the owner of the overalls?" says Malander.

Winking a great eye, Magnum says, "She threw a pan of dishwater at a customer's head."

"Crime does not pay," announces, Malander.

They all laugh. I also laugh, wondering whose overalls went in the chowder.

Malander's eyes slowly open-wide as he hovers at the antipodes of intellect.

Making a humble inquiry Magnum says, "I saw you playing basketball with Isawaddy, Mann and Pompa. Are they your new best buddies?"

"I like to play ball with them and their pangolin minds. Leo should have studied pangolins. Those damn Swirlopeds. He claims those things can fly. I think he's nuts. I looked them up in the encyclopedia and it says they hide out under rocks and logs. It doesn't even mention anything about them swimming, or whirling," says Malander.

"He's right. I've gone with him on several field trips. They do whirl and fly, and they also swim," smirks Magnum.

"Your wife's one hell of a woman," says Seabeck.

"Thanks," says Magnum. "She was working three days after giving birth."

"One hell of a woman," says Seabeck.

At my table I hunch lower over my beer. Feeling sad.

"Yup. Leo should put his foot down. I've told him so," says Malander. "But what's the use.

When Bauer says 'no' it's like hearing a mouse squeaking.

All the men laugh at the thought of me squeaking. Bastards. I touch my forehead, feeling warmth.

Volens says, "What great American said, 'Shit or get off the pot?'"

Banging his stein on the table, Seabeck yells.

Observing the spilled beer Magnum dourly comments, "Don't dribble."

Volens says, "The dribble; the revenge of Montezuma."

Magnum says, "Tijuana trots."

Volens says, "One way or the other, it's not coming out right." He asks, "What's a pangolin?"

Malander says, "They are scaly and horny."

Seabeck asks, "Are they full of fleas?"

Magnum, grinning, says, "Did Leo teach you about pangolins?"

"Pompa told me about them today. That man's a genius," replies Malander.

Volens sings in a kazoo voice, "While playing a pangolin, while playing a pangolin."

"Arrgh," says Malander clutching his throat."

"Drink."

Volens says, "No wonder I never stop drinking."

Despite these brave words, when the beer is gone they go home. Shortly after my friends leave, I pay my bill, walk around the block to my car , scratch my bearded chin, start the engine and drive home wondering all the way, what does Dylan mean when he sings, "Oh, the ragman draws circles, up and down the block?"

# CHAPTER 25.

## SERIOUS BUSINESS

I begin to put more of myself into my classes. My goal is to be the real me. No bullshit. Just honesty. My lectures change. I spend more class time discussing controversial subjects including the ethics of transplanting human hearts. I ask students, "Should people be subjected to operations costing tens of thousands of dollars that will only add a few months to their lives? Is such an operation necessary or is it mostly an ego builder for the surgeon?"

I ask Magnum, "Why should I lecture? The students can read the textbook."

"You're right except they don't want to read textbooks or listen to lectures. It makes sense to cut out the middle man and not lecture."

"You're right, we should cut out the middle man. On the first day of class we should pass out the textbooks. On the last day of the quarter teachers and students can have a grand reunion and discuss what has been learned."

Magnum says, "That shouldn't take more than about five minutes. After that we can all have a big party."

Not really wanting to do away with my job, I start taking students on field trips to forests, lakes and seashores. I worry that the class doesn't like me, because while driving the Blue Papoose bus I often sit alone in the front seat. The students sit in the back, sort of like it was them and it was me but it wasn't everybody together.

Most of the time the students dig the field trips. They appreciate my telling intimate facts of life. In the forest I say, "Did you know moss sperm travels through a thin film of moisture from the golf tee like top male structure to the sharp topped female part. Even mosses have fun."

In the marsh I say, "Look, a red winged blackbird. What are those other birds?" I wait, hope they will answer wrong.

"Sparrows, finches" comes a hesitant male voice.

Pleased, I reply, "No. They're female red wings, members of the harem of this mighty potentate of the willows and cattails."

The male redwing, red epaulettes flashing, dips low and gives a pure fluid call. Hovering in the warm sunlight the sound ties together cattails, wrens and a duck's splash.

Later back at the campus I cook up some Labrador tea collected in the marsh. Experiencing a gentle high, Johny Petrus says, "What a trip." He laughs.

Sometimes students greet my sincerity, my love of nature with laughter, as if the hike in the woods or across a marsh was a joke. This bums me out. I have never learned how to handle mockery.


Often I give D's to my favorite students. Many A and B students seem to be narrow-minded as if they are wearing blinders. Cattle greedy for A and B oats. They seem to follow orders as unquestioningly as steers led to the slaughterhouse. I begin to read poetry to my students. I read them parts of my journal. I want to be a person instead of a mere presenter of facts.


Selections read included: The tide's going out. A one legged hunter said, "It's been a poppin and a pingen since two thirty;" A vandal destroys

hundreds of fine panes of ice; The sun goes down on a landscape of thin
sheets breaking off grassy ice buttes next to drift log stumps. Lower
down older fragments have joined, the sharp shards are smooth again.
From all over come brittle cracks, long slow cracks, quick ricochets, and
sounds of a glass house slowly breaking apart.

How different this is from the marsh in June when green aphids
suck thus creating marsh plant caverns. In June the grasses and sedges
are dirty, flat. The green is veiled by silt and covering grasses. In the
wind is the sound of grass on a meadow. A green stalk carries white
flowers almost above the grasses. A candle blooms. Sedges hang seeds
down like bundled up caterpillars. Grasses send up seeds like flags. On
the opposite bank willow leaf underbellies, exposed in the wind, are
silver.

My A and B students write down every word of these observations
in case they will be on a test. One said to his neighbor, "Professor Bauer
is wasting our time."

The lectures include valuable information that I abstract from
scholarly journals: The more deer eat the more they poop. Wood ducks
do not like to live in poorly constructed nest boxes. Hundreds of wild
swans have died in the lower Coeur d'Alene River Valley from poisoning
by heavy metals including lead, zinc, and copper washed down from
nearby mines. The swans feed on aquatic vegetation. Poison gas in
granaries repels and kills mice. It also repels scientists. Malayan rats
rarely cross open areas during a full moon (Perhaps they are afraid of
vampires). Beheaded female Drosophila flies show retarded mating
behavior. They can live headless for several days and manage to fly and
preen themselves when headless. This offers proof that the preening
behavior of females is among the most basic of all behaviors. The males
of some species of fruit flies attempt to mate with female flies whether
or not they possess heads. This reminds me of certain human females
who can also preen, strut, giggle, swallow champagne and mate after
losing their heads over a man.

# CHAPTER 26.

# IF MAN WERE SATISFIED THE WHEEL WOULD NEVER HAVE BEEN INVENTED

I am selected to be the chairman of the Satisfaction Committee. Finally the rest of the faculty recognizes my ability. Imitating the Gallop poll, we prepare a list of questions that we distribute to the faculty.

After the return, I tabulate the responses. The results please me because they confirm my expectations. I am sure the data will be helpful to the administration, which is always saying they want to know faculty opinions.

We release the results in a thirtyeight page report marked-TOP SECRET: Survey of Humaluh Valley College Faculty Morale.

The day of distribution I become very popular. Malander and Magnum shake my hand with a flourish and pound my back. Malander says, "An outstanding job Leo."

"It was all of us. A committee effort," I say.

Magnum says, "I recognize your writing style. You wrote the report. It's an objective, gutsy, report. Something you can be proud of."

"Thank you," I say. I am glad my friends recognize my ability. During the day other faculty members seek me out and thank me for saying what needed to be said. I imagine myself, as a result of the survey, being nominated and elected president of the faculty. We also receive negative feedback from a few people. I discover two notes in my box:

Dietrich Eckart, the director of planning, wrote: "I have been working long hours and have not taken a vacation in years. I am incensed at the way your questions were slanted so as to produce an anti-administration response."

The second note from President Davis read: "Leo. Please come and see me at three o'clock."

I am there promptly at three wondering what's up. After knocking, I hear, "Come in."

As I enter the room, the president stands up, causing the presidential chair to whack the wall. Reaching out, pointing the presidential finger at me, Davis says, "Leo. Why did you do this to me? I've been your friend."

I halt when I see the presidential finger. Standing halfway to the desk I reply, "Doctor Davis. It's only a questionnaire. It can assist you in improving Humaluh Valley College. Using faculty opinions can help you improve morale."

Davis humphs. "Improve morale. Ha." He picks up a copy of the questionnaire. Waving it, he says, "This document will destroy morale. It can cancel out all of the progress of the first two years of my administration. And I thought you were my friend."

"I am your friend. We did not attack you. Our goal was to maintain complete objectivity."

"Objectivity Bullshit!" says the president.

I glance at the rubber tree. The soil is wet; the tree is artificial. Another of life's mysteries.

As I leave the room I think, why is it so easy to piss off the president? I thought he wanted input from the faculty. Back in my office I attempt to try to understand the president's fury by rereading the survey and the faculty comments. Several of the teachers had written words to the effect that the administrators were dedicated men. Men especially dedicated to filling their own pockets and bellies, so dedicated to meeting their own needs that they were unresponsive to the needs of the faculty.

I began to understand the president's fury, though I still remembered words from a Davis speech. The president had said, "I encourage free speech. If people speak out fascist boots cannot march." I visualize lots of marching Humaluh boots.

On the Friday after the release of the survey I thirstily accompany eight of my friends to the *Schnitzel Haus*. Lifting dripping glasses they sing, "Hooray for Leo. He's our buddy through and through. He's got guts, he's true blue. Hooray."

"It wasn't just my report. We worked together as a committee,"

Girodias leans forward, his owl spectacles reflecting the lambent red candlelight. "You can't fool me. You wrote the essays. You put the whole thing together."

"Our committee decided upon the questions: The answers were written by faculty."

"Davis is madder than a thrice thumped hornet's nest," says Magnum.

"Don't worry. You've got friends," says Volens with a voice of authority.

"We'll support you right down the line," says the gravelly voice of Seabeck.

"You did what should have been done a long time ago," says balding Apfelboeck.

"I'm glad you did it," says Magnum.

Malander says, "Those pompous fools have been revealed. On every count they fail. They jammed merit pay down our throats. We voted against it, but they went ahead. If you've got friends on that committee, and if you do them favors, you get advanced. That's merit?"

"Merit, schmerit, bullshit!" says Seabeck.

"Yes a faculty committee," says Malander. "It gathers information, deliberates, recommends and sends a fat file to the administration, which deliberates, recommends and sends a fatter file to the board, which decides if I am meritorious enough to receive an extra two thousand dollars a year for five years. Meanwhile to pay for this bonus the rest of us get less."

"Merit badges for my skull," says Alfo.

"Merit badges up my ass," says Volens.

"Merit badges for kissing ass," says Malander.

"Lots of money for kissing ass," grumbles Seabeck.

"What are the criteria?" I say.

Malander answers peering through the glass revolving between his fingertips. "I applied this year. An evaluation committee was formed. Two were appointed by my chairman and I appointed the third."

"Can your chairman appoint your opponents or enemies?" I ask.

"That can happen," grins Malander.

"You can be torpedoed in the beginning when you meet with the committee and they decide which of nine areas should be emphasized. They include: cooperation with the administration, loyalty to the administration, enthusiasm for college programs, cooperation with colleagues, personal appearance, professional competence, fulfillment of teaching and institutional duties, professional conduct, and accessibility to students." Malander gulps more beer.

"You mean, you get merit pay for combing your hair and cooperating?"

"You're bright today Leo," says Malander. Swilling down half a stein of beer and belching he continues, "The committee has to OK the areas of emphasis. Then like a terrier you trot around the campus seeking recommendations. Student evaluations are optional. If you want them, they may be included. The more love letters you accumulate the better your chances."

"If you don't associate weeth zee right class of people, your chances go down zee tube," says Girodias.

"It pays to be nice," says Alfo.

"I'll try to use my accomplishments. I've spent my time teaching, not ass kissing. Next year I'll submit love letters."

"*Tres bien, monsieur*," says Girodias. "*Amour toujour, toujour amour.*"

"So the committee turned you down?" I say.

"Not exactly," says Malander. "The evaluation committee, which contains friends of mine, recommended me. Unfortunately, I lacked supporters on the Merit Pay Committee that includes coaches, scientists, and vocy techy types. They turned me down. I felt like a black in Alabama with an all white jury."

"Can you appeal?"

"Sure. You can appeal all the way up the line, but what's the use." Malander flops his hands on the table. "They already had all the evidence. I gave them newspaper clippings of my art exhibits. Last summer I had a one-man show at the Charley Gallery. I've brought in artists who have demonstrated how to throw pots and how to paint. Most of the student opinionaires were favorable. A few of the little bastards said I was too critical. One said I was boring. Perhaps I should take them to rodeos and car races?"

"That's a good idea. I'll drink to that," says Volens. "Hey give us another pitcher," he yells. He looks into Malander's face and says, "Seriously, I'm concerned about you. You belong to the Elks Club, don't you?"

"No."

" Rotary?"

"No."

"Have you invited the administrators in for tea and crumpets?"

"Of course not."

"No wonder you didn't get merit pay." Volan's eyes twinkle above his smirk.

We leave at eight. I get hell from Cleo for leaving her alone on a Friday night. Watching leaves fly away from branches, I admit, "I should have phoned," while thinking, has Cleo become my mother?

Saturday afternoon Doctor Eagleton praises me for starting to pay attention to feelings and needs, and lauds me for my courage.

Three weeks after the release of the questionnaire the faculty is ordered to convene in the auditorium for a president's forum. I sit in a comfortable blue chair. Only administrative leaders sit in the first two rows. Between them and my friends and I are clusters of administrative supporters, many of them on merit pay. The malcontents sit in the subdued light in the back of the room. Some teachers following recidivistic urges and straining their eyes correct student papers or read paperbacks. Many of the faculty near me laugh and comment as the president speaks. I imagine it is similar to simultaneously hearing English, French, Russian and Chinese at the UN. Thrigwhistle passes the time doodling, drawing jet planes, trains, kangaroos, and elephants. Barnaby sketches his colleagues, emphasizing chins, noses, teeth, toes, bellies, and ears.

I listen to the crisp voice of shiny-faced dean Mann say, "Faculty, It gives me great pleasure to introduce our president. As you know he is a man who has devoted most of his professional life to Humaluh. Today our president will discuss employee satisfaction. Please listen well to him. Elmore knows what's good for us." The dean, mellow as a rum soaked Cuban cigar, waits for the president, who stumbles slightly, on his way to the podium. After they shake hands, the dean sits down and the president humbly brushing away applause speaks: "welcome, welcome, welcome to another president's forum. I am glad to see all of you. I enjoy these times when our small family meets and reasons together. If you have any questions during my talk please speak up."

The president is the image of up to date fashion in his new burgundy sports jacket.

"I have your best interests at heart. I am very proud of all of you."

Volens blows his nose.

"Raise your hand if you have a comment or question." He looks alert and fresh in black pants and white shoes. "As I was saying. I have your best interests at heart. Each week I work to insure we have the best community college in the United States. We are top notch. Recently there was a so-called survey of faculty morale. The poll was done by neophytes unskilled in asking and evaluating questions. The poll was designed, whether on purpose or by accident, to produce biased results."

Davis seems to stare at me for a moment. I examine my fingernails and slouch.

"Nevertheless today I will discuss the results of this questionable questionnaire as if they were valid. Apparently on the surface many of you appear to be dissatisfied. Half of you work at outside jobs during part of the year and you claim you have to do this because you don't make enough money here. I would like to remind you, though I'm not on your salary schedule, I work hard trying to get the highest possible salaries for you. I admit; most administrators are on merit pay. However, we have an excellent administrative staff. It is imperative that our college attract and retain top notch administrators."

Malander whispers, "They're attracted all right. Like yellow jackets to hamburger."

Unaware of his competition Davis continues, "It is imperative, as I said, to reward excellence. It is imperative that our superior deans and division heads stay with us."

"Like ducks, they are too fat to fly away." whispers Malander.

Clutching the podium Davis says, "Some of you think the administration is more concerned with the welfare of the administration than the welfare of the faculty. In this you are dead wrong. We are very concerned for your welfare. Very concerned."

I recognize Seabeck's muffled, "Bullshit!," from several rows back.

Rearden, a favorite of the president, enters the auditorium and walks towards the front of the room. Spotting him, Davis loudly says, "Rearden, I allow no one to come late to these meetings. It's not right. You will be on time or else."

Angry at the personal attack, Rearden bellows, "I'm sorry Elmore, but I was with students. The reason I'm here is because of my students."

The president's reply is an explosion of words. "Rearden," he screams, "this is more important." Rearden shuts up and slips into an aisle seat. Acting as if there had been no interruption the president continues, "Actually the study showed, more of you are satisfied than dissatisfied. Nearly all of you want to remain. Most of you think that the morale is bad yet you want to remain?" Having posed the enigma he looked puzzled and says, "Why?" Elmore's voice lifts, "Perhaps you like our sabbatical leave? Not bad. Every seventh year some of you can go off to study in Austria or Leichtenstein. Not bad. And all full time teachers get the summer off. You like that, don't you? You're not like us administrators. We have to work in the summer.

"Many of you don't like the way we assign night school duties, but you like the extra pay. Many are dissatisfied with the quality of the students, yet everyone likes their paycheck.

"Because of the students you get paid. Don't ever forget that." The president flails the air to emphasize the importance of the students.

Malander softly whispers in my ear, "The purpose of a school is to give jobs to teachers, And to feed a bureaucracy. Each group protects itself and feeds upon the others."

I silently agree with Malander. He switches his ears back to the president who is saying, "You don't like us to evaluate your performance. What do you expect us to do when the board says, 'Justify your payroll.' Heaven knows I try. I fight to keep your jobs, yet you complain."

Competing with Elmore Davis and the rhythmic pulse of the heater fans Malander whispers, "Fight fiercely dear Elmore."

Davis is saying, "Measure up. Shape up or ship out."

Sounding irate Volens interrupts the president, "Why are we overstaffed? The faculty doesn't do the hiring. We should not be punished."

Looking like an innocent lamb, the president says, "It's not my fault either. Hawthorne doubled our faculty, but I'm the guy who has to face the music. I don't like it and if you don't like it that's tough. Some people are going to have to go and that's that. I'm stuck with the situation. Is that OK with you?" Leaning over the podium he stares angrily at Volens who asks no further questions. As a rock of reason, the president continues. "As I was saying. You like our wonderful valley. You are dedicated. You have freedom to teach the way you want to teach. The classroom is yours." The president looks into my eyes.

Pacing back and forth on the stage he says, "Some of you are unhappy. Some people would be unhappy in paradise. Think about this. How much work would get done if everybody was satisfied? If man had been satisfied the wheel would not have been invented. You would never have gone to college. I would not have left Leeds, Alabama. It is only through dissatisfaction that things get done." Having given up this precious kernel of personal philosophy, the president benignly smiles towards his staff. "Are there any questions?" he adds."

We faculty like restless lizards want desperately to crawl away. No one dares to ask a question. The meeting breaks up.

A few teachers go up to our leader and compliment him.

Davis modestly admits, "Yes, it was a good speech, wasn't it?"

# CHAPTER 27.

## HELL NO I WON'T GO

It probably isn't good for my career, but we have freedom of expression in America. A man has to stand up for what he believes. It seems natural for me to join the protests against the Vietnam War at the Federal Building in Duwamps. They are held on Columbus Day in October so there are no classes. Millions are opposed to the war and want our troops to come home. I didn't think twice until marching around the Federal Building, I look into lenses on dozens of still and movie cameras. I wonder, will they attempt to use our photographs to prove we are subversive? Will the videos be on television? Will the college administrators, and the Board of Directors see my picture on TV? I am not very tall. A tall person would stand out like a giraffe. Yet when we turn corners, the cameras, the video cams photograph everyone in our breaking curving row.

What will the administration do if they see my photograph on television or in the newspaper? Will I get fired?

I try to maintain a low profile: even though short I feel like I am a giraffe. Have you ever seen a giraffe try to hide by creeping through short grass? Actually I've never seen a giraffe hide, but I still think of giraffes.

Several weeks later, Johnny Petrus, one of my students, asks me to represent him at a conscientious objector meeting. Perhaps I should have consulted with friends first, but thinking my job is to support my students, I say yes, of course.

Because the hearing is to be held during class time I ask Dean Mann for permission to be off campus. He seems to think it's a big deal. He calls in president Davis who says, "What will the people in town say?"

I say, "I won't tell them."

The president does not smile as he says, "We have to think about our community relations."

"Can't we think about the students?" I say.

Mann says, "What will you do at the hearing?"

"I'm supposed to play the role of an adviser, that's like an attorney." I say.

Dean Mann says, "We have to discuss this. Your classes are also important."

Davis says, "Each class missed is a tragedy."

I ask, "What about the Kennedy visit? Lots of teachers and administrators went to hear Robert Kennedy. That was on a school day."

"Petrus is no Kennedy."

"Our college was a co-sponsor of Kennedy's visit. Weren't all of those missed classes a tragedy? What makes those absences acceptable and my absence forbidden?"

"We're not forbidding you to represent Petrus. However we have to spend some time considering the ramifications of such an action. Wait here. We'll be back shortly." Says Davis. They left me stewing.

I think, you men are each making tens of thousands of dollars a year and you have nothing better to do than hassle me. I want to yell through the door, "I just want to do a favor for a student."

They return after about fifteen minutes. Davis walks over to me. I put down the Reader's Digest. Davis says, "You can go. Just keep a low profile. If I was you I wouldn't tell anyone about your testifying at the hearing."

Mann says, "Although divided on this matter we have decided to let you go. We won't be able to pay you for the missed time. As you can see, we are more liberal than you may think."

"Thank you," I say. As I walk away I think, I would have gone anyway. Those bastards take what should be an automatic yes and make it into an affair of state. I want to do something for my fellow man, who happens to be a youth, a student, and they object.

We are driving to the hearing in Duwamps. Johnny and I wear suits. His mother, white haired Mrs. Petrus and his girl friend Sally McGuire wear serious dresses. As we drive I tell them about my confrontation with Davis and Mann, adding, "We used to wonder why the German people were quiet. At first they wanted to keep their jobs, and not get hurt."

Johnny says, "The quickest way to settle an argument is to kill your opponent. It all seems simple. Just use enough napalm and claymore mines and again there will be peace. That is a stupid concept. This war makes me so sad."

Mrs. Petrus says, "His older brother Frank died in Korea."

Johnny says, "I'd like to know him now. He was thirteen years older."

"Violence escalates or dissipates. Your objection is an act of peace." I say.

The Federal Building looks like a big orange brick beehive. There are numerous plazas extending down the slope to First Avenue. After parking, we take an express elevator and easily find the hearing room. The examiner is a soft-spoken gentle man whose hair is streaked with white. He asks Johnny, "Why do you want to be classified a C.O.?"

"War is against my religious convictions."

"The FBI resume indicates philosophical reasons for your objections."

"My objection is religious."

"We will mark your objection is based on religious beliefs as Exhibit One. Johnny, do you want to state any additional views?"

"Not now."

"Mrs. Petrus, we welcome statements from parents. We are quite concerned with sudden conversions. They often happen after the draft board starts breathing down someone's neck."

Mrs. Petrus, a gentle woman emanating love looks at the examiner and answers, "Johnny was the middle child of five. We came to Cascadia in 1940 from Iowa. Johnny was born in 1946. My husband changed from farming to mechanics. He can repair anything. We had to struggle but things were easy for Johnny."

"Are you a religious family?"

"We are very religious."

"What religion?"

"We don't indoctrinate our children."

"Did Johnny go to Sunday school?"

"In high school he went with some friends to the Baptist church and sunday school."

"Do other members of the family hold similar views to Johnny?"

"He has his own views. His older brother has stopped speaking to him. His other brother Ted died in Korea. His sisters are angry with him. They are patriotic. I support his views."

"How many brothers are there?"

"We have two. His older brother is in the service in Viet Nam."

"Does Mr., Petrus agree with Johnny?"

"He feels Johnny should make up his own mind. He is an electrician. A good man."

"Johnny, would you be willing to do alternate service?"

"I would do alternate service for a humanitarian cause."

"Before coming to this meeting, were you told to shave and look conservative?"

"No."

"Sally, you have presented a statement?"

"Yes."

"Are you a conscientious objector?"

"Yes."

"Because of your religious training and belief?"

"In part."

"Is Johnny sincere?"

"Yes. We go on long walks together. We try to figure things out. We often listen to folk singers."

"Johnny, has folk music influenced you?"

"Only a little bit. I like Pete Seeger."

"Mr., Bauer, would you like to say a few words?"

"You already have my statement. Johnny became my friend while he was a student of mine. He enjoys reading Thoreau. He likes children. He is a good person. He is against the war."

"Are you a C.O.?"

"I am a veteran of the Korean War."

"Mr. Petrus. I will read everything carefully and review your application. Would any of you like to say anything more?"

Mrs. Petrus speaks, "Children should have freedom to make up their own minds."

"Thank you all for coming." The examiner shakes everyone's hand and we all leave the room. Mrs. Petrus takes us to dinner. We eat pizza.

Johnny continues with his studies, and worries about his status. He is declared an official conscientious objector on June 6th 1967. A year in the future Robert Kennedy will be assassinated. At that time sobbing students in a sociology class at the University of Cascadia had asked to be excused from their final exam. Their professor told them, "We must meet our responsibilities."

When I heard that, I thought, I must investigate the definition of sociology.

# CHAPTER 28.

# LET'S SELECT A TEXTBOOK

The summer of 1968 we return to Wisconsin. We get a television and watch the coverage from San Francisco. The hippie movement is taking off. We would like to be where the action is. Cleo and I work on our marriage. I do lots of boating with Karl. He is turning into an excellent swimmer. He is much better than I can ever hope to be. We water ski without my getting pneumonia. I read the *Grapes of Wrath*.

We return to Duhkwuh in the fall of 1968. Not long after our return the biology staff meets in Isawaddy's office. "We will try to keep this meeting short," says Isawaddy. "We are busy men. This meeting is to select the textbook for general biology." Pompa, Jackson, and I, listening to our leader, are as close as barnacles on a Puget Sound piling. "We will continue to use the same laboratory manual." Isawaddy holds up a green stapled paperback.

I clear my throat. My colleagues look at me. I think, that book confuses me and I'm the teacher. Shall I tell them it is rotten? That it needs a drastic revision? "Just a tickle," I say.

"We have good news," says Isawaddy. I look up. "Bobby Pompa and Dean Mann have written a textbook. *Biology for Everybody*, based on our program. It contains the most extensive coverage of the DNA Litany available. Fortunately we can get preliminary copies in time for winter quarter. I commend Pompa and Mann for their mighty accomplishment. It goes without saying that I highly recommend the selection of this book."

Pompa leans back, bearing a gigantic smile.

I say, "I also want to commend Pompa and Mann. In many respects, it is good to have a book written primarily for us. Many students would also enjoy using a book written by their professors. Despite all of the many advantages of the book, however, I don't want to use it." Like a poisonous serpent the words have crawled out of my mouth. The room quiets. I think, if I use their book, I will have to begin my lectures by saying, according to Pompa, according to Mann. Students, biology is synonymous with DNA. That's what it's all about. If you want more information, consult the experts in the next office. And as for me, I don't know shit. However, according to Mann, according to Pompa. Who am I you ask? Bauer is the name. My nights are spent in the contemplation and memorization of the immortal words of Pompa and Mann. They are the reincarnation of Aristotle. No. I shall not be the donkey's ass to be paraded about by Pompa and Mann.

"Well I want to use it," says Jackson. "It is the best book available for General Biology."

"Here, Here" says Pompa. "Sure it has a few bugs. That's to be expected. They can be taken out in the next edition." I think, that's a good time for the bugs. Oh the bugs go in, the bugs go out, the bugs play pinochle up my snout.

"Thank you," says Pompa smiling.

"You're right Robert. The bugs can be removed," I say. Hunching forward, arms on the table, I am immersed in the swill of my body odor. "I have no love for the book we're using. When I came in today, I had intended asking for a new text. However I'm scared by this decision. If we all use *Biology for Everybody* it will be impossible to switch later on. I want the freedom to choose my own textbook. I don't want to be locked in. I've always believed in the freedom of choice. I don't want to lose it. Please. Let the choice be individual instead of departmental." My anguished voice rose.

One early reviewer wrote, "one of the finest biological encyclopedias ever written." His sharp eye showed the irrationality of my position. One reviewer had written, "Surpasses the works of the famous French biologist Buffon." I recalled the learned Buffon and his description of Tartars, Turks, Negroes, Hottentots, the porcupine man, dwarfs and curious giants. He also gave an excellent description of the Oran-otang, the pongo and the jocko.

To enable the reader to form his or her own opinion, a few excerpts taken at random from *Biology for Everybody* follow: "It is highly probable, traditionally as noted, the discoveries, the explanation, perhaps the best fundamental problem, before we begin, is characterized by another major important accomplishment, a very controversial topic. We might say art blossomed, biology bloomed, the general climate, we might say, if we examine for easy reference a popular theory, a major accomplishment of one man, two men, three men. Besides, it has been found, it has been suggested, it has been observed in the preceding, the foregoing analysis, from a biological standpoint, from a biochemical standpoint, recently it has been discovered, the animal cell commonly has, the plant cell commonly has, the structure we are all familiar with. To continue, a cell constitutes complete from a chemical standpoint, in the body, within the muscles, the tissues, many instances are known, many tissues are involved, and a comparison can be made perhaps. The concept. Thus we see, thus you can see, there is also of equal concern during analysis another important characteristic in general in the description.

"Before proceeding, remember that there is now the essential characteristic we learned that it is probably apparent up to this point when we examine the role of another extremely interesting factor. Everyone knows, it is believed; one significant difference should in the process be noted. In another case, before discussing a varied group, another extremely interesting factor up to this point is probably apparent. Remember that.

"It should be stressed, we recall from a previous chapter, historical records indicate in some cases if those that must be remembered as noted earlier are certainly important, so we see, as we just noted, we must hasten to add, overwhelming evidence in the preceding paragraphs, as we have said, it is interesting, we can sense it must be remembered, if those we are already familiar with in the study of a relatively uncomplicated example, so you see we must hasten to add."

Instead of voting, my patient colleagues agree to meet again so as to give me more time to read the book, and to compare it with other textbooks.

During the week after the meeting I notice a reduction in the number of cheery greetings from the other biology teachers. I think, perhaps they resent my request for independence.

At the start of the next meeting Isawaddy says, "We're meeting today to select our textbook. Leo, would you like to say anything before we vote?"

"Thank you," I say. "It is my belief that a textbook should be literature. I have compared *Biology for Everybody* with some of the great books. There are great differences. Consider some of the beginning words from great writers. In Ulysses you can read, 'yes, that's the man; I know where; who says I? Bloom says he; Is it that white-eyed Kaffir? That's where; He's a bloody dark horse himself; mind says I; There you are; Goodby Ireland; so anyhow.'

"As an indication of variety in writing, the *Annotated Mother Goose* by BarinGould states that 'out of an average collection of 200 traditional nursery rhymes, there are '21 cases of death, 14 cases of stealing and general dishonesty, 16 allusions to misery and sorrow, 9 cases of children being lost or abandoned, and 9 allusions to poverty and want.' Clearly there is much variety and emotion in Mother Goose. Information is conveyed also as is shown in the poem, '*Mackeral Sky, Mackeral Sky, Never long wet, and not long dry.*'"

My voice rolls over my slouching colleagues like a lawn roller over mole holes. "Listen to this Grimm tale, 'How dare you come; Alas; The anger of the witch; in his fear; Rapunzel the most beautiful child; It happened a couple of years later.' And *Huckleberry Finn*: 'I read considerable; I didn't know day was so many un um; I says; Ain't dat gay? They don't do nothing; No: is dat so; Of course it is.'

"And Job in the *Old Testament*: 'Now; at the hour; A shiver; A breath; someone stood there.'

"There is much drama in *War and Peace*: 'Anatole used to; then he recalled; I am not such a fool; Pierre was; It is all, all her fault.'

"And kindly Uncle Remus: 'Wiiles I wuz; One time; Who; De Mad man; De Blacksmif; De next year hit pass; Well, den.'

"And that great man of letters Winston Churchill: 'The Japanese have; in this interim period; the resources; But we must steadily aim; Not only then, but in the interval. It was; I must confess; I ended thus.'

"Carl Sandberg wrote: 'John Wilkes Booth; He drank hard; the son; to the hanging of John Brown went.'"

"Gibberish," mutters Pompa to Isawaddy who breaks in on me. "These examples from literature have nothing to do with biology textbooks."

"Sorry," I say lifting my eyes from the pages. "I also have excerpts from biologists including Rachel Carson." Pompa winces. "She wrote, 'Use of poisons; If we are troubled; we can polish our floors; The Department of Agriculture.'

"Sigurd Olson wrote: 'Before me; Gradually the streamers; Within an hour; I skirted the weak ice; Now the shores were bold walls of rock, barren, burned over, and desolate.'

"Aldo Leopold wrote: 'It was a bolt of lightning; Next morning; we mourned the loss of the old tree.'

"There is much beauty and emotion in the writing of these people," I say. "I want beauty and emotion in the books I read."

Isawaddy, using the same slow patient voice he uses with his children, says, "Leo, biology is not supposed to be beautiful or emotional. Biology is a science. We deal objectively with facts."

"So. Is the DNA Litany factual?" I say in a loud steady voice.

"Leo, " He spreads his hands. "I cannot see how a person can teach biology if they don't believe in the litany"

"John, the whole concept, the entire litany, is only fifteen years old. How can you believe so much in something so recent? You are like the early Christians."

"It's much the same. We and they found new knowledge."

"How can you separate your truths from myths?"

"I resent your questions," snaps Isawaddy glaring at me.

I lower my voice. "You question my beliefs, I question yours. Why can't we accept the right of the other person to have his own thoughts? We are not so different." I hear a clock tick. I hold up a book. On the green cover, gold words say, *General Biology and Life*. "I would like to use this text," I say.

Isawaddy takes the proffered book and flips through the pages. "I'm familiar with the book," he said. "It's shallow. Our students deserve greater depth."

"It has a much more extensive treatment of ecology. And look at this beautiful picture of a blue whale."

"Yes, the whale is interesting but the text is deficient in its treatment of DNA."

"It has much information on animals and plants."

"Animals and plants are only a small part of our course. They'll learn about them when they're juniors and seniors."

"But this will be the only biology class for some of them. Let's satisfy their curiosity about the natural world."

"I'm sorry Leo. But you know we don't have time to cover that material. We've talked about that before. Now let's vote."

Of course I lose. The meeting is over. All beginning classes will use *Biology for Everybody*.

Driving home I yell through the rain-smeared windshield, "*Biology For You*, my ass. Academic freedom, bullshit. Screw the Helix. I believe in falling leaves, in diving ouzels, in butterflies."

"I have to use their fucking book," I tell Cleo. "Maybe now they'll start inspecting my notes. So much for academic freedom."

"Those shitheads," Cleo stomps the floor. I move to her, burrow towards her center. She twirls my curls.

After hearing of the adverse decision, Malander invites me downtown for crumpets and tea. The crumpets, a new menu addition for the Schnitzel Haus, are moist and smell nice and yeasty. Joseph says, while applying butter and marmalade, "Your position regarding textbooks is debatable."

My forehead tightens. I don't need this, I think, twirling my tea bag.

The munching Malander continues, "Go with the flow."

"Go with the flow. Bullshit. If those assholes stress the Smerzkapop mechanism that controls the totoproprioomnireceptors in the toe of the three-toed rabbit, then I've got to stress the same damn thing. Do you want life to revolve around, to center on totoproprioomnireceptors in the toes of three toed rabbits?"

"I've always enjoyed the Smerzkapop mechanism myself," says Malander. "The whole thing can be like a mantra."

"Mantra my ass," I say choking on my crumpet. "You wouldn't know a mantra if it smacked you in the teeth."

"Why not think of *Biology for Everybody* as a breakfast cereal?"

"What? To go with your mantra?"

"Yes. You've got the idea. Consider breakfast foods. They must go down easily and not cause allergic reactions. Therefore they must be bland. A textbook is much the same. Cereals contain a balanced array of vitamins, roughage, protein and fat. So do textbooks. After Pompa and Mann are done with the cooking, other experts will dry and break up the parts further before they and various additives are stuck on bleached white paper along with full color illustrations. Despite all this work, there will still be students afflicted with allergic reactions including diarrhea, colic, constipation, flatulence and rolling eyeballs terminating in a comatose condition whereby they will be impervious to a snapping finger."

"So they will die?"

"No. Unfortunately there is a cure. The teacher physician merely must take a hard backed eraser in each hand, walk to the side of the student, separate the erasers as if they were cymbals, and bring them together with a great whack!"

Never knew you were so smart," I say.

"Other tricks can include opening windows and dropping solid oak beams. If you can wake our students you can wake corpses."

"Sometimes there isn't much difference," I admit.

On the way back to the campus I think, Malander invited me out to cheer me up, but I'm not sure. I must oppose my colleagues, but how? Can a decision be reversed? How can I oppose authority? Can I survive as a teacher if I oppose the bosses?

# CHAPTER 29.

# A LITTLE CHAT AND THE EXHALATION PROCLAMATION

A smiling Pompa pops into my office.

"Too bad about having to use our book," he says. "It's just one of those things. Don't take it seriously. Hell, other people have selected most of my texts. Don't worry about it. In fact, I'll tell you what I'll do. I'll buy you a beer out of the profits. How's that?" he laughs.

"Thanks. Thanks a lot," I say as I think you screaming asshole. The drawings of Biology for Everybody look like they were done by a team of spastic monkeys.

Early Monday afternoon there is a knock and four soft raps. I slowly open the door revealing Isawaddy's face in the wedge of light. "Please step into my office," he says. "I'd like to have a little chat with you." I think, Christ, what now. A little chat. Sure just a little chat.

A moment later I am seated across the hall. Isawaddy looks into my eyes. "Leo, I'm disappointed in your performance. I'm not alone. Some of your students have asked me to teach your class."

"Name them," I snap, thinking, damn, this comes of my move towards independence.

"Their names are not important. There are other things, and I'll be the first to admit, some of what I say is hearsay. I am passing this on for your own good. This is not easy. I've heard that you run through the woods laughing with your students."

"Is something wrong with having fun?" I say.

"Did you sit by the river and eat caddis and stone fly larvae?"

"Try them. They're tasty and juicy. Fishermen use them to catch trout."

"You have unscheduled field trips?"

"They were picnics on my own time."

"Some of the students felt they were required."

"That's their problem."

"After finding lilies poking through the snow, you ate them."

"They were crunchy."

"You whistled at marmots."

"They whistled back."

"One day you had a jug of wine."

"I didn't bring it. I was doing the students a favor by carrying it. They were tired."

"I think you are corrupting your students."

"Heck, I'm a babe in the woods. I doubt if I could corrupt anyone. I wouldn't mind trying it with a few of the coeds, but I'm too old and unattractive for serious debauchery."

"Please be more serious. Don't you care about your career?"

"Sure I care. I just like a little levity."

"Apparently you've told students that memorizing facts is a waste of time. Students have memorized knowledge for thousands of years. Who are you to disagree? Would you replace facts with intuition? If students followed your advice, who would do the research, the studies that help people stay alive?"

"John, research doesn't require memorization. Science needs value systems. Nazi scientists performed any research the state required.

Tobacco companies pay for research that says smoking is healthy. Research is not sacred."

"Today in the United States scientists are highly ethical and research is objective. We would not knowingly hurt people. Research animals feel little pain. Your kind of ethics would cripple science."

My eyes open wide, trying to recover lost ground, my voice level, I say, "Let's return to the picnic. I'm sorry I wasn't serious about your remarks. The students planned the whole thing. It was their idea. We danced across the meadow because we were happy. We ate insect larvae so we could better understand trout. The students had some wine along. I advised against it. Several were over twentyone. Some of the girls asked about Swirlopeds so I went into the woods with them. They helped me herd Swirlopeds into nets. One girl was angry because she couldn't go along. I couldn't take everyone. As it was I had a mob. I was worried the Swirlopeds would spin away. Maybe you heard about the noise. We banged on some old pots. It was getting dark. We sang songs so nobody would become frightened."

"I have some tape recordings of your lectures in which you howled like a monkey? Should I play the tape?"

"Why not. I have a good voice. I won't deny it. Of course I howled like a monkey. Howler monkeys maintain territories by roaring. They don't bite or scratch and they have no Vietnams. If we want peace in the world, it is imperative that we learn to howl like howlers."

"Do you teach that monkeys are more advanced than people?"

"Sometimes they are."

"On another field trip you snapped up mouthfuls of mustard flowers."

"Try some. They are sweeter than avalanche lilies."

"Are you a cow?"

"I only munch. I don't moo."

"Professors should maintain their dignity."

"We also cooked and ate nettles. Was that criminal?"

"There is a more serious charge. Your DNA Litany is only one hour long."

"So I've shortened the litany."

"You've created a litany of your own."

"I've added a unit on ecology."

"Do you follow the course outline?"

"Certainly, with a few minor changes. Some parts are expanded. I've shrunk others. The whole thing fits together nicely."

"Did you add eagles? Did you really have the entire class get up on chairs and perch for an hour? After that, let me tell you, they had their doubts about you."

I thought, if I were an eagle I'd shit on your head.

"You laughed like a loon."

I think, ha, ha, ha, ha, ha.

"You've taught your students to communicate with crows."

I think, If I was a vulture I'd peck out your eyes.

"You have missed some classes."

"One morning ice covered the road. I couldn't make it up the hill. Snow was falling. I don't own chains or snow tires. Another morning my car wouldn't start."

"It's your responsibility to get to the college no matter how bad the weather. We are here because of the students."

"John, when I finally got to the campus, the place was deserted. The students didn't get to class either."

"You're not a student. We expect more from our teachers."

"John, why don't you admit that your real complaint is the Satisfaction Report? My committee came down hard on merit pay, and you spent a lot of time on that proposal."

"I've forgotten all about that."

"Or is it because I don't want to use *Biology for Everybody*?"

"That has nothing to do with our discussion. The quality of your teaching has been deteriorating for a long, long time." He said long, long time as if he were a tolling bell.

"I disagree! My teaching has changed for the better. I've put some of myself into the course. I bet that's what you object to. You want me to keep in step."

"Don't be foolish. We're not the army."

"Your real objection is, I'm bringing life to biology."

"That's not the problem. Let's get down to specifics. Instead of emphasizing cell division, you protest people multiplication."

"Do you know that Raymond Dasmann has a ten year old daughter?"

"What about it?"

"Well, during her lifetime, six million new people have settled in California. Doesn't that frighten you?"

"Why should it? That's California. We live in Cascadia."

"In the middle of the 18th century there were 750 acres of land per person in California. Now there are only 5 acres."

"So California's shrinking," Isawaddy laughs. "What about the milk? Why did you tell students that milk was bad for them?"

"In parts of Brazil people become blinded by powdered milk. They lack the right enzymes and use up their vitamin A. This milk poisoning is an example of what can happen when we interfere with natural systems. Milk isn't always good for you."

"We've got a dairy farmer on our board of directors. Why don't you tell that to him?"

"He probably knows about it already."

"You spent three days talking about endangered species."

"The lowland gorilla is one of our closest relatives. Each year the population gets smaller. It would be terrible if they became extinct."

"You act like you're a close relative."

"They're part of our heritage. What have you got against our relatives?"

"I'll ignore that. You're probably an atheist too. We can't talk about that. Let's go on. What do blue whales have to do with basic biology?"

"What good is basic biology if blue whales become extinct? Oh, in regard to religion, I'm a Unitarian."

"Whether you're a Unitarian, Baptist, or Catholic your job is not to save everything that swims, flies, or crawls."

"While the living world dies we spend weeks studying the movement of atoms. That should be the job of a physicist. We spend three weeks learning about macromolecules. That should be the job of the biochemist. We give two weeks to the behavior of cells and only two days to the behavior of animals. Two weeks on the behavior of chromosomes and one day on animal societies. One week on the contents of an atom, and one week on communities, ecosystems and the biosphere. The origin of life, which is theoretical, probably took an instant. Astronomers should teach it. It gets as much attention as the evolution of life that has lasted billions of years. We focus on one event, the minute, the ultramicroscopic, and give short shrift to that that can be seen with our own eyes."

"Leo, to understand the ecosystem you have to understand biochemistry. If a species is threatened by disease, you have to understand the disease. Besides there's television. Every week our students see someone like Jane Goodall with primates or Niko Tinbergen with ducks. They can learn all about those things on TV. Molecular biology is different. Because it's more complicated, it can't be learned from television."

"John, I'm not talking of eliminating the molecules. I just want a balance."

"Some balance. You're turning your students into tree huggers."

"Sure. And we smell fir and spruce needles, and touch the earth and taste river water. Last week I asked my students, what do you remember about your childhood environment? They recalled grass, trees and the smell of rain, and berry picking with their parents."

"That's in their past."

"Well I want to give them another chance."

"You're hopeless. It's like I've got a teacher in my department from the nineteenth century. After taking your course the students will be unprepared to take advanced courses."

"They'll be better able to run the government."

"You're not telling me anything new. We've known about evolution for a hundred years, but we don't have to beat the kids to death with it."

"And we've known about molecular biology since the 1820's when Wohler synthesized urea. So should we concentrate on piss? Each plant or animal is something special. It is wrong to think of them as bubbling chemical retorts. A biologist is not a stirrer."

"Biology is a science. For a science to be respectable we have to be able to predict."

"You're right. I predict the extinction of hundreds of species."

"The beauty of biochemistry is its predictability."

"And the beauty of biology are changing patterns. The Life Sciences have a noble history. Each chemical reaction has a limited lineage. Sulfur burning today is the exact same thing as sulfur burning a million years ago. But the horse of today, is not the horse of a million years ago. Horses change and life changes. The biology of the horse is more than the chemistry of its hooves, and whether or not they can be used to make glue. The chemicals serve the horse, they give it form, but a horse is much more than a vat of chemicals. A horse eats grass and makes shit, so what. Should we replace the noble history of the horse, with a focus on molecules? Our students have to memorize chemical reactions, which are so new that each text presents the information with different terms and molecular names. Why can't we go slow with biochemistry or give it a course of its own? Why is it necessary to short change the known in a rush to replace it with the unknown? We are forcing our students to gallop, with blinders on, straight at the frontier of knowledge."

"You're very eloquent Leo. Unfortunately, you're on the planet at the wrong time. Fifty years ago you would have fitted in perfectly."

"I am not alone. George Gaylord Simpson has similar opinions. He thinks molecular biology may be a fad."

"Of course he does. He's an evolutionary biologist."

"John, do you deny his contributions?"

"No. They were right for his time. The new has to clean house. There is not enough time to cover everything. Time is limited. There is not enough of it. There is only so much time, and I have no more. I've got to go. I've got another meeting. Excuse me."

"I came here because of animals and plants, not because of molecules. People can study molecules in the city. Here we have wilderness. Why must the molecules intrude?"

"You knew about our emphasis on molecules when you came."

"John, I was hired because of my knowledge of natural history. Let me teach it?"

"Perhaps, if you go along with us, we'll go along with you. We may add a natural history course in the future. But as for now, you're the new man. Teach our way or get out. It's that simple. I'll give you some advice. Stop worrying so much about the survival of the big cats and whales and start worrying about the survival of Leo Bauer. If you don't adapt, you'll become extinct. That's part of evolution, and you believe in evolution, don't you? Well adapt or disappear. Travel our road, or leave. I've got to go."

"So I must go with biochemistry. Ring a bell and the dogs salivate."

"Look, it's up to you. Conform or leave."

"It isn't easy to leave. I love the land, water, and mountains."

"Then get back on track."


My gorge overflowing, I slam the door and return to my office for my jacket. Instead of going home I walk to the woods, and go to my favorite stump. While seated I write the Exhalation Proclamation. I decide to take my case to a higher authority, my fellow teachers. When the proclamation is completed, I return to the campus and get some stainless steel probes from the laboratory. Walking with them and a rock hammer I go to the DNA Totem and roughly hold the proclamation against the metal pole. Fingers contracted on the handle of the hammer, I hammer away. The nails flatten. Fortunately I find a wooden 2X4 enclosing an entryway. While fastening the document to the wood with firm blows, the vibrations hurt my fingers. It is as if the molecule is fighting back. After the parchment is attached, I walk away, leaving the words to be read by students, administrators, townspeople, teachers and crows.

## THE EXHALATION PROCLAMATION

I, Leo Bauer, a biology teacher at Humaluh Valley College, have been in a state of robotry. My freedom of choice has been stolen and my creative energy sucked away.

Yet I believe, when a man believes himself utterly lost, light breaks. Forgive me my fellow teachers that I the scum of the earth should dare to solicit your support. May you look upon this speck of dust and hear my plea. I can be silent no longer. A college cannot get strength out of the blood and hides of sheep.

From this day on, in accordance with the Magna Carta of Socrates where emblazoned on a green backing are the scarlet words ACADEMIC FREEDOM, I Leo Bauer do hereby declare that henceforth I shall teach according to the dictates of my professional conscience. Be it so ordered that this freedom shall be recognized and maintained by the guardians of academic freedom, including teacher's associations, unions, and The Crunch and Munch Society.

In recognition of liberty, I hereby charge the biology department with depriving me of academic freedom. A statement of my charges will be immediately delivered to the president of the Humaluh Valley College Teacher's Association.

Upon this action, sincerely believed to be an act for justice, under the banner of academic freedom, guaranteed in the Cascadia Professional Rights and Responsibilities Act, I invoke the considerate judgment of good people everywhere and consecrate my life to the memory and ideals of Henry David Thoreau, Socrates, John Dewey, A. S. Neill, John Holt, and George B. Leonard.

In witness whereof; I have hereunto set my name and affixed the seal of Socrates.

Done at Humaluh Valley College in the Winter by a teacher.

Leo Bauer

Next I write a short note to President Davis:

Most respected Elmore. In regard to my proclamation I offer myself and all that I am. Call, recall, approve, reprove, as may seem good to you. I will acknowledge your voice.

Leo Bauer

Upon reading the proclamation Isawaddy writes a note to the president saying, "Bauer must be drunk. He will feel different in the morning when he sobers up."

Paul Dallapicola, the president of the Humaluh Valley College Teacher's Association telephoned Davis and said, "Bauer is a brilliant chap. The whole row is due to the envy of his colleagues." Dallapicola called an immediate meeting of his executive committee. They gave the job of investigating my charges to the Satisfaction Committee. The special investigators included Barnaby Thomas of the art department who was to serve as chairman; Thomas Thaumaste, speech; Thomas Seabeck, electronics; Bev Frazier, chemistry; Tom Mun, economics.

This was the first major investigation ever undertaken by the association. Therefore they hoped to invest a great amount of time talking to me and interviewing my past and present students. Meanwhile, having read the proclamation, many of my fellow teachers patted me on the back and said, "You sure have guts. Keep it up. Don't let em push you around."

Because of this strong support I was optimistic. I was distressed however by the coldness shown by Isawaddy, Mann, Jackson and Pompa.

The day after the proclamation I give an inspired lecture. I say, "Oh my students, look at the natural world. If a flower bores you, look longer. If you see nothing worth looking at in the leaves, in the water, look closer, look longer. If while driving you see little of interest in the countryside, drive slower, open your windows, park. Walk away from the road. Look at the land. Listen to nature's messages. Sing this chant:

Look at the life around you. Look up, down, out, around.
Feel the life around you. Feel up, down, out, around.
Smell the life around you. Smell up, down, out, around.
Taste the life around you. Taste up, down, out, around.

"Oh my students. Think back to Thoreau. 'Thus we behave like oxen in a flower garden. The true fruit of nature can only be plucked with a delicate hand.'

"Let us mourn man's flight. Thoreau said, 'Thank God, men cannot as yet fly, and lay waste the sky as well as the earth.'" After my lecture I lead my students outside where we walk quietly through the forest looking, listening, smelling, feeling and tasting.

That afternoon in the laboratory I talk about eagles. We, the class, perch on chairs imagining we are eagles. Our arms become wings, toes became talons, noses beaks and hair feathers. The room is full of silent eagles. This was at the time of the Wyoming massacre when hundreds of eagles met death by gun and poison at the hands of killers paid by the raisers of gently baaing sheep.

I tell a little story:

Baa baa black sheep, have you any wool?
Yes sir, yes sir, three bags full.

One for my master, and one for my dame
And one for the little boy who lives down the lane.

I play the role of an independent investigator and ask, "Why were the eagles slaughtered?"

They reply, "We need the money from the wool."

I ask the dame, do you approve of the slaughter of eagles.

She replies, "I'm not sure if the eagles kill many sheep, or if they should live or die."

"The little boy says, "Don't kill the eagles. Let them fly. Let them fly."

And the master says, "Let them die, let them die."

During the same period of time a group of eagles sits on the banks of the Humaluh digesting salmon while observing the rapids.

Late Friday afternoon I ask Magnum, "Do you think I did the right thing? Was I wrong?"

Twisting his mustache, lips quivering with indignation, Magnum answers, "Of course you did the right thing. I was wondering when you were going to assert yourself."

# CHAPTER 30.

# UNSIGNED NOTES

An unsigned note appeared in each faculty box:

QUESTIONS NEEDING ANSWERS ABOUT TEXTBOOKS

Fellow teachers, consider your personal ethics as instructors. Answer the following questions:

1. If someone forced you to use a particular textbook, would that be an intrusion into your classroom freedom?

2. If you wrote a textbook, would you require fellow teachers to use your book?

The day after the first note a second note appeared:

Leo Bauer would be a better teacher with more freedom. The teacher's right to choose a text should be a God given right. How can a teacher's class be in harmony if he has to use a textbook he despises?

When a committee chooses textbooks, the vine of knowledge gets wrapped tightly about itself like a strangler fig; new growth is prevented from reaching the light of day.

Another note read:

Bauer is like a long distance runner dashing down a track littered with debris. No one can run fast if they have to jump up and down, over and under, this way and that, hither and yon, into and out of lots of crap.

A supporter of Leo Bauer

A fourth message read:

I've got a new course to teach this quarter and they didn't give me any preparation time.

Each time I turn around the amount of known knowledge doubles, so I've got to learn more.

If I ain't got enough time to prepare my students will sleep in class because my enthusiasm will depart. I've got to have time to dig in the clam beds of knowledge.

A fifth note said:

Our thoughts need a sounding board. These notes are it. Finally we have a faculty newspaper. There are no Humaluh men of power soliciting the opinion of the common faculty. Many of us seek more than money from teaching. We are part of a large organism. Feedback should travel from teacher to teacher, from teacher to administrator, from teacher to student, and back again. I am grateful to Leo Bauer for getting the ball rolling.

Hopeful Supporter

A sixth note said:

Bauer needs the entire support of the faculty. He shouldn't have to consult with the other people in his department every time he takes a step. His battle belongs to all of us. Ponder this question my friends. Bauer is not alone, is he?

Six copies of the note ending with, Bauer is not alone, were placed in my box marked with a big red YES! Another note addressed to me said:

DO YOU HAVE TO PUT THESE DIATRIBES IN OUR BOXES? IF YOU'RE SUCH A HOT SHOT ENVIRONMENTALIST WHY DO YOU WASTE SO MUCH PAPER?

# CHAPTER 31.

## THE INVESTIGATION

The investigation took four weeks. The verdict is announced in a letter sent to me with copies given to Chairman Isawaddy, Dean Mann and President Davis. The letter states:

### THE BAUER INVESTIGATION

In reference to the charge by Leo Bauer that his academic freedom has been lost, it is the considered opinion of this committee that his charge is correct.

The right to select textbooks is a basic right of every teacher. The right to have autonomy is also a basic right. May truth reign eternal.

To like yourself you need freedom. If you have to ask to go to the bathroom, how can you like yourself?

We interviewed many students. Some of their comments follow:

Someone just walking in would think he was off his rails. That's what made the class interesting, his wild enthusiasm.

Who else on campus would howl like a howler monkey?

He is conscientious.

He is mad.

He knows his subject well.

Sometimes he is late.

He is often early.

He listens to me.

He could be more organized.

His hair is too long.

He gets carried away at times.

Sometimes he is depressed.

He is often joyful.

I saw him picking his nose.

He squeezes pimples.

His pants need pressing.

His tests are too hard.

His tests are Mickey Mouse.

His lectures stimulate me.

He teaches what is important.

He has given much outside time to me.

He showed me how to roll over rocks and roll them back again.

He cares about me.

I don't like the man.

A poor teacher.

Class was always interesting.

He encourages students to talk.

His personal knowledge contributed more than any text could.

He has done a good all around job.

Good sense of humor.

Always tries to answer questions.

He is very knowledgeable.

He is a Dum Dum.

He dislikes the DNA Litany.

He is a real person.

Too much bullshit. He should stick to the text.
Sometimes he is silent.

The majority of the students we interviewed thought Bauer a competent instructor. Some may claim that these young people are unsophisticated simpleminded gullible kids. This committee disagrees. Often we do not give young people credit for their wisdom and honesty. Overall the students liked his class, thought he was adequately prepared, and said he was fair.

From our interviews we could find few who thought him incompetent. Several however thought he was mad. However, our research discovered no contradiction between madness and competency. We read many biographies and discovered that many great men and women were mad. Madness seemed to give them a view of the world unseen and unavailable to most people.

In conclusion, we recommend that Leo Bauer should have the freedom to choose his own textbooks and should have autonomy in his classroom.

Barnaby Thomas, Chairman
Thomas Thaumaste
Tom Seabeck
Bev Frazier
Tom Mun

The fly network reported back to me. That evening Elmore Davis read the report while eating crackers in bed. He said, "Florence, This report is lacking in scholarship. A rush job. No good. No good at all. Florence frowned. The cracker crumbs were keeping her from sleeping.

John Isawaddv, normally a peaceful man, read the report in the mail room. Leaving work early he drove home, kicked his dog, threw tea on his wife, yelled at his children, and went to bed with a headache.

I read the report sitting on a concrete bench. I drive home singing silly woozily songs.

Walking into our house, I cartwheel into and send Cleo sprawling. She frowns big time. She relents after I pick her up, embrace and kiss her. Cleo says, "Whoopie. Let's get drunk and celebrate."

Karl laughs. Cleo gives him a glass of Coca Cola with a Maraschino cherry.

I am happy all week. My classes are cheerful places. I walk with a spring in my step. People must see the sparkle in my eyes. Each afternoon, when arriving home, I pet Fang and kiss Cleo. We had started going to a marriage counselor because of the stress at work. However, because of the stress of work I have not gone to the marriage counselor for weeks. I play with Karl for the first time in a long time. He is six years old and needs his daddy more. We build Lego castles and I tickle his belly. While laughing he shrilly yells, "No Daddy, No, No, No."

Some additional documentation had been included with the report. A special concern of the committee had been, what was the effect of a man like me on impressionable young college students?

My uniqueness was demonstrated by notes taken during one of my lectures by a student, who admitted doing a bit of daydreaming. In the boy's mind I became an ancient Chinese teacher. As far as the committee knew, I had never visited China. However the possibility existed that perhaps I had been Chinese in a previous life. The student's notes follow:

Professor Bauer stands at the blackboard talking to the chalk lines. His drawings cover the board. Over them are written words, forming a palimpsest. From isolated words images form in my mind. Oriental music intrudes from the next classroom. Inexplicably I am suddenly in China in the Shin Dynasty, at a time when Chan Chan Chin is studying the tragedy of thousands dying from typhoid. Chinese symbols glow red against the black depths of my mind. They include sketches of houses, rapid impressionistic sketches written from top to bottom in columns. The sloping ceiling of the lecture hall darkens.

We are inside a Chinese hut lit by oil lamps. Moxa smoke travels towards heaven from a burning ember in the master's hand. I am a disciple studying yin yang and the ancient five elements of wood, fire, earth, metal, and water. My teacher's hair is thirty-two feet long and pure white. An herbal doctor, he only charges patients who stay well. "A dead man has no bills." His voice drifts through ancient passageways deep in the Peking Palace. His words are measured as carefully as remedies. "Too much salt make too tight kidney. Waste product too difficult to go down. Sweat and urine very similar. Animal food make more waste product." He pronounces animal aneeemal and says "animal protein take more kidenee, more diffeecult to cure." His ears seem to be listening to small far off sounds. He says, more salt, heart beat more strongly, blood pressure go up.

In the next room a freaky organ plays bouncing up and down the scale as if a Schweitzer or J. Power Biggs is at the keyboard. Drums bang. Cymbals clash. Bauer erases the blackboard. Waves of chalk remain on the green sea. His forehead is smooth. An old man, he is ageless. Bones show beneath pliable skin. Arteries spread over the back of his hand like a river delta. He asks, "What is the symptom of the beginning of a yang disease?" Answering his own question he says, "Strong pulse, high fever."

"He bends over and searches in his cloth bag. Manuscripts are unrolled. He reads, "Yang illness also have body, feet, cold, head with pain from fever. The higher fevers are yang. The cold yin phase can end in death."

He continues with a paradox. "Sometime very hot, hard work, sweat, yin. No sweat, yang." He pronounces sweat sweet. He gives me important advice. "To bring down fever take cinnamon tea, peony root, ginger, and liquorish. This also make more urination. If no sweat give Mao or Kuzu root tea. Thirty minutes after tea take one cup of soft rice. Keep warm, lie down, rest."

Following Bauer's advice, I rested. After that class I had much more respect for my professor, because he gave me insight into another culture.

# CHAPTER 32.

## A PRESIDENTIAL SUMMONS

I am relaxing after being vindicated. Spring is turning into a pleasant time of year. Cleo, Karl and I spend a Saturday playing on the beach near the Devil's Gateway. It seems like a long time since we have had a relaxed day together. Cleo naps, her head on my chest. We talk about having another child. Karl needs a sibling.

Cleo says, "He spends too much time alone."

I say, "you are right. He is always daydreaming."

Cleo says, "Let's give him a playmate."

I say, "Let's go for it."

While Karl naps, she and I go under the covers. Listen to the waves and currents. Consummation is easy. Just takes a day at the beach.

Within a few weeks she has much morning sickness. She gives up her daily running. Takes it easy. I start doing more chores such as cooking meals and washing clothes. I stop having long sessions with the Crunch and Munch Society.

One morning, not many days into the quarter, a note from Davis is in my mail slot. I wonder, Perhaps the president wishes to congratulate me. As I enter the president's office I see Dean Mann at the right hand of the president and Isawaddy on his left. I take a seat next to the president's secretary. On the seat next to Theresa McGowen is a tape recorder. A notepad is on her lap.

I think, oh shit, I'm in for it. My breathing quickens as if I had been climbing a hill. The president speaks. "Leo, you have been accused of incompetency. The other members of your department don't want me to renew your contract."

I think, "those bastards want blood." I stammer speak, "There has been an investigation. The Satisfaction Committee investigated the charges I made against the Department. I won. The committee agreed with me."

Oh, the president on this day is as smooth as an ocean liner sailing to Hawaii. "The investigation by the faculty committee was shallow. I have decided to ask three other people to investigate the new charges brought by the department against you."

I think, "Dammed if they don't look like serious old buzzards. The meeting adjourns. I go to my office to think and write:

How would anyone feel if they were in my shoes? This morning I woke happy. Hundreds of thoughts happily tumbled through my head, eager to be put down on paper. Soon we will have a second child. Cleo will be happy taking care of the baby. She is great with baby talk and has been reading women's magazines like crazy. Oh, I was going to teach such a great course this quarter. Then I read that simple short note. I went to the meeting, unsure, but not pessimistic, because I had won.

Then however Davis said, "Leo, the department wants to fire you. They told me, "You are incompetent."

I didn't have the guts to say, what about you guys. When's the last day any of you has done a real day's work?

How would anyone reply? Let's imagine me, dressed up in a fancy suit, walking down the street and stopping someone, maybe you. Without wasting time on hellos, I say, "we've decided to fire you. You're incompetent."

You protest and say, "I'm not incompetent. You are." "Consider what you are saying Mr. Man in the Street. Do you really think you can effectively confront accusers bearing superior credentials? Two of my accusers, as an example, own PhD degrees. Each of them is stamped competent on a parchment hanging on the walls of their offices, like beef stamped prime in blue. Each of them, or at least Mann and Davis, has taken high-grade shit for at least eight years. They have polished and licked boots. Superlative students, each of them graduated Magma cum kiss ass. I admit. I was bodacious; I was audacious when I told them I knew how to teach. Why who was I? I was a mere particle of grit in the academic treadmill. But I didn't know that. I didn't understand that they were the masters. I should have shut up and followed orders. But being myself, I had to speak out, and now, of course, they are dedicated to getting rid of me. So I ask you. How do you like the morality play?" You say, in reply, "don't teachers have power? You've got a faculty organization. You have a Satisfaction Committee."

I say, "well woo hoo for that. I guess I don't have to worry any more. Woo hoo. You are right; I have lots of power. Yet how can I fight a president who says, that the investigation was shallow? Davis said, 'I have appointed an administrator, a teacher and an unbiased citizen.' Damn will we ever have fairness. Ha. The president does the appointing and he says the committee will be unbiased. Will this shit never end?" Closing my journal I walk away without waiting for an answer.

Arriving home I walk to the liquor cabinet and pour a whiskey glass to the top. Cleo watches. Her smile departs. Hesitantly she asks, "What happened?"

"Again they want to fire me." My voice is flat.

Pouring herself a shot she joins me. I am quickly getting drunk. Her obstetrician advised her to have two daily drinks of alcohol during her pregnancy. She follows the doctor's orders. The phone rings. We ignore it. I say, "Honey, it's just more bad news. Let it ring. Let it ring."

Cleo says, "Ding, ding, ding." In bed, we hug as we float off to sleep.

The next morning I robotically dress and drive to the college. Arriving late, I meet with my class. It is the first meeting of the quarter. Without a smile I say, "Welcome. I hope you enjoy biology this quarter." A robot outlines the assignments and tells them about the course. Forcing himself, the robot answers possible questions about grading and dismisses them. In going out the door the robot overhears one of the new students, say, "My God, what an up tight teacher. I'm dropping this course."

The previous afternoon, unknown to me, the Satisfaction Committee has become incensed when they hear what President Davis has said about their investigation. They stalked into the president's office. After my first class I hear about it from Barnaby Thomas.

Thomas says, "Davis, mighty man, pushed himself backwards in his swivel chair. The chromium armrests reflected the late afternoon sunlight.

"As chairman I said, 'Our study has been very exhaustive. We have talked with past, and present students. No one can be more thorough. With few exceptions the students thought Bauer extremely competent plus being a hard worker."

"Gabberheist" spluttered Davis. (Don't look for this word in your dictionary).

"Thomas Thaumaste conceded, 'Some of them said Bauer is eccentric, but that made the class more interesting. He certainly wasn't boring.'

"Bev Frazier said, 'Our committee checked Bauer's class outline and compared it with the outline used by his colleagues. We determined that he covered the same material with the addition of a unit of ecology.'

"Tom Seabeck said, 'Bauer asks essay questions. He uses just a few multiple choice questions, he calls them multiple guess, and he never uses true or false questions that are apparently used by the other members of the biology department.'

"To prove the dimension of their scholarship the committee placed eighteen inches of papers on the president's desk.

"After carefully measuring the stack Davis said, 'Yes, I can see you have done a scholarly thorough investigation. Therefore I will not have a second investigation.

"'I have decided to allow Bauer the right to choose his own textbooks.'

"Our committee members feeling vindicated hugged one another. We even threw our arms around the president.

"You could see Davis was proud of his decisive act, which has ended the matter once and for all. To conclude the affair the president has scheduled another meeting."

Driving home my red cabbage mind tumbles memories of the past week. The committee said I had no academic freedom. They said I should be allowed to select my own textbooks. They told the bastards to get off my back. After weeks of hell, and cold stares, the whole thing is over. I am vindicated. I am supported.

Back home, my depression over, I say to Cleo, "I've won. I can get back to teaching. We can relax. Let's go out to dinner and celebrate."

The next morning, alone in the mailroom, I read a note from the president. Oh great. Another damn note. What can this one be about? I am still foggy from the drinks of the night before and from the confusion of the events of the last few days. There is a 2 pm meeting.

In the meeting my brain quickly clears when I hear the president say, "Leo, from now on you can choose your own textbooks."

Davis says, to Isawaddy, "I want you people to find common ground and work together?"

"I'll try," says Isawaddy in a low voice.

"I'll work on it," I say.

Agreement being reached the meeting is over.

The next day I go back to my teaching. Because of the earlier trouble winter quarter had been out of whack. My organization of lecture notes, a perennial problem anyway, was more disorganized than usual. While the investigation was in progress it had been impossible for me to concentrate.

With the attempt to fire me, of course, everything has gone to hell. So much of my time has gone to planning my defense. I have not given Cleo the support she needs during her pregnancy. I have not spent time with Karl. Will I be able to spend any time with the baby? Can I give Cleo some breaks in the heavy responsibility of motherhood?

Seeking to eliminate tension and produce harmony I send a note to Isawaddy:

John. I want to teach in a way I was rarely taught. I want to challenge my students by stimulating their curiosity. I hope to introduce them to the world of books and ideas. I don't want to perpetuate a system that has turned off so many students that thousands are rioting in California. I have no dislike for any of you. You all have pleasant personalities and are highly qualified.

I however have felt boxed in. Recently I broke out of the mold. In order to split away however, much of my energy has gone into offensive action. I now want to stop being offensive. I want to improve myself. I'm going to change my course by replacing lectures with discussions. I want my students to ask their own questions and seek solutions in their own way.

I also plan to use overhead projectors, tape recorders, slide projectors, movie projectors, television and single lens reflex cameras. The president told me to teach the way I want to teach. I am glad that you now agree with our president.

I hope we can establish better avenues of communication and support one another before the students. When we downgrade one another before them, we all suffer. In the Salem witch-hunt and in the French revolution only a few were accused at first. Later the blood freely flowed.

If we establish decent ground rules, many of our differences will disappear like paper tigers.

Your Colleague, Leo Bauer

My appeal was returned with a small paper note stapled to the corner initialed by each department member. The chairman wrote, "Leo, there are some valid suggestions in your memo. Yes, in life and in work, each of us must be able to work with his fellow man. However too much non-conformity is counter-productive.

"Submit your choice of a textbook. I will consider it."

John Isawaddy

# CHAPTER 33.

## NEW LIFE

A few weeks into the summer of 1969 I drop Karl off to camp with his friends. Summer should be a good time for Cleo's pregnancy. I must stay close to home.

She has lots of morning sickness. She craves ice cream and milk shakes. It's supposed to be over after three months. I feel useless at home. I don't know how long I can handle her moodiness. Often I hear her throwing up in the bathroom. I should go to her, hold her. When she is nauseated she wants privacy. I cook the meals. She is often not hungry. I fail at tempting her to eat. Finally I open some cans of stew or something and leave it at that. Yesterday when I gave her some broccoli she yelled, "You should have known that broccoli makes me sick." A couple of nights ago she craved Chinese takeout. I went to get some but the restaurant was closed. Not much nutrition for an expectant mother. She stopped at the co-op for salad. When they weighed her plate it weighed over two pounds. The mound damn near reached the ceiling. She has replaced running with walking. The doctor advised walking and less exercise. She said, "What in the hell does that damned doctor know?" One day, when out walking she stopped and took a nap in a neighbor's yard. Damn that was a weird thing to do. She goes to sleep early, by 7.30. Karl runs around looking for things to do. I feel like such a jerk sometimes. Actually I feel helpless. Pregnancy is the territory of women. We men normally are like wolves padding around the periphery.

My study is turning into a nursery. She has a strong nesting instinct. Has painted the baby's dresser yellow. There are stick-ups all over of elephants, lions, tigers and bears.

While bicycling I see yellow waves on a green sea, buttercups, corn sprouts, peas flower. Wisteria, in feminine grace blooms pale this cloudy day, some azaleas are red, some are pink.

My God, a Saint Bernard is upon me. My heart stops. Am I to be devoured at the side of this busy highway, to be dog food or a sandwich; my legs to be the meat, the spokes and fenders toothpicks? Each red reflector will migrate to a new position, one on each side of his muzzle. From now on the dog will have glaring red eyes.

The next day: From the top of Gazebo Mountain I see a wide red tractor birth a dark brown line as it moves through the spring dried soil. Drying gives this land dark rich patterns, slowly changing as one rainless day merges with another. A heavy spring rain would wipe the slate clean; the zephyrs could again sketch changing images.

From my lookout the cows are white and black rocks are scattered on green felt. When yellow is in straight rows it says daffodils. When evenly distributed, like corn flour shaken from the cook's hands, the yellow yells, we are *Agoseris*. We are prolific, successful, and beautiful, we are not like those insipid daffodils; delicate items of commerce, too delicate to live alone for long, phony and greasy, their fulfillment is to meet the scissors.

Now in the upland woods yellow, I can see the star flash white of hawthorns and the shiny dark green of Douglas fir. Closer to the forest floor grow prickly Oregon grape and saw edged Salal.

Off now to the dike, wind whipped whitecaps are roiling the shallow shores creating a brown strip between the green marsh and the blue salt water. When the wind commands, white waves appear. Cloud shadow arbitrarily blocks out entire farms in darkness, ye, verily so shall ye be chastised for slicing up the land. The punishment is short lived and the farms are once again sunny. Dust streams and billows from big blocky road building dump trucks. The trucks are yellow like dandelions and daffodils.

I walk along the beach to where Karl is camping. The boys are sheltered on a sand bar against the bank, nestled amongst flood-tested willows silver this windy day. Their roof is a tarpaulin tied by the side to a willow and staked to the bank above.

Karl proudly tells me, "We used roots to tie with. See how strong they are."

I bend a root over my knee. "You're right. They're strong. Did you get wet?"

"Oh, a little."

During fall quarter, Cleo and I focus on the pregnancy. I confess I have zero interest in shopping for baby things. She is drawn to friends who have recently had babies. They are at our house in droves. They drive me crazy. They bring stacks of baby blankets. She had saved two baby blankets from Karl's baby hood, some embossed baby silverware and a knitted baby jacket. She has had a baby shower. She goes to baby showers. Everything has to do with babies. My study is transforming from a place where I can write lectures to a nursery. There is a crib. Above the crib a multi-colored mobile rotates. My work area is gone. I can no longer concentrate. There is a baby swing, an infant carrier, a folded up crib. I am inundated with baby stuff. I have never been good at arranging celebrations, yet much of Christmas is up to me including the cooking of the turkey, the mashing of potatoes and mixing of stuffing. I like lots of herbs so that's what I use, plus onions, and dried bread.

Her abdomen sticks way out. She waddles like a duck. She says, "I'm scared."

Hugging her I say, "You'll do fine. Just a few more weeks."

It is wintertime and Cleo's time. It is January 10th, 1970. I am excited. Between pains she feels good. The contractions have started. Now they are ten minutes apart. I drive her to the hospital, just a few blocks from our house. Hold her hand during admittance. She is nervous and excited. They bring a wheelchair for her. Her forehead is wet, shiny. Her face shows pain. I hold her hand. She squeezes my hand. They take her away. She doesn't look back. I am not allowed in the room.

Slipping out for some air, I walk to the river and observe wind blown white caps. The current must frustrate these river waves. It is a stand off. The current moves to the sea. The white caps emerge yet stay in place, or move forward just a yard or two before settling to ripple to wave to ripple. Now our unborn child is fighting a current. In a short time the passage through the birth canal and the struggle to the surface.

I have been those whitecaps trying to emerge from the river of life, ebullient, sucking in oxygen. All too often the current has captured and carried my angry protesting self towards a maelstrom. Now Cleo is in a current, fighting to enable our child to emerge.

How strange to watch the current patterns change. A few bits of leaves and twigs move downstream in seeming contradiction to the waves moving upstream in the counter current. We all pass through the breakers. Soon another will join us.

Over my head highways of curdled milk point north. A white rod emerges from the dark gray mass and forms a route within the solid southern sky. To the west there is blue and some snowball clouds are piled along the horizon. The killdeer cries, take cover, take cover, run, hide. The crowd of horsetails cowers. Green, they sound like dry grass in the wind. Their segmented vertebrae are rooted in the sand of castles. A train calls. The wind dies. Life is good on the riverbank.

Upon returning to the hospital, I ask a nurse, "How's she doing?"

"She's in a lot of pain."

"Can't they give her a spinal?"

"I'll ask the doctor."

I beg. "Please let me witness the birth."

"That is against the rules."

The delivery takes a long time. I imagine her moaning in pain. Begging for the spinal. She is within a room closed off to me. Her forehead must be covered with sweat, she must be crying. Perhaps a nurse is squeezing her hand saying, "It will be over soon."

My first view of our second son is through a glass window. A nurse stands holding the pink, shriveled little guy for my inspection.

We name him Arthur, not because of the king, but because it sounds nice and can be shortened to Art.

During the joyous homecoming, three days later, our king is gently placed in his crib. Above him I watch the mobile made by Cleo twirl. On the walls are colorful Haitian pictures of lions and tigers, lots of bright greens, blues, and oranges. The lions and tigers look noncommittal. No hostility.

When Karl sees the baby for the first time he is interested. He says, "I'm glad it's a boy. We can play ball together." As the weeks pass he seems disappointed. The baby crawls, gets into his things. His stuff has to be on shelves.

"The baby can't do anything useful. Can't even catch a ball," says Karl.

I get into my second adventure in parenthood and even learn to change diapers and hold the bottle of milk. I had never changed Karl's diapers. I wonder, are diapers the origin of bonding?

With the expansion of the family, my work area is gone. No longer can I type lectures in private. The baby might wake up. When the baby wakes up he cries. I can no longer concentrate. Books once shelved in the study have been carted to the college or stored in boxes in a recently rented storage locker.

Cleo focuses on the baby. It is as if I no longer exist. I miss her caresses and sex. It seems years since we last had sex. Our intimate conversations are gone. Karl and I talk but he is not an adult. Our conversations focus on kid stuff. He misses his mother. I bet he resents the baby. Karl watches lots of television. I hate the sounds of Sesame Street. I miss the Smother's Brothers. I like to watch the Huntley Brinkley Report. I admit, I am a life long hard core news junky.

# CHAPTER 34.

## RUN OVER BY A TRAIN

Everyone loves a clown; today two of our teachers are jesters wearing red, green, blue and orange pants and shirts and blue and white jogging shoes. Alfo Narf has straight white hair and Nolen Volens has curly black hair and fine white teeth. I appreciate their humor.

Arms out like wings, Alfo runs at me as if attempting to knock me out of the sky while going:

u u u u u u u u u u u r r r r r r r r r r r r r r r r r r rrrrrrrrrrrrrrrruuuuuuuuuuuurrrrrrrrrrrrrrrrrrrrrrrrrrrrrrrrr rrrrrrrrrrrrrrrrrrrrrrr   rrrrrrrrrrrrrrrr   rrrrrrrrrr   rrrrrr   rr rrrrrrBBBBBBOOOOOOOMMM. Wings crumpling he smashes into me. If we become seriously hurt we have to care for our own wounds because the college has no medical corpsmen.

I am more appreciative when Nolen as an old man comes up to me in a sort of dance saying, "I say please sir. Can you give me a quarter? I'm down on my luck and have not eaten for a verrry verrry long time. You see, I used to be a teacher, but now lad, I'm down on me luck, and I'm so verrry verrry hungry."

I reward him with a quarter.

Today another incident. It is a warm spring day. I lie in the sun contemplating strategy for my environmental groups. If only there was a brilliant psychological way to convince the businessmen to join with us in preserving the rural landscape? Chewing a stalk of grass I hear a distant train whistle. The train gets louder. It sounds as if the train is heading right for me. Frightened I curl up in a circle of protection. Whistle blowing, steam emissions sounding, a grinning Nolen races past, continues chugging his way across the campus. Having nothing better to do, I follow him through the student lounge, down the corridor, past the student rest rooms, past the faculty rest rooms, and down a corridor into the faculty lounge where he quietly takes a seat near the president.

I sit at one of eight triangular hardwood tables. Looking at the wall I wish the monotony would be broken by a reproduction of a painting by Cezanne, Caravaggio or van Gogh's sun flowers. I peer, through the windows, barely able to see above the bottom tiers of frosted glass. Getting up, standing on my toes, I peer out past Henry Reardon. We look past the food service garbage cans, as a mini-skirted coed walks proudly chest thrust forward as she strides towards the library. Malander joins us. We murmur appreciatively when a gust of wind lifts her skirt above her waist, and the girl too late, pushes the fabric down to her thighs. Unaware of her professorial audience she continues to the library.

Show over, I head for the coffee urn. On the way I scan the plywood stand holding teacher union pamphlets describing retirement plans, insurance policies, travel packages, group auto insurance, discount tire price lists and other matters of concern to scholars.

Coffee in hand, I sit at one end of a larger L shaped table formed of several small triangles. President Davis is talking. "A hundred million dollar state bond issue will be on the ballot. If it fails programs will have to be altered or dropped. No new buildings will be constructed. We will have to lose excess staff."

The men at the table listen carefully. Most are wearing colorful well-tailored suits. Their shoes are polished and their pants are pressed. In back of me there is another conversation. Mary Jamison says, "I think it is terrible. Students too lazy to work form delegations and complain about us. If they don't like a test or a lecture they complain. They are not for anything, they are just against." Others at her table agree. They discuss the good old days when teachers had power. If a student didn't study he or she flunked. No one asked the students, did you enjoy the lecture. Did my test please you? No. Oh my. What a shame. What a shame.

I listen to the gentle gnarring of the old refrigerator used by the secretaries to preserve yogurt, Jell-O, salads, and tomato juice. I have often thought it would be a good place to keep beer.

Mary says, "Today I have to be a whiz and compete with TV personalities. My students in their cozy apartments watch Chariots of the Gods. This film converts them to the belief that thousands of years ago space men landed on earth. My students say there is proof, there are drawings of space men sitting at rocket controls, and photos of ancient airfields. They sit like bull frogs in my philosophy class. I swear, when they leave their minds are as Empty as when they came in."

My attention shifts. The secretaries are having a good time near the refrigerator. They are laughing. Alfo has become a cash register. Hitting several keys he pulls a handle. A bell rings and a drawer pops open. Carefully extracting some bills he says, "Here's your money. For you sir, and for you George. Now the college can build the Machiavelli Building. Finally Davis can give scholarships to barefoot boys from Leeds, Alabama. Don't worry sir. I've got plenty."

Davis rewards Alfo with a weak grin; returns to the discussion of the bond initiative.

Alfo goes to the refrigerator, takes out yogurt and dill pickles, walks over to an isolated table and eats his lunch. He has a special love affair with kosher dill pickles. He sucks noisily on the long triangular slices.

After carefully placing my cup in the disposal tray, I leave the molded plastic chairs and walk to the student lounge; seeking a one to one discussion. Unfortunately it is two thirty and the students have all gone home.

# CHAPTER 35.

## ROAST BEEF, SLAVES, SNAKES AND SUZETTE

eeking culture I phone Cleo, say I have work to do. After dining on
*boef au jus* I return to the campus to attend a concert. The music
department, although divided by discord has enough coordination to
have a quartet play strings, lean towards each other, lean away. I hear
in the violins, violas and cello thousands of snow geese, crying people,
a solitary lark, a flock of black birds, laughing children, crying adults,
and giggling lovers. The number concludes as hands slowly leave the
strings.

During the concert I write on my program: I know what really goes
on at concerts. Backstage a mouse named Bear looks for his mate Fluff
who is sleeping on the strings of a cello. The quartet turns a page. Miss
Suzette in an emerald silk gown scratches her cheek and continues to
play her violin. That itch must have been a long growing urge. If she
would have halted in mid movement shock would have pushed through
the audience. Thank God she waited. She was close to disgrace.

The music turns martial. The head of the palace guard is a confident
fellow. Look at him swagger. He leans this way and that. He orders his
men loudly about.

217

Now Suzette is a queen. Head forward she cries, "Spare that captive." Changing her mind her head jerks in condemnation. "To the alligators with him!" Now she lulls us with a lullaby.

Restless snakes slither beneath the seats. Scaly skins scrape concrete and wait in scattered spirals. The music turns martial. The head of the palace guard is a confident fellow. Look at him swagger. He leans this way and that. He orders his men loudly about, and calls softly to one man.

The head of the music department, tall Dr Peabody sits facing us. A cook, he pushes his hair from his sweating brow. From right to left he examines the feast. With a flourish he lifts a long thin knife. With rapid strokes he slices portions of meat for the diners. A heavy thick juicy piece for that old fatso. A dainty bit of bloody rare for the delicate wine-sipping mademoiselle. Many huge rude slabs for the boisterous rowdy dowdy soldiers. I see a little girl. Red slacks swisting, she wanders past the snakes. Tongues flick, stalup, stalup, stalup.

Handkerchiefs wipe sweaty brows. The concert is over. The musicians proudly walk to the wings. We all clap. I give each of the three non-poisonous snakes a goodnight pat and go home.

# CHAPTER 36.

## PLEASE COME TO A MEETING

Immediately after mid terms I receive a note from the president. "Please come to a meeting this afternoon: 3 pm."

Puzzled, perplexed, paranoid and confused I spend twenty minutes crunching ice with Magnum who says, "Don't worry, he just wants to have a friendly little talk."

I say, "Everybody's been so friendly. We're close to French kissing."

At the appointed time I enter the president's office the way I would have gone into a Duwamps skid row alley at night. I blink into the cloud filtered winter sunlight streaking over the president's shoulder. I sit opposite Dean Mann and Chairman Isawaddy. I think, how pleasant, another courts martial?

Mrs. McGowan switches on the tape recorder and begins scratching her pad. Forehead tight, face grim, Davis says, "You have been charged with insubordination."

Giving him a sick grin I say, "When was this alleged incident?"

Davis says, "at the last department meeting."

Davis suddenly standing walks next to me. Squinting in the sun I look into his face. I hope he will not fall on me. "Oh Christ, I disagreed with them. Is that illegal? If that's insubordination I'll eat my microscope slide spread with tuberculosis bacilli."

Davis asks, "Did you tell them you wouldn't follow the course outline? Is this true?"

"I'll follow the outline if we all agree on the minimum basic information."

Davis ponders while I in silent fury remember the meeting. I say, "They ignored my suggestions. I said we should emphasize ecology. They said students need the basics. I said each teacher defines the basics differently. You guys majored in molecular biology. To you those are the basics. Nothing else is of significance. I said, different strokes for different folks. And I disagreed with the lab book. Told them it was a cookbook. That's insubordination?"

The president looks to Isawaddy, "John. Will you sit down with Leo and agree upon a common core?"

An unsmiling Isawaddy says, "We'll try to work it out."

Davis looking at me says, "Leo. Will you try?"

"Of course I'll try." I say without enthusiasm. Think it is easier to pick up a glass of water. Either you pick it up or you don't.

Davis smiles. Perhaps he thinks he has solved the problem and has acted decisively; the insubordination charge has dissipated, the core has been strengthened.

As we walk out of the room Davis says, "I hope you're all as glad as I am. This dispute is finally resolved. It's about time. You all know how much I dislike quarreling in our happy family."

After the meeting, I walk into the woods and ask a tree, "Can I make ice cream with curdled milk? How will it all come out? He says it is solved. Bullshit. Have I reaped what I sowed?

"What about our lab manual? I remember the day that part time secretary was typing her head off copying dissection instructions someone else had published. We are in the western USA. The original material had been used in the east. It was blatant thievery. Jackson said he forgot to ask the author. Nevertheless he told the girl, "put my name down, here," and the secretary complied. And just like that, Jackson became the author of another publication; soon he will be collecting royalties.

"I have complained to some of the other teachers, and my friends. They listen and agree with me, saying, "It is unethical to copy other men's work." But they won't interfere. Professional courtesy allows word thievery. Doctors protect doctors. Politicians protect politicians. Pork fat, hog fat, everyone a fat cat. Get whatever you can. That's my advice. Get it fast. Get whatever you can. That's the American way. From her mountains, to her bank vaults, white with foam. Am I without sin? Buddy, buddy with the students, that's me. I lack proper professorial formality. Too disorganized, I criticize before my mind is in place. I drink too much. I lack humility. Bless me father for I have sinned. Since my last confession father I have become an agnostic. Oh Daddy Laddy and the Big Spook. I am just a pile of junk."

That night after the baby is asleep I tell Cleo, "Today they again wanted to fire me. We had a discussion, Davis said, 'this dispute is finally resolved.' No one smiled. Will this thing never end? I no longer believe the words of Davis."

"We've got to get out of here," says Cleo, getting up to tend the baby who has woken, is crying. He probably has a stomachache. I haven't been spending time with Karl. He must think he is an orphan.

The next day Isawaddy and I agree to add a unit of ecology to the outline. The entire department will use the revised outline.

After the agreement I sit alone in my office staring at my Swirloped collection. My gut hurts. Pressing my stomach I wonder, am I getting an ulcer? I should go back to the president and say, that solution is no solution. Can't you see they hate me? They want to nail my hide to the wall and scrub the sinks using my mind as a Brillo Pad. Who am I fooling? If Davis were here now, I would stay quiet. I'm mostly mouse.

I drive home. Cleo and the boys are out. Without undressing I wrap myself in blankets and think, will life never get better? I've tried to be a good person but everything turns to shit. Wanting to sob my guts out I can't cry. My stomach feels hard as if a giant fist was pushing against my diaphragm. Clutching the pillow I dimly hear Cleo open the front door, wonder, will she sympathize with me? Pour me a drink? Say poor little boy? Now she sides with me and condemns them. Can our marriage take this conflict? I should quit. How can I quit? We have payments to make; the house, furniture. Yet it would be better to quit than be fired. It would be better when looking for another job to have quit. Another job? I can't afford to quit until I line up another teaching position.

I can shoot myself. What would Cleo do with the corpse? Wilted flower, she'd seek sympathy. Soon she'd be laughing again while I'd lie rotting. Slipping beside me, Cleo whispers in her courtship voice, "What's wrong?" She caresses my hair and whispers, "Don't worry so much. It's been settled. The president's on your side."

"How do you know?"

"I was with some friends. They told me. They heard the president was going to settle things in your favor."

Talking into the pillow I mumble, "Once I believed in Davis. But this thing will never end."

Cleo bounces up, "I'll get you a surprise that'll make you feel better." I hope she'll return in a peignoir. A moment later she comes to me with an amber old fashioned. I suck the sweet cherry.

The next morning she shakes me. I burrow into the pillow. She says, "Don't give in. Be strong. Go to work."

I try. I get up. I don't eat; have no appetite. The sky is heavily overcast. On my way to the college I drive jerkily, as if in a tunnel. I am only peripherally aware of other cars. A car ahead of me gently brakes. I slam on my brakes to avoid a collision. The brakes stink.

At the college I am a rat in a hostile world. Sliding along the corridor walls I try to keep away from people, push them away with downcast eyes.

In the lecture room the students must wonder about me. After class a student asks, "Is anything wrong? Don't you feel good?"

I reply with a tongue of glue, "I feel fine." If I would have told the truth I would have said, "I want to cry. Twice this year they've tried to fire me. Did you know that? I have a new baby and they keep trying to fire me. Can you understand? And you students want a ball of fire. Can't you understand? Don't you know what they are doing to me? They are torturing me. I want to go home and sleep. Can you understand?"

Depressed, part of me realizes that things are better. Another part of me distrusts everything.

During the next weeks I get to school late. I correct exams but get them back late. My grading becomes inconsistent. I make mistakes in addition and division. Forcing myself I get my work done. It is a joyless effort.

I overhear the students. They are bitching about their up tight teacher. Several drop my classes. I hear one to one from friendly students, that others have advised friends, "Don't take any classes from Bauer."

Isolated and withdrawn, I cannot help my students, my family or myself. My misery twists within.

I return to Dr Eagleton. He prescribes Elavil, a trycyclic antidepressant. The pills make my mouth dry. I keep trying to swallow. During the day, because of the medication, I occasionally dribble in my shorts. I worry about the stench of urine. Can the students smell me coming?

I want to sleep and at times only to sleep. I sleep an entire weekend. I give zero help with the baby. I doze through evenings and struggle to stay awake during the drive to the college.

The drug works. Like a frozen flower softens in the warmth of the sun, I change thanks to biochemistry. The worries, the many troubles that have been shoving me down, suddenly turn to fluff. Euphoria overtakes me. In my altered state I no longer give a shit. Again relaxed I prepare for classes. Sometimes I laugh.

After five weeks, disliking the pill caused bad taste, dryness, dribbling, and other real and fancied side effects, including problems getting hard-ons, I discontinue the pill. I am pleased when I discover I can function without medication. Trying to regain the respect of the students, I spend hours listening to them in my office and in the lounge. I hope they will support me.

I devote more time to local and state environmental causes and write clever well-researched essays on nuclear reactors, state parks, air and water pollution, and environmental education. I give presentations to meetings of environmental organizations. I help Cleo with Arthur.

On weekends I drive the highways, stopping to photograph examples of air and water pollution. Each shutter click of visible acrid air gives me pleasure.

While my position within the college erodes, my standing among regional and state environmentalgroups grows. While one hand of society is raised to slap me down, another hand is raised in praise.

I read Job in the Jerusalem Bible:

"How dare I plead my cause ... For he whom I must sue is judge as well…He, who… wounds and wounds again leaving me no moment to draw breath, with so much bitterness he fills me.

"Shall I try force? Look how strong He is. Or go to court? But who will summon Him? Though I count myself innocent; am I innocent after all? Not even I know that; and as for my life, I find it hateful.

"Nonetheless I shall speak, not fearing Him... Since I have lost all taste for life I will give free rein to my complaints. I shall let my embittered soul speak out."

After reading Job I write: The ultimate minority. The ultimate minority is one. The ultimate minority is one person rejected by everyone. It makes no difference. So what if the person denied has caused his or her own rejection by assuming the role of scraggly puke, blabbing word mumbler, drunken recluse. It is the same if the person denied is rejected because of an accident before birth, is flesh without beauty, motion without coordination, sound without intelligibility. We lump these people without discriminating against creed, sex or color. Rarely do we reward those pulsating moveable lumps with so much as a mere glance. After our look they are again ignored, unless we give them the magnanimous gift of words, our piddling acknowledgement. What about the lump that is I? I am sobbing but no one hears me. Looking at me, people must say, what a grouch.

I hear another voice. The voice yowls, "go forth whelp of the wolverine. Leave. Go to the ocean. Keep to the cover of the forest. Follow the surf rattled rocks. Swim the small rivers. Float on logs across barrier waters. Keep moving. Go where the fish are plentiful, the waters warm and clear, where the long legged waders spear fish.

"Leave. This life of yours is an asylum. Leave the mortgage. Let some other idiot take it over. So what if you lose your equity. Once lost you won't have to worry about losing it. You won't have to worry about taxes or the loss of everything by fire. Termites can gnaw someone else's timbers. Windstorms can break someone else's windows. The monthly payment. Let it go. Let it go.

"Leave your wife. She lifts you when you're down but downs you when you're up. She is as miserable as you. Crying and sobbing, no one hears her. She won't decide. It's up to you. Leave her. Leave your sons. You're not much good to them. Let Cleo find a good role model father for them. A man who relishes daily going to work. Who delights in mowing the grass. Who is a good citizen. Who supports industry and development.

"Leave your books, boxes, and bottles. Leave the accumulation of generations, the family archives, the knowledge of the ages. Leave technology. Go north loping like Lobo the wolf. Go north like a long necked loon in the moonlight. Drink in the raindrops. Let your hair blow in storms. Laugh at the wind. Laugh with the moon. Laugh in the waters of small fast streams. Poke your nose through bubbles. Drape your face in seaweeds. Make a belt of vines. Eat strawberries warming in the sun. Eat fresh flopping fish. When the tide is out shuck and eat a hundred oysters.

"Forget how to read. Forget the radio, television, and stereo. Forget electricity, oil, automobiles, trains, planes, and boats.

"Look at people living beyond. Look at haystacks and distant campfires. Listen to dogs barking and train whistles."


For some strange reason I feel like writing whenever I am most miserable. The next night I write in a cocktail lounge. I know Cleo will be pissed I am not with her helping out with the kids and keeping her company.

It is a challenge, it is fun to nurse my drink. With concern in her eye the barmaid, another Florence Nightingale, asks me, "Sir, would you like another drink?"

When I say, "No thanks, I'm leaving soon," she minces off as if I've hurt her feelings.

What a farce. TV commercials say, "Stay sober, don't drive if you drink." And then we reward people with smiles for pouring booze down our willing swilling sucking throats.

Every day we hear, the more we buy the better off we are. What's sauce for the goose is sauce for the gander. Gobbling sweet cereal, sweet soda, our swilling kiddies dream of the day when they too will swill buckets of beer. No wonder we have a compulsion to guzzle, gobble, fart, and belch.

In the new world all dainty sippers will be taken out and executed. Fill the till. Swill that beer. Slurp those martinis and Manhattans. Think of the skyline, the amber sky of Manhattan. Tom Collins. Tom and Jerry. All good fellows hale and well met. Tom, Tom, the piper's son, had a drink with a little rum. Tom was beat he could not eat, the rum flowed down and sloshed the feet of Tom, Tom, the piper's son, who had a drink with a little rum.

Give us this day our culture made mellow with the euphoria of booze. Listen to Florence yell, whoopee. Look at the fun we're having. In the mirror she sees wrinkles, the reflection of her eyes. The euphoria becomes swill ritual as the wrinkles march and bivouac. That parchment proclaims our history seen in the smoky Manhattan where molecules transmit candlelight and hoped for romance. On a good humor morning the boozehounds howl at a moon, which is disappearing. When it is gone, they don't know where it is, and look in Manhattan or its simulacrum.

After comprehension has diffused in the candlelight and the flickering lamp goes dark, after I close my journal, the waitress lifts and pushes and pulls me out the door. Finding my car I crawl in the back seat and sleep to sobriety.

Waking before remembering, I am surprised to discover myself in the car. It is Saturday morning and I have no appointments. While shoppers pass I write:

Decent Americans know where their bread is buttered. The problem is not the outsider but the insider. When bread is dropped it always falls on the buttered side. While swallows soar men's minds go glooomph. We must have universal freedom including freedom from religion; freedom from employers; freedom from parents, mates and children.

A new system must develop. The old system will shrivel away. The schlock of administrators tumbles forth like Pea silage from grabber grabber trucks. The old homilies flow like rancid butter on hot muggy days. Consider state and local politicians. God no longer burden us with such mediocrities. The bitching of we millions is like the prayer wheels of Tibet. Who is listening?

The following is for our six top administrators:

Six pompous fools
Suck twelve fat thumbs and six sticky lollipops
Floating unaware
They are in the Sea of Hopelessness
Waves smash them. Their hands clutch the rocks
Of the Mountain of Optimism.
The crash of the surf is so loud they cannot hear the avalanche.

When I get home Cleo gives forth mighty envenomed scowls. "Stop feeling sorry for yourself. I refuse to put up with your bullshit. You've got to change your attitude."

# CHAPTER 37.

# I THINK OF WISCONSIN

I agree with Cleo yet in the time of my trouble I think of Wisconsin, of the days when as a youth I lived carefree in the woods. I remember those summer days when my canoe and I floated far from shore near the strange snag pointing to the sky like a finger. The treetop once grew from the forest floor, was covered by water when a low dam created the lake. It served as a beacon telling me where to fish for walleyes, and where to tie my boat.

I slept, warmed by the sun, my back against the curve of the stern. My canoe was of cedar and canvas so the waves sounded natural. Later I bought a more practical, less aesthetic aluminum canoe and heard the reverberation, a sound like tin, tin, tin throughout the hull. While bobbing on the waves I read Shakespeare and Thoreau.

One Winter I walked, ran and slid across the frosted frozen jigsaw puzzle Lake. The air was clean, scented of pine, fir, and spruce. When snow fell, I followed animal tracks and knew where each fox burrowed, and where to expect an enraged chickaree who would shake in fury while seemingly stuck to the dark gray trunk of a white pine. Some of these pine squirrels lived up red scaly Norway pines. When in fast retreat their feet scratched the scales; sometimes dropping spiraling to the duff then stopping, and turning screaming, the hell with everything except we chickarees. Other tracks were of voles who upon leaving the snow covered tunnels challenged the owls *mano e mano.*

Sometimes while walking deep in thought, my eyes snapped open as ruffed grouse cannon balls hurtled through the sky and hid beneath snow covered branches.

At night I listened to the sap steaming from logs I had cut of maple, oak, birch, and poplar. I saw cities burn in flames, elves dance, castle lights glow, dragon's glare, cat claws scratch. Later in the evening, still listening to cracking sounds, I left the fireside to crawl beneath the covers to read in bed with light from my birch bark framed light. Early in the season I read mysteries, adventure stories and science fiction. After several thousand pages my reading speed increased and I switched to the classics. Some months I finished twenty books. It was a pleasant way to fall asleep listening to the fire and the waves.

In the morning when I woke, my face was lit red and blue from bits of colored glass inserted in openings between the logs. The colors also glowed the logs next to the bed. Outside the birch leaves shook in the morning breeze. The patterns shivered in the room, and the memory shivers my back today. Other light patterns, never to be duplicated, were reflected from the lake to the ceiling.

I still can catch a whiff in my memory of the sweet fern on a warm summer day, and clench my fists recalling those strangers who came to shoot my friends the grouse, deer and fox. I hated when the water skiers frightened the ducks and loons. The fury of their waves smashed silence and stole tranquility. At such times, while daydreaming, I thought how easy it would be to pick off such noisemakers with a thirty-thirty. However, I would never really use violence unless people or something else attacked people I love.

Some nights, before going to bed, I held a flashlight while on my knees, and peered beneath the pier watching the glowing red eyes of crayfish advancing over the rocks in that plankton specked water.

During storms, the tall white pine tossed as if possessed by forest spirits. On calmer days I climbed that tallest of all trees. From the top, while tightly holding the thin central spire, I saw a lake far away in the marsh. During times of forest fires I climbed my tree and watched the flames and smelled smoke.

At night, especially during storms, I thought of the tree. Would it lose its top or be struck and destroyed by lightning? During storms lightning lit the bedroom. When thunder cracked it seemed to threaten to break our windows. If in bed at such times, getting out of bed I watched the lake and waited for a bolt to part the furious waves, to turn the water to steam. I often wondered, if the tree is hit will the trunk stand? Perhaps a furious spiral of energy will spin down the trunk, blasting away chunks of bark, exposing the shiny slippery cambium. And if the tree falls, while suspended in air, will it hover above us like an angel of death, before descending to the roof to join us in a fatal embrace?

Imagining destruction did not make me want to destroy the tree. Although our fate was in its power, I would never cut it down. If the tree was killed we would have lost the spirit of the forest. Something Aldo Leopold wrote eloquently about.

During the pregnancy we sold the woods and cabin. Part of my heart was ripped away from me. At that time, rationalizing, I said, "Oh, we can't keep the land in Wisconsin because we live in Cascadia. The taxes are eating us up. The cabin is rotting because we cannot take care of it. It needs work. The eves should be extended so water won't blow on the logs in a storm. There's so much to do, and it's so far away." So we sold the place, I sold my birthright for seven thousand dollars. Such a paltry sum. Of course depression came upon me, thrown in with the depression caused by work, by Cleo's moods; like drifts of dirty snow piled drift upon drift. If I had been a friend of Caesar, I would have stabbed him. If I was capable of selling the cabin, I must be capable of any treachery including murder.

Now I want to go back home to Wisconsin. Cascadia has brought us misery. It is stupid to remain for another nine months of rain and overcast. The college does not give a shit about me. At home tension congeals the air. I want my cabin back. I want to go alone to Wisconsin and sit on the shore and watch the Northern Lights reflecting off the lake. Often the entire northern sky was a pyrotechnic display as if the fingers of God were giving the earth an electric massage. The sky was illuminated for me as it was for Indians and wolves, and I sold the land.

# CHAPTER 38.

## THE PURPLE FRINGED SLOT

I have come early to the campus. A fog covers the land. Pine needles are bearers of tiny drops of water. The cars have their lights on: each car sounds important. Internal combustion imperfections are magnified including the chug altered by a pinched tail pipe, a leaky muffler, or an out of tune engine. On the campus distant figures are soundless. Nearby walking figures transmit their imperfections. One drags his feet just a little, another lacks confidence, a third clicks along.

I am taking notes on a faculty bulletin. While listening to my feet I stumble. I jump back struck by the full force of the air raid alarm. I hear no bombs. It is quiet except for the siren slashing through the fog. Six administrators run past. Dean Mann is the point man. The vice president and three division chairmen follow him. I run after them. There is no smoke or sound of breaking glass. Maybe the fog has eaten the sounds of fire and explosion.

We reach the administration building. I go inside and join hundreds of students and staff staring out the windows. It is good to be in the crowd. It wouldn't be good to meddle in whatever is going on.

Squad cars, blue and red lights flashing, swerve into the parking lot. A longhaired youth breaks from the shadowed cars and runs toward us. A cluster of policemen fumbles for their pistols. One cop drops his wallet; another sends a handkerchief and keys to the grass. They stop, retrieve their possessions, and smartly turn to their cars. Using roofs for support they brace themselves for the best shot.

The boy stops in front of me, on the other side of the glass. Saliva runs down the corners of his mouth, mats the sparse auburn beard. He is gasping. His eyes bulge.

The police have left their crouch and are running towards us. I hope they don't shoot. The youth's hands, flat against the window, are stained with nicotine. They seem to pulsate against the glass until he is yanked away and thrown to the ground.

The president is to the left of me. His face is red. The other administrators are by his side. They are all watching.

The police jerk the boy's hands behind his back and snap on handcuffs. Pulling him by the wrist cuff chain he is brought upright, leans against our window. While he strains to keep supported they pat his pockets. Gritting his teeth the boy yells, "You apocalyptic pigs." The boy looks disreputable. Perhaps he takes heroin or amphetamines. I have read that amphetamines make your eyes bloodshot. His eyes are bloodshot. Perhaps he is on downers. Downers make some people anti social. Maybe the president kicked him out of college for going barefooted in the cafeteria. Perhaps he threatened the president's life. Even so I'm glad no one shot him. He ought to have his chance in court. I don't like these guns.

The police are excited. Excited people don't reason things through, they just react. Now the police calm down. They seem to be enjoying themselves.

An officer runs up carrying a leash that he snaps onto the handcuffs. Laughing he jerks the line and spins the boy away from the window. They reach the squad car, the boy hobbles. A sergeant wraps the leash around the boy. He hands the end to the custodian of campus parking who yanks the leash. The boy is spun into the back seat of the car. Two officers hop in. Siren wailing they race off, almost colliding with a tow truck. The tow truck stops in back of a dented 59 black Ford pick up. The driver attaches two hooks to the back of the frame. He winches the back of the truck into the air, and drives off with his orange lights flashing. Soon he has vanished in the fog. The president's purple fringed parking slot is again empty. Justice has been done. The people around me are leaving. I'll go to my office and work on an examination.

# CHAPTER 39.

## MY DAYS ARE NUMBERED

In zoology lab I say, "Write about this shark." The students feel the sandpaper skin, the teeth, and the slippery liver, smell oil and resist smelling formaldehyde, and explore the spiral gut. Instead of giving them lists of what I want them to see, I have them write accounts of what they see.

One day when they come into class the students read:
In red ink: The Whistling Oyster
In purple: The Trembling Sea Squirt
In blue: The Palpitating Jellyfish
In crimson: The Anxious Anemone
In violet: The Crestfallen Crayfish
In orange: The Cruel Crab
In pink: Wrestling Rabbits

Students study petted rats and yelled at rats. The criticized rats snap at the hand that feeds them. The waltz rat is very intelligent and runs the maze in 38 seconds. The hard rock rat seems addled and loses the way. The exercised rat is fast. The slothful rat's legs are atrophied.

They watch a spider spinning a web and a caterpillar eating leaves and fashioning a pupa. The assignments take many hours, but I have banished time by covering the clock with a photograph of the sun.

I teach my students that people photosynthesize, and require natural sunlight to produce the light hormone that elevates the spirit. I say, "Windowless buildings are an abomination. A lack of sunlight replaced with flickering fluorescent light gives people tired eyes and headaches, and depression."

I write a letter to the students, but never deliver it. Dear Students, it is terrible to hand in a paper and never get it back from your teacher. There should be no excuse for this yet there is an excuse for everything.

Please excuse me. I have been in a struggle with the administration. I stand-alone. They are trying to fire me. My energy goes into erecting lines of defense. I am not paranoid. This has happened. My days are numbered. While concentrating on survival, it is hard to get all of my work done. I have read all of your papers, but the next step, that of returning them to you, that step seems impossible. I have too little energy.

I'm sorry.

Despite success with my students, Isawaddy changes the schedule. I lose the biology and zoology classes. It no longer makes any difference whether or not I can select my own textbooks. There is no more biology for me.

In spring this biologist miraculously becomes a physical scientist. My new teaching load consists of daytime physics laboratory sections and one night class in ecology. You already know how I feel about physics.

The laboratories are a cinch to teach. One lab is like another lab. Monday's laboratory is like Tuesday's laboratory, is like Wednesday's laboratory is like Thursday's laboratory is like Friday's.

Instead of rejoicing in my good fortune, I am outraged. Lecturing had given me pleasure. As a scholar I had enjoyed abstracting information from books, and preparing visual aids and handouts. My students had frequently complemented me on my slide shows of exotic places like Zanzibar.

Independence gone, I am under the supervision of Ollie Ivar Sharp, a newly minted Ph.D., hired six months earlier to improve the general education physics class.

As you know, my poorest grades had been in physics, although I had enjoyed micrometeorology, geoecology and chemistry. It could be argued that I should be motivated to do a good job, because teaching the laboratories is a way to prove myself. Instead I resent being switched out of the area of my competency. I doubly resent having to work with and under someone new to Humaluh.

After I become a physicist I often arrive late to classes. I am so despondent. My insignificant background in the physical sciences does not help. My teaching of the laboratories is less than mediocre.

In the middle of the quarter, Sharp writes a note to the Dean of Directed Instruction:

Leo Bauer is indifferent to the teaching of our physics laboratories. He could have responded to this opportunity with greatness. He chooses to act otherwise.

My condemnation would be complete except that I have talked with some of his ecology students. They say he was enthusiastic, stimulating and dedicated. Those students regard Leo Bauer as a Master Teacher of Ecology.

I respectfully urge that Bauer not be allowed to teach more physics laboratories. Instead, please encourage him, allow him, and command him to develop a Humaluh ecology program, or else assist him in finding a position elsewhere as a professional ecologist. Surely there must be a use somewhere for a man of his talents.

Ollie Ivar Sharp

I am angry when I read my copy of Sharp's letter. Upon reflection, I become grateful and optimistic. I think, perhaps this letter will cause a change in my career.

I apply for a sabbatical leave. My letter to the Sabbatical Committee says:

My psychic batteries are low. I need a recharge. To pick up my spirits I want to take my family on a steamship to the Mediterranean. To boost our spirits we will become friends with the locals, dance with the Turks, break glasses with the Greeks and eat cheese with the French.

To better understand the decline of the American Earth I shall study the ruination of the Mediterranean Basin. To learn about deserts and desert tribes, I will ride a camel, and watch the Sahara expand. Through observing logging of the slopes above Florence I will learn how deforestation gives oomph to Italian cloudbursts. After weaving palm fronds together I will form a raft to float my family through Florence, taking special care to observe the art treasures near the *Piazza Della Signoria*.

To prepare for this journey, I have read several obscure manuscripts. My camera is loaded. Our bags are waiting.

I receive the answer in three weeks: We were forced to consider many outstanding proposals, and yours, although meritorious, was not chosen.

One of the successful applicants was my friend Thrigwhistle who proposed to touch the vertical words on Shakespeare's tomb and breathe in the spirits, vapors and mists while, reciting:

Good frend for Jesus Sake, To dig the dust encloased heare, blest be ye man yt spares this stones and curst be he yt moves my bones.

Impressed by Thrigwhistle's success and example, I go to a meeting of the English Club that is held off campus at a coffee house. Some of the people had been drinking. While there I meet a coed. Her face flushed pink she watches the guitarist. Noticing me, she says, "What's your name?"

"My name is Leo."

"My that's a nice name," she says. A little later, interrupting the guitarist in mid song, she says, "That music has soul. You really have soul, don't you?"

The guitarist stops playing. "I don't know much about souls except the ones under my feet," he says.

As the guitarist plays she vigorously shakes her head and shoulders keeping time only a little behind the rhythm. She turns to me and says, "How unusual the last days have been. I've felt good for five days. Tomorrow will probably not be a nice day. I've had too much to drink. We partied before coming here. Just a little bit."

She lurches to her feet like a rocket misfiring. I think, she might topple over on top of me. I imagine her acneed forehead getting closer, her forehead smashing against my forehead, the popping pimples smearing my face.

She tilts back to the vertical. Again she is ready for takeoff. "What's your name?" she says.

I say, "My name is Leo."

"My that's an interesting name."

I am glad she is drunk. She is probably past the stage when someone will try to screw her. If she went with someone she would be like a manikin. Her Levis would be pulled off like a parent pulls muddy clothes off a small child. The blouse would be unbuttoned, the bra unsnapped as a chore, a duty, by a teen aged supposed lover trying to be a man. And during the masturbatory fuck, perhaps she might open her eyes and ask, "What's your name?"

A youth named Will reads a story titled Rondo:

I smelled something burning. I thought it was the beans. I was in the midst of reading a book. Actually I was nearing the inconclusive conclusion so I didn't want to stop. I kept reading. The smell of burning became stronger. Finally I could no longer ignore it. In exasperation I got out of bed, put down my book and walked to the kitchen. I had been correct. The beans were burning. The water had boiled away. I took the pot off the stove and let it cool. Taking a second pot, heavier than the first, I scraped the top layers of unburned beans from the first pot into the second pot, added water, and placed it back on the stove. I added water to the first pot and scraped the burned beans, about a cupful, into the garbage. The beans were white on top and black on the bottom. It was like a conglomerate riverbed. After dumping the burned beans, I put water into the pot and left it to soak. I went back to read. As I neared the end of the book I smelled something burning. I thought it was the beans. I was nearing the end of an inconclusive conclusion and didn't want to stop. I kept reading. The smell of burning became stronger. In exasperation I put down my book and walked to the kitchen. My hypothesis was correct. The beans were burning. I let the pot cool and then scrape off the top layer of good beans. After adding water I scrape away the bad beans. The pot looks like a window to the dark with dozens of moths seeking the light inside. I let it soak and put the good beans with water into a third pot.

I set the pot on the stove and turn the burner to medium. Back to my book. I am almost on the last page when I smell something burning. What would you have done in my place? Of course I kept reading. I wanted to finish the book.

Several in the group say words like, interesting, original.

Although gratified by their praise, Will seems resentful towards his drinking buddies. Lately they have been of little help to him.


During the writing portion of the meeting I write: The Friday afternoon teacher conversations are like listening to a tape. The minds of most teachers are as shallow as a sun-baked riverbed. The teaching profession pits ego against ego, a contest with the winner unannounced. Wobbling around the ring, we are so blinded by the light we cannot see our minds flitting in frantic spirals around the cobwebbed rafters.

Committees. When committees decide how to educate the young, they will only produce hum ahum, humahum, humahum hum. Most of teaching is a song and dance act. A routine by marionettes. If we had huge bulbous noses, red cheeks and oversized polka dot bib overalls we would be complete.

Gertrude Stein said, "A rose is a rose is a rose." Because I am a biologist, a biologist, a biologist, my profession, profession, profession and the system, the system, the system neatly box me in. The microcosm that is I is smothered in transcripts. When bureaucracy controls the classroom learning jumps out the window. I might be happy in a department of naturalists. Here I grind my teeth. Like a hiker who has gone uphill all day, I wait for the trail to level. At a time when many are close to their fellows, I am estranged, an outcast.

When I should be accomplishing much, I tread water. I consider the alternatives: Life cannot always be this pointless. There must be more for me. I am trapped in a time of national experimentation. The ecology proposal has gone nowhere. Perhaps I can switch. Why can't I teach Mexican Americans or Native American Indians? By helping them learn, I may again feel significant.

Must I take more graduate courses before I can jump into another cell? Perhaps somewhere there is a new life. I am stuck and want to become unstuck. The mud is too deep. Can I continue? I want to sleep at night. I must be around friends. It is too hard to work among enemies. In the time of the Medici, people poisoned their opponents. Now we destroy their faith and hope.

I must make a decision. Next year I'll go back to college and major in English. Like someone who has been taking drugs, I will kick the biology habit. My drug the dead dog dream of biology is of the past. Once antelope came to look at me. Bull elk bellowed, whistled, charged, tried to kill me. Beaver whacked pond puddles with flat tails, miracles were in pond water and the sea at night was molten churning fire. That was all an illusion. Academic biology is real; it is a place of facts, and closed minds. My departmental colleagues are one colony, a single organism. There is no room for another life form.

If I ask, perhaps the president will give me an unpaid leave of absence. My friends in English will help me. I will study in the learning center until I become flawless at capitalization and punctuation. Can I really accomplish that? I will sell the car. Cleo can get a part time job. While she works, I will watch Arthur and Karl.

Until I do this flocks of geese will avoid me, afraid that I'll shoot and pickle them.

I write two requests for leaves of absence. In one I say I want to go back to graduate school to work for a master's degree in English under Bernard Malamud. I mention that as an undergraduate I had minored in English and had worked on literary magazines. Unfortunately I forget to mail the letters.

If I had lived many years ago, I would have become a universal teacher studying and teaching all things in the manner of Ebenezer Cook, former poet laureate of Maryland.

I worry about switching to English. I had never learned how to diagram sentences. I consider becoming a philosopher, but give up that idea because I don't know how to define words like synesthetic isomorphic parallel communications.

I studied the other faculty in an attempt to discover which teachers were happiest. I assumed that the teachers who had been at the college the longest would all be happy and secure.

I discovered however that the first happy families had separated into an in-group and an out-group. Nine of eighteen still here are in the in-group. Strangely, each of them is in excellent health and is also an administrator.

The other nine original teachers are in the out-group. None of them is an administrator and all are in poor health.

Upon discovering these strange new facts, I leave the meeting and enter Thrigwhistle's office. His colleague, one of the out-group, is staring into the wastebasket. Instead of being jubilant at my discovery, he says, "So?" shakes his head and redirects his attention to the wastebasket.

After additional study I conclude that no women are in the in-group. All of the innees are males who had coached a sport. None of the out-group has coached. All of the in-group are in science or technology.

My conclusionsare inescapable:

1. Coaching develops administrative ability in men.

2. The humanities make people sick in the middle ages.

3. Never having coached a sport, I must expect cancer, hardening of the arteries, or other health problems.

4. In order to advance in academia women must grow male genitalia.

# CHAPTER 40.

## A FACULTY PARTY

My findings make me low down at the next faculty party. Home life is deteriorating. Cleo and Arthur are off to the side surrounded by women. I sit and brood. At times someone comes booming over to whack me on the back saying, "How are things going, old buddy? How are you doing changing diapers?"

Wanting to say GO FUCK YOURSELF, I always force out, "Great. Things are going great. I love diapers. Never know what I'll find. The baby's great. Just look at him. He has healthy lungs. If you're lucky you'll hear him sing." By lapsing into silence and delaying my response to succeeding questions, I manage to get my visitors to wander off and bother someone else.

Thrigwhistle is different. I never resent him as he comes over in the guise of an old man softly saying, "Leo my boy. Would you like some tea?"

After a visit from Thrigwhistle, I join the crowd and write my observations on a sheet of butcher paper I ripped off the table. This party is at the local gas company. The room is brightly lit, mauve and sterile. The floor is linoleum and the food is potluck. There is beer from a spigoted pony and wine in jugs. There are no top administrators. Most of the vocational teachers and their wives are present. The welders and mechanics are wearing suits. There is a delegation from the science division. The humanities division is poorly represented. In each humane couple either the man or the woman seems depressed. Romeo's wife is sullen and Alfo's wife morose. To cheer up his dark haired wife, Alfo Narf challenges Nolen Volens to a tricycle race. As they circle the room Alfo's nose appears damn near buried in the base of Nolen's butt crack. Although Alfo wins the race, his feat fails to cheer his wife. Malander's wife, wrapped in black cotton is isolated. If a great frog kisses her she may again become lively and beautiful. The teachers of writing sit as if they are unwilling participants at a reading by Harold Robbins.

While drinking out of plastic glasses, we listen to music from a phonograph. The records include fox trots, a little rock, not much Latin American. The men are getting drunk while most of the women remain with Cleo and Arthur. The women stay sober. Things liven up when music is played from Zorba the Creek. It seems as if every faculty member and every faculty wife loves the Greek music. A line forms of people holding hands, facing left, and facing right. The musical is a smash hit on Broadway and each one of us wants to go to New York to catch a performance. We throw our glasses to the floor but the plastic bounces. I would like to be like Zorba who lacked a single passive bone. Though in his sixties, he danced to exhaustion. By contrast we merely talk about Zorba or dance the line dance while not knowing the correct steps. Of course Zorba would not have worried about exactness. He would have just danced, and pulled one of the wives off to bed.

As an experiment, I attempt to engage people in serious discussion. My efforts are deflected. No one wants to talk about Vietnam. By eavesdropping I learn that all are successful. They are liked by their students and appreciated for the extra help they give. Their lectures are unique. Despite the excellent job they are doing, the administrators blame them for declining enrollment.

A week after the party while in a faculty meeting I write: Coolsam complains, we are using the SCAN phone too much. Ten minutes are spent complaining about and trying to find ways to stop students from skipping classes.

If I was a student and it was a warm sunny sleepy Indian summer day, I'd be outside drinking beer, tossing Frisbees and making love in some hidden place. November through February, on those dreary days, it makes sense to sit by a fire somewhere smoking pot, drinking wine and occasionally retiring to the bedroom to fornicate. It would be irresponsible for them to get out of bed and drive on ice covered roads. If parents would only realize how many lives are saved just by sleeping in, fucking and drinking. When the sun reappears, it is natural and reasonable for students to take to the hills, lie in the grass, drink beer, soar Frisbees, play cards, chase each other, and roll around in the grass and screw.

Shortly after the faculty meeting, I am elated when Sally Thompson trots to my evening class with hip huggers, scrolled in red at the top rim of her pushing forth bra are the words, "I love you." After class she says to me, "I come to class because this is important. Days when I am absent, I paint, or lie in bed making love with my boyfriend. So professor Bauer, please realize, when I come to your class, it's because I really want to be here."

Another coed says, "I think most classes are boring. Your class is definitely not boring. You're one of the best. But I don't have much time and I do have a B average."

I find it is hard to be firm with the firm girls though I am disappointed by their absences.

On the way to physics lab I rip open an envelope. The message reads, "A lively physical day for you." I say, "Shit. The God damned things I get to read."

I want to tell the students my feelings but I keep quiet.

A long thighed mini skirted coed writes on her essay:

"I'M AVAILABLE NOW!"

I think a moment. Damn. Does that mean what I think it means?

I read a brochure puffing my colleague's text:

The book you've been waiting for. Should be required for every college freshman. This rigorous monumental easy to read beautiful text is hard to lay aside. A brand new approach to contemporary biology

Allows fantastic creativity by presenting all information in discrete boxes.

Printed in fine clear ten point bank gothic type.

Contains over 500 pages and forty thousand definitions.

Prodigal use of photographs.

Eighteen colors.

Profuse use of graphs, overflowing with line drawings.

Trenchant analysis of our oscillating environment. Covers all the highlights including the DNA Litany, genetic engineering, frontal lobotomies, fungal hormones, and sewage sludge.

READ WHAT OUR REVIEWERS SAY

A radical change from other textbooks
Refreshing organization
A well-integrated text
A masterpiece of biological epistemology
Expands student horizons
All the salient facts
A wealth of information
An impressive scholarly work
Will become a classic by next year
Gives DNA its place in the sun
Will revitalize any course it is used in
Appeals to the terminal student

Carefully extracting a large booger from my left nostril, I swirl it over the shiny brochure, crumple the paper, and deposit it in the wastebasket.

# CHAPTER 41.

## REQUEST FOR A LEAVE OF ABSENCE

Forgetting my ire, I join the Schnitzel Haus gang, who with beer in their mitts comment upon the blurbs, testimonials and other guarantees of quality by which the reader is guaranteed an outstanding textbook.

I say, "Our text reminds me of the testimonials for pills which are sent to physicians. They are similar. A book, like a pill or suppository, is designed to trigger as few allergies as possible, and should be easy to take." Malander agrees.

Buoyed up, I decide to act decisively. That evening I write and the next morning deliver a letter to the president. I feel like I am a compulsive obsessive stuck record.

***CONFIDENTIAL***

With sadness, in bitterness, I ask you to grant me a leave of absence for the coming school year.

I am sad for our college, strangled by the narrow wisdom of scientists and technologists.

I am bitter. The Satisfaction Inquiry said my charge was just. They vindicated me, yet their findings were thrown back into their faces and again you requested my resignation. Our continuing contracts are worthless.

One man cannot hold out alone in a war of attrition. My opponents have the real power. They own the office of the Dean of Directed Instruction. Supposedly objective, that office serves as a scalpel to remove independent faculty.

I have remained because you said you liked me. If you had said I was a terrible lazy person, I would have left a long time ago. Because you consider me to be salvageable and the committee says I am a success, I am in limbo. Cut off from heaven, I stew in purgatory.

What is my crime? Am I such a threat?

I must go away and lick my wounds. Give me a leave of absence before I am destroyed.

Three days later I receive a hand written reply from the Office of Elmore Davis:

Leo,

A request for a leave of absence must be read during a board of trustees meeting. Your memo was marked confidential. Do you really want a leave of absence? If you do, you should write another letter.

I understand your feelings. Let me reassure you. On the basis of what has been presented, I will never support a move to dismiss you.

Thank you fordoing an excellent job during the last few weeks.

The note was signed President Davis.

Knowing of his support, I decide I will not apply for a leave of absence and will remain at Humaluh Valley College.

When I get home I tell Cleo the good news. She says "Humph." Karl is watching TV and Arthur is sleeping.

# CHAPTER 42.

# THE PROPHECY OF FRANCIS BUTLER

My happiness in getting strong presidential support is marred by the return of Francis Butler. Walking across the quad after my class I see an unkempt man in the sunlight at the base of the Helix clothed in an unraveling gray sweater, brown pants with ragged bottoms and jogging shoes. After recognizing him I am shocked by Butler's face; white jagged lines separate pink and sallow patches of skin. It is hard to imagine how he had survived the bullet ripping through his skull.

Red beard quivering, Butler screams, "They took my brain. Pffaffkaff keeps it in a jar on his desk. Poor Pffaffkaff. He can no longer walk barefoot in his library. Bone fragments prick his tender soles."

I think, this poor confused man has forgotten the president's name.

Butler paces the concrete as if he were a tiger in a cage. I wonder, did he follow the same pattern in the institution? When tigers are released back into the jungle, do they still pace in rigid rectangles? Do they circle right or left? Is the direction they travel different in the northern and southern hemispheres?

"Leo, why do you stay in this institution?" yells Butler. "You can leave. There is no imperative to slice sand sharks. Do you enjoy pulling the wings off flies? Is there pleasure in cutting up monkeys? You monkey. Me monkey. You do not see. Me see. You think you're free. Listen. I'll tell you why I had to return. None of us are free. Something, some compulsion drives every man and woman. You, they, no one must forget my brain."

"Francis, you haven't gotten the news," I say. "My problem has been settled. There's peace in biology."

"Peace? Smeace. Dogs snap at me. Beggar them. Last night while I slept blood dripped, ran sticky. Came from a cart, ran over the polished boards. The board slept, bored while Pffaffkaff licked my blood. By the sun's light, oh can you see, I'm way past dawning? Look at my face. It is split and ripped. A bulldog tore my forehead open, pulled scarlet ribbons, scarlet ribbons with my hair. Oh on that day my cheeks were red and rosy. A white eyeball rolled to the side pocket."

I shift anxiously from foot to foot. Wonder, did he escape? I am very curious. "Butler how did you get here?"

"Last night I got off the bus. Slept in the woods wrapped in this ski jacket. This morning I walked to my beloved campus. The dogs were frantic. I am lucky I was not bitten. I'd hate to get hurt."

"That's a two mile walk. Good for you."

"Oh Leo. Laugh with me. Let's play music. Stick a flute down my throat. Why do you look away, are you seeking leaves and clean snow? Why look away? On my belly I will lick the snow and chew grass. I applaud divorce and death. I shall go gay to funerals. I congratulate failures and will praise to the dew my dying. Let us sing. Join me. Skip, skip, skip to the dew, skip to the dew my dying, but first get to the butcher as fast as you can."

Hearing enough nonsense I wave goodbye and rapidly walk away. Butler waves goodbye. Reaching home I quickly walk into the house. Cleo looks up. I say, "Mixed news. Butlers out. He's completely mad. His mind is focused on hate and horrible images. He used to be a pacifist. Maybe that's good. If he had been a fighter, after the bulleted destruction, he might have become a killer. Now not peaceful, he raves and howls."

Cleo huffs, "I don't want to hear about sickos. They ought to lock up loonies. And you, who are you to say he's harmless? Are you a psychiatrist?"

Karl is listening. That evening at bedtime he asks, "Dad, do you wish we had a pet werewolf with teeth down to here?" His fingers trace a line from lower lip to chin. Pointing to an empty pair of shoes, he says, "What would you say if those shoes started walking? Vampires can jump fifty feet. I've jumped twenty feet."

"You have not."

"I did. Remember the rock and the sand?"

"By the river. That was a long jump, but it wasn't twenty feet."

"I did so jump twenty feet."

I look closely at my son's mouth. I say, "I see no fangs. Don't think about vampires. Think of the river. On the day of your jump the water was clear as glass. There was a deep green pool. Sleep well my son. Think of the green pool." I turn out the light.

Later, trying to sleep, I keep hearing Butler's voice, like the hiss of a snake. I see a face, a skull with patches of skin stuck on as if with glue. I am almost asleep when a hiss causes me to lift my head. Cleo says, "Go to sleep Leo. Go to sleep," in an angry voice.

I say, "Damn it, I was asleep when you woke me." I turn my back to her. I dream of werewolves.

The next morning, although it is sunny outside, I consider canceling my coffee break. I do not want to see Butler. Remaining in my office, I try to read the text. My mind wanders. Giving up, I walk across the quad, and stop at the Helix. Butler is yowling, his voice unpleasantly harsh. A small crowd watches him the way people stare at a circus freak. Butler says, "My skull is cracked. Pieces of my brain lie on his books, on his table, on his floor. Perhaps he hopes my brains will turn to wine. My brain ferments. Who will drink the wine? Leo. Will you drink from my skull?"

I shudder. The thought upsets me.

"The sand grates on the vault of my skull. Can you feel the sand? When Pffaffkaff walks the floor his feet push against the grains. He dumps the sand on his floor to protect his feet from fragments of bone. He is afraid my teeth will bite him." Butler presses upon his temples with his fingers. "This skull is hollow. A thought comes from the void. Feel the edges of bone, Leo. Touch my head. Feel the vibrations."

I jump. A feeling of repulsion up-wells. "No. No. I don't want to feel your head. I don't need to feel your skull."

Butler turns and faces the administrative offices. He raises his hand as if it holds a wine glass. "Pffaffkaff drink. My cup is full. Drink. Drink to your barefoot past. Drink to Alabama. Drink to your mindless present."

I turn my head, there is no Pffaffkaff.

"Oh. A bee is in my head." Butler pushes against the top of his skull, presses hard. "My head is a kettle drum and the bee goes boom! I wish the bee would go away and come again some other day. Leo and Cleo. How mellifluous." He removes his hands. "Grapes. Clinging grapes of wrath warm in the sun waiting for the harvest moon. They wait for the time of smashing. Oh give thanks. The juice is in the barrel. The wine master sips. Oh look. He frowns. The grapes seemed so fine. Why does he frown? Perhaps the yeast was bad. A foul mould has spoiled the brew. A viper is coiled in the vat. Her slippery scales scrape the walls. Her tongue waggles. She sweetly calls, Taste this wine. Take a chance. One drop is so sweet it can dissolve gold and eat through titanium."

"Francis, you are talking nonsense. I am happy. Cleo and I are happy. Our sons are happy. Things are getting better for us. Why don't you walk in the country? Go talk to some cows!"

"No I will not talk to cows. I am my own man. I have a bullet degree. My skull is my diploma. Listen to my lecture. A, B, C, W, X, Y, Z. Come when you're called. Do as you're bid. Shut the door after you come in. One thing. Do one thing at a time, and do it well. If you dig a ditch, dig the best ditch. Enjoy baseball our national sport. If you get a donkey and he doesn't go, whip him. No, no, no. Its time. Quickly now. All little boys run into the barn, get under the hay. Students. You are my students. You are my sunshine."

A laughing red headed coed says, "Yes Francis. I am your student and your sunshine. If you'll have me, I'll be your old lady."

"I need no old ladies. I want young ones. Girl. What are teachers made of?"

"Snakes and snails and puppy dogs tails?"

"You're wrong. Teachers are made of sneers and leers. A wasp stung me. Stinger in hand he walks the halls. Listen. He says, Hello. Helloooooo. Helloooooo. Helloooooo. Listen to his lullaby of Hellooooo. He is like a grandfather. Does he pat us on the head? No. Perhaps someday? In the month of May he may pattahead, pattahead, pattahead. Patta red head, patta fat head, patta baldhead, shiny head, long head, wide head, cabbage head, patta patta pattahead. Poor me. Brain bye bye. Bye bye. It was just too hard to keep raising the mocking bird, the warbling bird. Oh, I cooed, fuck you, fuck you. What a surprise to those with balls and them that crawls. Listen to the talkatalkatalkers. Listen to wisdom."

I say loudly, "Please Francis. Quiet down. People are listening. You called the president a bastard. You gave him the finger. That's not nice."

"Our voices demonstrate the results of years of experience counseling stooooodents. I understand. I understand you. Sure. Ha. Listen to them understand, Listen. The mourning bells are ringing. Ding, ding, dong. Tick, tick, tock. Listen, they say. Francis, Wake up my boy. Come to your senses. They, where are they? I'm looking for them. Hold out your hands say, Francis, take our hands. Pat my back. Pull up your knees. That's good. Fetal position. Oh look at pretty little Francis. Francis, now you can talk. Go ahead. Talkatalkatalkaway. And after anger is all out, we can go with flowers to the faculty lounge where we will sippasippasippa cup of coffee. And it's such a lovely day for a coffee break. My God. Tension. Here comes Pffaffkaff. A tisket a tasket, let's put him in a mellow basket, and take him to a deep deep well and throw him far away to hell." Butler slips into the woods. The crowd breaks into small groups, most of who go to the cafeteria to sip a beverage and discuss the improvisational performance.

Later that day President Davis reaches the Helix, listens to the metal clang in the breeze. He is unsure how to handle Butler. In Cascadia it is okay to be crazy provided you don't harm yourself or anyone else. The law does not give the president authority to have Butler returned to the institution unless Butler threatens someone's life.

The rumor mills are chattering. Davis wants to keep his distance from the deranged ex choirmaster.

Back in my office, I could not understand why Butler was so fascinated with we Bauers. Why did he keep calling attention to my past troubles? Who had told Butler about the conflict in biology? When had he met Cleo? At the salmon barbecue?

Beetles have difficulty crawling from logs that are being consumed by fire, and swallows smack into lighthouses. In the same way I keep returning to the newest campus attraction. The next day it is raining. There are fewer students clustered around the strange figure on the bench. Flapping his arms, Butler reminds me of a caged starving crow I had seen in Wisconsin by the Flambeau River. The raucous voice pokes into campus nooks and crannies. Raindrops run over the frizzy redness of his beard and cling to the long hair hanging matted over his eyes. The left eye, made of glass, points away from the right eye.

"Do you like watching me Leo?"

"You have an interesting face."

"I bet I do. Later today look at your own face. Your brow, once smooth, now wrinkles from worry waves. Your hair is streaked with gray. Once your eyes were curious. Now they look like dull glowing coals. You bite your lip. Don't want to show anger, do you? Like a marsh you like clean air. Biology has turned brackish. Hydrogen sulfide bubbles to the surface."

"Worry about yourself," I say. "Don't think about me. My battles are all in the past." I march angrily into the forest and disappear behind some trees. Some of the students are open mouthed at my anger. Those who do not know about the conflict in biology will soon hear details from friends in the cafeteria. There is lots of entertainment at Humaluh Valley CC.

Once out of sight of the small crowd, I creep back to the forest edge and lay in a depression behind a huge rotting umber log. I listen as Butler, like an angerhawk, directs his shrill voice towards me, though I am hidden. I peep over the ferny top.

"I have a prophecy for Leo Bauer. He will again meet with the dean and the dean will again say, I am your friend. He will again meet with his division chairman, and the other chairman. The president will say, I am your friend. However they will in addition, as a consequence, regardless, nevertheless, even as you well know and are aware, the problem as you no doubt agree, this institution, fewer students, enrollment is down, you must realize your performance, personal problems, student complaints. Of course some admire you. You have followers. Nevertheless, on the balance, overall, consider the situation. Understand our position. For a long time we have been your friend. Have you any ideas? What should we do? Come, let us reason together. We do not hate you. We like you. Most assuredly we will mourn your passing. However most severe economic problems. Your dissolution means savings of eleven thousand three hundred and thirty three drachmas. Using these and other funds, with wise financial management we can with scrimping hire part time replacements, reduce course offerings, take this and other savings, in the aggregate a magnificent sum, super total including labor tax, birth tax, marriage tax, life tax, death tax, coffin tax, funeral tax, burial tax, and thumb tax all subtotals, through addition, subtraction and multiplication $26,664.00 saving or enough money to hire an additional full time administrator.

"Do you understand? We are your friends. Goodbye. Our best wishes. Have a happy new year. Love to the wife and kids. Joy to the world. Good by dear friend." Butler laughs jovially, sounding like Santa Claus.

I wonder, Can I have him committed? Perhaps I can make a citizen's commitment, like we make citizen's arrests. Maybe a phone call this evening will do it. I don't want the students to listen to this nonsense. They might be superstitious and believe.

Butler turns serious. "Oh my dear friends. Leaving that meeting Leo will probably think they are his friends. He is so naive," He chuckles for an instant, then looks up in shock. "No. I cannot laugh. Someone has stolen laughter. Should we consider the administrators? Are they human? Do they have feelings? Certainly. They will not laugh at your dissolution. Imagine them looking sad. Listen to them: Poor Leo Bauer is dead. The struggle has killed him. He lies in the parlor, the funeral parlor. Can you see him? Look." Butler points at the ground with his long thin arm. He slowly moves his arm in an arc across the horizon while saying, "A burying beetle, a sexton dressed in black chauffeurs the Cadillac meat wagon. The beetle speaks. 'Listen. What a shame. So young. In this hour of your bereavement, several options. Difficult to talk. I know. You're all choked up. Nevertheless we must decide. Choose. Choose what your beloved Leo would have wanted. Consider your needs. This model, fine stainless steel mirror finish. Mourners can see reflections of falling tears. Don't forget, concrete vault required by law unless you're on an Indian Reservation.'"

I feel bad imagining myself dead. I wonder if Butler's precognition is accurate. Butler sings in a high falsetto, like a boy at summer camp, "Oh the worms stay in and the worms stay out and the worms play pinochle on his snout." Holding his hands out, palms flat to the sky he says, "Excuse me? I thought we should consider the worms. Leo was a naturalist." His voice becomes somber. "Memorial service. Sad. So sad. Time for the testimonial. Dear brethren. Our departed father, friend, brother, wage earner, husband. What's that you say? Only a wooden box? Didn't want to spend more. I know. Wot a shame. Wot a shame." Butler sobs in a weak snively way.

Tears dried, Butler assumes a rhetorical voice. "Poor old Kalija Bauer. Poor old young worried chewed up thrown out bone. Now and at the hour of your termination, of your death. Death in the jumbled garage with the doors closed and the car running. That last sudden high from Elavil overdose, holy holy face blot from gunshot, the warm salty flow from sliced wrists. Oh ponder that last drink. Go grandly, soar in a magnificent leap from the Devil's Shortcut to the rocks. Splot!. Splot. Wot a shame. The bottle broke emptied; the wheels spin on your jolly jolly car in the ditch. In hospital drug heaven your skin yellows and a toe falls off. My friends anything but old age. That's no fun. So sad, Look at his face. Dead. Why did it have to happen? He was such a nicea, nicea, nicea, nicea person. True. He had problems. That's why we had to let him go. Hated to do it. In fact we, all of the administration are very sad. Smell the roses. The president picked them himself. Smell the carnations. The faculty has sent a huge basket of red and white mums. Sniff, sniff, sniff. And the dean, our good kind dean has sent violets. Sweet violets." His voice rises on the lets. "Sweeter than the carnations."

"Oh poor unhappy Leo. If there was only something we could have done. We did whot we could. Poor fellow. He's happier now at the hour, at the ticking last second, at the first silent second of his death. Let us pray for the soul of our departed brother." Imitating an organ Butler plays Bach funeral music. Da da dum, da da Dum, da, da da da da da dum, da da da da da da dum, da da dum, da da dum.

"Let us now listen to Leo Bauer. In his grave he talks." Butler's voice becomes loud and bellicose. "In my grave I bellow in rage, grind my teeth and bite my lips to shreds. What else should I do? I can't Sit up in this wretched box. I will smash the wood with my enraged skull? We will drill some holes in the coffin lid. I have to breathe. Fragments of bone, to mix with spines of Hawthorne. Sucking air into rotting lungs. We hear his voice. I sing of my brothers with putrescent bubbling. Oh the man who knifed me is my friend. He's a buddy through and through. When he bit off my balls, he was my buddy too. It's OK. You can have a bite. Chew, chew, chew.

"Forget about Bauer's fate. My outsides are like Bauer's insides. Look at my shriveled eyes. My bony frame. My emaciated face. Before Bauer left us, I too was destroyed, in spite of, because of, in deference to you my friends. Thank you for all your help. And now as I bid adieu, this is the time I must grieve thee, for the best of friends must part. It's so sad. So sad. I'm all choked up." He softly cries. Raising his head silently he watches a gull fly from horizon to horizon. He softly sings, *Hush a bye baby in the tree top* and walks away.

I wait a few minutes, then head into the woods to emerge behind the cafeteria where I drink a Seven Up. My stomach is upset. My head hurts. My forehead is tight.

I keep away from the campus madman for the next few days. At night I wake up several times thrashing about. Listening, Cleo says later, she heard me sing, "*The worms come in, the worms go out. The worms play pinochle on my snout.*"

I try to sort my thoughts out in my journal. In addition to writing about my recent fears of death, I write: Francis is different. Say what you will the man is original. He is crazy. I wonder if I am going crazy. Cleo notices I'm now affected by full moons. Francis says whatever comes into his mind. Isn't that supposed to be healthy? It is bad to be repressed. Yes he is crazy. Crazy people scare the hell out of me, not because I think they're going to hit me, but because when I'm around them I tend to imitate them. Whenever I'm around Francis, part of me starts thinking the way he thinks. I'd be the wrong person to work in a mental institution. I'd probably identify more with the inmates than with the staff. This is why I must avoid Francis Butler and stay away from cuckoos.

I know what he says is meaningless, and won't come true; nonetheless, his words are disturbing.

I am in my office Wednesday trying to think of some way to lure Butler away from the college. I wistfully recall the days when sailors were shanghaied. Perhaps I should sneak some amyl nitrate out of the lab and create a Butler Cocktail; offer it to him as a gesture of eternal friendship. I can drag him to a boxcar and ship him north across the border: They can always use another Canadian Mountie.

"Oh hell," I leave my office and walk over to the Helix. Butler is there. The day is sunny, fat clouds above, humid and oppressive.

Butler looks deeply into my eyes. He says, "Mann and Isawaddy are in the chemistry lab watching an orange retort. I peek through the window. Bubbles of carbolic acid are popping. The foul vapor is sucked away by fans.

Listen. They are making an oath.

'Not for seven years may Bauer again teach the young. He may not touch the furred ones or watch the scaly creatures. Instead may he do what now repels him. May he stuff the envelopes, add the figures, work in windowless buildings as a clerk, becoming all that he has condemned. May he not get paid for his writings or earn another dime doing what he enjoys. When in the future anyone writes for a reference, the truth shall be told, that the man's destiny is clerking, that he shall be tossed off Darwin's Mighty Road. May his dogs have puppies by caesarean section, his plants wither and his life become routine. That'll teach him to give us static. May landlords evict him and his banker charge him high interest rates. That'll teach him to give us static. May he lose on every real estate transaction. May his savings vanish and his income decline. May his optimism turn to cynicism. May what gives him joy give him sadness. May women mock him, and his listeners yawn. May his travelling cease. May he nightly grind his teeth worrying about money and health. May his hair fall out, his car break down, and his clothes grow shabby. May the environmentalists reject him. Let him become lonely. That'll teach him to give us static.

"'Because we are a forgiving administration we shall be kind. Let him not be covered with boils. However, let there be a few more additions. May his canoe sink and his books get moldy. May calcium spurs form in his joints and alcohol give him no pleasure. May his hamburger catsup squirt on his shirt and his soup dribble and stick in his beard. May women criticize him. May his BVD's get ink stained and lose their elasticity. May he scorch his omelets and burn onions. May his Lettuce get limp, his bread get moldy and his taste buds aestivate. May his mattress get lumpy, his phonograph become armless, his glasses become scratched, his ears fill with wax, his hearing vanish, his tongue get coated with green, and his teeth hurt and get covered with tarter. May he piss blood, get strange lumps on his chest, and have ulcers on his guts like mushrooms on manure. May he become afraid to look others in the eye and may his voice quiver. That'll teach him to give us static.

This curse will last from anon until all nine planets line up after the sun disappears.'"

During Butler's recital most of the students have been grinning and giggling.

My reply is loud and clear, "May your bullshit cover your ears and float you on a tide of horsepiss, with cow manure, out to sea on the waters of the mighty Humaluh. May you be taken out to sea, may crabs eat your flesh, may your bones be used as drumsticks by cannibals, may the world forget you ever existed, may your remnants wash up on a beach in California after an earthquake and may a tidal wave obliterate your landfall as people say, what's zat?"

Butler asks, "Leo, do you accept your curse?"

I say, "Francis do you accept your curse."

He says, "I am a musician. Your curse lacks music. Do you accept your curse?"

"I'm a scientist. I don't believe in curses!" I say expelling my words with such anger that drops of my spit fall on Butler's shaggy red beard to glisten in the sunlight.

Wiping his whiskers with his fingers, Butler says, "Leo. Who are you?"

"I'm a halted wanderer," I say.

"Who else are you?"

"I'm a professor. A teacher of the young."

"Are you alive? Let me touch you. You look like a faggot. I'm a faggot and I want to touch you."

"Don't you dare faggotize me. Keep your mitts off."

"Are you really a man? Do you breathe? Can you fart? Who are you?"

"I'm strong as a bull. Women love me. I'm a great lover. My voice is weak today because my ego is low."

"You're full of shit."

"You will always ve a slimy slug."

"You're wrong. I can be anything I want to be. If I lose my job, I can become a truck driver, a commercial halibut fisherman, or a logger. If I want to I can become another Zorba the Greek. I'm dammed if I'll ever become a clerk or a laborer."

"Once you could do those things, but now you are a pile of uncoordinated bones lacking ligaments. You are nothing. You will be whatever I prophesize"

"Watch me, I'll show you what I can do." Shucking my lethargy I cartwheel across the quad. Upon reaching the far side I screech to a halt on my feet and say loudly. "I will ignore him. His prophecies are bullshit. I am not superstitious. This is the twentieth century. Let him plague other people. I am rid of him. If I see him again, I'll say be gone Satan. Be gone Satan. Be gone Satan. That'll take care of the Butler problem."

True to my word, from that day on I kept out of earshot of the deranged ex choirmaster and took wide detours around the little group clustered near the Helix. When discussions with friends mention Butler, I change the topic. I forget about the dumb prophecy.

# CHAPTER 43.

## A SIMPLE SOLUTION FOR TRANQUILITY

Two weeks before the end of spring quarter my telephone rings. I hear the gentle voice of Mrs. McGowen "You are invited to a meeting with President Davis."

Her words hurtle me into a cess pool of anxiety. I find my way to the meeting through swirling brain fog. Taking a chair I wait for new news of my fate. It seems as if I am always waiting for word. As if I no longer have control over what happens.

Isawaddy is smoothing a sheet of paper. He reads to me, "A delegation of students came to me. They said, 'Mr. Bauer is incompetent. Our physic's laboratories are dull and confusing. Our examinations come back late.'" Isawaddy rolls up the sheet, sticks it into the pocket of his sport's coat, and continues. "As you know Elmore, Students are very important to me. I've checked the preregistration list. Bauer's laboratories are short of students." His voice turns soft, lulling, "We know Leo has had more than his share of problems. But, the reason we teach is the students. Bauer must leave biology and physics. This problem cannot continue."

I feel like I am in the dentist's chair. The dentist says, just a prick. This won't hurt much. I push on my thumbnail until one pain is replaced by another. I wonder, is Davis now capitulating to biology and physics. Those labs are mechanical. I hate telling about crystal lattices and I don't give a shit about how molecules come together. My physics includes shimmering color; the spectrum through a prism. Looking through a kaleidoscope. Turning two wheels. The outer one of blue, red, clear triangles. The one closest to the three mirrors green, orange and frosted Paisley. My physics are fractals, the patterns of pine cones and the spirals of sea shells: The fragmented parts are each exactly like the whole.

President Davis clasps and unclasps his hands as if he is trying to squeeze the problem away. Looking at his desk he speaks with gravitas. "We all know the background of this matter. There is merit on both sides. One side is not all right, and one side is not all wrong. I have spent much thought and have worried long about the discord in the Science Division. Leo I realize that you have trouble working with people and are too ready to go your own way.

"I also realize that the biology department has boxed you in. You haven't been able to teach the courses you have wanted to teach, therefore you have been frustrated.

"This matter must be resolved. I will stake much of what I am on the final resolution of this issue. It has divided our faculty, ruined our sleep, broken friendships, and is bad for our college.

"After giving this problem my full attention, I have reached a solution."

Of course I lean forward. Relishing his moment of triumph the president hesitates, says, "Bauer, You must leave the Biology Department." His hand waves a calming signal as I look up in alarm. "You will like your new assignment. Congratulations Leo. You are the new director of our environmental program. Congratulations." Getting up from his chair Davis strides around the desk, comes over to me and shakes my hand. I force a grin. He grins. It is hard after such a long struggle to believe in my good fortune.

With a single decisive stroke the president has solved the problem. We all shake hands and happily talk as if there had never been discord.

The news spreads. Fellow teachers congratulate me. Everyone says how happy they are. Finally the troubles are over. I can't wait to tell Cleo. Now I can devote all of my energies to working on ecology. All that day I break into occasional bits of song.

The good news brings out the Crunch and Munch Society Marching Band. They trot the campus sidewalks and corridors, cheeks puffing, trombones and trumpets blasting, drums booming, following Tom Magnum's inspiring lead as he om pah pahs his tuba, glistening full mustache, resplendent; his new red velvet performance vest glowing in the sunshine. The chorus sings:

> We will have peace in the valley.
> Thanks to our noble president
> Tranquility has come to Humaluh.
> Humanities welcomes environmental studies.
> Hallelujah, hallelujah, hallelujah.

I softly say. "It sounds like Christmas, Haydn and John Phillip Souza and the U.S. Marines are in the land of the Humaluh."

The bands corny song continues:

> Joy
> Our president has triumphed
> With wisdom over ignorance,
> Scholarship over mindlessness
> He has discovered a solution
> Let us be happy.
> Glory, glory, glory.

I run alongside the band, next to Alfo. He and I tumble, twirl and spin cartwheels. Students smile. Birds sing. The sun breaks through the clouds. The world is happy.

Later that afternoon, at our house, Cleo is reticent to enter into the universal joy. I say, "Don't be a party pooper." Building a log fire I sit by the flames sipping brandy, smiling, imagining my glorious future creating an ecological empire.

Later that evening, while dining at the Big Steer Steak House, the board of directors toasts the president's solution with sparkling burgundy.

The Cascadia Teacher's Association newspaper headlines:

**TEACHER'S ASSOCIATION WINS ACADEMIC STRUGGLE. THERE IS PEACE AT HUMALUH.**

I meet with Dean Mann Monday to receive my new job description. Walking into his office, I imagine myself to be a man of destiny. Mann neglects to tell me that many of my new duties had been thought up and agreed upon at a meeting in the Schnitzel Haus where the Dean and Bobby Pompa pleasantly plastered and hysterically chortling attempted to surpass one another in inventing interesting tasks for the new chief of the Humaluh Environmental Program.

I mumble, "The road of life has hairpin turns."

Dean Mann, super friendly asks "Would you like a cup of mocha?" It was the first time I had heard the steam of his new office espresso machine. A minute later I huddle with the Dean as if we are pals. I shift my look from the Dean's face to the piece of paper on the coffee table. Mann says, "Leo, your life is really going to change. We've got some important assignments for you. You'll be in the Humanities Division under Joseph Apfelboeck. You will be expected to attend all Humanity Division meetings. To help you plan the evening environmental studies program, you will meet several times a month with J. M. Keene, the Director of Continuing Studies."

Mann gulps a mouthful of coffee and continues explaining my future with amazing specificity. "Because your environmental classes will be taught in the science classrooms, please continue to cooperate with John Isawaddy in the use of equipment and space. You will move into the big leagues by meeting regularly with representatives of the University of Cascadia to ensure the easy transferability of your courses to senior institutions. You will be able to learn more about acting when you meet with the people in drama to arrange the details for the annual Environmental Symposium that you will chair. A generous budget of over two hundred dollars will enable you to bring nationally known speakers to Humaluh.

"Community groups and schools will appreciate you for the non credit ecology workshops you will develop and lead in Duhkwuh, Canaltown, Ship Harbor, Quimper and Salmontown.

"You will, in addition, apply for grants from the Federal and Cascadian governments for environmental education. You will use the funds you receive from these grants to develop a comprehensive environmental curriculum for our college. After you develop the curriculum, I will have to check it over. I expect no problems with the process." The dean gives me a heart-warming smile. How could I have ever thought evil thoughts about him?

"Make sure you check with me at least once each month, so I'll know how you're progressing. You won't have time to be bored. For additional stimulation we've split your teaching load between the Duhkwuh main campus and our satellite Quimper campus."

Upon hearing of my duties, I say, "I'm flattered by your confidence in me."

"I'm sure you won't let us down," says Mann. "Oh. I almost forgot. There are just a few more tasks I'd like to show you."

We read the additional tasks, making up the Deans List, while sitting side by side like old friends.

THE DEAN'S LIST

ETHICAL TASKS:

Teach coeds birth control in the privacy of your office.

Befriend them by giving them foams, creams, gels, and condoms.

Convince local Catholics of the merits of the loop, the pill, abortion, sterilization, oral sex and masturbation.

Talk local evangelists into saving energy by bathing with friends.

Research the practicality of initiating the taxation of new products to pay for their disposal down the road.

Convince Penneysaved, Side O'Beef, Grosshamhock, Dutchshoe, Earthmole, Wadzook, and Bangfender to contribute ten percent of their income to an environmental endowment fund. Using those funds construct an environmental museum. If you succeed, you shall become the curator.

Convince the state legislature to Support the Death Penalty for those convicted of wasting energy with electric knives, automatic window openers, electric purple grapes and other wasteful devices.

POLLUTION TASKS:

Discover how industry can cut air and water pollution by eighty percent without upping the cost of their products. Organize and march with the state grocers on the state capital and demand mandatory returnable bottle legislation.

Initiate research at Humaluh on the development of a carbolic acid formaldehyde resin to use in the manufacture of pressed wood chipboard at the human body temperature of 98.7 degree Fahrenheit.

Bury a new Luxury SUV contributed by a local car dealership.

Measure the auditory pollution of rock bands and encourage the county health department to close them down when the decibel level goes over 100.

To show the evil of water pollution, throw dead fish in the river.

At night, shine arc lights on factory smokestacks to discover the exact time of pollutant release.

To stop air pollution in the valley, raise the height of smoke stacks of the pulp mills by one hundred feet.

To reduce anal emissions, distribute carbon cork filters to faculty and students.

ENERGY TASKS:

Persuade the AEC to construct giant windmills up and down the coast.

Develop a nonpolluting car that gets 80 miles a gallon.

Encourage the grounds crew to trim the grass and weeds with hand mowers. Have the crew trim blackberries and vines using Namibian goats.

Block the construction of the Kickapoo Dam. Delay the Alaskan Pipeline.

Develop a safe way to bring 900,000-barrel oil tankers past the Ten Thousand Islands off the mouth of the Humaluh. Perhaps your students can investigate the feasibility of moving the islands so as to avert danger.

TRANSPORTATION TASKS:

Arrange a compromise between the supporters and the opponents of the SST. Convince the Humaluh Port Commission to construct a local landing field for the SST.

Convince the trucking industry to ship by rail.

CONSERVATION TASKS:

Merge the U.S. Forest Service and the Sierra Club.

Tell Japan and Russia not to kill any more of the big whales. If your advice is ignored, build a campus aquarium to preserve a breeding pod of the last blue whales.

Establish a brain tank next to the whale tank where scholars can solve the major ecological problems of our era.

Use junk mail for your stationary.

Transplant the endangered Redwoods into sanctuaries spread across the southern United States.

Supervise the relocation of Alaskan seals into marine waters where they are wanted. Provide conseling for the seals to raise their low self-esteem.

Encourage students to attend the Duwamps opera and stick chewed gum on coats made from wild mammals.

Stop the wind from blowing the Oregon Dunes out to sea.

Put bricks in toilets.

Eat beavers and save trees.

## PLANNING AND LAND USE TASKS:

Supervise the construction of satellite cities around Duwamps separated by forests and lakes.

Gently twist the wrists of realtors until they agree to oppose the future commercial and residential development of shorelines.

In the dead of night destroy Duhkwuh's riverside business district and convert the land into gardens, walkways, and outdoor restaurants. Disclaim any connection with the college if you are caught.

Meet with Ralph Nader and James Buckley to plan national ecological priorities for the future.

## ADDITIONAL TASKS:

Ask the Ponderosa pines in Los Angeles why they are dying.

Stop the annual emission of 200 million pounds of salt spray, 40,000 pounds of cosmic dust deposition, and the release of 24 million pounds of earth dust from and on our county.

Lower the Humaluh Dam.

Have praise services conducted by recently widowed praying mantids for black widow spiders mourning their mates, and ladybird beetles for the loss of their homes.

I go home immediately after the meeting, show Cleo the list of my new duties, and say, "Let's celebrate."

Cleo turns into a party pooper by saying, "You fool. This is impossible. You can't do all of those tasks. It's a set-up"

I say, "You're wrong. This is my big chance. Why are you always such a wet blanket?" I grab a bottle of brandy, stomp to my study, and celebrate alone.

Now Cleo and I are avoiding one another.

During the summer, I work like a slave preparing environmental lectures and laboratories, reading environmental books, and taking still and cinema photographs of vegetation, wildlife, shorelines, smokestacks and factories. I want to prove myself to the administration and Cleo.

# CHAPTER 44.

## ALL POTATOES AND NO MEAT

Burning the midnight oil, I focus my energy on the new assignment. After creating a complete environmental studies program on paper, I take my proposals to the Dean. The dean takes my proposals to the Directed Instruction Committee. I am not at the meeting. Tom Seuss, the student representative, told me later what happened.

"Bauer has put a great amount of time into these proposals," said the Dean. "I commend him. Unfortunately, there are too many potatoes and not enough meat."

"How can we have more meat? What do you recommend? Mutton or rabbit?" asked Tom.

The committee voted to have another meeting. Two weeks later, when I see Seuss at the water fountain, I amble over and ask, "How is my proposal coming?"

"We're still discussing it," says Seuss.

I say, "You'll have graduated, and transferred to the university, gotten married and had five kids by the time you guys approve it."

Seuss says, "I voted for it. The dean throws roadblocks."

A couple of week's later standing at the urinal, eyes straight ahead, I read, "This is probably the most important thing you've done all day."

The voice of Seuss intrudes, "I'm sorry, we rejected your proposal. The Dean again said, 'too many potatoes and not enough meat.'" I shake myself, zip up, and leave the urinal forgetting to thank Tom for the news. Walking into Mann's office I ask, "How are things going?"

Mann says, "Sorry, it has to be rewritten."

I say, "How can I develop a program if you say no to everything I suggest?"

"It wasn't me. It was the committee," says Mann.

"Hell. You're the committee. They listen to you," I say.

After meeting me the dean had coffee with the director of planning and Seuss. Making a sour face, he said, "The problem with Bauer goes back two years. That man just doesn't want to work with other people."

"Why don't you call him in for a little talk?" said Eckhart.

"I have tried to talk and to work with him, but it doesn't work out. We'll have to find some way to take care of this problem."

After meeting with the Dean, I have coffee with Malander. "My environmental program was turned down. I got the word at the urinal."

"Were you pissed off?" says Malander chuckling.

I glare at him. "I thought you were above punning. You are lucky. The students have to take your classes. As for me, I have to entice them. I have to be sweet to everyone. When I meet someone in the hall, I say, take ecology, and he or she says, Whaz zat? Next Sunday I'm going to church, just to get recruits. The girls. The pretty girls take only required science courses. The Voc Tech students take only required academic courses. Science students won't take more science."

"Talk to the counselors. Take them out to dinner."

"Hell. The counselors think elective courses are a waste of time. They go by the book."

"Do you have any students?"

"Yes. I have some humanities majors. They take a perverse delight in taking electives."

Malander moves closer. His voice acquires a confidential tone. "Other than your recent meeting with the dean, how are the two of you getting along? Has he ever forgiven you for not using the book?"

"Usually he's friendly. Last week his secretary gave me the environmental file. It contained a little letter the dean had written to the University of Cascadia. Delightful. The note said, Leo Bauer is our coordinator of environmental education. We've had some differences but are confident his courses will merge with your expectations."

"Can you imagine? The man's an expert with left handed complements. He destroyed any impact I might make on those clowns at the U. No wonder I'm ignored."

"Nice man," says Malander. "Don't take it so bad. It's not as bad as you think. He did say 'your courses will merge with theirs.'"

After saying goodbye, I wander off.

My aggravation with the dean continues to the next day when I hear that my old friend from physics, Dr. Sharp, has won approval of a new program. His request was on a half-page note written on a napkin. The committee accepted it on the first go around.

I am amazed how long I hold up after so many reversals. A lesser man would explode. Consider the missile business. An expert can program a missile to explode at a particular point and a specific time. Another expert, if given the data before the explosion, can say exactly where and when the missile will explode. Human affairs are more complicated. No one has ventured a guess as to the hour or second when I will hiss like a flare, ssszzzt like a fizzler, and blow up like a cherry bomb. Most of my colleagues actually expect me to muddle through, and I guess according to their expectations I am continuing with my normal progression or regression, although at times I seem to be irregular in my movements as if I was having trouble with my propulsion system.

Although I distrust business, I think I would have been better off working for a large corporation. My new courses would have been called a new product line. The firm would have devoted thousands of hours to the design, manufacturing and publicity of the new products. In the event of success, I would have been promoted. After a clash with the Division Director, I would have either been fired, or given a transfer, new duties and three assistants.

I know the humanities division will not be paradise. My new colleagues are overworked, teach large classes, receive less money for supplies and have fewer teaching assistants than the science teachers. I will compete for limited funds.

Once the Environmental Studies Program is approved, I will be the only teacher. I will have no one with whom to talk, plan, or dream. There will be no one to tell my fears unless I spill my guts to someone like Malander.

I write a note to Apfelboeck thanking him for his help. I add, "I want to become part of the decision making process. Please halt my isolation."

In a return note Apfelboeck wrote, "I understand and will help out."

At the end of my first year in the new division, I am given a dittoed form to evaluate my division chairman. I write, "I have been too isolated from the teachers in the division to make many comments. Apfelboeck seems like a nice man, he handles paperwork efficiently. He seems fair. This is what I can say about Joseph Apfelboeck."

At the same time I was judging, I was being judged. A mother came storming in to Dean Mann. "You should have told us that John was doing D work."

"I'm sorry Mrs. Randall. We only send home the final grades."

"John told me all about Mr. Bauer. That mans eccentric. No wonder John got a D."

"I'm aware of Bauer's eccentricity. We're trying to do something about the situation, but the teacher's union is very      powerful."

"I was so proud of John. Why he spent an entire evening with my daughter Joyce, clipping photographs and typing the report. And he's a hard worker. He puts in twenty hours a week as a bus boy."

"He sounds like a fine boy."

"You've been nice about this injustice. Even so," she looked the dean in the eyes, "John's mother and I will complain to the board if the grade remains the same."

"I'll see what I can do," said the dean.

After meeting with the girl friend's mother, the Dean called me into his office. Sitting across from me he says, "Leo, Randall's girl friend's mother is all riled up. If you don't change his grade she will go to the board."

"If you want me to change it, I will change it."

"Good. It's important to have good community relations."

"I agree. The D was too high. I'll change it to an F."

"John's mother will also go to the board."

"You should have seen his paper. His lines were quadruple spaced. They hang in whiteness. He scissored most of the report out of magazines. Should he get a C for that?"

"It's your decision."

"I required a ten page report. He typed twenty lines separated by pictures."

"A picture's worth a thousand words. He's got well over ten pages."

"Do you want me to give him a C?"

"If it goes to the board and you lose, it'll be another strike against you, but it's your decision. I don't care what you do."

"Thanks for the advice," I say in a sullen voice. The next day I walk to the registrar and say, "Change this grade to a C."

Most of the time I am not vindictive when I give low grades. Students have to earn a D. Many of the D students are my favorites. Some of the poorest students are fantastic in bull sessions. The D, therefore, was not a rejection of John Randall by me. The rejection came after I gave the youth the C. After that, I no longer spoke to him. Randall, by contrast, seemed quite jovial, and tried without success to engage me in conversation whenever we passed on the quad.

Bobby Pompa was aware of my new ecology class, which finally was approved.

Sally Thompson told me, "I asked Dr. Pompa if ecology would be a good class for me?"

"What did he tell you?" I asked her.

"He smiled and said, 'Sure, if you want to pick up tin cans and bottles!'"

"That son of a bitch," I said.

My class was concerned with more than picking up cans and bottles. In fact I hate picking up trash. One day a book salesman found me in and we chatted. I told him that early in college I had majored in journalism. He asked, "Have you ever thought of writing a book?" By the time he left, I had halfway promised to put together a book of ecological readings. Now if I can only find the time.

I often show films. In the logging film students became chain saws, and yell Timber!

To better understand engineers I showed an earth moving film, in which they became roaring trucks and bulldozers.

In the jungle in South America they were howler monkeys, parakeets, and tapirs, and in Africa trumpeting elephants and laughing hyenas.

Nevertheless people continued to mock me as shown by the note in my faculty mailbox that said: Leo. Have you ever thought, if we did away with cars the highways would be covered with horseshit?

I was tolerant of most of the faculty except the engineers and teachers of business courses. This was unfortunate, because the engineers were trying to solve some major ecological problems relating to the use of energy. Despite criticisms, the college engineers had designed and built a gas powered water wheel for moving water uphill, and had in addition constructed a huge fan that was used to propel sailboats.

I was more humdrum in my approach to the saving of energy. I tried to get my students to use existing technology. One project was to get people to bicycle to work. When Johnny Petrus applied for work at a grocery store he mentioned, "I'm going to bicycle to work."

The assistant manager said, "If you bicycle to work, the manager won't hire you. Once one of our employees rode a bike. By the time he got to work he was too tired to stack shelves. He also lacked the energy to run when he parked shopping carts. Why don't you buy a car?"

"I can't buy a car," said Petrus.

"Why not? Don't you save money?"

"I don't have a job. If I had a job, I'd have some money. Then I could save some money."

"And you could buy a car?"

"Yes," said Petrus, neglecting to say, I wanted to ride a bicycle for ecology. To reduce green house gases.

I overhear two students discussing how to finance a college education:

"I'm trying to enroll."

"What is the trouble?"

"I need a government loan."

"So why don't you apply for one?"

"I can't get it unless I'm enrolled."

"So?"

"I can't enroll without the government loan."

"So what else is new?"


I write in my journal:

I saw Red today. She is sexy in a waitress miniskirt. She was in my first biology class. "It's been a couple of years." I said, "Do you miss Humaluh?"

Examining her fingernails, she said, "That funny farm?"

I remember her for her intellect. Today she tried to be funny. She said, "Its better to have a bottle in front of me than a frontal lobotomy."

I didn't laugh.

Earlier, in class, a boy about eighteen couldn't understand a continuum. I wanted to go on to other material, but he kept saying, I don't understand.

It was like an obsession with him. Most of the class quickly understood how populations merge with populations. Like a dog wrestling with a stick, he wouldn't let go. I wanted to go on to other material. I had programmed myself to rush through the definitions and get the linear stuff out of the way, but he was confused, stuck on a term that was not essential to my presentation. Running out of time, frustrated, I steam rolled over him by saying, "We can talk about it after class."

Later, in talking, I noticed he was nervous. His hands were sweaty. He asked me, do you spank your children?

I said "occasionally," and felt like a monster. When I asked, "Were you spanked?" he said, "Often, with a belt." He looked like a whipped puppy.

Trying to justify myself, I said, "after a spanking I give a hug and say I love you."

"You equate punishment with love?" he asked.

I said, "Once my son Karl walked across a bridge while balancing on a railing eighty feet above some train tracks. I gave him one hell of a spanking for doing that; then I gave him a big hug. Sometimes they go together."

"Maybe," said my student.

While eating a cinnamon roll I overheard students discussing my grading. "You have so many points, see, and if you get enough points you get an A."

"Did you say you need 25% to get a C?"

"No. You need 50% for a C."

"Rough class?"

"Yup."

"When do you have your final?"

"We don't have finals. For our last test Bauer makes us flap our arms and act like crows."

"For your final?"

"YUP."

"I'm going to sign up for ecology."

"I have a half day tomorrow. How about you?"

"So do I."

"Its a rough life."

"Yup."

"By the way. Does the name Pavlov ring a bell?"

This conversation is an oversimplification of course. On the final exam a youth wrote, "Crockodials are endangered in Florida canals. Crockodiales evolved before prehyrsteric birds." When asked about alternative futures for civilization, he wrote, "Atomic bombs could eliminate all problems. They'd kill everybody and we could start over." One student was optimistic, "My house will be made of logs. I'll cut the logs myself and raise my own food. I don't know about the rest of civilization, but I'll be OK."

I asked the students what grade they thought they had earned. The replies included:

"There are 26 letters in the English language, 16 in the Mayan, 14 phonetic sounds in the Greek. Choose one. Who cares?"

"I think I deserve a high C or a low B. The knowledge I gained in this course is really a lot more useful than a lot of the technical crap taught in most courses. I really wanted to go on those field trips, but I had to work Saturdays and Sundays to get enough bread to go to school. See you next quarter. I enjoyed this class."

"I want a B because I want to transfer to the university of Cascadia, and I need the grade point average."

"Sorry I didn't put myself out on the term project."

One student was grateful to me for giving him a passing grade when his scores fell after the death of his father.

Other replies said:

"Didn't take the course for a grade. Made a contribution. Be my guest."

"If the grade for this course is determined by what the individual has learned, I would say I rate a B. If you determine the grade on group participation my grade should be somewhat lower."

"Give me a B please because when I was in class I was active. Also I spent a normal amount of time on my class report. I was unable to come to all classes because of reasons I was unable to control."

Cindy Bogsman wrote: "B is for Bogsman. C for Cindy. C+ for mediocrity."

A note in violet marker ink said: "I think that somewhere this class got off the track, and we all spent a lot of time airing our respective biases. It was all very interesting."

Another note made me feel like the pope: "Although I don't need the credit, I would appreciate your indulgence if you give me an incomplete until you receive my paper that I can mail in three days."

One youth who had not read any of the required class readings wrote, "I believe I have participated in almost every discussion this class had. Although my attendance wasn't great, I feel that when I was here I put out 100%, I think I deserve at least a C grade."

I imagine myself in 1980. I have left teaching for a better job. Wearing a blue pin stripe suit, I sit at the front table of the Cascadian Power Company waiting to testify in favor of a nuclear reactor. My mind contemplates the time later in the evening when I will sit by the fire in my quarter of a million dollar waterfront home. The fire dies down and I toss on a handful of dollar bills for warmth. The servants have all gone to bed. There is work to do. I play a tape of the hearing. Gritting my teeth, I listen to the objections of some irrational local environmentalists. They have made my life miserable lately. I worry about getting an ulcer. No telling what those fanatics will do. They might even bomb my house. But why should I worry. My company will build me another.

# CHAPTER 45.

## WHAT IS OUR LIFE?

My sixth teaching year is our eleventh marriage year, my eleventh year spent in colleges and will be the twenty-fourth year I have spent in school. I am thirty-seven years old. It is 1970.

A Duwamps radio announcer, Sidney Blackburn, said, "You can tell a lot about a person by looking at their shoes."

It is therefore time to take another look at Cleo and me.

In 1970 Cleo is for women's rights. She is also an obsessive housekeeper. She hates my possessions as much as my grandmother hated the art objects collected by her husband. Cleo hates my dedication to work, says I never make time for the family, and do not help her much when she fires or markets the clay beer mugs she moulds with her hands. Each cadmium blue mug is a man with fat cheeks and full laughing mouth and a gigantic full mustache. Her mug men do not resemble me. Perhaps they are modeled on a former lover. She went with a plumber until our romance. Perhaps the plumber is on the beer mugs. They do not show a biologist, researcher, ecologist, harumpher, or pshawer.

I admit, I don't take her craft seriously. Hell, what kind of an artist can only make things when their confidence is high? And when she gets angry, she becomes one of the furies, smashing the mugs flat on the table. She does that when the clay is soft.

Often when we talk she asks, "Do you agree?"

She gets furious when I respond, "What did you say?" Hell, I do have a hearing loss. Not much, but enough to make a difference.

When infuriated she stalks from the room.

I think she wants a man like her father. He used to bounce her on his knee and talk of Winnie the Pooh. Her father, a friendly mid Victorian art historian resembles a diplomat instead of a teacher. His self-control is commendable. At a party he sips his drinks, stays sober while others got drunk. I'm sure he looks down on me for getting plastered at parties.

Cleo also despises me when I get drunk. She has called me a slob, a drunken slob, has refused at those times to let me into bed. Unfortunately when I get loaded lust comes forth. She says, "Look at yourself. Your hair is wild, your breath smells like a brewery, you have a weird smile, and then you have the audacity to come to me as my lover?" At those times she pushes me away as if I am a dog who has been rolling in manure.

Not to give you the wrong idea. Cleo also drinks. When she gets high she is carefree, she laughs. To hear her talk I get drunk at every party. I admit, it is nice to have someone who can drive me home. It is good to unwind once in a while, to carouse like Hemingway.

I fondly remember those days in upper Wisconsin when my friends and I entered bars yelling "ROWDY, DOW, DOW, DOW, DOW." Most bartenders accepted us. We weren't thrown out of many taverns. When it happened it was for flagrant violations.

I admit, one bartender was really mad. I got behind the bar and poured a round while he was in the back room. He had yelled, "you rotten bastard, get out. I'm calling the cops." He spluttered like the spigot of a pony running out of beer. I led my friends in one last "ROWDY DOW DOW DOW DOW" as we ran out the door.

Normally I am a reliable citizen. Now I never even whisper rowdy dow dow dow dow, but I am wistful of my early twenties. In those days I caroused, now too often I brood and drink alone.

In the marriage bed, I am stung by rejection. Sometimes at parties I flirt. No harm in that. While dancing with the wives of other teachers I have gotten hard. That's natural. Damn, they push back. I like slow dancing. I think it's natural with guys. When she rejects me, my machismo wilts like celery left out of the fridge, except when I am slow dancing with someone else's wife.

On nights when I have been rejected I often sleep alone on the white Naugahyde coach. The nauga is the only mammal that sheds its hide without harm. We paid only eighty-two dollars. It had been damaged in shipment. I plotted assignations on those nights. Say to myself, I'll show her. When my punishment went on for weeks, I imagined moving to a land filled with shapely women lusting for my body.

When dating, when courting, she loved me for my free spirits. At parties I laughed, turned somersaults, poked fun at the community. Yelled "ROWDY, DOW, DOW, DOW, DOW." She liked that nonsense at first. Liking the contrast between her stuffy serious father and I. While a teen she wanted her Daddy to let his hair down.

Several years into our marriage she realized she despised men who made fools of themselves at parties.

I mocked her modesty when she wore high-buttoned dresses. She resented my earthiness. Said when nude, "Stop looking at me that way. Are you pervert?"

I envied the truck driving men married to Polish Catholic women. On their way home men like that stopped off for a few beers near their work on Milwaukee's South side. From what Milwaukee friends told me, coming home late at seven thirty or eight those men received dinners cooked just for them. After the kids were in bed the man and his wife went to bed and the woman inhaled her man's breath with the smell of beer, garlic sausage and beer nuts; and she received him as if he were a king. Now that's the way to live. Of course, I'm not a truck driving man. I behave more like a dog being chased whimpering from delicate flower beds by a mistress who is worried that her doggy will pee on her lilies of the valley and drool on her nasturtiums.

Sometimes when rebuffed for several weeks on end, I get dressed up and go to town seeking a woman. I hope no one reads this stuff. A few times in a haze I have succeeded, have gone with a stranger to a motel room where I have pounded away; my feeble way of dealing with rejection.

Later bolder, while at a faculty picnic, I screwed the wife of another teacher. She and I went off to the woods to look for mushrooms. I'm not going to go into any details. It's a private matter. Actually, we did it on the dry moss and lichen. The forest floor, quite soft, reminded me of a Sealy mattress. She was worried about wasps and spiders. It kept her from relaxing. It's not as easy as you might think. We worried about being caught. She was anxious. We were hidden, tucked away behind a thicket of salmonberries with light orange berries.

Cleo's mother wore expensive clothing with bracelets, rings, buckles and bangles resembling those that Cleo had worn when we dated. Later on, Cleo learned of my puritan streak. She adapted, learned to dress plain, stopped wearing lipstick.

I was sort of mixed up. I rejected Puritanism verbally yet expressed it by saying, "the simple things are best. Women who devote their lives to making themselves beautiful ignore their minds and become vegetables."

I valued objectivity.

As a convert to my goofy secular Thoreau faith she wore Levis and even bought a pair of heavy duty hiking boots. She used those expensive boots once. Her preferred footwear are running shoes. She is a fanatic about jogging.

At first in our marriage we thought we were flexible, like a fluid or amoeba, which could acquire any shape. We did shift, yet our change was towards rigidity. Cleo accepted some of my dismissal of what I called functionless clothing. She acquired a closet overflowing with exercise gear, shirts, shorts, and sweatshirts in addition to lots of dresses, skirts, blouses, and expensive hand crafted silver jewelry. When things started deteriorating, as if to spite my wishes, she went more and more towards the impractical. She took a cashmere sweater camping, and it became loaded with twigs, burrs and debris.

I guess Cleo hoped that a miraculous transformation would come to me. She hoped I would change and become like her father. On his way home from work he would buy bouquets of red roses. He would get babysitters and take his wife out to dinner. The maitre D would take them to a table lighted by candles.

Oh at times I tried to be romantic. I would help her off with her coat and pull her chair out as she daintily sat down. Damn it, she isn't that dainty. Her legs are muscular. A detective couldn't find an excess ounce of fat on her bones. Before checking the menu, while we sip wine brought by the wine steward, I have admired her jewelry, praised her unblemished skin, remarked upon the slimness of her figure, and called her teeth a string of pearls. Yet that kind of thing grew old for me, how often could I vocalize that stuff?

I like to wear wear clothing shredded at the elbows and knees. I often wear mud caked boots that she despises. When she sees dirt on the floor she says, "You've carted in more shit."

I wish she would understand my position is precarious. I have to work long hours and be dedicated so that my job will be secure. The time when I can ease off is in the future. At that time I hope we can love and accept one another; and Cleo will eagerly wait for me to come home, to come to bed and make love to her.

Of course we expected Karl to be a well-behaved child. When he is bored or angry he prevents me from concentrating on my lectures and stops Cleo from reading.

Sometimes when rush cooking a meal Cleo hands part of the job to me. I resent having to do women's work. In addition, I admit, I have never appreciated babies. During their early years I wait for the time when my sons and I can talk intelligently. I look forward to hiking and camping with them when they are older.

Cleo mourns not going to college. I know she missed having a time of freedom. The first pregnancy was unplanned. She has talked of former boy friends who had proposed marriage or other adventures to her. Sometimes she confides in me, she tried to imagine life with them, considering each in turn as if they were horses on a merry go round. Sometimes they were magnificent stallions. Seen from a different angle they were plow horses despite carnival music. She told me, I had been the best of the boys she had dated, including the plumber whose grandfather came from Italy. He earned good money and never read books.

Sometimes I think all of us are waiting for some future time when we will play, be happy, and loving. I often believe, the present is bad but the future will be exciting. We are like early Christians living for death and heaven, except we are agnostics. We do not believe in a heaven with angels. We seek our heaven on earth. Life cannot always be so grim, of this we are sure.

Meanwhile I read Sexus by Henry Miller and imagine a heaven in the land of fuck. Cleo reads Lawrence Durrell and dreams of romance in Alexandria.

Karl imagines heaven as a place where he has lots of friends to play baseball with. Where he is always the first person chosen. Arthur experiences heaven when he is fed, hugged and rocked.

Unfortunately no angels have brought heavenly messages and each of us has to pursue our dreams nestled in clean sheets and cushioned by soft Cleo fluffed pillows.

Lately Karl plays with some brass shells he found and talks of explosions. He often has tantrums and fights with other children. We worry about him.

I am sure that after ten years of marriage Cleo is convinced that all men except her father are bastards. Sometimes I think that all women except my mother are bitches. Perhaps that is why we stay married. We men are with the bitch we know and the women are with the bastard they know. Would another mate be better?

I continue writing a summary of our lives:

I, a free white middle class male have tried to do right by doing the following:

I went to grade school though hating it.

I went to church when I didn't believe in Catholicism.

I went to high school though I was bored.

I tried to be a good son and often broke my mother's heart.

I took college courses I despised because they were required.

I got married because it was expected of me.

I spent five years of doing unpaid research.

I became an expert at things I knew little about.

I often dress the way I am supposed to dress.

I bought a house with a mortgage for happiness.

We bought a rug and car on time payments.

We follow the advice of experts who know what's best for us.

I smile at people I despise.

I resent the newspaper saying we environmentalists are impractical.

I take a lot of crap from people.

I teach students who have been turned off to school since grade school.

Battling over ethics with bosses, I win yet lose, yet win.

I stay at work, often in misery, because I mustn't fail.

This is my life; is this a life?

Feeling a need for a long break, Cleo plans to spend the fall with her parents in California.

# CHAPTER 46.

## YOUR EYES ARE THE EYES OF A WOLF

I go more into the forest seeking the mystical experiences I remember from childhood. I use a tall red moist partly rotted cedar stump for a kind of pulpit. Deep fissures divide it into a series of skyward poking prongs. Bent nails, some rusty, some galvanized, dot the wood. Candy bar wrappers, old box fragments, and pieces of yellow, red, white, green, orange, speckle the forest floor. An eye of light reflects from a broken glass hurricane. The shards are from wine bottles, soda and beer bottles, and mason jars.

Children's axes aided by nature's mold have formed the stump seat. Not comfortable, it feels like the one legged stools used by horse race spectators. To stay seated, I have to wedge my rump into the notch. Insecure, I half expect my feet to slide over the mold and my ass to fall while my head thuds against the still hard clay scraped of humus by walkers. The inner walls are like sedimentary rock eroded into deep hollows and speckled with dust and wood fragments. The indented layers are perforated with elliptical beetle tunnels. Small cedar fronds cling to the fibrous projections and declivities attached with silky threads. Douglas fir tridents and maple seed samaras vibrate above patches of fungal white, pastel algal green, moss green, oxidized white yellow pitch warts, orange mould, and orange white weathered cedar. Sunbeams illuminate long fingers of dust forming airways for gnats and flies.

In the moonlight the colors disappear. The paper glows as if it is phosphorescent. The forest floor is cleansed at night. The sky can be seen through cedar branches gently veiling the moon, stars, sun and sky, breaking raindrops to mist. On the Honda rutted trail mud pools reflect moonlight, cloud light and the sparkling reflections of elderberry, salmonberry, fern, and maple. Nettles grow along the trail edge. The better to keep me alert.

In March when the nettles sprout there are white trillium flowers, red Indian plum blossoms, and creamy push tassels pungent in the morning sun unless the night has been frosty. During the first days of April, fiddleheads unwind like coy coquettes pulling nylons up elegant legs.

Now when springtime has arrived in this Cascadian coastal realm, there are no ice jammed rivers, no dripping icicles, no sudden changes. It is as if the sleeping vegetation makes a decision to wake up and send forth new green leaves. I laugh tickled by the bellies of uncurling leaves covered with soft white fur, listen to pill bugs crawling on many legs through warming rotting leaves and crumbly sand and lay on my side watching Fang piss, shit on, and sniff a pile of broken beer bottles, empty plastic bleach and detergent jugs, egg, potato chip and soap packages, cartons, tuna, tomato and bean cans, and a stenographers note pad bearing the name Tammy.

Perhaps Tammy's Daddy saved money by not going to the dump. At any rate, many of the empty containers hold remnants of soap thus indicating a culture that frequently bathes and washes.

A yellow helmeted driver purrs past on his bright orange Kawasaki. Standing in the sunlight, I wave, Fang barks, the youth waves back. Butterflies appear, summoned by the fates of April fools day. I hear a plaintive chirping. A bird flies. I say, "Bird. You have no intellectual decisions to make. No need to question a worm squirming red and glistening on greening leaves. You just open your beak, bend down, pick up Mr. worm, tilt your head and let your former companion slide down your gullet. It is natural. Ahh. Ha. Bird. Can you tell me what is natural for me?"

I kneel, study a rock. Write in my journal: From a darkened pseudo volcanic field rock, fairy cordial cups are ready for filling. With green spiny centers a forest of amber moss spears fends off attacking spiders, flies, bumble bees and grasshoppers who, while trying to land say, "Tee hee, haw haw, that tickles," before hurrying back into the air.

In this micro forest there are scattered rocks that bear forests of moss plants pointing spear tops skyward fending off in moisture films attacking whirling, fan mouthed rotifers, twitching protozoans and snapping amoebas. And in the middle of these small forests, there are grains of sand boulders, carrying on their sides fungal hyphae, which repel or devour hordes of bacteria, bacilli, and cocci. And in the middle of that forest, there may be specks of stone, boulders, bearing on them wild living crashing forests repelling invasions of particles smaller than viruses and so on into and through the eye of the needle is infinite life on every boulder including that wild hurtling rock called earth, which is but a pebble in a cosmic field.

I speak to my congregation of sparrows and pill bugs:

"And God shall come again and walk the earth and mankind will not recognize him. Doubters say that if God came to earth he would be mocked by Catholics and called a blasphemer by evangelists who would say to him, 'We follow the Bible, and you, ignoring the holy words claim to be God.'

"When they ask, 'How can you be God?' Answer them. Say loudly, 'I am God, I am God, I am God.'

"They will say, 'If you are God, why do we doubt you?'"

"Men always doubt the truth."

"If you are God, prove it. Make that tree burn."

"God is not a forest fire. God is belief. God is love. If you love me, and believe in me, then I am God."

"I deny you and do not love you."

"Then I am not God. You and your beliefs and perceptions create or destroy me."

"Well, maybe you are God, but I don't trust you."

"Do you trust your feelings?"

"No. I doubt myself."

"Work on this. Say, we are all God."

"Me God? Oh no. I'm not God. That would be blasphemy."

"We are all God. You are God."

"How can I be God?"

"God is love. If you love you are God."

In starlight while the sparrows sleep, I say to the bats:

"Become the essence of love, become love and you become God."

"How can I be love?" Say the bats.

"God is belief. If you believe you are God, you are God."

"People will deny that I am God, even if I am God, so why be God?"

"You batty bats. Do you think God's existence is determined by a vote of the bats?"

"What should we believe to be God?"

"The truths of mass consciousness. pk,pk, pk, zzzzzzzzzzzzzzzziiiiiiitttt. Doooon, dooon, dooon. Glung, ob, ob, ob, ob, zzz zeeeest, zz z yeeeng, yeeeng, yeng, zzeezeedeedeedeebizzzbzzpsst, sizzzzzzzzzz, zang, zang, zanggggggg, zannnnggg, zaaaannngggggg OOOOOOOOOOOOOOOOOOOOOOOOOOOOOUOUOUO UOUOUOUOUOUOUOUOU.

"There is a wolf in the sunlight, in the moonlight. Your eyes are the eyes of a wolf. Fang, why don't you rip my throat open? Because I feed you or because your nose is wet and mine is dry? Fang, Wolf. Your feet have pads and claws; mine have concentric circles. Mine are tender and yours can run through the snow without hurting, unless the snow is crisp and cuts into your pads. Your eyes are more beautiful than mine. Your hair is finer with a richness and softness, and mine is old monkey fur. Monkey see and monkey do, but whatever I see, I do not do. For I have left you monkey, and I have left you wolf, and I have discovered truth.

"On the wings of Simulconsciousness, Wolf and I run through the sky in GREAT BIG STEPS. GOING UP, going down and AROUND, ALL AROUND.

"We float in the BLUE SKYYYYYYYYYYYYYYYYYYYYYYYY YYYYYYYYY IN LINE UPON LINE UPON LINE UPON LINE UPON LINE UPON LINE UPON LINE UPON LINE UPON LINE UPON LINE UPON LINE UPON LINE UPON LINE UPON LINE UPON LINE IN LAYERS ABOVE THE SNOWY EARTH AND THE SLEEPING PEOPLE ZZZZZZZZZZZZZZZ ZZZZZZZZZZZZZZZZZZZzzzzzzzzz.

"WHO SUDDENLY TURNED OUT ALL THE LIGHTS, we can't see and so we FALL, not through the STARS, to the ground below

L

0

W

E

R

"Until we land in foggy celestial specks of ice clouds, and the rings of Saturn are around us moving faster and faster, we are in the centrifugal forces; we whirl around Saturn and the reds and purples and violets become a flickering violet blue white light brighter and brighter as it moves towards us from the center of Saturn, hot white boiling white hot center, and we whirl straining to escape, confused by the celestial dust, deafened by the high grinding of the rings frictioning on one another, there is heat, loud shrieks, cries in the violet blue white night, my spine shivers, the wolf howls, drums beat, an explosion throws us OUTTTTTTTTTTTTTTTTTTT and we hear the cries, cries, cries, cries as we float through the vacuum of space.

"CONGRATULATIONS MEN AND WOLVES.

"You've successfully tested space. Space has passed with flying colors. Wolves have proven their value to mankind. Therefore we will let one wolf live.

"YEAHHHHHHHHHHHHHHHHHHHHHHHHHHHHHHH!"

"The streets are filled with people. The castle is decked with flying banners, and waving pennants. Knights in armor proudly ride through the walled city. The people are singing, "HI HO, THE WOLF CAN LIVE, THE GOOD OLD WOLF, THE SPACED OUT WOLF, HI HO THE WOLF CAN LIVE, THE WOLF CAN LIVE, THE LUCKY WOLF CAN LIVE. THE WOLF CAN DANCE, THE WOLF CAN SING, THE WOLF CAN DANCE, THE GOOD OLD WOLF CAN LIVE.

"THE FURRY WOLF, WITH RICH BROWN EYES, WITH RAYS AND RAYS, WITH GLEAMING EYES, TO SEE IN THE NIGHT, WITH BIG LONG NOSE, THAT SMELLS THE SMELLS, WITH SOFT FUR PADS, AND SOFT BROWN FUR, HI, HO, THIS GREAT OLD WOLF CAN LIVE."

During all of the excitement, the wolf with tail between her legs runs off, mouth frothing; after pushing frantically between some ladies in gowns who instinctively back away, she runs whimpering down a narrow cobblestoned street without stopping to smell a time honored urine splattered wall, without stopping to pick up a meaty bone by the abattoir. Running, whimpering, the wolf runs across the bridge spanning the moat with only seconds to spare, for the cry is out,

"THE WOLF HAS LEFT, OUR ONLY WOLF, OUR SACRED WOLF, OUR DEAR OLD WOLF, OUR DEAR OLD WOLF HAS FLED.

"SAVE OUR WOLF, RESTRAIN OUR WOLF, BANG THE GATE, BLOCK THE BRIDGE, SAVE OUR WOLF, SAVE OUR WOLF."

The steel gate smashes down upon wolf vapors swirling in the morning mist. Reaching open country, the wolf continues and finds a forest, some dead logs, moss, and a gentle stream. Then the wolf sleeps, and the time of wolves comes again. Midnight howls dart to the souls of mankind, children cling to their mothers next to their fathers, and the wolves in a pack under the clear bright moon joyously run over the snow. Above them, the forest branches are sharply outlined against the moon's fullness. And the time of the wolf is a time of smoke and fire, and sweat and labor, and man and wolf both live. They live, my God, how they live."

# CHAPTER 47.

## SAVING THE DEVIL'S GATEWAY

In spring of that same year, 1971, a solitary figure leans against the green railing of a bridge crossing the Devil's Gateway.

The tidal current forms a maelstrom in the rocky gap separating Humaluh County from the island of Quimper in Gateway County. Sometimes powerful commercial fishing boats, caught in the churling water, have been fed to the cliffs.

Engineers bridged the gap in the nineteen thirties. Now tourists stare at the currents while speeding through the gap in a tour boat. They think they are safe from the rocky cliffs.

Troubled people are magnetized and mesmerized by the whirlpools. They drive to the fir green bridge, park in a pull over. Walk towards the center, stop, empty pockets, and climb the low railing. Cars slow and stop; drivers and passengers watch as the figure tilts off the railing, falls out of sight 220 feet to the hard swirling roiling spirals which they join for an instant to then disappear. The broken object, sometimes clinging to life, is carried by the tides and found by men or crabs and cod. Only two have ever survived the jump, and they were pulled out of the water like dazed bruised wet rats.

My neighbor, when a brave stupid teen ager, with his buddy emptied pockets on shore where the girders perch on concrete, and carefully crawling on their bellies they slid over those rivet warted green steel girders, carefully angling up, leveling some, to commence carefully angling down, trying not to steal a glance at the currents. Sometimes they faltered, fought dizziness, before completing their crawl.

My neighbor told me, "I have been terrified of heights ever since that dumb day we crossed the Devil's Gateway."

I asked him, "Would you ever do it again?"

"Not for a million dollars."

Today on the bridge a strong wind causes me to brace my legs. Wet from rain, I make my way to the center of the bridge. My hands sliding along the bumpy green steel surface I stare grimly at the whirlpools and think over the events of the past year. How easy it would be to climb the railing and jump.

Crossing the road, I look at the small island that divides the incoming current. I have been fighting Cascadia Power. They have just released their proposal to construct a nuclear reactor on that rocky island. The press release said the reactor would produce one million kilowatts and have very little effect upon the environment, because much of the reactor would be constructed underground in the rock. I wonder would the steam stack also be underground puffing towards the center of the earth? Scientific studies are to commence to determine any possible adverse affects on marine life. The reactor would take in forty-degree water, warm it by fifteen to twenty degrees, and return it to the Devil's Gateway.

A plus for the reactor; the water will be warm enough for swimmers. As for me, I don't give a damn if they create a giant bathtub, sauna, or hot tub.

Almost as soon as the ink dried on the news release, we formed a *Save the Devil's Gateway Committee.* Our members included people from Duwamps who planned to retire in waterfront homes, and year round residents including fishermen, loggers, teachers, contractors, shopkeepers and executives. I got a kick out of one man. He had recently retired from Cascadia Power. He had been an executive.

Some of these people, NIMBY environmentalists, enjoyed watching eagles fly past or perch in trees near the edge of the water. The people and eagles enjoyed spending leisure time observing the bridge, sea gulls, boats, winds roiling the water, and storms.

No sooner had we organized the Save the Devil's Gateway Committee, then we heard of another plan. Developers wanted to transform the shores of Elysium Lake into a Planned Unit Development designed to house thousands of people. Condominiums were to be constructed on the ridges above the lake and house trailers were to be placed in the valley. Elysium Lake was adjacent to the Devil's Gateway. The lake and protected harbors near the Gateway were my favorite canoeing waters.

I inserted a short notice in the Duhkwuh Tribune inviting opponents of the real estate projects to come to a meeting of the Save Elysium Committee. The meeting was a major success. I was elected president. We decided we would collect signatures on petitions, write letters to the editors of in-state newspapers and attend Humaluh County Planning Commission meetings. A month after we formed the Save Elysium Committee, the local paper came out with a plan to fill in 7700 acres of tidelands on Humaluh Bay so as to construct eleven thousand condominiums to meet the housing shortage in rural Humaluh County. Apparently some of our fifty thousand residents were without adequate housing. The county planner opposed the development because it would change the land use from agricultural to residential and would upset the overall development plan of the county. He said, "We don't need a thirty two million dollar development in our small county."

Several months later an editorial in the Duhkwuh Tribune commended the county commissioners for their courage to support progress including the reactor, the planned unit development on Lake Elysium and the Humaluh Bay real estate development. As if this wasn't bad enough, those hoping for progress again reared their snorting heads out of the valley silt when plans emerged to develop a four hundred and

forty acre recreational complex on the Humaluh Indian reservation
adjacent to the Humaluh Canal.

I got totally furious when the planner was fired. At one time I had been
convinced that the planner was selling the county down the river. I realized
how wrong I had been. He and I had been roughly playing in the same
ballpark. It seemed dumb to turn the county into a bedroom suburb for
Duwamps (sixty miles away). With the one voice of reason in the county
government gone, I decided to recruit allies. I invited all of the major
environmentalists in the county and Duwamps to a meeting in my home
while Arthur slept and Karl played outside. Cleo joined us and provided
iced tea, crackers, aged Tillamook cheddar, Brie and Camembert.

We formed The Humaluh Environmental Council or NEC. It
immediately became the most powerful environmental organization in
the county. I was elected president.

Instead of congratulating me and wishing me well, the editor of
the Duhkwuh Tribune ran a headline stating: SAVE HUMALUH
COUNTY FROM THE ENVIRONMENTALISTS!

In response to the editorial, Jeremiah Wiggins formed a Save
Humaluh County Committee. Wiggins said," All those other save
committees are made up of people from Duwamps. Some of them are
from California. They are outsiders. Their leader is a carpetbagger from
Wisconsin. Listen to the local people. We want jobs. We don't want
our children to have to go to Duwamps for jobs. Progress is inevitable.
Join the Save Humaluh County Committee. No fuzzy thinking. No
membership fees. Just good common horse sense." Wiggin's remarks
appeared on the front page of the Tribune.

I thought of writing a letter to the editor pointing out that Wiggins
had been born in Carbondale, Illinois, and the editor came from
Manhattan, Kansas.

County people were pro and con on the projects. Those living close to a proposed development became instant environmentalists. As an example: Before retirement the leader of the Save the Devil's Gateway Committee had been an attorney who initiated condemnation proceedings against people owning houses in the path of future power cables. One of the men he had evicted had screamed, "I hope someday you lose your home the way I've lost mine. God damn you to hell."

When the power company attorney retired, he and his wife built their dream home overlooking the Devil's Gateway. Two years later the reactor plans were unveiled. The power line transmission corridor would march across the shallow water directly in front of their picture windows. Only the view, an intangible, would be altered. After hearing the news, slumped low in his chair, he had asked his wife, "What are we going to do?"

After our group was formed, these folks joined and immediately became busy going door-to-door soliciting cash and support to oppose his former employer. In the coming months his skills were useful and effective to us.

Each of the committees had been formed in anger. The members resented the fact that plans long in the making were suddenly dumped on their heads. Because time was short, lacking basic factual information, we had to act fast. We suspected collusion between the developers and public officials. Some of our people would jump up during planning commission meetings and yell things like, "You guys are trying to railroad this thing. What's your hurry? You don't like to listen to us citizens, do you? You only listen to the developers, don't you? What do they do, pay you off? Don't you people realize, if a reactor is built it might blow up and kill all of us."

The Tribune praised the engineers and architects for well thought out proposals. How it would make dollars and made economic sense. There were lots of figures, easy to understand drawings, and reasonable conclusions.

Meanwhile, I taught the people in the Save Committees how to perform scholarly research. The people opposed to reactors studied the technology of nuclear power. They learned how to follow the power company's charts and drawings and came up with their own charts and drawings. Our own expert from California refuted a power company expert from California. Our Save attorney refuted the power company's attorney.

Those of us opposing the real estate developments discovered how land use decisions were made. We discovered, to our chagrin, that we liked the concept of Planned Unit Developments or PUDs.

At the Humaluh County Democratic Convention it was resolved and passed: Be it resolved that this convention supports the construction of nuclear reactorsin downtown Duwamps.

At the Republican Convention the delegates voted to support the construction of a reactor at the Devil's Gateway.

Five years earlier a copper refinery had been proposed for an island five miles north of the Gateway. It had been blocked by a citizen lawsuit. After the expensive defeat, and long court battle, the county commissioners did not want to make mistakes. They wanted to make sure their decisions would stand up in court.

Our county has become polarized into those for and against development. There are many struggles: The war in Viet Nam: Four students have been slaughtered at Kent State protesting our invasion of Cambodia. That was their right. The National Guard shot them. My battle with the college administration continues. Much as the nation is polarized, I sense a polarization at the college of those for me and those against me. And I wonder. What else can go wrong?

# CHAPTER 48.

# THE DUHKWUH MUGGINS MALL

The Tribune headlines: WORK BEGINS ON FIVE MILLION DOLLAR MALL.

"Its a bad idea," I tell Cleo. "A small town doesn't need large shopping centers."

The mall, fathered by Jeremiah Wiggins, was being built on the flood plain on the edge of town. Wiggins said: "Our mall will enable county residents to buy at a discount. We will have chain stores from New York City and Los Angeles. There will be a motel and space for 5,000 cars in the parking lots."

Some months earlier, I had told the Humaluh Environmental Council, "In our city the butts of the buildings face the river. We should spin those buildings 180 degrees, and move them back one hundred feet. A developer should construct a promenade along the shore. Attractive outside tables will allow people to sip fine wines and keep tabs on the sand bars when the river is low. During a flood, while sipping an aperitif, diners can observe the water covering bushes, and clearing the city of riverside house trailers. Wagers can be made on the progress of assorted logs, branches, bottles, and horse trailers. When the river is clear, strollers can watch fishermen on flat bottomed boats, chattering kingfishers flying undulating paths, and swallows on the sweep. When the sun sets, the old folks on benches can stare at the orange sky. At night lovers can thrill to the shimmering lights of the moon reflected on the rippling water."

The Tribune in reporting my talk said, "The ecologists want to play spin the bottle with our downtown buildings." The paper ignored the part where I had praised the downtown. I had said, "I appreciate being recognized by the shopkeepers. It is like visiting aunts and uncles, because they accept you despite your faults and they recognize your face. I will like the downtown even if we don't rotate the buildings."

Shortly after the new mall opened, three Duhkwuh drugstores went out of business. Within the year a clothing store burned down and several other stores folded. The new mall transmogrified the downtown into a wasteland of empty shops.

The downtown merchants, whining in futile rage, were antagonistic to their new competitors. Wanting to keep new mall businesses out of the Chamber of Commerce, Anthony Thompson, one of the old timer chamber members, vowed, "I'll quit if we let them in."

Thompson and the other merchants did not remain passive. They sent an ultimatum to the city fathers: PULL OUT THE PARKING METERS! Mayor Hausfuss, a progressive man, cooled the fire by yanking the meters, replacing them with signs saying: FREE COURTESY PARKING.

The merchants devised a unique way to attract people to the downtown. Anthony Thompson, who had just returned from a visit to India, said, "Let's build a copy of the Taj Mahal."

Accepting his advice the merchants funded the construction of a white concrete Taj Mahal on the site of the former garbage dump across the river. Canals, cut at right angles to the river, produced excellent reflections of the domes, only occasionally marred by floating garbage and gas bubbles rising to the surface from the detritus of the past.

Bowing to the reality of the mall, I take my students on tour. We stop on the way. As we peer out from within our small bus, I say "Look at that big old soooper market" We read a large red sign: YOU'LL LEARN TO BELIEVE IN US.

"Hallelujah," I say. "Business gets religion."

We eyeball the roofline. The sunken roof sprouts air conditioning units that resemble low refrigerators. Hollow ventilating shafts remind the students of periscopes.

"The Duhkwuh Muggin's Mall is named after the first mayor of Duhkwuh." Turning off the ignition, I push my glasses down the bridge of my nose. "What is a mall?" I ask.

"Shops," blue levied white bloused full bosomed Sally McGuire says.

"Let us consult zee books," I say. "Ah. Zee dictionaree says, zee mall is a promenade or walk, and eet is usually shaded. Et cherie, eet is often zee street with shops and zee street ees closed to zee vehicles and eet has zee tables and bottles of wine and zee pretty mademoiselles walk past weeth tweesting heeps while zee gentlemen loooook and say ooooo la la. Now mes enfants. What do you see?"

"Monsieur mon professor. I see zee beeg parking lot," says Sally.

"Do you see zee trees or zee promenade?"

"No mon professor," she flutters her eyes.

"Now let us go into zee bowels of zee mall," I say.

After parking and getting out we pass through automatically opening doors entering a promenade lighted with fluorescent lights.

"Mon professor. Regardez," squeals Sally. "We are on zee promenade and zer are zee plants." She triumphantly points.

" Oui, oui," I say. "And lo and behold there are plants, a tree grows in a red wood box and is for sale. "I apologize, I steel desire zee glass of ruby burgundy to loooook through while I watch zee ladies and listen to zee violins."

We enter the bright well-lighted grocery store. We must look like wistful strangers homesick for the smells and colors of the little markets back home in Europe or Africa. Picking up and examining packages of food we act like dumfounded wombats. Our day's math lesson: "Is a package of fifteen and one half ounces cheaper per ounce than another package weighing eight and one half ounces? How do you convert grams to ounces?"

Tony Ragatoni sings, "Oh tell me why, the bread never moulds, and the pie in the sky never rots?"

Sally winces.

The astute store manager, Dudley Dewbunny, recognizing an invasion, briefly orbits our group like a satellite. Realizing most are students, he leaves us alone at the shelves where we resembled curious marsupials.

While my students are writing lists of product ingredients, I hold a package above my head. "We have here the solution to the dilemma of the packing house. When they ask, what do we do with the extra fat and assorted scraps of meat? They hear a voice from the heavens shout. Grind it up, toss in food additives, when embalmed toss and shove it in a plastic skin, call it All American, tell people to stick it over a fire and partially incinerate it, cover it with mustard, catsup, onions and relish and say, Uum, Uum, Good."

Skipping the checkout lines, I lead the shabbily dressed students into the cut-rate department store where Dudley Dewbunny, four assistant managers, three floorwalkers, and two detectives place us under surveillance. Doing their duty, the men in pinstriped suits, moving along parallel aisles, shadow us.

Despite my saying, "Please be couth," the male students give the King's English a severe test.

"Hey, will you look at this shit? It'll break before the poor kid gets it home."

"This plastic tractor is too much. Christ."

"Remember to tuck it into a wall socket every night."

An internal combustion engine roars to life. After a jackrabbit start, the toy racer smashes into a puffed plastic pillar. The managers, guarding the Barbie Dolls, cringe from the smell of gasoline.

The student driver runs from the scene of the wreck saying ,"I didn't do it, I didn't do it," and almost collides with a group of men in pin striped suits before halting, entranced by the wetting mechanism of dolls.

Rodney Rapshot, examining the wreckage says, "These things should be labeledGuaranteed for one hour." After thinking about it for another minute he corrects himself, "No. It should state: GUARANTEED FOR ONE-YEAR PROVIDED THIS TOY IS NOT TOUCHED BY CHILDREN OR USED BY ADULTS."

At the end of the aisle, Rodney Rapshot pushes down what turns out to be the ignition switch on a moon rocket. He jumps back as the rocket in a flash of fire, smoke and sound, momentarily hovers just above the floor, to suddenly shoot roofward in a massive cloud of smoke, piercing the ceiling like it was aluminum foil, before disappearing. People are coughing. Dudley Dewbunny has lost his cool. He is yelling, "When I catch the son of a bitch who ignited that rocket, I'll cut off his balls." To add emphasis and support his manager Jeremiah Wiggins picks up a toy chain saw, and pulls the cord. His staff jumps at the roar.

Jeremiah, hands in his pockets, walks to the Tahiti Lunch bazaar. It is his lunchtime.

Retreating from the toy department, our class moves to the aerosols. "This stuff is neat," I say, picking up a blue container. "Parents spray it on pans to keep them from sticking, and kids squirt it down their throats to get high. A multi purpose product."

Randy, a ready volunteer, helps Sally examine vaginal douches. He says, "Would you like a little demonstration?"

"Maybe later," she says, grinning.

Belinda Brown says, "What's in it?"

"Look at the contents," I say.

"They're not listed," says Belinda.

"They're exempt from the law," I say. "They're usually harmless unless you have allergies."

"Doesn't everyone have allergies?" says Belinda.

"It is supposed to contain Hexachlorophene," says Randy.

"When they fed that stuff to rats, it turned their brains into Swiss cheese," I say.

"I'll be fucked," says Randy.

Hearing the profanity the managers move into our aisle; mingling with students. They see me filming stacks of plastic bowls, dishes, trays and pans that resemble a Martian City. As my camera whirrs there comes about a great managerial convergence. Dewbunny, The Green Berets film starring John Wayne fresh in his mind, interrogates the cinematographer. "What are you doing?" His waggling index finger pokes the camera lens. The camera continues to whirr.

"Sorry." I look up, then look down and continue. "Just filming pots and pans."

"That is forbidden. You cannot take pictures in this store." I turn off the camera. "How can I get permission? I'm making a photographic record of the sixties and early seventies."

"Write to our headquarters in Dallas. They've never given permission yet, but maybe they'll make an exception in your case," says Wiggins with a chuckle.

"Thank you," I say. Sweetening my voice a bit, I ask, "Can I shoot the last thirty seconds? I'll leave it with your camera department for processing, and when it comes back, if there are any top secrets, you can censor them out."

"No!" screams Dewbunny. "You cannot film in our store. No. No. No. No. Now please go. Get out. Leave." It is apparent that Dewbunny is a bit riled.

I say, "We're going. Don't shoot," as I back, under his glare, out of the store.

This incident brings out another facet of my life. I have heard rumors: some people suspected that I am a secret agent of an industrial espionage ring, skilled in karate and trained to kill. Perhaps I learned my skills from secret agent Maxwell Smart. When the hand held movie camera stopped whirring, was another camera triggered from it's lair in the cave of my nostrils? Did each bristly sideburn hide a tape recorder? If I am an industrial spy, the college field trips are a clever ruse. If I am not a spy, are the trips worth the ill will they engender in the community? The problem goes beyond my restrained behavior, blemished a bit by my penchant for saying humorous things, sort of lighting a match to oiled waters. My students seem compelled to ask embarrassing questions, as if all of the businessmen are bad.

The field trip to the oil refinery also went bad. The students had asked questions about a tragic accident the previous year that had killed three workers when hot sludge poured out on them as they opened a metal door. The workers had assumed the sludge had cooled, after all it was hours after the plant had been shut down after an alert. After that unwise uncompassionate discussion, a student asked, "Isn't it unethical to base our nation's energy policies upon an excess consumption of limited energy?" Another student said, "Money? Isn't your company kind of a monopoly? How much research are you doing in solar power?"

On another tour the students had laughed at the blue flame at the sewage treatment plant, joking that those were burning farts.

I have always believed in the benefits of asking questions, but the students are like young bulls, and impossible to control. They even criticized the generation and storage of chlorine in big blue tanks at the pulp mill, forgetting that chlorine helps produce the salt of the earth. Of course there had been that chlorine leak, the gas had spread over parts of the city, there had been a few deaths. This was before my time in the land of the Humaluh.

Wiggins had the opposite view. His head vibrating like a balancing rock in the wind, he apparently told the chamber, "The young should be taught to appreciate and support our capitalistic system. They don't know enough to question or criticize. They can do that when they get older." He was also on the College Board. Once he had told his fellow Humaluh College Board members, "Criticism is a chisel directed at the heart of the cornerstone of democracy. Youth must have faith in the fundamental goodness of business. Without business, people will stop buying. Without business, there will no longer be America."

After we leave the store, on our ill-fated tour, Wiggins yells, "We should investigate that man. What's his name?"

A clerk stops watering a bouquet of red plastic chrysanthemums long enough to say, "Bauer. Professor Leo Bauer."

While the clerk continues his watering, Wiggins writes Leo Bauer on a scrap of paper, which he carefully slips into his wallet.

The Tip Toe Tulip affair is worthy of mention at this time. Although not of my doing, the incident affected the college staff and student body.

A week after the mall tour, a student wearing a sport coat and tie asked Dewbunny, "Can we put a poster in your window?"

"What's it about?" said Dewbunny.

"It's for a contest sponsored by the tulip growers."

"The tulip growers? They're in the chamber of commerce, and they're fundamentalists. Fine people. Put up your sign. I like to support student activities."

Wiggins had almost forgotten the incident when Miss Tilebrown rushed into his office yelping like a terrier. "Mr. Wiggins. Those pictures are terrible."

"What pictures?" said Wiggins.

"Those terrible tulips." Heels snapping across the floor, she led him to the mall hall where they joined a crowd pushing forward to study photographs on a poster. Wiggins saw grinning fat cherubic students wearing tulips, which barely covered crotches. A smaller photo displayed fundaments that were almost completely exposed, taken while the models touched their toes smiling demonically as they faced the camera.

Happy at the attention received by the poster, Harry Marcus, the putter upper, stood beaming from the right edge of the crowd.

Catching the eye of Dewbunny, he gave a little wave.

Dewbunny rushed towards Marcus like a bull after a bullfighter in Ensenada. "Who's responsible for this filth," he screamed, grabbing and shaking the suddenly serious youth.

Marcus briefly considered being angry in return. Gave it up after a quick analysis. "You gave your permission," he said.

"The tulip growers?"

"Yup, the tulip growers."

"I've changed my mind." Releasing Marcus, Dewbunny re-entered the store, ripped the poster off the window, crumpled it into a ball, and smiled at Marcus, who grateful for his life and freedom quickly left the mall.

Dewbunny complained to Wiggins, who acting as if his daughter had just been defiled in the window, dialed the college administrative offices. "I want to talk to Davis. I don't care if he is busy, this is Wiggins." He broke three yellow pencils while waiting. "Yes. Business is fine. I'm calling about your students. Why do you allow obscenity at Humaluh? Are posters with fat naked students your idea of fun? You're not aware? You don't even know what goes on? Well I'll tell you. It's the Tip Toe Tulip Contest. Students have put up obscene photographs of nude male and female students on our mall windows." He listened a moment then said, "No. You can see everything. They are wearing tulips, but not much is left to the imagination. How could you let that happen? You better find out. Call back with answers. Goodbye."

Before Davis could investigate, he had to answer his telephone. It was the principal of the Duhkwuh high school. Davis said, "You're advising your students not to go to Humaluh? Is it the Tip Toe Tulip Contest? No, of course that wasn't my idea. I just found out about it. Well how am I going to know everything that goes on around here? Just have some faith. We'll take action. Heads will roll."

Davis, being a scholar, set out to find the facts. Dutch bulb growers had donated the tulips. The bulb growers, who believed in flowers and God, after becoming outraged at the photographs, withdrew their sponsorship of the contest and demanded the return of their tulips. The flowered and flowerless students had been photographed in back of the gymnasium. The winner of the contest was to be chosen by three coeds wearing lava lavas. The high point of the contest was to be the auction where the audience would bid on the tulips, which would be plucked by the winning bidders from the hides of the winners, Mr. Tip Toe Tulip, and Miss Tip Toe Tulip. It was anticipated that as the bidding advanced, the remaining tulips would grow in value.

Davis examined a copy of the Twit that had just been published with an entire page containing photographs of students cavorting in tulips. Although the most strategic parts of their anatomy were covered, bellies, chests and portions of rumps were uncovered. The article said, "Ziegfeld Follies, Roman Orators and Tiny Tim move over. You've got competition."

Davis attempted to find the dance and newspaper adviser. Mr. Girodias however, perhaps suffering from a foreboding of doom, had become ill shortly after okaying the contest. Davis called him on the phone. "I don't care if you haven't seen the photographs. You're supposed to know everything that goes on with campus publications. What? So you've got diarrhea. That's bad but obscenity is worse. Be in my office in thirty minutes. I don't care if you've got the runs. Be there."

Upon arrival, Girodias slumped on the couch like a wet dishrag. He cringed as the president yelled, "What are you, some kind of pervert? You've done it this time. The board wants my skin. You better look for another job. Be at the board meeting tonight. We're going to decide your fate."

Girodias stood up, said, "I've got to go to the bathroom," and ran from the room. After twenty minutes in the head, he drove to the Schnitzel Haus where he initiated emergency stress management.

In the Schnitzel Haus Joseph Malander and I tell him to stop drinking and sober up for the board meeting.

I say, "Don't forget to tell them about freedom of speech; the protections of the Constitution; the first amendment. I think it's the first."

"Use reason," says Malander. Tugging on his mustache he adds, "It should be between the students and the board. Students should be responsible for their own actions. Nailing your hide to the wall would be a miscarriage of justice."

"I like the photos," I say. "There's nothing wrong with nudity. Our bodies are beautiful."

"Your body is beautiful?" snorts Malander.

"Sure my body's beautiful. And what the student's did was funny. They can laugh at their flabby butts and bellies, which is more than we teachers can do."

Later that night at the board meeting, Girodias heard two of the board demand his resignation. Another thought he should be arrested for perversion.

Davis nodded vigorously as if to indicate, yes, those are my thoughts also.

Mr. Wiggins, a believer in positive thinking, offered a way out. "Replace the Mr. Tip Toe Tulip Contest with a Mr. Wholesome Contest. The most wholesome contestant will be the winner. Contestants will wear suits and have their hair cut short. To keep his job, all Mr. Girodias will have to do is guarantee that the students will cause no further trouble."

"And if there is any more trouble, out he goes," said Davis, whacking the table with his palm.

The night of the dance was pleasant enough. The two chaperones, a ticket taker, and the campus cop, thoroughly enjoyed the luxury of having a large ballroom and band all to themselves. The students were at a beer party on a farm just outside of town, where they were having some sort of tulip auction.

# CHAPTER 49.

## NEWS AT THE SCHNITZEL HAUS

The Schnitzel Haus meetings, like meetings everywhere, usually resolved little or nothing. To attend a Schnitzel Haus Meeting a teacher didn't have to be invited: He just had to be male and show up.

One day when he has shown up, Malander says, I have heard from on high, "They're planning on firing six faculty. English is overstaffed. Music and the fine arts are overstaffed. Science is overstaffed. To decide the best way to reduce staff, the administration is hiring two new administrators. One will help the dean; the other will handle public relations. Two secretaries will be hired to assist the two new administrators." He gulps tannish foam off his beer. "Its obvious gang. The only way to survive is to become an administrator. Watch me. In a year or two I'll be with them."

"Heaven help us," says Girodias. Having just recovered from a bad siege of diarrhea, he is grateful to again be swilling beer with his friends.

Red lights flicker on Malander's glasses. I cringe at the thought of having to report to Malander. Thomas Thaumaste farts. Alfo says, "That's the most intelligent comment I've heard all day." Seabeck belches.

"At least administrators don't fart and belch," says Malander.

"Neither do women," I say.

"They won't succeed," says Thaumaste, his voice redolent of the Roman Senate.

"Davis won't last long, anyway," says Magnum.

"Not if he doesn't exercise more," I say.

"Maybe they'll all die," says Thaumaste in a prophetic voice.

"Let's hope so," I say.

"Don't get your hopes too high," says Malander. "Administrators outlive teachers."

"Davis is dedicated," says Magnum.

"Dedicated to making money," I say.

"He has much knowledge," says Magnum.

"Yes," says Volens. "The knowledge to save pennies."

"I thought I moved ahead when I left high school teaching," says Apfelboeck. "When I developed a program, maybe I wasn't encouraged, but I sure as hell wasn't obstructed."

"You should be in my shoes," I say. "I face the forward line of an ex football team. Sometimes I think you're the only administrator on my side. You are, aren't you?"

"I try to remain objective," says Apfelboeck. "By the way Leo. The next time around, why don't you become an administrator?"

"Davis says we should be glad to be here. Lots of teachers are out of work," says Magnum.

"According to Malander, that trend will continue, isn't that right?" I say.

"Don't cry over spilt milk," says Malander. "The handwritings on the wall. Teachers are becoming obsolete. Think it over. While there's still time, join the administrative team, like good old Apfelboeck." He pats Apfelboeck on the shoulders. Apfelboeck bows. "Join a growth industry. Study the British navy. While the tonnage of ships declined, the number of admirals increased."

"On skid row they call all the Indians chiefs," I say.

Seabeck says, "I'm glad you know all about skid row. Were you studying our graduates?"

"I believe in field work," I say.

Seabeck says, "At the last faculty meeting, our committee demanded no additional increase in administrative positions. The president turned purple and screamed, 'don't you realize we're overworked?' 'So are we,' I yelled back, and we glared at each other. And they ask for suggestions. If he tries that bullshit again, I'll go back to industry."

"We're lucky about one thing," says Malander. We've finally got the Widget man."

"Management by objectives," says Magnum.

"You must have a sharp step, square shoulders and a twinkle in your eye," says Alfo in a clipped military voice.

"Hail to the wonders of business," says Seabeck, raising his stein. We all drink to his toast.

"We'll teach with programmed instruction," says Girodias.

"Wow," I can't wait for the future. I read all about it in *Player Piano*," I say.

"And we won't have to waste our time teaching," says Magnum.

"That's something to be thankful for," says Malander.

Girodias says, "I move most solemnly that we award the Pedant of the Month award to William Z Widget, the president of International Widget. Although Mr. Widget has never visited a community college, he is well qualified to be the new director of the Cascadia State Community College Board."

I recall Widget's statement to the press. "There is little difference between manufacturing widgets and educating students. A widget contains wheels, bells, wires, transistors, gears, and light emitting diodes. We can program a widget to do a specified number of tasks. Each additional capability however, costs more money. In the same way, a student, comprised of nerves and muscles, also requires X amount of dollars to learn each skill. We educators must discover how many dollars are available. We must decide which tasks are essential for our students to learn. The non essential must be dropped."

"I agree," I say. "Widget deserves this award. I am very impressed with his product, which beeps, rolls merrily along, turns upside down for some belly scratching, stands, circles, and when kicked licks its owners hand. They make excellent pets, use little electricity, and require no rabies shots or pet licenses. If his next product, the controllable student, is equally successful, Cascadia will continue to be a leader among the states and countries."

"Huzza, Huzza, Huzza," we yell, giving the award by acclamation to William Z Widget.

After I leave, I heard later, the remaining Schnitzel Hauser's, knowing my feelings had been hurt by a lack of recognition at the college, applied vast energy in hammering out an award for me, to be awarded at a special ceremony to be held on the summit of Trash Mountain, Indiana's version of Pikes Peak.

Going into the imaginary future, when the time came for me to receive the award as Environmentalist of the Heap, I ran away. Reporters, fascinated by someone who turns down something, followed me into an open space between blackberry bushes just out of smell of the mountain. The cameras zoomed in on my face, which was barely visible because I was sitting with my knees pulled in to my chest, my fingers covering my nose and eyes. The reporters asked, "In your writings you advise people to face up to the world, yet you ran away. Why?"

"When in a crowd, although in the center of things, I am alone. I have to run away and hide."

"But you were about to be made Environmentalist of the Heap."

"I felt alienated."

"You tell people many things are wrong with our society. You tell them how to live, and yet, you are, if you'll pardon MY saying so, in many ways a failure. How can a failure tell other people how to live?"

"Vincent Van Gogh was a failure. Now he's great."

"Are you going to cut off your ear?"

"Do you want me to cut off my ear?"

"I am a reporter. Yes, I would like to see you cut off your ear, if we can get it on camera. If you do it now, it will make the five o'clock news."

"You'd like that. Professor cuts off ear, tosses it to reporters. Reporters catch ear."

"Professor Bauer. You've got it wrong. We're not your enemy. Our business is the gathering of news. Some men exploit the mineral resources of the planet. We mine the fables and follies of people, dogs and cats."

"I am also a miner. We are kinsmen. We exploit the same mother lode. I treasure ecological nuggets and mourn damaged natural cycles. We are in the same business."

"You have been denounced for your so called opposition to traditional American values. Do you love or hate America?"

"I love America. I don't want to leave this land. But I hate sticking a price tag on everything."

"Are you a communist?"

"Of course not. That's worse than capitalism. If the communist state wants something destroyed, it is destroyed, be it forests, rivers, or people."

"What do you believe?"

"I believe in enlightened social democracy, some private property, some shared property. I believe in solid organization from the top and total freedom and communalism at the bottom. I believe in strong morality and occasional orgies. I believe in sobriety and ribaldry. I believe in the love of one woman and the love of many women. I believe in brotherly love."

"What is the first thing we must do to solve our nation's problems?"

"We must all cartwheel at the same instant all over the United States, and all over the world."

"Cartwheel?"

"Yes. If each person cartwheels, we will have a good society."

"What about the disabled? Will you exclude them from society?"

"We will teach the disabled how to psychologically cartwheel."

"We have the freedom to cartwheel now."

"No we don't. Today only the children have the freedom to cartwheel. If a teen-ager tries a cartwheel, his friends will roll on the ground in laughter and his parents will say, why don't you grow up? Grown ups never cartwheel. The major problem of our society is, we are afraid to cartwheel."

"Are your children good cartwheelers?"

"My children never cartwheel. They're afraid someone will see them."

"Excuse me Professor Bauer. We must go. An enraged young son has a knife at the throat of his widowed mother. He plans to cut her throat because she was good to him. If we get there in time, we can videotape the throat cutting in time to make the six o'clock news."

"I wish you a successful throat slashing. So long and anon and anomie."

I start a fad. It begins with, did you hear the news? A variety of answers follow including:

"The president got an award."

"What award?"

"A large degree of diarrhea."

"They sure are loose with that degree."

"There's a new course."

"What's it called?"

"Mnemonics, but they forgot to put it in the catalog."

The next time we meet Malander says, "Poor Davis. He told me he's got a rough decision to make. He's got to lay off some faculty. Not his fault, he says. Its the recession."

"That's not new news." I say.

"No Administrators will be terminated," says Girodias. "No administrator has been laid off in the history of this institution. Faculties fail. Administrators never fail."

"That's because in the future they will be called giants. Buildings will be named after them," says Alfo. "Here's their grading system. Grade the administrators A for ability and the faculty M for mediocrity."

Malander says, "Listen, You've got them all wrong. They're actually humane. They're going about it scientifically. This should please you Leo. They are making a matrix analysis that will determine programs that make economic sense."

"How many years will this study take?" I ask.

"They plan to be done by January fifteenth. After completing their research, they will know who will stay and who will go. Don't worry. They'll only discard twenty five percent of us."

Although they were kidding, my forehead tightens and my gut constricts. So it begins again, I think. "We will be stuck in that matrix like insects in webs," I say. "They are the spiders, we are the flies."

"His former name was Chrome Dome. Now he is Spiderman," says Alfo.

"Perhaps they'll just flip a coin," says Apfelboeck.

"Or toss dice," says Magnum.

"Or have Atoruk run a faculty blanket toss," says Magnum.

"This was supposed to be my Utopia," I say.

"Utopia?" says Apfelboeck. "I used to teach in a high school. My department head, an idealist, offered me an administrative position. I turned him down because I wanted to teach. I taught honors classes and worked with superior students. Most of them never come here. They go straight to Cascadia University. Our staff was superior. Well, because I was ambitious, I came here."

"Welcome to the big time," says Girodias.

"And now you're a part time administrator," I say.

"Its the best way to develop my own theology and sociology classes."

"I came here feeling I'm OK. Now I feel not OK. I keep trying to believe. They destroy dreams."

"I put in my time and play poker," laughs Volens, puffing a massive cloud of smoke toward me. I cough.

"Don't sweat it Leo," says Magnum. "If your times up, its up. Don't make it into such a big deal. Any one of us can get a better job on the outside. Don't worry so much about change."

"We have some good people, Lots of grass, trees and modern buildings. We could have worked together. We could have been like Black Mountain, Antioch, or Reed."

"We could have been better, perhaps as good as Apfelboeck's high school, or Exeter," says Malander.

"We've gone the other way, that's for sure," says Magnum. "Our committees haven't helped. It was a committee decision to drop humanities and English as requirements."

"It starts with authority," I say. "I've always distrusted authority."

"Often its the toss of the dice," says Magnum. "Snake eyes. Time to move on."

"A carpenter can move on," I say. "With a hammer in my hand, at the first sniff of trouble I would have told them to shove it."

"As an academician, I can become obsolete just like that," Girodias snaps his fingers.

"It seems so simple," says Malander. "Just across the river there is other employment. Digging a ditch may be OK. We tell students their career options, yet who will tell us our career options?"

During the conversation, I look at a group of men at the next table. I think, we are much grimmer. They seem to laugh easily in white overalls. Are they carpenters? Their hands appear calloused. It's dark in here. Academic life is tense and full of drudgery. Even in summer, my graduate school Profs stayed in the lab when they could have been boating. It has been so for a long time. Carpenters create much that is beautiful.

At the next Pedant of the Month presentation, Girodias twirls both index fingers in an orbit around his ears. He curls his hands, bringing them in front of his eyes to form the binocular mandala, then he focuses on a spot on the rafters. Placing the imaginary field glasses on the table, he says, "I propose an exceptionally meritorious candidate, our esteemed world renowned scholar President Elmore Davis."

I shout, "Why?"

"In recognition of the decree, during the first day of his reign, in which he proclaimed our freedom to wear sport shirts on campus."

"Huzza, Huzza, Huzza," cries the company, whacking the table, roiling the beer which pours over stein rims, forming puddles on the polished dark hardwood table.

"As a clotheshorse, our president sets a fine example," says Girodias. "Today he wore a finely tailored light lemonade pastel suit; his shoes of polished crocodile hide were so bright they hurt my eyes. We are blessed by his example. He is the perfect person to emulate."

"You're right," says Malander. "The brilliance of his decisions boggles the mind."

"Yes," I say.

"The efficaciousness of his decisions requires corroborating information," says Girodias. His eyes bulging towards the glowing red table light shining through his amber ale. He polishes his glasses with his shirttail.

Magnum says, "Do events determine the greatness of a man, or does a man determine his own greatness? Did Humaluh County create Davis, or did Davis create Humaluh County?"

"I have a point to make," says Malander. "He may not be all that great. Board chairman Pyle told me, He's not the best, but he hasn't made any big mistakes."

"That's what I like," says Girodias. "Positive affirmation for our leader."

"Getting back to his greatness, did this cultural stew produce Davis's success?"

"Do presidents have the right to be mediocre?" says Malander.

"In my heart I believe they do. It's in the constitution. Deep down, however, I want my leaders to be special, sort of down to earth yet superior. I want him to remain superior until the cows come home."

"If he acts superior, the cows will stay away," says Malander.

"The cows come home every day. He should not act superior, but he should be superior. That's what I say."

"Earlier today," says Magnum, "I was with Pantagruel and Planning Czar Eckhart listening to Davis. When Eckhart asked a question, the president smiled. Eckhart's naïveté amused him. I watched as the great man poured his own coffee. How down to earth can you get? And he is a man of the people. He mentioned a meeting with other college presidents. One of them, Johnson, a libertarian idiot, told the legislature his college didn't need all the money they were getting. We were all stunned. Now he's running for the legislature."

"No wonder the legislature wants to reduce our allocation," I say.

Magnum says, "In that small discussion, the greatness of Davis shone like fluorescent fungus at night in a Minnesota forest."

I say, "I've seen glowing fungus in Wisconsin. Before we take a vote, let me tell you about his harp. To be fair, we should consider all the facts."

"That stringed thing next to his book case?" says Pantagruel.

"That's for decoration, isn't it?" says Girodias.

"Nope," I say. "He uses it. When he is all alone, he closes his office door, tugs the harp to the center of the room, sits and tilts it to his shoulder. He plays like a man possessed. Frantically plucking the strings he resembles a giant turkey vulture pecking the carcass of a mule deer." In my mind I observe the vulture plucking out an eye, and then awling into the brain. After taking a mouthful, he continues to the chest and rips out the heart.

"Leo, I'm not sure I believe your story," says Girodias. "It lacks veracity. Besides the president's tone deaf."

"No, I'm telling the truth. Watch him next time there is a conflict. He will run to his office. The door will slam. That is the time to listen. You will hear the strings shriek, snap, and writhe in agony."

"Come to think of it," says Girodias, "I have heard a twang or two."

"That proves it," I say.

"How long has he been doing it?" says Volens.

"I've heard from my old buddy Pyle. It started in graduate school. Afraid to confess his discontent he broke harp strings. It was his way to cope."

"No," says Volens. "He was too poor as a student. At that time, he smashed guitars. He only bought the harp when he became president."

Girodias says, "Perhaps he imagines he is like the biblical David, whose knees felt the soundboard while the twelve tribes of Israel and Goliath listened."

After making our decision, we adjourn to our respective homes.

# CHAPTER 50.

## MATE YOU'RE ON DISHES

In the spring of 1971 John Lennon and Yoko Ono held a bed in for peace in their Hilton hotel room. Jim Morrison was arrested for exposing himself during a show. Musicians are big news. Daniel Ellsberg released the Pentagon Papers to the New York Times on June 13th. The articles let out the news that four presidents have deceived the people. Of course there are protests in the streets. Jim Morrison of the Doors is found dead in his bathtub. Karl worshiped Morrison's music. Our main focus is taking care of and playing with the baby. Sort of just laying back and taking things easy.

Also that spring I get a letter. Congratulations! You've won a scholarship to the Purple Sage Summer Ecology Camp.

Again, good news. Life is improving. While Cleo stays home with the kids, I leave for Wyoming. I think she is glad to have me out of her hair.

My second day in the clear invigorating air I am on all fours peering beneath a rock, waiting to ambush a particularly fine specimen of feathered Swirloped, when I am surprised and enveloped by an avalanche of rocks surfed by a wild haired man. "Get out of the way mate," He yells as the two of us fall elbow to elbow and knee to knee.

"What in the hell do you think you're doing?" I scream in the face of the strange apparition.

"I could ask you the same thing. Let's get our introductions out of the way. I'm Reggie Clark. I know all about the West."

"You sound English or Australian. How can you be an expert on our West?"

"It's simple. I'm a voracious reader. I also watch movies, lots of movies."

"From movies? Amazing and astounding."

"You were on the field trip this morning. Let's be friends or else let's fight."

Lacking six guns we walk to the communal dining hall for dinner. I meet Reggie's wife Victoria. It turns out they both love open spaces and literature. Therefore I ask them to visit my wife and I if they ever get to Cascadia.

The high point of the Purple Sage Camp is a hike to the top of Mount Jake Jake Smith, named after one of the philosophical card players in the Washburn Yellowstone party. The one who stuttered. Wandering away from the Clarks and the tour leader Evert, I discover a meadow strewn with crystals of amethyst. It is as if I have discovered King Solomon's mine. I run from rock to rock, get on my knees, feel the crystals, bend my head low to look at reflections and miniature purple vistas. Ignoring voices calling me, I reach into my pack, grab a rock hammer and attack paradise. My pack filled with gems, I almost break my back returning to camp. On the way I wonder, what will I do if I fall into Jake Jake Smith Creek? Should I remove the pack and swim to shore, or take my chances with the load? I think of Jack Benny confronted with a gun-bearing robber. When asked for his wallet or his life, Jack said, "give me a minute. I've got to think." Lacking the bravery of Benny I keep away from streams on the return hike. Back in camp, when I show the gems to Victoria she asks, "Why did you take so many?"

When I return home to Duhkwuh and show the gems to Cleo, she says, "What are you going to do with all those dirty rocks?"

I keep some of the crystals in my study. They look like purple transparent towers or turrets with points aimed in a variety of angles.

In the fall Cleo says, "You've had your vacation, now it's my turn."

Leaving us to fend for ourselves, she leaves for Monterey, California to visit her parents. She hopes to drink beer in the Hog's Breath Inn. Unfortunately, she write later, their visit to the bar was ruined when she and her mother were arrested for eating ice cream cones while walking in high heels. The arrest seemed terribly funny to me. She got furious with my response to the incident. Her father bailed them out after they were booked. They spent only one hour in jail. She was considerate of us. The freezer is full of soups, casseroles and stews.

The Clark's pop in for a visit a few days after her departure,. "Remember us mate?" says Reggie.

Victoria is holding Virginia swaddled in a blanket.

"Good to see you again," I say. "Why don't you stay for a visit? Stay for the weekend. There's plenty of room. Cleo's in California."

Later that evening, her tongue loosened by beer, Victoria says, "I don't think much of a woman who leaves her children. I'd never abandon Virginia."

"She deserves a vacation. It's only for a short time." I say, inwardly pleased. We had such a good time over the weekend that it seemed more natural for them to stay than to go. Cleo phoned, "Moms in the hospital. Just a routine operation. I've got to stay a little longer and cook for Dad. I'm also going to play nurse for awhile."

The Clarks are not all peaches and cream. Reggie's wit is sometimes funny and sometimes acerbic. The barbed projectiles often stick to my cortex like hooked weed seeds grab fuzzy Pendleton jackets.

One of the Clark's habits forces me to take a stand. Reggie and Victoria are fanatical television watchers. Sometimes in a discussion, just as I am ready to make an important point, my heart turns to cold marble when I realize that my friends, oblivious of me, are joined by eye beam cables to the squawking box.

However when they are off shopping, I miss them and eagerly

await their return with crumpets and other specialty foods. I look forward to a lively discussion when they return. Upon entering the house however, one or the other invariably goes directly to the TV set, leaving bags unpacked and frozen food thawing. It is as if a spell has been cast and they are like prisoners in an enchanted flickering forest. Fortunately hunger, empty glasses, or power failures can break through their hypnotic state. Victoria, firm yet loving, is as far from woman's lib as the North Pole is from the South Pole. She tries to please her husband, yet in a disagreement doesn't give in when she feels she is right. Shoulders back, head up and forward a little, brown hair moving ever so slightly, she says, "Reggie, that's not fair. You said you'd stop at the market." Occasionally she stomps her foot in pique, but usually is controlled. Sometimes, though not often, her anger erupts, stopping just short of a plate-tossing cataclysm. Later she retreats behind the closed door and we hear her sobbing. Her good sense combined with her husband's wit are a good combination.

Their abilities give them a varied family job pool. He is a journalist. She a photographer and medical technician got a job at the hospital counting blood cells and analyzing urine while Reggie baby sits and changes diapers. On diarrheic days when Virginia cries, Reggie's face is a crinkled dried apple of frustration. Jumpy as a caged fox, on those days wisdom is in keeping away from him.

On good days he is happy. He has worked his entire life with never a break: School and part time work, one job after another, and then America where he met Victoria while visiting Albuquerque. They fell in love and got married. The immigrant had hiked and bird watched in Wyoming, and had known for the first time the long views over the Great Plains. He had enjoyed the isolation of the open spaces, and in Duhkwuh he enjoys the luxury of idle reading. Like a drunkard guzzling booze in a cornucopiac wine caller, he drinks my books with eyes and mind. Book skyscrapers by the bed gave silent witness to his thirst. Americana turns him on, especially tales of the old mythical west. Western movies are his religion. Let Sweden give intellectuals

Bergman's Seventh Seal symbolism. Let Italy give Gina Lollobrigida to the dreary leerymen. The United States can proudly acknowledge the thanks of the world for having created the hard drinking dead eyed gunslinger.

When Victoria disciplines children there is no room for evasion. Not a quiver betrays weakness. She says, "I want you to stop that. Now" She adds, "Or you'll go to your room." If the children persists, a boy pulled by her strong hand is a piece of fluff caught in a hurricane. In the prison of his room he is forced to contemplate his malefaction quietly, or howl, yowl and bang in ignored outrage until once again he behaves like a human being, and is allowed to emerge peaceful and subdued, carefully closing the door behind him.

During sickness, she says, "When you are sick, stay in bed." It had worked well when she grew up, and it continues to work well for the children in our household. Because of meager finances, meals though adequate, lack variety. Some nights a British potpie is served. Called Shepherd's pie, it is a concoction of ground hamburger covered with macerated potatoes. Infrequently we feast on steak simmered in red wine, consommé, onions, mushrooms and garlic. In the morning we often eat fluffy bright yellow omelets or fresh eggs boiled and properly beheaded. Arthur and Karl learn to scoop the salted white from the top. The lower half provides flowing, thick as blood, sweet salty yolk. Lacking eggcups we use shot glasses for egg surgery.

Before the arrival of the Clarks, I had considered omelets to be one of my specialties. The morning after their arrival, I proudly slid out a flat dense yellow disc that I quartered for my guests. Watching incredulously, Reggie asked, "What happened? Is it dead?" After that disaster, Reggie prepared the omelets.

Unknown to me, while I am away teaching, nearly every day, gutsy as you please, Victoria drinks a shot of Benedictine, my most beloved liquid possession. I had kept the bottle for years for special occasions, including Christmas, Thanksgiving and my birthday. It was sort of a ritual. First I would touch the dab of red sealing wax and the red ribbon.

Holding the dark green bottle against the light I gently sloshed the heavy thick fluid before pouring a thimble full in a hand blown light blue Blenkoware glass with a twisted ruby stem. After staring at my drink I take it to my nose for a sniff and take a sip, which I mull over before taking another. The day I discover my loss, I drink the last feeble shot alone. It was my last solitary drink in some time.

My time of mourning is short. Preferring to be a participant, I assist in the consumption and elimination of the remaining brandy, rum, bourbon, and Chartreuse liquor, which being quite ancient has survived two moves and has crystalline deposits around the neck. Soon the cabinet is bare except for some specks of dust, old stains, and a glob of gummy apricot brandy.

When together they talk their heads off, unless they are watching television.

Reggie, like an alert fox, is an expert at getting the ax. He tells me, "Mate, it's all right if you get it fast. Once you're canned it's all over."

"What about money?" I, the realist, ask.

"What's money? Jobs aren't that hard to get." Reggie reaches above the stove and plucks a new bottle of rum off its nest. Generously he pours each of us a shot. Sipping, he frowns, admits, "Once it was grim. I worked for a newspaper, and everyone knew the thing was going to fold. Towards the end, we worked for half salary. Do you think we saved our money?"

"Sure."

"You're dead wrong. Every day after work we got smashed. Victoria gave me hell."

"You guys were in the same boat. I'm all alone. Why, I'm in debt up to my eyeballs. My marriage is rocky."

"Why have you stuck it out?"

"We have a saying, you can't fix a leaky roof when it's raining. When the sun comes out, the roof doesn't need fixing. You've got to hold on to the shingles when the wind is blowing."

"Sounds like you're falling off the roof?"

"Don't you understand? I never could leave Cleo, although sometimes I feel I can't stay."

"You managed to tough it out so far."

"Part of me will never leave Cleo."

"What part will stay?"

"My body."

"What part wants to leave?"

"My mind."

"Where is it now?"

"My body?"

"Where is your mind?"

"Out there somewhere. Tumbling away in outer space."

"How was your mind before they tried to can you? In Wyoming you were happy."

"When I started teaching, the sky was blue, birds were singing, and the air was clean. I breathed deeply, and ran and skipped to work. I wanted to make biology fun. We even created scripts for things like the Scope's trial."

"The Scope's trial?"

"In Tennessee, they tried to fire Scopes for teaching evolution. A bible spouter, William Jennings Bryan, was the prosecution. Darrow made an ass of him, and Bryan died a month after the trial. Darrow got him to admit that he believed every thing in the bible, including the sun standing still."

"Doesn't it?"

"Maybe in England, but not here."

"Do you include that when you teach evolution?"

"I don't teach it as theory. It's a fact. Organisms are variable. Some survive and reproduce."

We had another shot and drank it down. "I've done that myself," says Reggie, throwing out his chest.

"You may be the missing link."

"Damn right I am. No doubt about it. And you also have survived.

I drink to our success. To the success of missing links" Reggie pours us each a shot.

"I'm drinking with you, but I don't know if I will survive." I stare at the blue Mexican shot glass recycled from telephone pole insulators and wonder, can I be recycled? "Once I was happy and optimistic," I say, "In the calm after their first attack on me I regained my optimism. After their second attack in my naïveté, I was still eager. After their third attempt, I changed. I became lethargic and pessimistic, perhaps forever. My faith in college teaching was gone. Bitter and resentful I knew I had enemies plotting against me. In those days, I didn't know the night before what I would say the next day. I arrived at the classroom door the moment class was due to begin. Before that time, I reviewed my notes. Now that they have given me classes I want to teach, and have removed me from the department, my head is clearing. When I was in the fire, my students thought, good old Bauer doesn't know what he is talking bout. He doesn't have a clue. Even the things I knew the most were unstructured. At other times I talked slow, haltingly, I was wasting their time. They didn't know. How could they? They didn't understand what was happening to me. The more I was vilified, the more I deteriorated. During my first teaching year, the word was, take Bauer. Later on, in my melancholic state, I wasn't aware. The best way to follow the changes in me is to follow the student evaluation forms. I still have them. Would you like to see them?"

I get up, eager to root through my files for evidence.

"I don't want to see them, but what do they say?" Reggie seems terrified of pouring through forms.

"The first few years, when I was learning how to teach, I knew little of my subject. At that time, students said I was well prepared and knew my stuff. After the trouble started, when I thoroughly knew my subject, the students said I was disorganized, poorly prepared, and didn't know my subject. I played right into the hands of my enemies."

"Excuse me," says Reggie. He walks out, bubbles the toilet, returns, opens the refrigerator, takes out a quart of beer, says, "Want some? The rums gone."

"Certainly."

Reggie fills two large transparent green Blenko glasses with lots of bumps. "Was everything bad?"

"Yes. Now things are better. I have created a new ecology course. Just before your arrival I received a great honor. The Cascade Environmental Foundation gave me a five thousand dollar grant. I now have money to buy movie making equipment, tape recorders, cameras, strobe lights, and a laser pointer."

"Why a laser?"

"I was curious. Like with kumquats. I've always been curious about kumquats."

"Kumquats?"

"All my life, I wanted kumquats until the day my mother bought me one. Since then, I've left them alone. It's good to get what you want, even if you want kumquats."

"Did the grant help you buy more kumquats?"

"The kumquats. That is my little joke. Of course, if I wouldn't have gotten the grant, I might have attempted to go elsewhere. It gave me the boost I needed. The newspaper wrote an article. My friends congratulated me. The administration was pissed off."

"They must have been shattered. The award meant you were competent."

"They were so pissed off."

"No congratulations?"

"Not from them. My notification of the grant was worded the way they broadcast marine weather reports. It was announced today, the Cascade Environmental Foundation has awarded Leo Bauer a five thousand dollar grant. Davis could have added, Bauer was selected over eighty other applicants from throughout the state. He could have praised me. God, I wonder what I have to do before people acknowledge me?"

"They pay you your salary."

"I don't work for money. I hate to struggle. I just want to do my work and be left alone."

"I like a good fight."

"I like a fair fight." I examine my palms, notice ball point ink smears like the marks on beef roasts. "When I was a kid my nose bled before a fight started. A little voice whispered, you're going to lose. I always had a big kid for a friend. I'd start something, and he'd finish it. I was never part of a gang. Even today, I have friends, yet I am alone. I mock other teachers for being in pairs, yet I long for a close friend. I wish you were on the faculty."

Reggie opens his mouth, raises his eyes and jabs his finger to his sternum. "Me" It sounded like the squeak of a mouse. His voice deepens. "Not me. I could be your worst nightmare. I never did like school. I have always given my editors shit. Fellow reporters don't like to do assignments with me."

"You're right. You have an acidic tongue. So do I at times. I have often been a failure. I liked college at times because I could succeed in college. Often professors praised my work. I was praised in Utah and in Oregon. I was praised for my work in my summer temporary jobs. When I was in my twenties, I seemed invincible. I even did well in the army. My grade school and high school teachers were a different story. I was at war with some of them. I was at war often with other students. I didn't fit in. The teachers gave me hell for not doing my homework, for not being neat, for flunking tests, and for not living up to my potential. God I used to hate school. Now look at me. I'm a teacher. I see my former self in the faces and postures of my students. Thank God I am not teaching high school."

"I never went to college. In England you can learn to be a journalist by working for a paper. School was a grind. I didn't fit in. I didn't fit out. No acceptance of my values. Hell, I didn't know what my values were."

"Well, at any rate, now you know your values." I smile.

"Leo, you're different than other men. If you adapt and become like everyone else, you will no longer be different. I like your craziness, your idiosyncrasies. If you adapt to gain acceptance, you will no longer be you. I like you because you are your own person. Don't compromise your uniqueness."

"Maybe that's why I remember so few teachers of my past. Was everything obliterated that was creative? Or was I too blind to acknowledge their uniqueness?"

"Society is threatened by unusual people. Schools are part of society. They are designed to force people to conform: To sit in office cubicles without complaining."

"I told Isawaddy a book should be readable."

"What a crazy concept."

"I opposed rote memory work."

"You were a definite threat."

"I told students to consider the entire environment."

"Triple threat."

"We went to town and looked at our community."

"Quadruple threat."

"They charged me with insubordination."

"Nasty you."

"They were right. I disagreed with them at departmental meetings. I guess if you disagree you are guilty of insubordination."

"You're irredeemable. A total wretch."

"After they tried to fire me, whenever they were out of town, I focused my psychic powers. With all the concentration I could muster, I willed their cars to crash. I wanted swerving, screeching, skidding cars with the metal bodies collapsing like accordions, and windshields granulating while within that mélange of those buddy, buddy people, the blood was pooling in dusty oily crevices, merging with cracker crumbs, apple chunks, orange peels and sticky hard candy. I could envision eyeballs pendant on red cheeks above shattered teeth. I delighted hearing them cry for their mothers, wives and children. I saw their brains, like grease in a grease trap, trickle through fissures, over ripped ears and matted hair while echoes reverberated within each cochlea. And the gasoline fumes prophesized their immolation, which would remove them from my world. If I would have been there, I would have lit the match."

"If I was a therapist I'd say you had a minor dislike of your bosses." says Reggie.

"Of course not. They are my colleagues" I shake my head. "I am not without loyalty. Yet I must admit. I didn't feel hatred in the meetings. Each time they said, 'We want to fire you,' a kind of mental and physical paralysis set in. I couldn't smile. It was as if a witch had put me in a trance. I heard sounds coming through muffled layers. When someone asked, 'Is there anything wrong?' I replied through fuzzy teeth, 'No, I'm all right.' The words fell out like cold clotted porridge.

My lips were rigid. My brain reptilian. My voice turned into mumbles. I could not at those times empathize with my sons or wife. How could I ask, looking into their eyes, have you had a good day?"

"We all need a little kindness. Someone who is interested in how our lives are going."

"I used to thrill when Karl yelled "Wheeeee" while I swung him. Or was it I who wheeeed? When under attack I moaned. My insides cried out, God, OOOOHHH It must stop. The hurt is too great. I wanted to have a mental breakdown. I tried to cry. I could not scream, I could not cry. It wouldn't come out. I wanted to run off to the woods, to sit alone looking at the sky and leaves."

"Why didn't you kill yourself?"

"I thought of killing myself. But I'm too curious."

Intent on listening, Reggie has forgotten to drink. This is very unusual. He makes up for the lapse by downing his beer, getting up, going to the fridge, and returning with another quart. "What masochism nails you to Humaluh? You've got a great mind and excellent credentials. What keeps you here?"

I grin, scratch my right cheek. "If I go now I'll lose the equipment. Remember, I just got a grant. I've got a professional Uher tape recorder and a Bolex 16mm movie camera. I'm in charge of my own program. I can't leave now."

"You have no boss?"

"I have two bosses. My new division chairman and the dean."

"The coauthor of the book?"

"Yes."

"Stop daydreaming. That man is your enemy. He'll dance on your grave. Get out."

"But I love the land, the mountains. I love the Humaluh."

"Leave this dumb community college. This tiny hick town." He snorts. "It may be a great place for butter clams, great blue herons, and mountain beavers, but it's a rotten place for you. Look at England. Intellectually it leaves America in the mud with the clams. My parents live there. But any fool can see the economic system is going to fail. The unions want too much. Everybody wants. England is not that wealthy. I left home for something better. You can also leave. Go where you are appreciated." He gulps his beer with passion.

"I live for the land, not the people."

"You aren't living! You're barely existing."

"I'm breathing."

"That's debatable. Victoria and I will have you declared a mental incompetent. Before it comes to that, if you want, we'll help you fill out some job applications. Except Victoria isn't here. Before she comes home, why don't we pay a quick visit to the Schnitzel Haus to finalize our plans?"

# CHAPTER 51.

## PARTY TIME

We drive to the Schnitzel Haus where we join an aggregation of men attempting to drink as much beer as possible before the price goes up at seven. Soon after our arrival Bob Jones, a cub reporter, joins us. He is fascinated by Reggie's hand movements utilizing Aboriginal, Italian and British sign languages.

Reggie is talking about his friend. "He's fantastic once you know him. Clip Cloff. Sounds like a horse going down the alley. Clip Cloff, Clip Cloff, Clip Cloff. And your new girl, she's pure ivory from ear to ear."

"Pretty illegal though," says Young.

"Delivered papers when she was thirteen. Now at seventeen she's normal as anybody," says Reggie.

"If she was older, I'd make her want it," says Young.

"That's a fine little body she's got, and she wants it now." Reggie turns to me. "She works downstairs with the accountant, says, 'I can't stand him. Every time I look up, he's looking at me.' I said to her, have you ever looked at yourself? Can you blame him? You come in, and he goes blush. Isn't that something?"

Tom Magnum wanders over to our table. I introduce Young as a reporter for the Tribune. "If you really worked there, you'd never admit it," says Reggie.

"Clark, I like you all right, except you're not human, you're British."

Magnum smiles and ambles off to join the other teachers. Food arrives. Examining the hot dry sheets of beef protruding from the French roll, Reggie says, "If a guy wanted to die, he'd eat here."

Young makes the mistake of admitting some ignorance of journalism. Reggie, an old timer at twenty-five, advises, "Fragments follow fragments. Anything you can get adds to the story. Only way you can go."

Between sentences, Young keeps saying, "Yes, I'll try that." Reggie asks me, "You know where I was last year at this time?"

"In England?"

"Yes of course," he chews his lower lip. "But I was working."

"I have to work at seven," says Young.

"That's the time that worries you mate," says Reggie.

"The job's not bad."

"You have my sympathy," says Reggie.

"But I like working."

"I had a thirtysix Dodge," I say. "It went everywhere. Through puddles and into the woods."

"To grandmother's house?" says Young.

"It ran until that dark, rainy night. Earlier we had been skinny-dipping. The car heated up and caught fire."

"Who were you skinny dipping with?" says Young.

"The mother of the new girl at the newspaper," I say.

"No wonder you caught fire," says Young. "Leaky muffler or leaky carburetor?"

"I parked, and the car died and I cried. I hung my head and crossed my hands."

"In memory of the dead?" says Young.

"That was a good year, " says Reggie. "I borrowed my first car. A guy came out of a side turn and runs into the old Austin." He roars his vocal engine and crashes his hands. "We got paid from the guy who wrecked the car. Then we returned it to the owner, gave him the keys and walked away. He couldn't see the damage. It was on the other side."

"That was terrible," I say.

"My companion had the mind of a criminal." Reggie pushes his head forward, feels his mustache, cups his chin, explores his ear, and folds his hand between the knees of his maroon nylon pants.

Reggie asks, "Have you ever ridden a motorcycle when you're drunk? Five miles mate and you're cold stone sober. Your whole life flashes in front of you. The visor leaves a tiny gap over your eyes like this." His hands form goggles in front of his eyes. "I'm going down the road, racing past a crowd of cops. I'm going ZZZZZZZZZZZZOOOOOOOOMMMMMMM. The cops turn. I look back at them like I'm a tourist. I go off the road, Bonk, Bonk, Bonk, Bonk. Did thirty yards of wheelie, and fell over backwards. The bike went Bzzzzzzzzzz, Bzzzzzzzzzz, Bzzzzzzz. A whole crowd was watching. That's when you start looking for a drain that'll accommodate you. Handle bars going the wrong way. You really feel silly. The cop above me was shaking his head. 'Well, you really bent that up, didn't you?' he said. Meanwhile I was getting smaller anti smaller."

"In France I had a Lambretta motor scooter," I say.

"In England we limit those to children," says Reggie.

"My entire squad was drunk, riding on my scooter. Like midgets at a circus, we grinned our way around a corner over some railroad tracks. We sort of laid on the steel and cobblestones laughing while the engine went RRROOOOOOAAAARRRRRRRR. Soon after that imbroglio, on another day, George, my best friend, hit a Renault hit on. He flew off the bike and over the car, rolled over, got up and complained about a scratched finger. The CO, chicken shit as usual, grounded all of the motorcycles. My Lambretta was less than a month old. For a long time, I spent my off duty time polishing while staring at my reflection in the green enamel."

"Your complexion hasn't changed a bit," says Reggie. "Speaking of dirt, downtown Surreys like Duhkwuh, only with people."

"Speak into the microphone please," I say, pushing over an empty beer glass. "Gentlemen, we have here Mr. Reggie Clark, who is not convinced that the Northwest exists. Maybe he'll tell us where the Cascade Broadcast hell is Surrey?"

Clark speaks into the glass, his voice resonates, beer sloshes past his lips and pours over to run down his pants. "Thank you for inviting me on this program. My boy you'd like it. It has the Mole River running into the Thames. It's part of a conurbation; that polycentric urban aggloberation which happens to include Longdon."

"Reggie, we have never heard such eloquence."

Reggie hands me the microphone. "Our next speaker is Mr. Leo Bauer, a man in the right place at the wrong time who makes picking up a pencil a ten minute job requiring a three man crew."

"How did you find out?" I laugh.

"You're a pretty elastic guy. Some people have a zero sense of humor. You reach half on a scale of ten."

"Tell us about the parties in England," I ask.

"One party was at the McFarlands. As a reward Mac got to keep the leftover booze, only Jim Hyde snuck most of it out the door, and he wasn't invited."

"I would have done the same thing if I wasn't invited," I say.

"Dick Brank was there and his eyes were like saucers. Hyde said, He looks OK to me, and I said, He looks all right to me, and over Brank goes. That was the last Christmas party Mac hosted. He's never forgotten Hyde."

"Neither has Jekyll," says, Young.

"I was at this party once, and was really phased out," says Reggie. "This bird saw me and asked how I felt. 'Oh pretty good, I said. I just feel great.' I saw this bird later in the week and asked her how she was. She said, 'Oh pretty good. I just feel great.'"

Listening to Reggie, I wished I had grown up in an English

conurbation which included Surrey. I like British humor. It seems wittier than American humor.

"Let's fade," says Reggie.

"For craps sake, you're not going?" said the cub, acting as if someone was stealing his pot of honey.


When we arrived late for dinner I appreciated Victoria's tranquility. Though we were beery and rowdy, she just smiled. After supper, I fell asleep at the set, so did Reggie.

Life was again meaningful. Despite the TV there were many evening conversations. The children also benefited from the attention, praise, and instruction of Victoria. When I took naps after work, if the children became noisy, her voice, tinged with exasperation and anger, firmly said, "Be quiet. Can't you see your father is sleeping?"

Manners became important at the table. The children were effectively subdued by adult power. My self-image rose to above ground level.

Once Reggie angrily yelled at me. "Hey. You're on dishes mate," and I yelled, "The hell you say. I did the dishes last night. Now it's your turn."

In the beginning when witnessing a verbal battle between Victoria and Reggie, coming from my passive aggressive family, I tightened up. I learned from observing the Clarks, that after a battle, tension dropped. Grudges were not held. I thought ruefully, the trouble with Cleo and I is, we hold grudges. We can't forget put-downs.


The next time Reggie and were attacking cheap Milwaukee beer at the kitchen table, I say, "I'm disillusioned about the college, but not about secretaries. Once in a while they type for me. They are the only efficient people on the staff. With jaunty stride and flouncing skirts they brighten drab offices. Their glistening thighs add a trace of erotica to an otherwise dismal place."

Peering owl eyed through his mug, Reggie says, "With women we live. Without women, how can we live?"

"Very clever. Except not all women are pluses. Some lacking frivolity are stodgy. In political discussions; the secretaries are conservative as squirrels. The most low salaried and exploited of the college workers, they frizzle and grouse about the people on welfare. Obediently they work and take orders from men. On the plus side, they do most of the administrative duties without getting grouchy. How unlike our administrators who react to an inquiry like poked rattlesnakes. When you ask them for assistance, they put you off. When you have an appointment, they are usually late like doctors. You cool your heels while they slurp coffee and munch warm cinnamon rolls. Lacking pomposity, the secretaries do not block. After I ask them for assistance, they reply, what do you wish done, how should it be handled, and when do you need it? "

Reggie closely observes his rum level drop. After it reaches bottom, he says, "I'll tell you one thing mate. I've had my battles, but I'm different than you. I've given more than I've received. When they give me crap, I say what I think. If they don't like it, I quit."

"Or get fired."

"Or get fired. It's happened before and it'll happen again."

"My superiors." I spit out the word as if I had spat up a fat slimy blue black slug. "The president, oh when he gases, I'd like to say, You're full of shit Sir! Instead I keep quiet and listen to his wind. We all are quiet when the dean talks. But he is clever. When he wants us to accept a new policy, he plants the idea among his friends, and lo and behold, it is reborn in the bosom of the faculty. They handled merit pay that way. The president said, "It is a necessity. I need evidence to present to the board. We must stop the chatter of complaining townspeople. We shall give plums to the super competent, and lemons to the underachievers."

"Actually, he gives figs to his opponents. We have the illusion of democracy. The Dean appointed a committee. Pens in their cute little pinkies, they drafted, with the advice and consent of the administration, a wretched merit pay proposal that was reluctantly and acrimoniously accepted by our stout hearted union."

"You better take a breath and drink some beer before wrestling with a word like acrimonious" says Reggie adding, "How'd you like to step into the president's shoes?

"I couldn't afford them and I want to save the alligators. They're made out of alligators. Give me more beer."

Reggie pours, and I gulp. Reggie asks, "If I was at the college, would they give me merit pay?"

"Certainly. If you took out your teeth you'd get merit pay so fast your head would spin. Hell. It pisses me off. The public gobbles it up. They are so scared of teachers who might be bad for their children. Anybody with a brain is a threat. One lady told me, 'My husband and me are not very bright. We never went past the eighth grade. It's scary though,' she said, 'to think of having children smarter than me and my husband.'"

"Your country's afraid of the intellect. In England we value independent thinking. Your society mocks the intelligencia. Mocks the eccentric individualist."

"Yes, knowledge is a threat to us Americans. We don't want our children smarter than we are. We want politicians who are average people with few skills or training or education. Just average dumb people. We worship self made men and women. Those who become successful without having to study or read books."

"I bet all America isn't like Humaluh. They wouldn't try this merit pay crap at a real college. Imagine offering that swill at Harvard," Says Reggie.

"I bet Harvard has merit pay," I say.

"If that's true, I'm returning to London."

"Preposterous."

"Rhinoceros."

"To scholars."

"Skoal to scholars." We slosh beer on one another.

"Up the president," I say.

"Up Harvard," says Reggie.

"To the librarian."

"Behind the stacks wherever she may lie."

"Let us give praise to librarians for they help us in our hour of need. Their firm hands guide us down the right path. Do you know why they do that?"

"I haven't the foggiest."

"It's part of their job description."

"That makes them unique, doesn't it?"

"Helping the faculty was left out of the dean's job description."

"A mere oversight. Ask to see it."

"I can't. I'm intimidated by him. Besides, what would I do if I discovered he wasn't doing his job?"

"You'd have him. Simple as that. You'd call him on the phone. Say, 'Dean. Come to my office immediately. Don't be late.' While you're waiting, practice yelling at the waste basket. Imagine his entrance. Just inside the door, when he sees you slouching, he'll give a supercilious grin and ask, 'what's on your mind, Leo?'

"You'll knock that out of him fast when you say, 'Dean, I've read your job description.' He'll blanch like steamed spinach.

"Ignoring his misery, you continue your attack. 'Sorry to say old boy, I'm very disappointed in you. You're not living up to your potential. Only today some of us realized, you're not doing all of your assigned duties. In fact, Deenie Weenie, we're thinking of putting you on probation. Have you anything to say to justify yourself? Speak up Deenie, don't stand there like a Ninnie.'"

"You're right," I say. "I'll call the dean into my office."

"Do it. Put him on the spot."

"I'll give him hell."

Grinning like a gnome, Reggie slides his beer glass in wild oscillations.

"No guts, no glory," I say.

"We'll drink to this mate," says Reggie, peering at me as like a weathered Gloucester fisherman. "If it fails, you can always become a journalist if you're willing to face the occupational hazards."

"What's that? Kill story editors?"

"No, editors are like border terriers. Lots of bark and little bite. After work, we used to meet at the pub. Once in a while an editor joined us. Ours is a drinking profession."

"I like parties."

"London's great for parties. Birds love parties. Sometimes, just walking down the street, we heard a party and walked in."

"Just like that, you walked in?"

"Certainly. We'd say 'hello. Thanks for the invitation.'"

"And you didn't get thrown out?"

"Of course not. There were so many people, a few more didn't make any difference."

"I think I'll go to the Surrey connurbation and go to parties," I say.

Out of beer, we transfer our business to the Schnitzel Haus where the conversation runs down hill. As our heads descend towards the table we become maudlin. Reggie tells me how much they like my kids and I tell Reggie how much we like them, and suddenly we are swept out the door by a bartender with a thin mustache. Driving home singing *Yellow Submarine* we inadvertently find ourselves on a highway heading out of town. We sound like two deranged tom cats until taking to the shoulder in a flurry of gravel we narrowly avert a head on with a semi. Regaining the correct lane, we realize we are heading towards Shiptown. This causes us to made a U turn, return to Duhkwuh, where we manage to park sideways in the drive. Narrowly missing floor lamps, piles of books, baby toys, chairs, and tables, half blind we seek our beds. Reggie, fully clothed, slides in next to Victoria without waking her. I of course sleep alone with my britches on.

The next day, or actually several hours later on the same day, although hung over, I feel a rebirth of optimism, as if the beer has washed tons of crap from my system. I decide to leave Humaluh Valley College for a better job where my abilities will be recognized, or else I will go back to school. The specifics are not important. What is important is my firm decision to leave. I feel better after leaping the fence of indecision. In the past I have turned defeats into successes. I will do so again.

The Clarks move on. In a splendid merger of hobby with profession, Reggie has accepted the editorship of *The Wild West Journal.* The dry-eyed departure is complete with hugs from Victoria and a handshake with Reggie. Virginia is sleeping. She is always contented, although she sleeps a lot. The visit was so short I never got to know her.

# CHAPTER 52.

# A BOUT OF CONFIDENCE

My self-confidence renewed I spout forth at the next faculty meeting as if I am a leader. I begin, "Friends..." Then I propose all sorts of idealistic stuff including, "We must equalize faculty salaries throughout the country so as to allow teachers to easily move from college to college."

After this remark, rosy cheeked Pompa laughs and whispers to Isawaddy, "He should try prunes. Its the best way to have a good movement."

After initially frowning Isawaddy grins.

"If all the faculty had the same salary, one teacher would not compete with another," I say.

"And the lion will snuggle with the lamb," says Pompa rhetorically.

"Why not make faculty meetings intellectually stimulating?" I say.

"He must have the wild idea that we're college professors," whispers Malander.

"Creative people need more rope," I say.

"Good idea. Let's hang the rascals," Malander says into his sweaty palm.

I say, "Do innovators always have to be in hot water? Should they be forced to leave because they're different?"

"You bet your sweet biffie," whispers Pompa.

I say, "the system should make it easier for each of us to find our niche. If teachers are not turned on to life, how can students turn on?"

Pompa says. "Students are turning on."

I say, "Teachers should be allowed to float from level to level. After teaching for awhile in college they should try high school, next grade school, and then back again to college."

"You're ready for kindergarten," whispers Pompa.

I say, "Our profession is too rigid. Certificates of graduation are awarded for being present with memory accounted for. Why are there no certificates for independent thinking?"

My voice is replaced with Isawaddy's lucid explanation of the new pension plan.

After the meeting is over, my compatriots and I meet at the Schnitzel Haus. I am patted on the back while my friends say, "You sure told em, Leo. Nice going buddy."

"Boing, Boing, Boing, Boing," says Alfo with foam on his lips. "I have important business. Let us give the Pedant of the Month Award today to a noted historian, Nebraska's pride and joy, a teetotaler, a faithful churchgoer, hasn't missed a Sunday since William Jennings Bryan, what a man. This quiet and modest person, our greatest cornhusker, you must realize by now is Henry B. Olmsby. He should, he must receive this award for his perfection of boredom in the classroom."

"Huzza, Huzza, Huzza," shouts the assemblage.

"I wish to speak in regard to the motion," yells Romeo, as he juggles three empty beer glasses, thus causing the immediate approach of a waiter who retrieves the glassware, and soon returns with another pale amber sloshing pitcher. Romeo pays, pours the round, and continues, "even though I'm a clown, my students are often bored. Imagine my surprise to discover that Olmsby's students are never bored, despite what Alfo has told you."

"Give me proof of your charge, or prepare to fight to the death," says Alfo. Fire flames from his eyes.

"Sheath your petard. My information comes from the horse's mouth." Says Romeo. "While crossing the quad, I stopped to chat. Olmsby was chewing on an apricot. I asked, Henry, are your students ever bored? I have to admire the man, for without breaking the suspense, he separated the pit, tossed it, said, 'Of course not. My students are never bored. They frequently complement me.'

"I was surprised at his effervescence. He usually talks with the enthusiasm of a golden Guernsey. I complained about my classes. 'Henry, last quarter I was plagued with class skippers, snorers, snoozers, sneezers and farters.' He listened with sympathy and gave me advice."

"Did you take his advice," I say.

"Of course not. I completely forgot his words until," Romeo drank more beer. "Damn it. I've forgotten everything."

"You were talking about Olmsby's advice," I say.

"I remember now. Right after I left him, I joined some students in the cafeteria. While they fattened on doughnuts, they talked of insurrection."

"We have anarchists?" says Malander.

"To be precise, Olmsby's students are in revolt. That morning they had infuriated Olmsby by acting the way my students normally act. He, prim man, resented their sleeping, laughing and farting, and yelled attention! Surprised, the students straightened up and watched their teacher. Apparently he looked befuddled. Perhaps one of the girls had her skirt hitched too high. He looked ludicrous. The students laughed. 'Won't you be quiet?' He asked. You know how laughter is. You can't turn it off like a water tap. They kept laughing. He felt humiliated. I would have felt the same, except he started crying like a baby hippopotamus. After his cry he felt better. The students apparently stopped laughing when he began crying. Feeling in control again, he yelled, 'I'm going to flunk all of you' as he stomped from the room. Alone, with nothing to do, the students selected a delegation. This group was supposed to go to the dean, except on the way they stopped in the cafeteria for some doughnuts, and invited me to join them. I asked them if they were protesting the flunk threat. They said no. They were protesting incompetency."

While listening, I wonder, is a similar group of students planning a protest to the dean about my teaching?

"Fortunately," says Romeo, "I managed to side track their campaign by seducing them with Casablanca. After the movie, it was too late for them to see the dean. The next day was warm and sunny. Their mood changed. They decided to give Olmsby another chance. The class continued in the normal hum drum style, and many of the students managed to get A's and B's, as a reward for scholarship."

"You have substantiated my motion," says Alfo.

"I drink to your sentiments," I say.

"It was nothing," giggles Romeo.

"There is a fitting climax to this story," says Alfo. "Last week Olmsby reached the peak of his career. At the awards banquet he was given merit pay in consideration of being an excellent teacher, a community leader, and a loyal member of the faculty."

"The case is air tight," says Alfo. "We teachers must give Olmsby our highest award."

"Huzza, Huzza, Huzza," we yell. The one time Nebraska sod kicker wins by acclamation. Cleo returns the day after the award. It is just before Christmas vacation. The boys and I are glad to see her. She in turn feels appreciated for the first time in years. She becomes irate, however, whenever I praise Victoria's parenting skills.

# CHAPTER 53.

## THE FLEA LABORATORY

The fleas have not eaten for several days and are ravenous. On this day the entire class wears shorts so as to create no barriers to interpersonal and interspecific communication. On the first walkover I, followed by my students, am like a magnet to glistening mica specks. Sitting on the couch I see the tiny creatures, wings folded, perch on young sweet ankles. The students feel a hint of movement, a tickle, and sometimes a jab of localized pain as a flea, pushing its shoulder to the wheel inserts three sharp stylets.

"Students, fleas landing on paper notepads sound like grains of sand falling on love letters. Some fleas quietly cling to house walls, resting before jumping to the skin.

I say, "Observe: walking across the middle of a rug attracts fewer fleas to our ankles than walking close to walls, drapes and furniture. Squatting, if you are sharp-eyed, you can see black fleas half a foot above the floor on corridor walls. Peering at you, the fleas crouch, heads lowered, resilin pads ready. When a volunteer marches past the wall the hooks will release, the resilin will expand, and the fleas will jump at 140 G's; thirty times the force tolerated by astronauts on their way to the moon. If the flea became human size theoretically it could jump

100 times the size of their body. The problem with this would be the landing. If you fell over 500 feet you would be all smashed up."

Demonstrating my flea attracting powers I march around the white Naughahide davenport. Drapes brush my legs. Because I am too successful, I call for flea spray, "Quickly," I say. Sylvia Thomas, spray ready, races to my side, hands me the spray. My adversary waits, compressed hind leg hooks engaged.

Pencils poised on pads the students watch. With alacrity, with just two squirts I destroy forty-two fleas. Wiping off the carnage, I thank Sally and walk to the front porch for air, just in time to see a jet of flame from a can of lighter fluid pop a flea. "Stop that." I bark. "I won't have cruelty in my class. There's no need for it."

Returning to the Naugahide couch, I kneel and point at a crack in the cloth. The students see subterranean passageways through yellowing chunks of foam rubber. As they watch, a group, actually a column of fleas emitting tiny sounds heads for me. I listen for tiny bugles. Sally again rescues me.

Done with killing for a while, I lead them from the stench of spray to the room's center. "Gather around me," I say. "Close your eyes. Imagine that you are furry fruit seeking primates. It is a time before towns, crops and golden retrievers. Swinging from branches, playing like children, you gather and munch sweet juicy fruit. Bellies full you sprawl in the sun, listen to the sounds of the forest. A friend comes over. All of you now please find a furry friend. Gently separate hair. Discover a flea. Bite it with your teeth. Grin in the sunlight."

Alas, I was the only one ungroomed and alone. I wait for ten minutes. "You may talk if you wish." Like flowers opening the students raise their faces and open their eyes. Johnny Petrus says, "I dug that. Can we do it again?"

"Next time I'm with my old man, I'm going to ask him to look for fleas," says Sally.

"You have nice fleas," says Johnny.

Scratching my ankle, I say, "In this way, before the wheel and machine gun, primates developed a concern for each other. Love began with searching for fleas. In that act is the warp and woof of the weaving of civilization; touch has come and too often in our culture touch is taboo. It is almost illegal to touch except for Frenchmen, lovers, and women touching women. If an adult touches a child, not his or her own, our culture labels it pedophilia.

"Now let us touch. Place your hands in the hair of a friend. With eyes closed, seek gently the flea while you are full bellied, full of fruits and nuts, and contented. Enjoy being in the forest of touch."

Forgetting all about fleas, a couple in close embrace, rolls on the floor beneath a table while I lick my lips in envy. Reasserting control, I announce, "I will now demonstrate my favorite techniques for killing beaked carnivores."

Spotting a flea on the well-tanned calf of auburn haired Joan Edwards I pounce with my thumb, sending her sprawling. "Sorry," I apologize. Keeping up the pressure the flea is trapped in the convolutions of my fingerprint. "Watch me," I grandly announce. "This is the grand FINGER ROLLLLLLLLLLL." Keeping the creature centered, I rapidly roll it back and forth as if I were a baker and the flea was dough. After nine and one half rolls over the soft light colored skin of Joan, I lift my finger. The students see a stunned rolled and balled flea.

Like a circus impresario, I announce, "It is now time for the FINGER NAIL CRUSH!" Picking up the flea carefully between my fingertips I drop it onto my thumbnail. Covering it with the other thumbnail I rock until the flea pops. The students clap. "A nine and one half flea roll is so effective that the flea dies from balling."

"What a way to go," says Johnny Petrus. The class laughs.

"I will now demonstrate a variation of the flea roll." I look at a flea on the white belly of Sally Thompson. She is clothed for the occasion in a two-piece ensemble of white short shorts and a flowery halter-top. Slurping my tongue along my index finger I pounce, my dripping finger catching the flea in a sea of spit. "There is a danger in using the flea spit roll. If you lick a finger that has been dallying about in crushed flea guts, you might ingest the eggs of tapeworm."

While Sally mischievously sings, "Where have all the young fleas gone? They tried to jump me one by one," I am thinking how nice it would be to join the fleas nibbling away at her belly. I say, "From the tapeworm eggs dropped onto the rug come legless larvae. They scrounge debris, cast off skins and flea shit." I think of a bright Camus green spring morning where a longhaired lady rides her prancing pony between rows of trembling aspen lining the Rue de Boulogne. "Fleas can carry the plague," I say.

Scratching pink little mounds (from the bites) Sally says, "Will I get the plague?"

"Certainly," I say. "Read Camus for a great account of what you will go through."

"How can I get it? How is it transmitted?"

"By eating infected fleas," I say.

She says, "Then I will definitely stop eating fleas."

"But you are scratching. In all your sweet innocence you are scratching your fleabites. That is the recommended way of getting flea shit into your blood."

She leans her brow on my shoulder, looks up, swings her arm, says, "by God, I've got the plague. It's all over for me."

Fortunately two first aid corpsmen hustle forward with some medicinal Boone's Farm wine. I give no permission. Soon everyone, including the surviving fleas, is tranquil and pleased as punch. If the reader would like to know more about fleas we can peruse my notebook for the following facts:

Itching: Itching a fleabite increases the urge to itch. A mild urge becomes an overwhelming compulsion.

Bathing with a flea: Fleas do not enjoy hot baths. A flea on your leg will climb up the leg to above the water's surface. He will float on the surface film. Fleas in too deep to climb out will cling and hold on. I guess they are good at holding their breath.

Flea Resuscitation: If the water logged flea is taken from the water within two or three minutes, he or she will be able to slowly crawl away from the tub. After a fifteen minute immersion the flea will appear lifeless when poked. The long glorious jumping legs will stretch almost to the abdomen. The beak like nose will point twitching towards the flea's chest. It is time to ask the Flea, "Are you alive or dead?"

It may be time to begin a deathbed or sick bed watch. Hours will pass. At that time you may have to send out for food and drink. The flea still lies lifeless. To prevent boredom you might want to get a poker game going. If you happen to look away from the cards for a moment you might notice the glistening abdomen. The flea might move his or her legs. It is appropriate to offer a non denominational prayer:

"We thank thee oh blessed mighty blighty bloated Flea in the heavens above for thy infinite mercy as you jump from cloud to cloud and enjoy, oh mightily enjoy, the glowing crepuscular infinite cusps of light, the sweetness, the most supreme ambrosia of all, taken ever so gently from the bellies of baby angels."

# CHAPTER 54.

## THE ROASTED PROFESSOR IS REMOVED FROM THE SPIT

Shortly after the start of classes in the fall of my seventh year I receive a hand written memo from Dean Mann:

Would you meet with President Davis, Joseph Apfelboeck and me at 3.30 today? Call and verify please. Thanks.

Rodney M.

Of course I could either have much faith or no faith in the meeting. There have been rumors that some of the faculty will be eliminated because of overstaffing. I remember the fellow forester at Utah State who received the Headless Ax award at the annual Forester's Banquet. Shotgun in hand, he had shot at the down swooping plane that unknown to him contained District Ranger Marshall. Perhaps there had been a valid explanation. Planes whirr. Grouse whirr. Maybe he thought the plane was a whirring grouse. And I. Is a double bitted ax headed towards my head?

I call Mann's secretary, "I'll be at the meeting. Wouldn't miss it for the world."

Mind clear, I go to the library; walk out with a portable cassette tape recorder. I walk, word carrier swinging, to the bookstore to buy a tape, consider, should my union be with me to face down the spotted laughing hyenas?

At three thirty five I walk into the President's office. Autumn sunlight glares through the window. Blinking I see Davis silhouetted against the light. Head bent, sitting behind piles of texts, documents, letters and memos; looking up, he smiles at me with tight fat lips. I wonder, will his mouth break? Will fragments, like broken porcelain, fall to the shiny surface of the desk to remain between the piles?

Davis speaks, "Please sit down." He sounds like a physician preparing to tell me, his patient, you have terminal cancer.

Obedient tail-less spaniel I sit and wait for the news of the day. To my left is Joseph Apfelboeck and motherly Mrs. McGowan. Mann is late. I remember the time of hiring when I soared like a hawk. Oh how nice, to be part of this little loving family. At first, were they impressed with my credentials? I wonder if they ever checked up on me. Mann had found out about my refusing to take more physiology. Ho. Ho. Ho. Happy family. Same name as a Chinese Lunch in Chinatown. My department happy family. My childhood. My Wisconsin family. My marriage. My entire life happy families. We have only lacked chopsticks.

This law rules the universe. Failure is normal. Seeds of failure are planted in children. For a while the vine flourishes; looks good then goes to seed. The fruits of autumn are different than the fruits of spring. Spring is the time of great expectations. Autumn fruits are reality. Dreading the future of this meeting I shiver, waiting, sensing, half sure this time the presidential ax will fall, will cut off my head. When did my career peak? I wait like a soft pendant peach in the sun. .

Mann rushes in. Holding my recorder I say, "It's ok to tape the meeting, isn't it?" (Nicht wahr mein fueher?)

Davis says, "It's your decision, his elbow bumps a stack of papers that fall off the desk. Attempting to pick up the mess, Mrs. McGowan and Apfelboeck collide. I feel like pouring black ink on the scattered leaves. The whiteness reminds me of the pictures of Jesus. I wonder, is it appropriate to ask Mrs. McGowan, Please, may I have some glue? Mrs. McGowan gently pats the white stack to neatness and replaces it on the desk.

The president says, "Mrs. McGowan, please get us a tape recorder."

*Manos a la obra.* While she is gone Davis taps his fingers forming a shaky teepee. Mann checks his pristine fingernails. Apfelboeck examines lines converging on the ceiling. I examine my lifeline. Seeking the end. Can't find it.

Mrs. McGowan returns. I pronate my palms to send out power. The spool leaves the tilting black plastic presidential recorder, bounces, unraveling across the carpet. I grin. Mrs. McGowan's fingers shake as settling to her knees she picks up the spool and carefully rewinds the thin narrow brown tape. I say, "Looks like a pile of worms."

She frowns. Keeps working. Announces, "It's ready."

"Turn it on," says Davis, the spools slowly spin. I press my switch and more spools spin. *Mano a mano.*

Davis forms a new finger teepee, looks serious, speaks. "Leo, based upon our enrollment projections and our matrix analysis, that is now partially completed, it seems to us at this time that we actually, probably will in fact, have to discontinue the environmental program."

Finally they have figured how to take decisive action. I nod, must look as if I understand and accept the president's conclusion, his wise decision, remember the time when as a child I got away with throwing tantrums, crying, screaming, saying, No daddy, no. Wonder, can I do it again?

Smooth as a suppository Davis adds, "Of course, unfortunately, this indicates, according to the analysis made, you understand, with the aid of a top flight consulting firm, that we will be unable to renew your contract."

"Does this mean I am fired?"

"No. It means we will be unable to renew your contract. It means you are being laid off."

"Permanently or for a quarter or two?"

"Permanently I'm sorry to say unless the financial picture brightens considerably."

I think of calmly replying, "You lying bastard." Fascinated with the presidents jerking mouth I listen to specifics spew forth like ticker tape.

"Your enrollment is low. This quarter your classes had twenty-seven students in one class, nine in a second, and eight in a third. The fourth class had only three students."

I create a Cheshire cat grin.

"Very low enrollment" agrees Mann.

"Low indeed" says Apfelboeck.

"Mr. President," I stand up. "Have you really supported the environmental program?"

Shifting his buttocks Davis says, "Dean Mann is responsible for the allocation of funds."

Mann stands and swivels on hard leather heels. "Careful study and analysis would confirm, we have supported your program as much as possible. Bear in mind, however, there are other classes on campus."

I say, "My program isn't in the catalogue."

Smiling Dean Mann offers a *bon mot*, "It will be in next year's catalogue."

With eyes wide open I shake my head. "I won't be here."

"Never the less, the courses will be in our catalogue." The Dean is triumphant with impeccable logic.

I sputter, "Yes, but."

"We assisted you in getting that grant."

"I got that grant myself. There was no support from you guys. Now the college will have supplies and equipment, but no class."

"Nevertheless, the environmental courses will be in the catalogue." The dean is glowing like a chunk of radium. "Your program is an expensive program."

"You made the schedule. You set me up. Did you expect my elective courses would attract half the student body?"

Davis stands. "Bauer. Students vote with their feet."

"Give me a chance. Require my courses for graduation."

"It's too late Leo, too late, too late."

I face Mann. "I didn't get much development time."

"You've gotten as much as other teachers. In case you've forgotten, there is a recession." Mann sits down with a sharp quarter turn. I blow air over my teeth. Our heavenly father Davis sings his lullaby, "We have given you as much as we could. In fact, I've been one of your strongest supporters. As you will recall, four years ago in a faculty meeting I said, Leo, your classroom is your turf. We gave you academic freedom. The Department wanted you fired because of incompetence. I stuck up for you."

Apfelboeck says, "A hundred and ninetyeight dollars was transferred with you when you came from biology. Isn't that true?"

"Yes Joseph. And this year I have received twenty four dollars to spend as I see fit."

Davis intercedes. "Leo, a major complaint with you has been that you are a difficult person to work with. You are a loner instead of a team member."

I say, "Mr. Apfelboeck. Have I fitted into your division?"

"We've had no trouble with you. You've been alone, but that's because you're not like the rest of us. I mean, you don't teach humanities. We took you in because of your troubles, and that was a good decision, but you haven't had to work with us. There wasn't a need for you to attend our division meetings. Your office was isolated. However, you fulfilled your divisional responsibilities." During his words, I think of the compassion of the Aztecs. For the year before the sacrifice they gave the honored victim four wives plus lots of flowers. They sang and danced with him before removing his beating heart with an obsidian knife.

The president speaks. "This is not germane. The problem is, ah, ah, as I've said before, an enrollment problem."

"Give me an equal chance. Remove all graduation requirements. Let me compete on equal terms. Let the students select."

"Leo, we cannot afford nor can we justify rash experiments with our curriculum," says Mann with gravity.

"Your fellow division members are in work up to their armpits. They have sixty and seventy students in each class. Consider them," says Apfelboeck.

"If you'd give me an equal chance, maybe I'd have sixty and seventy students in each class, consider the lilies of the field."

"We can't run a college on maybes. The lilies will have to take care of themselves. I can't tell teachers with heavy loads that we can't hire a part timer to help them because we have to pay a full time teacher to teach minuscule ecology classes." Apfelboeck's look says, aren't you ashamed of wanting to keep your job?

I, the non-businessman, plead a business analogy to one woman, three men, and two tape recorders. "When a new store opens, money is often lost during the first year. Money and time are needed to build the business. When a new product is developed, money is spent on research. When it is perfected it is advertized. With support, success comes in a couple of years."

"We gave you support." Says Davis.

"It was unreasonable to require me to immediately have full classes."

"We gave you the ball, you took it and fumbled," says Mann.

"How could I, teaching only electives, attract half the student body?"

"It was your challenge. You failed," says Davis.

" The Dean scheduled me into failure."

Mann confesses," Dietrich asked the other divisions if they wanted your help to develop environmental modules. None were interested."

I stare at the Dean. "Why wasn't I told? Aren't I the college ecologist?"

"There was no need to inform you because they weren't interested." The dean is smug as a pack rat in his nest beneath a Mexican Cholla cactus. "If you're interested, you can read about it in the minutes of the Directed Instruction Committee."

"We are masquerading. The deck was stacked. You and the Directed Instruction Committee are indivisible. You create, propose, chair meetings, lead discussions, act as if the committee decides."

"Poppycock Bauer. Our meetings are open. If you had taken the time you could have been there."

"If you would have told me the agenda, I would have been there. Hell. I'm the leading environmentalist in the county and you didn't involve me in planning my environmental curriculum."

The dean answers, "Read the minutes."

I feel like kicking over chairs, breaking vases, ripping books and papers, smashing the president's harp.

The president says, "You were a pioneer and a leader. I commend you for that. In fact, I cannot understand why your followers didn't flock to your classes."

"Doctor Davis, am I competent?" My eyes bore into Davis's eyes. He covers his forehead and chews his cracked lips.

"Your competency is not the issue. If I had thought you were incompetent, you would have been out the door three years ago. Our only problem is low enrollment."

I shrug, hold out my hands palms up. "Seven years ago I came to this college wanting to become the best biology teacher in America. Then I was told which textbook to use. Three times I was threatened with the loss of my job. With each new threat I felt more and more insecure. I admit, my work performance went to hell. My troubled mind was no longer quick and eager. Elmore. It is easy to be popular with students when you can smile. I tried to be loose, but inside I was tight. I could not control the real me. My up tightness and lack of humor drove away potential students. You are right. They did vote with their feet. Now other teachers are threatened. Many more are becoming up tight and less enjoyable. Students will find college less pleasurable, enrollments will go down, more teachers will be threatened with job loss, and so gentlemen, though I am one of the first, I will not be the last. You are dead wrong if you think eliminating me will solve your problems. After

I'm gone, you will be plagued with discontent." My bitterness out, I become quiet as a deflated balloon. The room is quiet except for the tape recorders. A cloud hides the sun. Through the window I see students playing tennis, leaping to hit the ball.

Davis clears his throat. Tries to speak. Swallows. Says, "Leo, I hope your bitterness will leave. You may think badly of me now, but I am your friend."

Mann speaks, "I've always liked you. I'm sorry about your troubles. I've tried to remain objective."

Apfelboeck speaks, "I've prayed for you in church. I took you into the division to ease a difficult situation."

I think, I've been eased and greased. Will they give me parting gifts, perhaps burial insurance? "Elmore. What benefits can I take with me?"

The dean leans back, crosses his legs, volunteers, "We give departing employees book gift certificates. Of course they must be used in the college book store."

I say, "Can I take my sick leave? Will I get credit for it? I've only been sick, I mean, away from work, seven days in seven years."

The president bites off the end of a Petaluma cigar that he lights. He puffs, says, "I'm not sure. It may be transferable if you are hired by another state institution within one year."

I think, It pays to become institutionalized. I say, "Am I entitled to unemployment compensation?"

Davis smiles. "I'm glad to be able to say, the last session of the legislature voted to have state college teachers enrolled in the program. You're lucky we're not a high school. If they lose their jobs they're out of luck."

" Will you give me good references?"

"As I've said before, I have no quarrel with your competency. You have been cooperative with me. My reference will not be bad."

Knock on wood, I think.

The dean speaks. "I can say that you have been a dedicated environmentalist."

Apfelboeck chimes in with more good tidings, "You have been very cooperative with the humanities division."

"The only negative thing about your work has been the conflict," says Mann.

"In humanities there has been no conflict," says Apfelboeck.

I laugh, wondering how could there have been conflict in solitary confinement?

"I won't be harsh on you," says the president. "However, this will have to be taken to the next board meeting. What are your wishes?"

"My wishes?" I laugh.

"What course of action would you like to take?"

"I have a choice?" My eyes are wide with amazement. Attempting to figure out what are my options.

"Yes, you have a choice. You can follow several courses."

"What, please tell me?"

The president wiggles his butt. Exhales a cloud of smoke. "We, ah, you see, this, ah, is very difficult. Very hard on me. I've become quite attached to you; sort of have had a fatherly interest in your career. You were too ambitious, but I've liked you. Nevertheless, the course we plan to follow is the one we've already mentioned, to drop the program and its staff, and so, ah, this is, ah, the course we plan to follow unless you elect to take another option."

"I have another option?" I notice the president's twitch rate has doubled, wonder, will the president explode when he reaches one hundred tics a minute?

"Well, you see it's possible, ah, that you, it's difficult to say, but you could offer another possibility?" Words wandering, the president coughs.

I stay quiet.

Mann moves into the void. "We've dropped programs before and had to let people go."

"What programs were dropped?" I ask.

"That information isn't necessary for this meeting."

"Why won't you tell me?"

"If you really want to know, read the minutes."

"Christ. Why can't you tell me?"

"Low enrollment."

"I'm not the first. Students have voted with their feet in the past?"

"Certainly. You're not the first."

Apfelboeck smiling says cheerily, "You're quite lucky. We've let you know in plenty of time."

"We've notified you well in advance of the deadline," says the president.

"Yes Leo. You are lucky. You've got lots of time," says Dean Mann.

I think, yes, plenty of time to get another job at another community college, so I can again get laid off. Not wanting to be a spoilsport I say, "Thank you gentlemen. Let's celebrate my good fortune. Will you join me for a beer? Or has someone bought champagne?" I laugh.

Smiling and relieved Davis says, "I'd like to join you, but I have work to do."

Muscles relaxing, grinning, Mann says, "I must be getting home. It's late. My wife will be expecting me."

Apfelboeck laughing says, "My wife would skin me alive if I drank beer today. We're going to a concert tonight."

"Then I will drink my beer alone," I say. Turning off my machine, closing the lid, I shoulder the tape recorder, shake hands all around and say goodbye as if I have just received a promotion. Walking away I think, it's all resolved. No more threats. Now I can relax.

I am in a quandary. Sick of the struggle I want to leave ASAP. I could have hired an attorney, yet who wants to throw money away? I could use the teacher's association. In the past, during the investigation, they sided with me. Yet my troubles continued. The false hope they gave me had given me courage to stick it out. I wished I had taken the legal route.

What I want now is a show of support by the faculty and the

students. I want people to say that I was OK and should stay, and that they, be they faculty or students, will fight for me.

Drinking a solitary cup of tea in the student union I resolve to see Ed Bellerophon the president of the Humaluh Valley College Teacher's Association.

I find Bellerophon in his office. He looks up, says, "Oh. Hello Leo. Good to see you. Sorry I don't have much time. Let's make it short. I promised my wife I'd be home early."

"They are dropping my program," I say.

Bellerophon leans back, clasps his hands over his curly hair. "Yes I know. It was discussed in the Instructional Council."

"Did you vote yes?"

"There was no vote. It was an administrative decision."

"Did you support it?"

"No. Certainly not. However, we do have a budget crunch. Our division may also lose some full time equivalents."

"It's all cut and dried?"

Bellerophon twiddles his fingers. "I'll write the board a letter of protest. How's that?" He says.

"Can the association do more? Can someone come up from Duwamps?"

"I'll check it out, but they're awfully busy. Now I've got to get going. Don't worry. I'll keep in touch."

"Thanks," I say. Thanks for nothing. The sponge has delivered. I bet there's an agreement between Davis and Bellerophon. One Bauerhead on a platter. The open sore can now heal.

My optimism leaves. Instead of sinking into depression, I behave as if I don't give a dam. I think, four years ago I asked my friends for advice. I'm still suffering from their counsel. I wish I had followed my primitive brain and run away.

During the next few days I think about meeting with Bellerophon. When my office phone rings, I wonder, is it Bellerophon? Will he offer massive support? Will the environmentalists occupy the administrative offices and close down the campus? What about the students? They won't let the administration drop ecology. No, the students are too radical for that. Hell, this is the era of student protests. This is the seventies. Students have closed freeways. They have rioted. What about the faculty? They'll go out on strike to save my job. They won't forget my work for them on the Satisfaction Committee.

On the pessimistic side I realize, the faculty have never gambled individual or collective security for another teacher. The earlier offers of support have evaporated. Now I get warmth and friendship from only a few teachers. The administrators are all against me. The students care about getting high and getting laid. The local environmentalists talk a lot, but won't stick their necks out.

It is as if my status has changed from that of valiant freedom fighter to Don Quixote fighting windmills.

A few days later, plucking a note from my mail niche, I see an announcement of a teacher's association meeting. There is no mention of the dropping of the environmental program.

Picking a pen from my pocket I write a letter to Bellerophon, then jam it into his mail slot, wanting to jam it up his butt.

Dear Ed:

A week ago, the president and his cronies politely told me that my program was being dropped. Isn't that great? We don't drop people, we drop programs; just like in Viet Nam. The military says, an enemy tank has been destroyed. They ignore people and talk machines and programs.

A week ago I came in and talked to you. I asked you to help me. Where is your help? Is it off flying with the cormorants?

In three days at the board meeting a group of people will "consider" the president's final request to terminate a program staffed by one man. What a farce.

Today I read the notice about the teacher's association meeting.

It said: Come, Come, Come to an important meeting. Learn, Learn, Learn more about Medical Insurance. Listen, Listen, Listen to the Blue Cross Representative.

The flyer forgot to mention only one little thing, the forthcoming elimination of Leo Bauer from our happy faculty.

Is my fate of so little meaning to our courageous union? Once you supported me. I thought what a great organization. At that time President Davis came through like a Harry Truman. He seemed willing to fight for me and came up with what seemed a brilliant solution.

I write to my union:

At tomorrow's meeting we will see how effective is our union. This fighting union at first opposed merit pay, now is led by people who are, on merit pay. You for example wear multiple masks. Not only do you lead the proletariat; you also lead the health science division. One day you determine who is to stay and who will go, and the next day you fight for someone's job.

You don't play favorites. The whole thing is done after a matrix analysis. Placed on a checkerboard, we teachers are moved to the correct square.

However I don't want to knock the organization too much. Members receive valuable benefits; including discounts on tires, batteries, automobiles and burial insurance.

Unfortunately, with no a job, I won't be able to afford the benefits, so please cancel me out. Drop me from membership. Thanks for all you've done. Goodbye.

Leo Bauer

At the union meeting, which I attend, in addition to discussing medical insurance the teachers vote on how to use the money budgeted for salary increases. There are two options: Divide the kitty equally, or pay each employee less; using the savings to retain teachers who are being laid off. The members vote to divide the money equally. Fight Harvard Fight.

Bellerophon reads my letter to his executive committee. Hearing my words, several angry voices yell, "Shame, shame." The organization's vice president says, "after all we've done for you."

Despite my nasty letter, the organization continues to support me.


Later at the board meeting Ed Bellerophon reads the following statement: While we admit it is legal for the college to drop the environmental program, we are deeply concerned because:

We don't like to lose a fellow teacher who has given this institution seven long years of service.

His dismissal may be the first of many. He came to this valley with his family, bought a home, and became a valued member of the community.

The state of Cascadia has failed this college: The environment is discussed on television. Shouldn't we instruct students in this vital area?

If the board goes through with this ill-advised course of action the HCTA shall assist Leo Bauer in his search for another job.

Sincerely

Ed Bellerophon


While the letter is being read I think, balls. This isn't a letter of support. It's a letter of appeasement. A sop to the top.

During the rest of the meeting, I study faces. I see pity. I want someone to hold me. No mother, mistress or wife comes forth. My chief advocate is a man I insulted a few days earlier.

The room is tight. We are packed like warm oranges in a crate. I feel more like a bystander than the leading man. During the drama, I'm not asked to speak, to say hello or say goodbye, to protest or to agree. Others speak for or against me. Mr. Fleisch, a Roman Catholic, sits there. Several years earlier when I spoke to the Rotary I had told

Fleisch, "Population must level off. Birth control pills and contraceptives should be given free to all the people throughout the world." Fleisch had disagreed and now would vote on my fate. Wiggins, the man from the mall looks especially hostile. Butler's former landlord Bob Pyle looks friendly, but he always looks friendly.

The board members are as strange to me as I am to them. I know they appoint and lay off teachers, but I don't have a clue who appoints them; perhaps the governor? They know little of what goes on; only what they hear in town or in conversations with Davis and Mann. When they arrive at important meetings they arrive empty handed. Waiting for each of them this evening is a loose-leaf notebook containing information. The folder beneath the notebook probably contains a summary, analysis, and recommendations. Most of the time they follow the recommendations of the president.

When the agenda gets to me, I listen intently, wonder, has a college board anywhere in the United States ever contained a writer, poet, artist or an ecologist. My peer group is not represented on this jury.

The vote is unanimous: the environmental program is dropped. They say. "The deletion of the environmental program and the dismissal of Leo Bauer in no way reflects upon his ability or performance. The ecology program is being terminated because of a lack of funds."

Magnum turns to me, "how did you like Bellerophon's love letter?"

"It was affectionate."

"Want to get a drink?"

"No. I must get away." I say.

I sense that old walrus Magnum, though on my side, is infinitely weary of the whole dismal affair.

# CHAPTER 55.

---

# BE A GOOD BOY LEO, ARF, ARF, ARF

For some screwy reason, instead of going home to Cleo, I go to the rusting twisted iron Helix. Butler is not there. Not having to cover my butt I pull a fifth of Canadian Club, from my backpack and take a gulp. I speak to the Helix. "You want something from me? I will not give you tears. I've learned man cannot stand alone. To survive, we have to belong to a herd.

"I was an eagle when I came here. For a while I soared. Now my feathers are singed. I thought I could see. I was blind.

"Imagine the talk in town. Braun the owner of the hardware store will say, 'Finally they got rid of Bauer.' Johansen the accountant, will say, 'He'll need another job, he's got to pay taxes.' The seller of nuts and bolts will say, 'Who will hire him? I admit, he's likable. His trouble is, he's against everything. That man is always questioning.' Johansen will say 'You're right. He is a boat rocking son of a bitch. Our kids need the basics. They don't need innovation. Thank God we got rid of him.' Braun will say, 'Environmentalists are always against progress. Why that man is against development. Development feeds my family.'"

Still sucking Canadian, I continue my monologue. "Sez I, Sez I to him. He sez, 'Now Bauer, you ain't got no livelihood. Maybe you are gonna have to go work for a living. Ha, ha, ha. You ain't got your cushy wushy teachy weachy peachy job no longer.'

"Well, one thing's good. I don't have to dangle no longer. I ain't gonna dangle no more, no more." Hearing buzzing I look intently at my arm. "Flies. Look at those flies. Those flies have more freedom than I've got. And I'm lucky. No matter how dark my thoughts, this ain't no Nazi Germany. We got no Hitler, no rocks through Windows. No teeth breaking. No fascist frivolity. Tic, tic, tic. Good Saint Nick, bearing bountiful gifts for good adults who have pledged allegiance to this empire, one college, with fringe benefits and human sacrifice for all." I take another swig. Pull a broken cracker from my back pocket.

"I take this host between my lips. Takes a lot to make a pound." As I chew, I think of the old time contradiction. "How can I swallow the victim whole?" God says, 'Now I am in your tummy. This way of dining needs no money." I tilt the bottle skyward. Listen to the alcohol bubbling. "I bet you're proud of yourselves. A job well done. You've gotten rid of the problem. It's easier than removing a spot on the rug. Out spot. Out. Out. Out Spot. Whack, whack whackarooo. Yap. Yap. Yap. Arfaroo. Barfaroo.

"Tenure. Boodle blood is on your hands. I thought I had tenure. Now you've pulled my toe. Think of the sacred vows all across this fair country. Your duty is to build a cake as fast as you can. Take the yeasty dough, pat the dough, mold the dough, stomp the dough, then pop the doughboy in the oven."

I lean into the spiral, tilt the bottle so it takes less energy to drink. Gulp. Gulp. Gulp. Gulp. There is a clanging sound as the bottle rattles along the metal edge. I call into the spiral. "Attention. You are now empowered to dispatch with utmost decisiveness. Cut off heads. Let the DNA tumbrels roll. Madame DeFarge. Your job is merely to knit. Knit a shawl to keep heads warm. You have three assistants. *Monsieur Davis, Monsieur Isawaddy, Monsieur Pompa.* The revolting committee is now in solemn session. With spiral smiles they decree helical impalement. *Achtung. Das ist richtig.* What say you?"

*"Uber"*

*"Uber?"*

*"Ugher. Muhger".*

"Hey boy, who asked you to talk?"

"My crime is defined."

"Your crime is not defined. This is a community of scholars."

"Ho, Ho, ho. Three flies on a roll."

"Crime against developers."

"Developers schmellopers."

"Crime against students."

"Ho, ho, ho. I've got your toe. The students like me. I've one for the bored. Show me evidence of having a loving relationship with at least one human bean. I can. You can't. Neener, neener, neener. You bastards smastards fired me. Excuse my language. I was laid off. I used to be stuck like one of those amino acids hovering above my head."

I am enjoying ranting. The tannin colored booze is getting lower in the bottle much as the cadmium scarlet sun is getting lower in the western sky.

"Yes. I was laid off, off of the amino acids. Laid out. Laid to rest. *Schlaffen sie wohl.*"

Time for an interior dialogue.

"Leo, How are you?"

"Me.?"

"You. How are you?"

"Sick."

"Well sick. How are you?"

"Fine. Just fine. Cut into little pieces, but fine."

"Leo. You can go elsewhere. They can glue you together with Administopheles glue."

"That would hurt?"

"Nonsense. You can become good as new, good enough to buckle my shoe. When I say well, you will be well. Have faith in the Helix. Do you believe? If you belive now you are well."

"Was I supposed to be sick?"

"You were stuck. Sick and stuck. Now you are unstuck. Together again."

"Together. All together. Come to me. Heave, heave. Thank you all."

"You're welcome. That's a good boy Leo."

"Arf, arf, arf, arf."

"Have a puppy biscuit."

"Crunch, crunch, crunch. Shit."

"Don't swear."

"Some fucker put gravel in my biscuit."

"What a shame. Poor boy."

"Arf."

"Take another biscuit."

"Arf."

"Wag your tail."

"I wags my butt."

"Fine. Just fine. Now go."

"Go?"

"Go off to another college."

"Hello New College. So good to see you."

"Where ya comin from?"

"Humaluh."

"Why ja Leave?"

"Big lay off. They closed down whole departments."

"I bet (said with doubt). What really happened? Leo, Are you a team worker?"

"I love teams. Tandem ponies sing dis song. Do dah. Doo dah. Doo dah day. Now is time to go along, tandem ponies sing along. How disgusting. The ponies are farting.

"We have a program for you. Thank the lord for the recession. Join the line over there.

Men and women with degrees. Pull down your pants."

"Left buttock stamped sir."

"What does it say?"

"Grade A sir. Prime scholar at your service."

"Oh damn. How in hell we going to retrain a scholar?"

"Sir. Will the purple stain my shorts?"

"Come along boy."

"Sir, I need another drink. I need Canadian dehydration."

"Remember the good old days down on the farm, the Leland Stanford Junior Farm?"

"Sir, look at me."

"Back on the farm."

"My eyes have seen the glory of the academic cities. I've seen fearsome casualties from jawbreakers, belly snappers and chalk screechers."

"Back on the farm. Way back, we all came from farms."

"Shit, piss, hog screams, blood, guts."

"Boy, now that this place is shiny sterile, time for your operation."

"Hell no. Don't. Don't."

"Squeeze testicles beneath ten tons, and what do you get?"

"Spasms. That old familiar feeling running down my spine."

"Whimper."

"Quimper France has English girls."

"Cry you dumb fucker."

"Me? A grown man cry?"

"The milk's spilt. Clean it up. Don't cry over spilt milk. Lose a million grab another pail. Remember the crucifixion. On the third day he rose, wings frantically beating, flew in triumph to heaven."

"What happens to me? Sea gulls come on this very day and shit on my head."

"Time to pray. Oh mystical meringue in the sky, so sweet the gently baked egg white."

"Give the child some sweets. Oh poor poor little boy."

"Those men are frowning at me. Maybe new employees? Campus security?"

"Cry baby, nya, nya, nya. Look at the crybaby. Leo. Be a man. Suck it in boy."

"Oh the good old days in the army. Suck it in. get in line. One, two, three to the rear harch. Oh I know a gal in Kansas City. She's got gum balls for her titties."

"Trouble with you Leo, you could never find those gum balls. Boy, You wouldn't fit in anywhere. You're neither flatfish nor barracuda. I've got an idea. Into the bowl with you. Step lively my son. Let's see. How do we turn this thing on? I'll try this red button. My it's noisy. Time to mix up a nice Leobroth. Nice nice nice brothiness. Bauergoo. Spoon you out like grandma's dumplings."

"A leary, a leary, a ten o'clock smeary, goes thisaway, goes keaseyway, goes my way, goes our way, goes in a way, there to stay to say, froth gets on my fingers. Huuummmmm. Doesn't taste half bad."

"Darwin, why hast thou punished me?"

"Because your hair is too long."

"I'm a wolf. Garoof, garoof."

"Are you really a wolf?"

"Garoof, garoof."

"Be straight with me."

"The wolf has flown the coop. The chickens tonight will lay their peckers down."

"Obviously our schools have failed."

"Stickastickastick. Reatin and writin and rithmetic."

"The PTA has failed."

"Join the PTA. Go to school. Watch the children dance. Cute. Cute. Cutsy cute."

"The parents have failed."

"Hello daddy, hello mommy."

"Sitzen sie."

"Nein."

"Well you're supposed to be well behaved. To lika lika Leica snap snap."

"They said, the boy has potential." Listen to what they said. They said, "He, the boy, the man talks, he talks he talks too much. Doesn't apply himself. Needs to focus. Zero in. Get a target. So I will obey their wisdom. I must create. Creation is ecstasy. I will have ecstasy. It is time for prayer. Protect us this day our rearly Administrators and forgive them their trespasses against us, for there is the kingdom, and the glory, and the good wines, and *hors d'oeuvres*."

"Can I have some? Wine is fine, brandy and candy are dandy."

"Stop your wineing."

"Whine, whine, whine, wine."

"Toura leura boola bungay. A pimple on his cheek, a wart on his meat. Smile away, smile away, its time to play to play with clay. Mold, mold, mold away, the fruit moulds, the tip of the mouldberger is visible."

"Give us this day our daily mould. Cover this culture with thy hands. God bless America from mould to shining mould."

"Let us have ninety nine percent fewer cavities within the brain."

"We are alone. Security has gone home. We are shiftless."

"May I cry?"

"You have my permission."

For the first time, I am brave enough to enter the Helix, to descend the stairs. I am delighted. There is a processional. The leading people have bold faces. I realize they are giant puppets with huge mouths and giant noses, large eyes and big cheeks. They are stately as they walk. The music is resonant. An organ dominates. I wonder, is E. Power Biggs playing Bach? I become part of the procession then sneak away. Soon I am again watching the huge faces from the periphery.

Some of us start climbing, holding on to stout iron work. There is some wrought iron in addition to rebar. Perhaps as the Helix was constructed my colleagues learned new skills. We are high in the air clambering. I grab hold of wrought iron grillwork and pull myself through. As I am slithering through, a young woman is trying to enter above me with her family. I tell them, "There is not enough room. You go first." After they are through, I ask some of those in back to give me a shove. I become a battering ram that is grabbed and pushed and pushed until finally I am inside. I have made it and no longer have to worry about falling to the ground, however now I am inside, what is beneath me?

# CHAPTER 56.

# THE DAY AFTER

I wake. Hear birds. They are purple red headed birds with fat thick beaks. The Helix is golden in first light. I sit up, smear my eyelids. Stand. Take another gulp of CC. Walk around the icon stopping when a particular image catches my fancy. There, there is the outline of a gyroscope. A shadow sphere is held together by wavy double lines, resembling the lines of the Martian canals. Resembling the tongs of Swirlopeds; the tongs of earwigs, all of which lack earwax, and waving antennae. I smack the molecule. The structure sings, the sound reinforced by a gentle morning breeze. I smell the resin from the nearby Douglas fir forest. I come full circle. Golden reflections blind me. Squinting I see diamonds, reflections from the lower curve. A girl's face, her hair is framed in a hexagon of pyramidine. I wave at her. She giggles and continues to her dorm. She is an adult. Nobody signs her in or out. Actually there are no dorms, only some cheap apartments. Somebody made lots of money off that deal. Moving on I see a plant. Was life evolving in the Helix? Looking up, there seems to be a staircase. I consider climbing onto the Helix. Shiver, remembering the snake pit from Hitchcock and from my childhood at camp. It started with a small snake. Next a bigger snake started eating the little guy by the head end. Then another large snake started eating the little snake from the tail end. I wish I had waited. Eventually there was only one snake. This I know. Horrible shadows. Looking down at cream-colored tile I see the shadow of a naked young woman. Small round perfect breasts.

The apocrypha: at a certain date every year on a sunny May morning there appears a vision, the outline of a naked woman. Helixes don't get better than that.

Growing from the tiled base the molecule is like a rose without aphids. Squinting I see men, victims lashed to the twisting uprights. Tied with wire lashings. The local S&M Association has been busy. I hear moaning. Blood runs down the twisting gold molecular edge. Too edgy for me. Let them have their pleasure. I push on the Helix. Perfectly balanced it revolves. The men above cry, "Have mercy." Still pushing I run as if adjacent to a school whirlyride. It reminds me of a corkscrew screwing the earth. I wait for the sound of grinding as it penetrates the tile, bores into the earth.

Pompa comes to mind. Pompa the lover of molecules. His body held together by tetrahedronal vertices. Each tetrahedron having places like handholds, places for atoms to grab hold. Pompa who couldn't get enough of kissing, kissing millions of geodesic domes, must be delighted with the millions of domes; like chicken pox.

I am Galileo reversed. While my colleagues follow the new science I am persecuted for seeking the past, when men believed in tree spirits and actually thanked the deer for donating its flesh.

Moving to, sitting on a bench, I imagine Mann sliding down a chute in the dust and rumble of thirteen tons of rock to disappear in the rock crusher. I enter the cab. I am in charge of the bright grass green truck, the backer buzzer tooting: I take on a new load of gravel. Drive up the hill. Tires pop rock against rock. Isawaddy is not happy. He waits on the edge of the road, tied neatly with blue shiny nylon cord. Wiggling frantically he resembles a grasshopper. My truck continues, low low gears humming, a slight bump, the rear view mirror shows a slight smudge on the road. I dump the gravel. Isawaddy has been useful. His sacrifice has helped form the foundation of the new academic highway.

I drive to the next job site where things are getting demolished. It is a pleasant cool morning. The drill goes tut, tut, tut; ratatat, ratatat as it enters Pompa's right eye. The see it all, know it all lens is cored on the left side. It is good to have balance. Each job has its own specs. Too bad about all those screams. That is one of the main problems with demolition. Some people don't have what it takes. After a push through the chest the pulsating heart is cored. Another success story for the pneumatic drilling curriculum.

Things have slowed down. Gotten bored with the coring? On to the backhoe. A big scoop and a major lift for Elmore Davis. In he goes, along with some odd pieces of roofing, into the bed of the dump truck. Exhaust belching we drive to the forest. I throw the bottle which shatters on a rock on the edge.

Finally in my stomping grounds. In the forest our orange coveralls are bright and cheerful. A couple of swigs of beer. Would you care for a beer Mr. President? You look uptight in your soft barbed wire cocoon. What's that? You say you will have revenge. Such an attitude. Vengeance is so unusual in a community of scholars, where everyone is dedicated to knowledge, to seeking knowledge. Mr. President. Set an example. Time to bring in the music and literature curriculum. The *William Tell Overture*. William S. Burroughs was a good shot. A bottle on your forehead. Pop, Pop. Pop. Glass and boulders are a musical combination. Ask any drunk. They know about such things. Oh, I'm so sorry. You've got glass up your nose. Reminds me of that song where the cabin boy lined his ass with broken glass and circumcised the skipper. What's that? What's that you say? You are not interested in songs. Oh, that's right. You're a history buff. The snuff of the buff is in the duff. Have a cold beer. Don't reach. On your forehead, pop goes the bottle. Pop goes the president. Foamy as the weasel. Just as long as it's all in fun, pop goes the weasel.

These daydreams might probably indicate to a psychiatrist that I might have had some minor resentment against authority figures. Perhaps I was unduly influenced by movies such as Fantasia as a child.

Curled around the crumbly trunk I dream about the Gymnasium. I am with the faculty and student body. The windowless gym becomes dark. It is so quiet you can hear a microscope slide drop. The band starts playing *Hail to the Chief.* The president enters from a side door followed by a single spotlight. Reaching the podium he stops, looks into the darkness, blinks, says, "My dear friends. I've called you together to lead you out of the darkness. Raising his hands he says, "Lights. Let there be lights."

There is an equipment malfunction. His voice squeaks sounding like a loose confused bat. Blinded by the spotlight the president looks for the Dean of Buildings. He begins pounding the lectern while screaming in Squeakese. Like a giant plump mouse he squeaks and squeaks. I start laughing. The entire room is laughing. I'm laughing so hard I might pee in my pants. The president points, searching for someone to respect him. He starts expelling foam. He slips, falls on his back. Lays kicking, waving his arms, squeaking. The laughter eases to occasional chuckles. The room becomes quiet. I wait for the second act. After waking, I return to sleep. Soon I am in a dreamland carnival. The band plays *On Wisconsin,* Grand old Badger State, We the loyal sons and daughters hail thee good and great. There is the march of the deans. The Dean of Directed Instruction wears a drum major's furry white hat. He twirls a baton, which he throws into the darkness, followed by spotlights. It is caught by the Dean. He takes a bow, twirls, and emits sparks like a Venetian spinning fire wheel. The next time watching the baton go higher, the people say, Ahhhhh. The baton seems to be sucked to the biggest spotlight that explodes with a rumbling boom. The audience Ohhhhhhs.

The Dean looks like a statue. Frozen in the beam of a new spotlight, his hand is pointed toward the ceiling. There is the sound of teensy weensy footsteps. A small child yells, "You broke the light. You broke the light."

The audience takes up the call, "You broke the light." A tossed student annual just misses smacking the Dean's open-mouthed mug to land to slide across the floor. Other annuals are tossed. The dean covers his face, yells, "Stop this. Stop this now. I'm going to check names in these annuals. We will rescind your Associate of Arts Degrees. Any faculty who throw up will lose merit pay. None of you will get to go to Disneyland."

The audience begins crying. The Dean yells, "Administrators, come out, come out, wherever you are. Help me put down this disturbance."

Pantagruel's voice echoes from a darkened hallway. "We haven't had time to prepare. Sorry about that. Sorry." At this point I wake up. Remember. Tuck my head on my forearm, return to the dream, allowing the plot to continue.

The administrative staff jogs forth from the dressing room. Some are gowned, some wear suits, a few are in underwear, the rest are naked. We hear the sounds of many feet. A triangle forms as arms upraised the administrators assume the standard administrative position to ward off attacks from the citizenry including incoming manuals and yearbooks.

"They look silly. Meow," says the little girl.

The audience meows. The dean rushes to the lectern, pounds for quiet. Says loudly, "All those on merit pay come out, come out, wherever you are. Quickly. Toot Sweet."

The superior tiptop of the faculty leave their seats, run to the Dean, and assume positions reminding me of fractals. All wear suits and ties. It is easy to spot superior teachers.

The Dean speaks. "Faculty, I'm disappointed. We must walk the narrow line. What happens in Humaluh must stay in Humaluh. Consider what has happened. You have hurt the feelings of our president.

He is a scholarly sensitive man not used to vulgarity. There will be consequences. No merit pay for two years."

Sobbing is heard. Joe Bibleo, a man with many children yells, "You can't do this unilaterally. Only the board can drop merit pay. There must be negotiations."

"The board will now meet," says the dean.

The corner of the room to the right of the dean is spotlighted. A group of men sit at a triangular table. "The board is in session," says the president. "Is there any new business?"

Doctor Fleisch, jowels quivering, speaks with rage. "I move, no new merit pay for at least two years."

"I second," calls a voice. Discussion follows. The chairman of the faculty negotiating committee says, "It has been moved, seconded, mussed, trussed, discussed. Is there a motion?"

"I have a commotion in the balcony" yells a voice. "No merit pay for two years."

"All those in favor say Aye."

"Aye."

"It has been moved, commoved, seconded, mussed, trussed, discussed and passed. Board is now adjourned."

The mayor, Mr. Hausfuss says, "I commend you. The community stands behind you."

The lights come on. The band plays *Poling up the River*; a bassoon conveys strokes.

The administrators jog around the room patting each other on their respective rumps. The little girl wearing a frilly yellow dress runs out, yelling, "Some of you are naked. Aren't you supposed to set an example?" The naked ones cover up their genitals. Some hold faculty manuals as protective cover. The board members are lined up at the water fountains. Those from the Midwest are at the bubblers.

The young folks start dancing. Their feet sound like drum beats. The bleachers tremble. The room shakes. There are popping noises. Broken glass starts falling to the floor. The falling scoreboard strikes some teachers. People cry Help. The clock stops. The music stops. The noble president helps wrap the wounded in gym towels before going to the podium. "I hope the press will not over play this small incident. Fortunately everything has now been resolved."

The Director of Facilities yells, "Maintenance men, man your brooms."

The band plays *Hail to the Chief.* Tuba players, cheeks ballooning, get into playing their role. The President marches chest out, belly in, towards the exit. His purple robes swirl to the side. The presidential seal balances happily on his belly.

I cartwheel joyfully towards the double doors. A cha cha line of students heads into the rain.

# CHAPTER 57.

## THE MAGIC SPECTACLES

Finally I get home. It is the middle of the day. Cleo is unhappy. A bottle of half empty Chablis is on the table. She is plastered. I say, "It finally happened. They've dropped me and my classes." She says, "That's not all you're going to lose." What does she mean?

I say, "Where are the kids?"

"They're with Mrs. McGrudder."

I go into the bedroom to read and think.

Enough about that job problem. Finally I have the freedom to teach imagination. I've got job security. They won't fire me a day earlier than the day specified unless I screw president's teen aged niece Sunday noon at the foot of the Helix. The administrators can grind their teeth. I am going to have six months of fun.

I shall call this term, winter. The next term I will call spring. Too bad my students missed fall when we could have lain on our backs watching the leaves change color as they fell. We could've smelled the leaf dust and the smell of burning maple and alder leaves. Now in the winter we will occupy cocoons and feel snowflakes melt on our eyelids. From within tents we will hear raindrops crash into the canvas and watch them melting slide. We will hug each other for warmth.

Spring is the time of miracles. We will watch yellow glacier lilies melt the snow and say hello bumblebees. Hello cabbage butterflies. We will smell the flowers, taste the nectar, hear the buzzing bee, look inside hollow trees, go to the beach, twirl and watch the water swirl the sand. We shall be leaping antelopes. As pinwheels we will whirl on toes while observing the horizon and forest blur.

Knowing my days are numbered I am like a dying person, who suddenly has the freedom to do anything. I have immunity. There have been movies made about having this gift. Do you remember the names of those films?

The administrators will behave like witches. Perhaps like Butler they will attempt to prophesize my future? With my reputation ruined, they will attempt to turn me into a Watchamacallit? If I go back to college and get new credentials will the same thing happen again and again? Hell. I spent half my life in college only to see it go all to hell. If I don't know how to survive now, how will I ever know enough? I've spent enough time in study. Now I must learn how to exist.

Hiding my devastation, I do not apply for other teaching jobs. Why should I apply? If I get hired my new bosses will be just like my old bosses. The first honeymoon year will be great. The second year will crumble.

I developed and taught ecology classes before there was much choice of environmental textbooks. By necessity I had to develop my own materials. Therefore, some of my laboratories and assignments may seem a little bizarre to you the reader.

Join me at night in my workroom. We will fabricate spectacles using lenses created by the Aurora Borealis Glass Company of Milton West

Virginia. Some have thick lenses, which convert everything into a blur. The lenses of others resemble Bucky's geodesic domes, the ones he saw as a child. I have the students put them on and describe what they see. While looking at a light bulb some of my lenses create a circle of eight lights. A church tower in the center of their vision becomes a circle of church towers. This is a great way to magnify the power of God. One face becomes eight faces. These should sell well to the Hindus. An ordinary sunflower becomes a Van Gogh color splash. A youth with one girl friend can become a polygamist. White light creates rainbows. A class with eight students becomes a class of sixty-four students thus pleasing the administration. I may choose to market the glasses to academia, the census and the military as a way to improve statistical counts.

I construct a pyramid with an eye on the front triangle. Placing their eyes against the eye, students can see whatever they want to see. When I place the pyramid against my ear I hear people whispering, they are lovers in the park, hidden from forever mates. A nose sticks out of the side triangle. The point at the base senses vibrations. By sucking on another point students can taste sweet, sour, bitter, salt, oils, vinegar, and desire. They experience trains, rockets, and waterfalls. I am teaching them how to get high naturally.

Join me in class. A modern Pied Piper I lead them dancing; gyroling to a health spa. To begin we do traditional yoga positions including sitting mountain, downward facing dog, the plank, the cat, the cow, the lion and the warrior before we move into shaker shaking, laughing crying, playful puppies, off leash terriers, running wolf, leaping dog, yowling cat, flying albatross, diving pelican, wiggling wombat and under water swimming water ouzel.

We sit on shiny mahogany benches in the koala room inhaling oil of eucalyptus. Toes on the wooden floor slats we bend as our lungs clear.

Forming a line of Sonoran desert lizards, we crawl into the 180° dry heat room. Tender rumps feel hot iron bench bolts. I say, "We are in the desert, who are we?" The students say, "We are Sonoran lizards hiding from the mid day sun."

We walk to the Vulcan steam room. Dots of water appear beneath hair forests, to run down our faces and join to slide down glistening chests and thighs to drip onto the slatted floor. I say, "Taste your sweat." They lick the exudate of capillaries from sweating cells. I say, "This is our link to the sea." We chant oooommmmmmmmmmmmmm. If this would be diagrammed capital O's would roll in arcs across the page line by line. When one person stops for breath, the others continue. The same pitch connects larynx with larynx, eardrum with larynx with eardrum. Joined with sounds we explore time. A coyote yelps, a puppy whines. An out of control spitfire dives to crash. Flies buzz in the meadow.

I say, "When your guts are weak and your head is cooked and your hands shake, leave this room, go to the pool of ice, dive in, float. When you stop vibrating, flip over the barrier, into the next pool. Close your eyes. Have trust. What are you? WHAT ARE YOU? What will flop the pool, float against the sand banks in the waves of the sea, bang you the log. Spin, spin. As a fish smoothly pierce the tidal rip, spin in the turbulence.

"Shed your fins. The water warms. You become the clam moving through sand, foot quivering, lengthening, undulating, you are an iridescent worm, sensing only light and dark. Circumflexing, the spiral snail twists into the vortex, slides on the vortical edge. Feel your spiral shell, as snail explore the vortex.

"I give you sight. You are frogs, open your eyes, jump. Harumph. Harumph."

We twirl past dizziness. Flopping on our backs we watch the ceiling lights, gently rock, hands touch, long antennae explore, claws feel one another.

"To the whirlpool," I yell. We jump, feel ninety degree bubbles jet from vents to press and flow around arches of our feet and push against our strong firm backs. Sucking in air, holding our breath, we bob, bump and bounce, hear roaring, become caught in the turbulence of a ship's propeller, the tangled cells sense the throb of power, we are carried by the current. Bubbles jet from vents. Sucking air, we bob, bounce and bump, caught in the turbulence, thrown off by the current.

On the edge of a pool we rest toes tickled by bubbles. I wrap my legs around the statue of Aphrodite, dive, until breath is almost gone. I spring into the air to the relief of my students. I say, "Hands beneath the water, your fingers form a net, look at the lights." They see prism drops. When they vary the opening sapphires, rubies and sapphires glow.

"Let us spin" I call, and we spin. Things in the room form a montage; *Pictures at an Exhibition.* "Oh statue, white light blue glass Golden glass Roman arch blue light red light golden light."

At the command "Twirl," they twirl, on toe tips gyrol and spin. The lights become orange blue green smears as the aquatic gyromancers twirl past dizziness. Flopping on our backs, floating, we jerk, calm and watch the ceiling lights rotating while we gently rock, hands slowly touch, our claws feel the antennae of other crayfish.

As we leave the spa we all are high on smell, touch, color, sound, and taste. A young woman walking past on the sidewalk calls to us, "Are you Pentecostal?"

We meet in the first clearing for the Whorl Gone Mad. The central person, the Whirlabout, spins, lifts arms, chants, whirs, rolls, whirs. We form a kind of whirlpool, our voices blending like moving winds. We are pulled up and down, in and out, spinning, touching down, gaining power. Late arrivals whorl at the edges. The group chants "whirroll, whirroll, whirroll, whirroll. We rolls that a way, we rolls this a way. That a way. Roll, whirl, whirl, whirlroll." When whirlers tire they hold up their arms and brace, support one another, fall to earth. They carry banners in the daytime. At night our torches frictionate, torch against torch. The men are called Whirlbones, the females Whirlpuffs.

They sing:
"Round and round we go,
"Spinning beneath the mistletoe,

"Love us now, one another.

"Love our Earth, the biggest mother."

As part of the rite of the Whirlypool, called the Whirligig by the students, we drive in the countryside past fields and forests to streams and ponds. We stand on the pebbled bottom of the stream or the mucky bottom of a pond. Hands touching the surface, we spin, see vine maples, Douglas firs, flowers on shrubs, sunlight sparkles, solitary orange leaves all merge. We keep it up until the whirlers become wobbler's fighting to maintain balance. One by one we fall, thrashing in the shallows like wounded fish. On our backs we see treetops maple green of maple, dark green of fir, patches of blue sky, while still spinning; sometimes looking through cupped hands. We give the call, change the sound by varying the shape of our mouths and hands to create a whorl gone mad. Sometimes we chant froth froth froth froth, frif froth, frif froth, frif froth, sounding according to some, like a giant Maytag washer.

Some nights we disappear in the moonlight in the mist. Arm in arm we howl.

In the spring during a heat wave the mudflats are steaming, the eelgrass lies in flat green rivers. Each student copies a creature. Johnny Petrus becomes a blue heron with a slow hesitating aristocratic walk. Ezra Cohn squishes through mud, feels the warmth between his toes. When the mud bubbles break he feels thousands of microscopic explosions.

Finally finished. The last class. No more Humaluh. Driving home I think of the last nine students. They made me feel good. One had said. "I'm not coming back. You and ecology have been my reason to be here." Another said. "You were my teacher. I will not return." Close to tears, I say, "I'll see you around."

I open the door, Fang licks my fingers, and yell, "Cleo. I'm home." Opening the refrigerator I get a beer, think, no going away party. At the last faculty meeting, Davis had said, "I wish those who are leaving a successful future. We thank you for contributing so much." He told me "thanks for the ecology program. Unfortunately it had to go in the belt-tightening." His words assumed we are all going on to better things. I lean back in the heavy oak chair, close my eyes, feel the fissures and rest. When I wake, it is dark. Still no Cleo. No kids. I get up, turn on the light. Wander to the dining room table. There is a note, which I pick up and read.

Leo. Your struggle with the department is over. Our marriage was never good. I've given my best to help you. I've seen you through to the end. Now, I'm bailing. I've taken care of the kids. You and I have been together for fourteen years. Now it's your turn. You won't be working anymore. You'll have plenty of time to be a full time daddy.

Arthur is at Mrs. McGrudders. When you need a sitter use her. She overflows with love. I'm empty. Karl is keeping me company on the drive to San Francisco. You can pick him up at the airport in a week. I'll send you the time of arrival. Don't try to get in touch. I'll be traveling. You know the song, *On the Road Again*. Take care of the kids. I'll miss them. This is hard on me. P. S. Have fun with Beatrice.

I think, how did she know about Beatrice Fox? That picnic? That was a one time event. I walk to the liquor cabinet and pour a small tumbler of brandy. "It's just as well. Our marriage was tense. We had some good years. It could not withstand the conflict at the college. I needed more support. Maybe no woman could have given me what I needed. And Beatrice. She's a brunette version of Cleo. They used to jog together. Seeking the runner's high.

I pick up Arthur. Mrs McGrudder is cheerful. Arthur is grouchy. I put him to bed.

That night, I have a dream: I am back in high school, carrying two journals, one red and one green. It is the first day. It is confusing.

I frantically search to find the homeroom and go up the stairs, down the corridor past the windows of a store with much chromium plated merchandise. I find the homeroom. My journals are on my desk.

Most of the students are getting lunch. I go out for a moment. When I return, my journals are gone. I become frantic and yell, "Where are my journals?" A student answers, "Oh, the teacher took them. He feels we shouldn't have journals in the class on writing."

I race off looking for the teacher, passing the store with shiny new kitchen appliances on display. The teacher is buying a Mars bar. "Where are my journals?" I yell.

He replies, "I have them. I didn't think you'd mind. I'll get them. Go and wait in the food line." I wait until the teacher returns and hands me the journals. "Here," he says. "They're not hurt. I copied them," he is smiling. I focus on his white crooked teeth; there are spaces between them. His white hair slants over his forehead. He keeps grinning. I say, "My journals are important. They contain my life." I feel as if the teacher is jealous of my writing. Instead of taking knowledge from him I am producing my own knowledge. The teacher resents this. Teachers always resent students producing their own knowledge.

A young girl is saying, "the police have been mean to me. They wouldn't have treated me that way if I'd have been an adult." She says, "They busted me."

It is strange being back in school. Is that the punishment for losing my job? Do I have to return to school?

Of course my life has changed. Arthur keeps asking, "When is Mummy coming home?" When I want to go out at night, I have to hire a babysitter. I don't go out for weeks. Arthur can't understand why his mother has gone or where she is. It is hard for me when I tell him, "Your mother and I won't be living together anymore. We are getting a divorce."

"What does that mean daddy?" He asks.

"We won't live together. That's all." I run into the bedroom and cry, overcome by waves of helplessness. How can I take care of a two and a half-year-old? As a teenager I had never wanted to be a father or be married. I wanted to be an explorer like Roy Chapman Andrews or Richard Halliburton. Now my life is going to be consumed by parenthood.

When Karl returns from California it becomes worse. Arthur cries over anything that goes wrong, and few things go right. Karl teases Arthur who immediately lets forth high pitched cries that drive me crazy. I can't handle his shrieks. It seems as if he is always crying. As if he is just a big exposed nerve. Instead of helping, Karl back talks. He doesn't talk about the loss, the separation, but is in vengeful rebellion.

I'm living on unemployment compensation and savings. There isn't much money. I used to go weekly to environmental meetings. If my fellow environmentalists had supported my program more I'd still have a job. They abandoned me. I will abandon them. Fang is my solace. We go on long walks. Sometimes Arthur comes along. On the walks he relaxes and is a pleasure to be with. When Karl comes along he fights with Arthur and Arthur cries on the walk so the walk becomes hell. I wonder, is Karl jealous? It would be easier with only one child. Karl is lucky. He has lots of friends. Lately he is spending more and more time with his friends. He often misses dinner. I would've been better off belonging to the Moose. They would have stuck with me. Moose always stick together. A herd of moose would've made a difference. United they would have bellowed together, "don't you dare fire our beloved brother moose."

What good were all of my environmentalist friends? Hell, I would've been better off belonging to the national Association of Manufacturers, the Rotary, or the Shriners. Man can't stand alone. He needs his fellow moose whether they make things or munch willows.

I still need support. Where the hell are my friends?

What are the Crunch and Munchers doing today? Is the Schnitzel Haus gang too drunk to call? The hell with them.

One afternoon I drop Arthur off with Mrs. Mcgrudder. Joyfully she scoops him up. He is happier when he is with her.

I drive downtown to a cocktail lounge. Murphy's Scotch on the rocks is delicious. In the early evening the band appears. It is pitiful. The black musicians have African hairstyles. The dancers are white with American hairstyling. Slits reveal hot pants. I watch students. A red-haired girl looks serious as her boyfriend's hands wrap her neck. Woozy woozy I think. They met yesterday. Tonight they will be in bed. I am so jealous. Whose neck shall I caress? Where lurks the one for me? I am a victim of age. Women in my age group have hair stacked high. Their eyes are dirty, their shiny legs are encased in nylons, which I like, with feet encased in polished leather. My feet are within dark waterproof shoe leather. The soles are thick and rough good for climbing and slippery rock. My legs are hugged by blue jeans. My hair is so long the emerging bald spot is covered. Does it make a difference? I am not a sex image. I am not with the Pepsi Generation. My laughter does not splash forth like TV commercials. Faces don't light up when I appear. I don't use Ban Roll On. I have no 24-hour protection. Woe is me. Sometimes I cook cheap steak costing 59 cents a pound. When I munch on asparagus spears my pee smells terrible. My teeth are not shiny white bright.

Those who've been undulating occasionally look at me with distain. They laugh. I miss the coeds. The girls of plain smiles and long hair, the bra less girls in blue jeans. If I asked these ladies to boogie, they would probably say yes, but later they would go to bed with their buddies. I could dance with that young lady, but I would not be her Johnny. My words wouldn't be enough. However, I can make more sense than those young men. I am loose, wild and free except for two children so what's the hangup? Aren't children supposed to be wonderful? Well they are. Dammit. Oh they are they, and I am me, and somewhere there must be a woman for me. Cleo's letter sounded as if she has had it. No room for reconciliation. She's through with me. I can understand where she's coming from. The years in Duhkwuh have not been wine and roses. We've had some good times. But the stress, damn it, the continual stress. She had to escape. I wonder, has she hooked up with her plumber friend?

The barroom hushes. The band becomes silent in reference to one of their number: the minimoog keyboardist, an integral part of their organization has just been busted in Duwamps. Fortunately the bar closes at two a.m. The good-natured bartender pushes we customers into the warm summer air. Outside befuddled, I wander like a ghost.

Although it is hard to walk, once in the car I am an excellent driver. I drive to the edge of the cliffs along the ocean almost hitting the railing twice. Somehow when I drink too much I often head in the wrong direction. In the past few years two other teachers were in trouble with the administrators. both died in car crashes while driving drunk. So much for strong characters. The higher mortality of the teaching profession. The end of the road for them. Are we the bad apples? Well, it is good to see the Humaluh flats. I have a kind of automatic pilot correcting me, guiding me to the freeway. Driving with the window open sobers me up. A few a few more miles, just a few miles more, the exit to home. Safely parking, I open a can of ravioli. It isn't good but it feeds me. I go to bed.

The next morning, driving to pick up Arthur, the smell of ravioli still swirls through my nostrils. I hate that aftertaste. It remains with me for hours. How stupid of me to have gambled with my life. Next time I won't drink so much. As I pick up Arthur, Mrs. McGrudder laughs. "You must have tied one on," she says.

That night I have a dream. My motor scooter has it's light off. I am looking for a particular store. I can't understand the traffic lanes. It seems I am going the wrong way. I turn off the busy street and stop at a restaurant. I eat a steak that has been soaked in gourmet sauce. It is delicious. I peel back some fat that is white, and thick, like whale blubber. Most of my steak is fat. I look over at the next table. Someone is watching me and grinning. It is Johnny Petrus. I say hello.

At my table people are talking. One man, a former student says, "my father was really strong. My father was strong enough to kill someone.

Because of this, I had to exercise every day. I had seen him work out with his heavy Dumbbells, his body glistening with sweat, muscles bulging. I said, Dad have you ever killed a man?" He said "yes." He also said he had fought our state legislature and had beaten them.

I left that dream. Went to another. I was seeking excitement in my dream world. We were all walking along the road. I carried many papers. The others carried papers. We all gathered at an important spot on a hillside. Some of my papers had fallen along the road. I went back picking up documents. I noticed many things that had been forgotten by the teacher. I ate food from one of the teacher's plates. Taking the dirty plate to wash, I passed the sink and dumped the plate in the soapy water. Near me were more sheets. It was like a camp of desert nomads. Walking back along the road I saw a man from a publishing firm. I said, "I taught ecology." I marked some dates. He said, "they are unrelated numbers." I mentioned to him that I was writing a book. He asked me some questions and wrote furiously in his notebook. I said I need a publisher. He suddenly became noncommittal. He was a heavy man. He seemed out of place. When I wake I am still in bed. I get up and go outside to check the weather.

A huge electrical storm is raging on the Sun. From here it shows as a solar flare during the daylight hours. Now at night the Northern lights are directly above me. They extend from the rise in the northeastern sector of the sky, which is flickering. The color is white. The vertical beams and fast-moving ghost images remind me of northern Wisconsin. I should return to northern Wisconsin. Tonight on the lake there must be a fantastic display. The lake and the sky will be having a game of catch. I turn on the television. Poor Senator Eagleton. His face shows such anguish, such torment. What is the difference between any of us and Senator Eagleton? So he had some mental problems. What's wrong with that?

# CHAPTER 58.

## SIMULSENSE.

No longer working, I let my hair grow long. I will pay more attention to my senses. I may become a Simulsenser. Unfortunately Simulsensers are gullible. If such folk are told that the Army Corps of Engineers is going to remove a nearby mountain to improve the climate, they become agitated and plan political action and revenge against the corps. Now everyone knows the corps would not engage in massive disruption of the earth. An example of a more practical Simulsenser is Zorba the Greek. Zorba is my role model.

The Simulsense Bible is the *Steersmen's Handbook* by L. Clark Stevens. They are people who delight in music, light, color and conversation. Their motivating principle is, do your thing, don't lay a heavy trip on someone else. As you probably know, the world's first Simulsenser was Adam.

I imagine myself in a new incarnation as a radio announcer: "Good morning. I'd like to invite you to Simulsense on the air. Our broadcast day begins before your birth and continues after you die. Traditional media, such as television, alters sight and sound: Even the applause is phony. Their product testimonials are fake love. Everything in traditional media is phony. Simulsense broadcasting includes the phony and the honest. During courtship, lovers say obvious things such as "you are the apple of my eye." Who wants an apple in their eye? "You are the perfect man for me. You are the perfect woman." They say "you are sweeter than honey." Honey is too sweet. Sweet stuff leads to diabetes. "You smell sweet as a rose?" Why don't they say you are covered with thorns? No one wants to fall into a patch of roses.

All of us can be Simulsense broadcasters. Each broadcaster possesses a different quantity and variety of filters. Observe my filters in the supermarket. I walk purposefully between shelves piled high with food. I think, I probably look suspicious. That clerk is looking at me. I can feel the pressure of his eyes on me. Although I'm not a shoplifter I feel like a shoplifter. As I pick things off of shelves and put them in my cart I see reflections of the cart and me on a big convex mirror above. Above the frozen foods a camera records my movements. It's hard to pick my nose in a grocery store knowing I am being filmed. Later on, after the store has closed, the workers will gather round the video and watch my nose picking. They laugh and giggle and laugh and giggle.

While worrying about being suspected of shoplifting, I amble past the frozen pies and Chinese peapods. Rebecca West comes toward me. I like her long hair and firm breasts. They are so fine. She smiles, says "Leo," places her hand on my forearm. Her touch is warm, her manner loving. Her eyes sparkle through large gold-framed glasses. I get a hard on. Yes, she broadcasts love and I receive pleasure, but I hold back. She puts her arms around me and gives me a hug. I want to hug back, but turn into a Popsicle. My arms at my sides are frozen. I become formal and retreat into linearity. You ask me why?

First, I am a former professor. I still have some standing in the community. Second, we are in a crowded public place. If we were in a private place I would want to jump her bones. Third, she is much younger than I. Damn. She is not long out of high school. I do not want to be considered a dirty old degenerate.

I am changing. Next time I see Rebecca, I will give her a hug. I may even try kissing her. I may go to bed with her. That would be nice. I will try to be a good Simulsenser. I hope she cooperates. As we mutually Simulsense, perhaps we will Simulsense in bed together.

This year, I have visited bars and searched for females. Boy do I get phony. I wear fancy Italian black boots with zippers down the sides. Can you imagine that? Tight striped pants and a sexy soft tapered soft shirt. I am broadcasting, look at me. I am the image of a sexy man. Watch me get you stirred up. I'm lucky I'm not caught and roasted. That's what happens to roosters. First they lose their feathers. My hair was cut in the mod way, whatever that is. I left it up to the hairstylist. The hairstylist, that's a joke. I go to the cheapest place I can find offering styling. They make me what I am. Cheap Snips. That is the name of the chain, Cheap Snips. Before going out I bath and dous myself with after-shave lotion. I must smell like a transvestite. How do I know what a transvestite smells like? I don't know. I've never knowingly smelled a transvestite? If I was next to a transvestite and I knew I was next to a transvestite I would run away fast. No. I must smell like a gigolo when I go hunting women.

When I ask a woman to dance, some of them interested in the false me say yes. While gyrating I look at them. Some of their heads are swollen from carrying, from bearing and wiggling rats. Those hairy ramparts are often sticky from stinky plastic spray. After holding those wreaking ladies, gasping for breath, I want fresh air. Looking into the eyes of one such woman the way is obscured by ashes. Her eyes look like polluted skies through sooty grates. Her lips are covered with wax. Her armpits are ravaged of their natural flora and fauna by the blade and deodorants. Artificial nothingness. An acrid cloud hovers. From her I sniff ointments, vaginal sprays and cigarette smoke. I wonder as I peer at her what is she really like? What would she look like after I gave her a thorough shower?

I talk to another lady. She says, I don't like my dress. I think, well then let's take it off. I look closely. It clings to her as if she is a cathode. Perhaps I can be her anode. How can I tell? She says, "I like parties. I have been to California." She is this and she is that. She never asks me what I like or where I have been. Yet when we dance we are very close. I suspect that she wants to go to bed with me later. But I dance with her just twice, and for the rest of the evening sit alone in my black shiny Italian boots with zippered sides.

Now I am more honest. I rarely wear my black Italian boots or wear ties. I loathe ties. They make me feel like a slave in neck irons, rowing a Roman galley through the waves of the Mediterranean. Getting lashed. My back is ripped open, the blood running down my butt.

My suits have been shunted to the hangers. They await moths. After the moths make them holy I will throw them all out.

Now my shoes are made for walking, made to walk through puddles, made to walk on slippery rain slicked rock. Made to last. My shoes are dry and comfortable. Wearing them I can dance, drive, walk in the snow and run. Instead of polishing my shoes I waterproof them. They look worn, but they are good shoes. They are my kind of shoes. They are honest shoes. They are not deceitful shoes.

My pants are good pants. They are strong. Some are drab. A few have patterns. Some are black. The cloth is tough. I feel like a man of the woods, of the mountains, when I walk in them. When I'm in the woods my pants accumulate the aromas and pitch from conifers, and camp fires, and wet moss sperm.

My belts are of thick solid leather. They are wide. A friend tooled this Western belt for me. It has fancy blue and red Indian designs and a big bright brass buckle with a coiled snake, which was cast at a local foundry.

My shirts are not me, but a friend Mike says he will make me a shirt of deerskin. The leather strips holding it together will travel wormlike up my sides and down my sleeves. When I am wearing that shirt I will have power and when someone asks me, who made your shirt? I will say, my friend Mike made this shirt. Yes I will be me in that shirt.

Other shirts for my future must be loose and comfortable. I hate feeling constricted. Some, like polo shirts will be knitted. My winter shirts and jackets will be woven woolen plaids and cotton shirts with paisley or solid colors dyed with natural dyes. The colors will flow from the line of the buttons. There will be no sharp corners. The pockets will be tough, but able to hold pens. All of my shirts will have deep pockets for long pens. The tough threaded buttons will last for years.

There was some conversation in the community regarding my clothing and aroma. Magnum overheard a conversation between women eating lunch in the Schnitzel Haus. He gave me their words.

"Bauer doesn't wear color coordinated clothing."
"He used to."
"Since his wife left he's gone to the dogs."
"She was a good woman. Always looked nice."
"He doesn't use underarm deodorant."
"He doesn't?"
"No!"
"Oh."
"I know it's terrible."
"His poor lady friends."
"He doesn't have any."
"I can understand that."
"If he gets a lady friend, she will have to put up with him."
"Women must bear the cross."
"We have to suffer and pay the cost."
"For men's transgressions."
"Doesn't he use rub ons?"
"No."
"Or misty sprays?"
"No."
"Anti-perspirants?"
"No.
"Anti-drying?"

"No."

"Germicides or fungicides?"

"No. He uses nothing."

"We must suffer for the sins of Bauer."


I agree with them. It is terrible, this I know. Because the advertisers tell us so. I developed a way to test linearity. I walk up to a pedestrian and say, "pardon me sir. I'm doing research for Universal Simulsense Corporation. Would you mind answering a few questions?"

"Thank you. Why do you get your hair cut?"

"Because it needs cutting."

"Why does it need cutting? Does your head get too warm?"

"It doesn't look good when it is long. Others will notice."

"I understand. You're getting your hair cut for others. By creating a better visual environment, you benefit humanity. Therefore you are a humanitarian and an altruist. A few more questions, if you don't mind. Does your head get cold in winter? Have you ever experienced pleasure when someone ran his or her fingers through your hair? Did this feel best when your hair was short, or when it was long? When you had longer hair as a child, do you recall swinging your head from side to side and feeling the hair tickle your neck?"

"Long-hair is for hippies and teenagers. I've got to look respectable. Long-hair is not for me, that's for sure."

"Why sir? Are you too old for long hair?" With great agility I suddenly sidestep an unexpected left uppercut, which just misses my jaw. Waving goodbye, I run around the block chased by the younger man who is overweight and huffing and puffing.

After my breathing slows, and he abandons the chase, I walk up to a man cutting grass. I have to yell to be heard above the self propelled power mower. "Pardon me sir. I'm with Universal Simulsense Corporation. Why do you cut your lawn?"

"What did you say? What did you say? I can't hear you, the damn mower."

"Why do you cut your lawn?"

"Because it needs cutting. You don't have to yell so loud,"

"I'm sorry sir. Why does it need cutting?"

"It gets too long."

"Do you like to touch the grass?"

"I like to lie on the grass but I hate cutting my lawn."

"Why do you cut it?"

"My wife, my wife, she likes the grass cut. She and the neighbors would raise hell if I didn't cut the damn stuff."

"Does your wife like to cut the grass?"

"No."

"Do your neighbors like to cut the grass?"

"We all hate cutting the grass."

"Why would they complain if you stopped cutting the grass?"

"If I stop cutting the grass people will think I am either lazy or sick. Property values would drop. The country would be thrown into a recession."

"Do you like birds?"

"Everyone likes birds."

"Do you ever see any birds in your lawn?"

"Sure. I see lots of birds."

"What kind of birds?"

"Robins. They eat the worms."

"Where are the other birds, the other kinds of birds?"

"They're across the street."

"Where?"

He points. "Over there?"

"By the for sale sign on that vacant lot? By the weeds and hawthorns?"

"Sure, if that's what you call those trees. In the morning that little place is full of birds. It's a great place to watch sparrows."

"Thank you sir. Have a good day. You have been very helpful to my project." Taking a different route because of my minor problem with the man getting frequent haircuts, I pass by several yards under aesthetic, and chemical attack by teams spreading chemical granules. Trucks are spraying garden beds with Agent Orange so as to obliterate wild flowers and other despised plants. I get into a coughing fit due to my allergies to insecticides and herbicides. Birds are gasping for breath. Moles are belly up in the opaque light.

I walk down the street and keep going until I am home. I put the new information into my journal along with my thoughts and dreams. I think, I might become a professional writer of journals. I will follow in the pentracks of Lewis and Clark, Anais Nin and Henry David Thoreau.

# CHAPTER 59.

## THE WRITERS ASSEMBLY.

U nwilling to work for an employer I decide to become a professional writer. I ask Nolen Volens for advice. Nolen says "Few novels and short stories get published. If you plan on becoming a writer realize, you will be a poor man to the day you die. Get used to seeing your children in rags. Women will avoid you like your face is covered with eczema, with blisters oozing and crusting like lava pouring and oozing from beneath the earth's surface." Disregarding his advice, I sign up to attend the *Cascadian Writer's Assembly* that is meeting at *St John's University* in Duwamps.

I drop Karl off with the Magnums, they have boys his age. I leave Arthur with Mrs. McGrudder.

Driving South to Duwamps I think, they'll be safe and happy. I Explore the Flying Fish Farmer's Market. I scan several rows of smoked piglet heads. The extended ears make them look like comical elves. Adjacent to them are shiny skinless tails of goats, calves, deer, horses, pigs, cats and oxen. I buy figs and fresh baked sour dough rolls. Ripping a roll in half I see a crab in the yellow center. He crawls out and snaps his pincers at me. I look into his stalked eyes and he crawls away.

The next morning after spending the night in a dorm, seeking signs, I agitatedly follow concrete paths. Briefcase in hand I ask a coed, "Where is the Writer's Assembly?"

"Try the union." she points. I take an oblique trail, walk up a pebbled ramp, enter a huge foyer, and stop at a table covered with brochures. A friendly middle-aged lady registers me. Wanting an interview with an agent or an editor I say, "I'd like to sign up for a conference."

"I'm sorry." Says a thin woman. "They're all booked up. You should have signed up earlier. Would you like to be put on a waiting list?"

I say "yes," while thinking oh shit. I sign up for a group session with a New York Editor.

Following signs I walk into the session called Analyzing the Novel. Two hundred and ninety three people sit in curved rows facing a group of card tables. I crane my neck to see. An elderly white haired man is talking. I take copious notes. "There are characters." Myself, me and I. Can't forget Mr. Fitz. Mr. Fitz Witz has wits. Has Mr. Fitz Fitz wits? On his wits sits Mr. Fitz Witz.

"A novel should contain a plot." Plot of ground. Square or round? Black or brown? Sterile or loamy? Sandy? Dry? Mucky?

"Words." Fuckety, fuck, fuck, fuck, fuck.

"The reader should be considered." Hello. Hello, wherever you are, go and pee on a far off star.

"Narrative." Hello Mrs. Onion. So glad to meet you Mr. Garlic. Have you had a good day? Fair to middlin. Mostly middlin. Sort of diddlin, I'm having a diddlin, diddlin day.

"Fast pace is important." On a rocket ship hurtling towards the sea, John and Mary shudder as they cleave the wine dark waves, Burgundy from France, nice bouquet. Still descending they are attacked by the Mer people with saw toothed beaks; those octapaquadrapanoodle nosed freaks entangle the ship in tentacles and begin ripping off the hatch. Soon the sea will pour in.

"Setting. The environment." If the ship is destroyed the radioactive belch gas will escape and pollute the seas, civilization will be destroyed. Therefore the Mer people must be defeated.

"Don't write a formula novel. However each genera has its requirements." Each of the eighteen hundred and thirty two genera of Swirlopeds requires food, air and water. With too much water they will drown. With too much food they will choke or become anorexic. With too much air they will dry up.

"As an example, the gothic novel." Have I ever read a gothic novel? I don't know. Was the *Hunchback of Notre Dame* gothic? Was *Candy* gothic? Is too much *Candy* bad for hunchbacks? Are hunchbacks out of style or will publishers still buy and publish hunchbacks. Are hunchbacks cheaper by the dozen? Can a hunchback discover romance? One for the money and two for the show, the hunchback and Candy are ready to go. "Give me your hump" says Candy.

"A final question." Are gothic novels written with talcum power or ink? Same question for Romance novels. If yes, what color ink is to be used?

Pondering the answers I had written I got up and walked to the Poetry Section where forty people sat in a circle on the floor listening to one another read their own poetry. Joining them I enjoy getting splashed with their emotions.

After lunch I join a session on How to Write a Novel. The panel includes a publisher, an editor, a writer and an agent. The author of How to Write a Best Selling Novel in Three Weeks speaks. Her wisdom flows like warm pea soup across the level room.

I write: Academic novels are corpses in the market place. *Death in the Afternoon.* Will this bull get me? Oh, ho, no.

A lady speaks. "I let my characters evolve."

I dig what you say, oh lovely British lady. From squirming Amphioxus worms with notochords come jumping lizards. Question. Does an old Amphioxus have arthritis and have to have regular visits to a chiropractor? After this is answered we can deal with jumping fence lizards and soaring frigate birds. Are any frigate birds frigid? Write in detail of the sex lives of frigate birds.

"Our stories must have optimistic endings."

I knew a lady once who taught Engfish. She cried whenever she read a story with a sad ending. In Engfish she watched the fishies swim.

"The lines most prized by Hemingway were yanked by Maxwell Perkins, his editor."

Question. Did Perkins have acid reflux?

"Know the editor and your story will be read." My god, an honest woman.

A male editor said, "I read everything submitted." Sure you do, liar, liar, pants on fire.

"We change the titles." At least you are honest.

A woman writer speaks. "I write and keep writing until I stop. Later I revise." Just another Kerouac. "I write every day from five in the morning until noon. I am compelled to write. When the impulse is gone I do something else. The first run of my novels is 6,000." A modest goal.

I am distracted by a sound in back of me, going retchita chazz, retchita chazz. I turn and see a thin bony white haired lady carefully brushing her teeth.

A male publisher speaks. "Ten percent of the new books are fiction. Super chains sell half of the books. They refuse to handle novels by new novelists. Operating on sound business principles they say, why gamble? Libraries, short of funds, are a poor market. Be able to tell a story. There is an oral tradition in the south." Always good to get new information. Alas we Northerners are too busy to sit on porches in Islip and while rocking sip mint juleps. Alas and alack, we have no fresh pecans to pick newly dropped from the newly mowed lawn or Spanish moss to evoke gothic tales. Oh my neck, it is hard to see the speakers. I dislike trying to stare through the backs of knowledge seeking ladies. If I ran the assembly the speakers would sit on cushions and float in the air above the audience. I would probably have to go to the Assembly of God to see such a sight.

"A first novelist normally earns $3,000 from his book." Not bad for three weeks work.

The toothbrush lady asks a question. "Does it help to go to New York and talk in person with the publishers?" Damn right it helps if you are young, curvy and desirable.

"What are the most successful books you ever published?" she asks.

"Sex in the Azores. Good literature sells," the publisher grins.

Following instructions, many of the ladies (most of the audience were female), and a few men, walk to the front of the room bearing questions on paper scraps. The line coagulates near the front table. I watch assorted shapes and sizes of rears, thin, wide, corrugated or smooth in green, red, navy blue, purple and brown jiggle forward to wait. The questions are divided among the panelists.

Additional information comes forth. "Negotiate with the publisher."

"When the story ends the fun begins."

"The editor and the writer should be friends." Just like in Oklahoma.

"A book has to be packaged like every other product." Give me a pound of potatoes, some detergent in an orange and yellow stripped container, and that novel with the red cover showing a muscled man swinging an ax while Elizabeth Taylor watches. I think it's a novel about real life. It includes six murders, one dope dealer, two beatings, six infidelities, eighteen scenes of fornication (fifteen normal and three perverse), all of which occurs on a night flying jet that will be blown up at midnight unless the hero defuses the bomb.

"Don't send off the whole book. Just send the editor a few chapters." Reminds me of the inventor of epoxy, who short on funds just sent off one tube of glue to the testing laboratory. They wrote back, the stuff didn't work. Later on when he had more money he sent the second tube.

While the panel summarized, I wrote my own summary. Don't write a first novel. Start with your second.

Towards the end of the Assembly I am lucky. I get to meet with a New York Editor who is kind and says; "I would like to see your book when it is completed." These words gave me much hope during the coming months and kept me at the typewriter when I might have been off having fun.

Later I told friends, "The best part of the Writer's Assembly was talking with the editor. He gave me hope."

I planned to return to the next annual meeting because the sessions had taught me the basic information I needed to become a novelist. I also resolved to take additional instruction elsewhere and scanned college bulletin boards to discover where I could attend a writing school.

# CHAPTER 60.

# THE BINKER BONKER SCHOOL

I apply for and receive a scholarship during this summer of 1972 to the Binker Bonker School. I am attracted to its location on a knoll in the desert, a place with clear air and diamond back rattlesnakes. I say to myself, I will talk to famous writers. In the cool dove cooing evenings and cheery mornings they will come and I will know them by their eagerness to teach me.

I imagine class in the cool of the silo. ICBMs hammered into pen points. What a great concept; to transform a missile site east of the Cascade Range into a writer's school. The land had been declared surplus. Edward Binker Bonker's political connections facilitated the purchase. He paid one million dollars for the acquisition of the missile silo, one surplus missile, one control room, various tunnels and elevators and some uninhabited acreage. Binker Bonker established his reputation as a lover of cats. In his pre prosperous youth his favorite cat Wernko, squashed by a road roller, had been entombed in Duwamp's asphalt. Embittered yet motivated by the accident, Edward Binker Bonker commenced offering canned tuna to stray cats for food and oatmeal for bedding and Scottish visitors. Running out of energy with the continual pitiful meowing of what turned out to be thousands of hungry cats ambushing him whenever he turned a corner, and the howling of the resultant high population of coyotes seeking cat food and criticized by the thought to be liberal mayor, he switched his philanthropic urges to befriending stray writers, who rarely meowed while begging.

He became a millionaire by producing Binker Bonker machines, which with varied assortments of pulleys, scoops, mechanical arms, conveyor belts, motors, buzzers and lights could do just about anything. After once in the money, two for the show, three to get ready, and four to go establish the non-profit foundation he purchased the missile base and silos before complete deactivation.

The foundation used five thousand dollars to hire artists to paint fine murals; pictures of peacocks, eagles, crop-dusting airplanes, and cats on the walls of the faculty lounge. Three thousand dollars were spent hiring poets to write original poetry in glow green ink on the walls next to the pictures. One example of the high caliber of the work was the painting of a cannon. Dangling from the tip of the barrel was a jock strap engraved lovingly with the word FATHER. One ball fell to join a pile of balls on a large apple pie in the open hands of a bony short white haired old mother. On the ceiling foot high hand printed letters said: BOOOOOOOOOOOOOOOOOOOOOOOOOOOOOOO OOOM. It was a long ceiling. Additional funds were used to hire a secretary and a director.

The director, Alexander Williams, used fifteen thousand dollars to hire top novelists. He used twelve hundred dollars to hire top poets and two hundred and fifty dollars to buy a horse because he had learned to ride at a riding stable on the east side of Lake Duwamps.

Some of the top novelists refused to come because the pay was too miserly. All of the poets came appreciating a change of pace from other employment including dishwashing, cooking, logging and the selling of insurance.

After leaving Arthur with Mrs. McGrudder, and Karl with the Magnums, I head away from the seacoast. On the way to the base I pass long ridges of crumbled rock of the Skookumchuck Formation scooped out for the extraction of coal. I enter the still fenced base in the chill of the evening and park across the street from the barracks. A small dark blue jeep with a white roof and two warning lights is parked behind a gate. It looks much smaller than my memory of military jeeps during the time of Korea when I was protecting my country in France. After climbing paint peeling wooden steps, and walking across the wide porch, I carefully open the heavy wooden door. My steps snap the shiny floor. I knock on the second door. Above my fist a small window is covered with newspapers. The door opens wide. A young woman's face protrudes languidly like a desert poppy, though she is blonde not orange. "Hi," says she.

"I'm looking for the writer's school."

"This is the women's wing."

"The women's wing has an office?"

"No silly. This isn't an office. It used to be an office. Now it's my room."

"I'm sorry. Where should I go?"

"Out to the porch and through the other door."

"Thank you. My name's Leo." Already I am glad I have come. She looks like a writer. Through strands of disorderly long hair I perceive a typewriter and books. Her window is covered with newspapers.

Smiling demurely she says. "I'm Sybil. I write poetry."

"I'm writing a novel." Observing her soft white slacks and rawhide sandals, I think, she looks like a poet. Sort of resembles Emily Dickenson. I bet she's not over one hundred pounds when wet. The dry Sybil does not invite me into her room. I realize Emily would have also left me standing in the hallway. Sybil does not inquire more about my novel and I do not inquire about her poetry. The silence too awkward to maintain, I thank her and walk to the porch, coming into the building a second time. Laughter echoes past a red beard across white tombstone teeth. I expect to hear, Ho, Ho, Ho and a bottle of rum. The pirate swaggers over, extending his hand like a cutlass, and says, "Welcome, I'm Pete Blackstone."

"I thought maybe you were Blackbeard?"

"Nope. Too far from the water." After failing to remove my arm from its socket, Pete says, "Come in and have a shot."

Gulping the delicious Captain Morgan rum, I wait a moment before lowering my voice, "I need a room."

"Take one."

"Which one?"

"Anyone that's empty."

"Which ones are empty?"

"All of them except this one."

"Where do I get a key?"

"The doors are unlocked. Each key will unlock all of the doors. Tomorrow if you want one you can get a key. Why do you want a key?"

"To keep out burglars."

"We ain't got no burglars. Come."

"Where?"

"I'll help with your kit." Starting to feel slow-witted I am pleased at Pete's offer. I like being helped. From the car we ferry in the electric typewriter, Writer's Handbook, Writer's Yearbook, Writer's Digest, Poetry Primer, experimental novels, bond paper, yellow pads of legal paper, eraser, stapler and sleeping bag.

I carefully open the typewriter case on a small desk built so airmen could write home. I plug in the cord. Place my books on the dresser. Ask Pete, "Are there any chairs?"

"Nope. No chairs. I use a fruit box. Would you like one?"

I accept a red delicious box. Relaxing now that my writing studio is open for business, though nagged by doubt, I test the box, which is shaky. Pete leads me back to his studio for another snort. While warming ourselves we hear footsteps. Pete sails forth with a laughing welcome. I join the welcoming committee, which grows and thrives as more men arrive. We go to bed at two am after the rum bottle is empty.

Hearing birds, I open my eyes and look out at blue sky gaily marked with mare's tails forming arcs across the heavens. It feels good to be away from the overcast skies of Humaluh Land. Hearing laughter, in BVDs and T-shirt, I push open the door, smile at bleary-eyed smiling Pete, who says, "Good Morning. Did you sleep well?"

"Of course, though I've forgotten my dreams. I'm hungry. Where's the cafeteria?"

Pete says, "There is no cafeteria."

"No cafeteria? Where do we eat?"

"That is a valid question. They canceled the cafeteria. It was too much hassle."

"I'll bring in my Coleman stove. I've got food in the car. We can all get together and cook. I've got extras"

Frowning Pete says, "Follow me." We pad to the barren front entryway where capital letters proclaim:

NO FOOD OR COOKING ALLOWED IN BUILDING-Smaller letters say, Sorry.

***P.S. If we cook in here the fire insurance rates go out of sight. Sorry.

Alexander Williams

I groan. "If we can't eat, we'll die."

Pete yowls with laughter, enjoying my anticipation of misery. "Don't feel so bad. The mind is more alert when it's not contaminated with food. You'll make it. You won't die."

"You're wrong. I will die." I say, a far cry from the young man who once hiked six days eating only cheese, bread and Spam.

"People fast for weeks and feel better for it. Drink a lot. That's the secret. Think of the ancient Chinese drunken poets. Li Bai was one of the eight immortals of the wine cup. Another poet Li Po drowned when he tried to hug the reflection of the moon in the Yangtze River. Closer to home a Cascadian poet wrote poetry on napkins. After he fell into the Humaluh his friends collected the napkins and published his stuff." Still chortling Pete puts on boots, leads us, in a sense his crew, into the church based in a Quonset hut, past the organ to a pew. People are standing about in little clusters getting acquainted.

At Ten after nine, a thin man splits from a threesome and walks to the altar. "Welcome," he says. His hands shake. He reminds me of a Sears's jigsaw. "Please sign up for the workshops of your choice. All workshops will be in various levels of the Intercontinental Ballistic Missile Silo. This was the first liquid propellant missile that could be launched from underground. This missile was equipped with a nine-megaton thermonuclear warhead. This is 600 times more powerful than the blast that wiped out Hiroshima. The missiles are 103 feet tall. An empty missile still sits in the silo. The silo is 147 feet deep and 55 feet in diameter. We can explore all eight levels if we wish. According to the government they haven't been deactivated yet, but who can trust the government? Same thing with the New York Times. They claim the Air Force is still using ICBMs and they can be launched in seconds, but they're a liberal rag. You can't trust the Times. They were activated on New Years Day 1962. You can specialize or alternate. Don't trip. Each evening, at eight sharp," he laughs, "we will have readings in the chapel. Our staff writers are available for consultation in the Control Center, which has three levels. Use their time wisely." His speech over Williams sits down. I, a neophyte novelist, sign up for the workshop of Johnson Silverbow, a man resembling an Indian brave galloping past the skull and scapula of a long horn in a painting by Charles M. Russell.

Following him, I recall Will Roger's words, "We just don't raise no more of his kind of men." Silverbow easily pulls open the blast door weighing a mere 6000 pounds. It is recessed deeply in concrete and steel. The door reminds me of a modern painting of concrete with a wide stainless steel frame. A stenciled sign reads, IF BLAST DOOR BECOME INOPERATIVE CONTACT MCC FOR ASSISTANCE. I wonder who in the hell is MCC? After walking down a long lime green corridor lit by fluorescent ceiling lights we enter the Level Two Control Center which is mounted on eight huge springs. The whole building can move side to side and up and down. The combination to the controls is in a safe secured with two combination locks. It takes two people to get in the safe. The launch clock shows Greenwich Mean Time. Zulu time is the same. A 28-volt DC power system is in use. The batteries hold enough power to run the whole launch. Even though the system is deactivated a woman wearing an air force uniform sits at the control panel. It looks like she is sitting in a dark grey Lazy Boy arm recliner. I peer over to see if she is using a footrest. I don't see any. She says, "Welcome to the 666 Strategic Missile Squadron. Please don't touch any of the switches. If someone uses the wrong combination on the lock it takes 40 hours for the reset. You have no worries. If there is a direct hit on this site you can crawl out the airshaft. This system is much more reliable than the Atlas Missile which used liquid oxygen. It took 15 minutes to get off the shot. It had an internal guidance system. This missile is hypergolic. A home chemist can simply mix potassium permanganate and glycerin to produce a hypergolic compound (I wistfully remember my teen-aged years when I used potassium permanganate to soak my feet to kill athlete's feet. It colored the water purple and dyed my feet brown. This impressed the girls. I used glycerin to facilitate the inflation of giant soap bubbles). A leak will cause an explosion and the fuel is highly toxic. For the chemists among you who wish to construct their own missiles the fuel used is Aerozine 50 and dinitrogen tetroxide. It takes only one minute to send the ICBM missile on its way to one of three targets. Oh let me think. What city shall we select today? This is why some of us want to have peace. Please be careful during the class sessions. A man dropped a twelve pound socket wrench one day that fell eighty feet. Upon landing it punctured the fuel tank thus causing an explosion, one fatality and 21 injuries." I make a silent vow to drop no socket wrenches during writing classes. There are two red glowing buttons in front of her and a black phone and a grey phone. We walk down a corridor with dozens of large sagging steel conduits above us reminding me of a nest of giant stainless steel Spirobolid millipedes. We take an elevator to reach the our assigned level. We take a few additional steps on a ladder. Our feet tunk tunk on the steel steps as we enter a world lit by 100-watt bulbs. I look around. We are standing on a large grating, a platform stuck to the walls of a huge concrete cylinder. In front of us is the missile. Feeling vibrations I stare at the iron bulls eye in the center of the far off floor. I shiver. Realizing that the United States Government would not create anything unsafe, I become less afraid. Sitting cross-legged in a circle we look at Silverbow. Outside hidden from our view the sun must be rising, the desert warming, fence lizards are crawling into position to wait for flies, while diamond back rattlesnakes initiate countdown to coiling. Meanwhile I shiver. It is sixty degrees Fahrenheit so as to keep fuel from premature ignition. I look to the base of the missile; see lines where water shoots out to cool the missile during launch so the whole thing does not get so hot that it blows apart. I think I see a few wisps of steam at the foot but cannot be sure.

I sit on the platform in the pose of a meditating Buddhist the tips of my thumb and index finger touching in the root chakra mudra, my notebook on my lap. I check my pockets to make sure my coins, knife or wallet will not fall. Too late a penny falls. Later I hear a faint tick. I hear a faint yelp from one of the students in the classes below us.

Silverbow says, "Write I remember:"

I write, in church the organ played Bach. The priest ritualized. Near by were girls, breasts wrapped in linen, legs disappearing beneath plaid woolen skirts hiding the white triangle. Another time, at the party the older youths laughed as she frolicked full of beer, she spun, her soft skirt flaring. She took my head, firmly kissed my virgin mouth. Pressed her tongue past white teeth. Gutsy my tongue pushed hard, ran the polished smooth shiny line of her teeth. Her lips swept my lips while our hips pressed. I held her waist. Feeling my growing strength she kissed my nose said, "You learn fast little Leo." When they all laughed I wanted to run upstairs to my room. The next girl in my life was less experienced than I; offering shiny lips pressed against mine, she hid her tongue.

To this day, as now in this silo, seeing skirts my blood warms, flows, with wanting. If the lights go out I could take a woman, if she was willing, on this steel grating before asking myself, can they hear us? Will my knife fall through the grate?

Silverbow talks, "A writer merits respect." I think, respect. Inundating me with words aunts and uncles said Leo, it is good to want to write but you are a grown man with children. Accept your responsibilities. You are forty years old Leo. It is fun to write but Leo think of your family. Get a job. A job. What is my job? The job of a baby is to eat, shit, sleep and grow. People love babies. What is my job? I am not a baby. Hat in hand, open, inverted, inwardly I cry, "Please sir. Will you buy what I sell?"

"What are your wares?" The confident grey suited man asks. "What do you sell? I need matches. Do you sell matches?"

"No sir." I answer.

I write. Please read my writing. It is worthy of respect. Silverbow said so.

"Boy, you forget easily. Remember that E in college English. In high school your grades were so low you were only unsurpassed by the mentally incompetent. Your grammar was atrocious. I don't think you ever learned how to punctuate correctly."

"Ha. Though they expected me to fail I proved them wrong. In the English part of the GED test I was in the eighty-second percentile."

"Leo that meant eighteen percent were above you. The skills test after the army proved your grammar was terrible. Remember that term paper on Gulliver's Travels. You got a D."

"That was the teacher's fault. He ignored content."

"Leo, what is your content? What is inside of a Leo? Would you buy a house built by a carpenter who didn't know how to drive nails? D work is D work. It's on your transcript for any prospective employer to see."

"At another college it would have been a C. Those Jesuits were chicken shit. I got knocked down for Chicago Tribune spelling. What's wrong with spelling though tho?"

"Leo, come off it. You write nonsense. Discover the world. Forget fantasy. Join your working cousins. Be positive. Become a banker or sell vacuum cleaners. Make something of yourself."

"I want to, but I cannot. My career got side tracked. Remember in the second grade I was tried, judged, condemned."

"Respect your craft." Silverbow's words washed away the relatives and neighbors until respect my craft remained. I've kept journals for years. I'll name them in order: First the Unicorn, then the Troll, Narwhale, Zebra, Gazelle, Peter Pan, Queen of Hearts, Little Sheba, Rin Tin Tin, The Jokers Wild. Actually to be truthful their names go: one, two, three, four, five, six… Creative don't you agree? Respect my craft. People say what do you do? I say, I write. They say, have you published? I confess No. They realize they are talking to a failure. I am a failure until I am not a failure. Others continue to judge me. Sounds good to say respect your craft, respect yourself, however no man is an island living to himself. I need input from friends. What I need are some high quality sycophants, or elephants. Where will I find this respect?

"Respect is in the same locked box as happiness, within you."

It's easy for you to say. Of course you're right. It's so simple.

We break for lunch. I hear the tunk, tunk, tunk of our feet on the grate and the stairs to the elevator, to the corridor, through the Control Center, down the corridor and into the sunshine.

I join Pete for a hearty lunch in the dorm of crackers and Kraft cheese." (I hate Kraft American Cheese almost as much as I hate French Fries which are not French)

Pete says, "In fiction we learned how to plot a novel. Want to listen to my tape?"

I say, "Later."

After our gourmet lunch I return to the silo, following the line of students through the blast doors. Again moving away from the edge of the platform I lean against the wall and sit on the grate. Also cross-legged Silverbow says, "Write."

I write sixteen pages. The session is over. Back again up the lift, through the blast doors, through long corridors; watching the overhead snakes reminds me of the snakes without.

The other students and I eat a delicious supper of crackers and Velveeta cheese. After supper we hear Solomon Stein, Gertrude's son, read a chapter from his novel *Mother*. Stein, a sophisticated witty easterner, who had grown up in Paris, had written about a boy and his strong Jewish mother and her affinity for holding salons. Apparently her matriarchal power had been beneficial to him; *Mother* has been on the New York Times bestseller list for eighteen months. When Stein halted he was immediately asked a question by weasel faced Karl Pearson. "Mr. Stein, how many words are there on a typical page of your novel?" No sooner had Stein's answering lips stopped vibrating then clever Karl Pearson asked another probing question, "How many words are in an average chapter?"

Early the next morning after a filling breakfast of crackers and peanut butter, I sit cross-legged on the grate next to Silverbow. He says, "Please write, I recall:"

I write, I recall my father, too busy, the great depression, what pressures. He could have lost house and business. No time for little kid me. Besides, I was always in trouble.

"If the boy would only apply himself." That's what dad said, that's what dad wrote. That photograph. Squinting in the seventh grade, already I was a wizened old man. Eye trouble. A well known Cause of bad grades in some kids. I acted up. Yet I read. That might have affected my schoolwork. Why those clashes with authority? My father and I. Was he mine? How could my father have been mine? I did not direct or manipulate him other than pulling forth his anger.

He'd say, "why do you keep asking questions? Why do you do these things? Why torment me? God. Try to be a good boy like James Schwartz. He never defies his family. Never says why?"

"Dad? They reward him, stuff him with ice cream in cookie crust cones, take him to the zoo: They all go to baseball games."

"Son shape up. Do your errands. Take out garbage. Shovel snow. Rake leaves. Your mother lets you get away with murder."

"Dad, Dad, why am I so fouled up? Am I crazy? The boys spit on me. You say, learn to fight. From who will I learn to fight? Who will teach me? Jack Dempsey? Joe Lewis? Will their photographs teach me the motions? Don't you know I am a coward?"

"Son get your nose out of those books. Play ball."

"Dad you've never taken me to the games. You're always wearing that scratchy wool suit. We can't play ball when you wear that suit. You talk forever of business. You say, "We need money." I think, where is my father? Working for the Yankee dollar? Not like mother and daughter. Mother loves me, this I know. Baby of the family. Sickly. Cough, cough, cough. Pneumonia. Poor boy. Bad kidneys. Maybe an artery is choking off the urethra. Poor boy. If it gets worse we'll have to operate. Snip, snip, snip? It might be dangerous. Germs all over those hospitals. No safe anti-biotics until 1945, when two Brits came through. No penicillin or streptomycin in my kidhood. Father in bed. Old man's arteries. Too much fat, not enough exercise. We searched seeking health in America's clinics. Learned to like one another your penultimate year. I saw you two days before the end; connected to tubes, catheters. Back to the base I scooted.

Telegram.
COME HOME. YOUR DAD IS DEAD.

"Mother you are all alone by the coffin. Even the flowers, carnations, smell dead." Since then I have never liked carnations. Outside the air cold, land of snow and ice. Carnation gagging me that day. I remember. The widow, my mother, gentle widow. I the youngest. "I love you Leo. That's a good boy." Mother you never cringe when I sit down. You are afraid to gush over me. Anyway I hate oily lady gushers, lady kissers, clutching clutching lady fingers.

You in turn lingered sweetly, lovingly. Doctors infused your system with chemicals. Your glory hair fell out. Emaciated, sitting quietly how well did you look? How could I tell you? Was I supposed to be honest then? You died, could not live long alone surviving your husband, my father. Was that it or did you want to live a long time-alone? I recall the tears on both those nights. After death I was alone in bed crying.

The class waits for frantically writing me to finish my memories. Some laugh. I flash resentment. Ignore them. Keep writing.

After mid day crackers and salami, after our walks to and from the launch site through blast doors, the assignment is to write: I like myself: I leave the page blank.

After class, no evening sessions, I see Sybil on the porch. Walk to her, attracted by her pale narrow face framed with antique bronze colored hair. We decide to go to town for a sandwich. She twenty-one, I forty-one. We drink beer. I am nearly broke: joyful to be with a young woman, I buy. Later, arm in arm we walk across the porch; kiss goodnight. Nodding to Pete and the other guys drinking in the hall, I go to bed; dream of Sybil. Half asleep I caress the sheets.

In the morning we eat crackers and cheese and drink illegal tea. At the early reading, with crumbs on my shirt, I listen to Stein read about the portrait by Picasso of his mother. After the applause, tactful Karl Pearson asks through parchment thin lips, "How much money did you make on your book? Do you have an agent? How much do agents cost? How do you get an agent?"

Belching like a dyspeptic hippo, Stein answers reluctantly. If I was in Stein's shoes I would initiate the requisite moves to throw Pearson over the railing, as part of a scientific study to see if he can glide nine stories and make a soft landing on the concrete pad on the edge of several red and black discs. Perhaps, as Pearson drifts, I can yell, are you almost to the bottom? How does the air feel against your face? Will you write about your experience in your novel? How much will you earn from the book?

After the reading I am glad to return to the cool war womb. Silverbow says, "Write, I wish:"

I write, I wish my father had taken me for walks. We did stand by the window together watching fireworks arcing forth on the fourth from the State Fair in West Allis Wisconsin. Five months later fire destroyed thousands of linear feet of wooden cattle barns. The walls fell over in great hay dust explosions. Cattle bellowed, screamed. Other days I screamed sobbed quietly in my room, an outcast. *Persona non grata.* At times outwardly, at other times inwardly crying, who will play with me? I wish father had tossed one baseball to me, yet I feared the ball. With other boys I was scared it would smash my four eyes. I thought, mother, mother, get angry. I want a change from all acceptance on your part, all rejection on his. I remember your dialogues.

"Don't be hard on him. He's good boy."

"Good boy, my eye. If he keeps on this way he won't amount to anything."

They fought over my miserable flesh. If childhood had been happy, I am convinced life would have been easy. If my father had not given his life to his business, maybe I'd respect businessmen. I despise money, work, and commerce: Perhaps my fatal flaw. I shall die penniless of starvation. My objective has always been the impractical. Oh Lord, I know not what I feel forced to do though I think I know why I do it. I merely want to be happy. Oh where is happiness? Life always turns out the same. Most of us get a tub of shit. Remember that pessimistic child? Receiving a giant pile of horseshit for Christmas he says, "Shit!"

The optimistic child receiving his gift of shit yells, "Wow, Whoopee. Yippee. Hooray." Jumping up and down with excitement, tears of happiness running down his cheeks, he realizes that with so much shit there's got to be a pony. And so I say, "where is my god-dammed pony?" I'll snap my fingers. Wait for the pony to gallop to me for cheese and crackers.

The woman, the special woman, if she comes will she say, "Leo. Leo. I love you Leo. Your eyes are brown and green pools, your hands the hands of an artist. You make love better than any man on earth. How fine your shirt is, your hand made shirt. I read your novel and was inspired. Leo I could not put it down."

"Yes it is rather good, isn't it?" I will say to that most literate horse.

"Ladies and gentlemen, our guest tonight is Leo Bauer, author, a man who has been compared to Joyce, Nin, Vonnegut, Homer, Cervantes, and Rabelais. Have you anything to add Professor Bauer?"

"Oh it was nothing. Merely a work of genius from a man of conscience. I wish they'd stop the intellectual inquisition in Cuba. Free the Isle of Pines political prisoners. How can mere poets hurt the great Fidel? Joseph V. Stalin and Adolph Hitler bulldozed artists and paintings into piles of rubble. You guys crushed my daughter Freedom. Remember that so called Saint McCarthy? Back then in the Wisconsin taverns they said, If you don't like it here go to Russia.

To Russia, to Russia,
Home again, home again,
Jiggidy jig.
My warm embrace holds a bouncing pig.

On the way home passing through Paris the train stops. I take a horse drawn cab to the *Bois de Boulogne*. Clop, clop, clop, clop go the horses. The horses say, "whineeeeee."

*Mademoiselles. Bon Jour mon cherie.* Like Monarch butterflies on butterfly trees they seek Bauernecter.

The power of Leo. I love all of you. My kisses will stay on your lips forever. I'd like to be with you under the bridges of Paris. *Vous tous savoir faire mademoiselles*, you know how to make me feel like *une grand monsieur. Il en fera a sa tete.*"

I see your look. No I can't afford champagne. If you don't want tea I'll go to Japan.

"What's the matter, you no like Japanese girl?" My eyes dissolve to a sandy Zen garden with furrows. She comes softly to me. Slowly we sip. *Watashi wa, ocha o, nomimas.* My cells relax, nasal membranes undulating, she soaps my shiny back. *Watashi wa. Kanajo no opai o.*

Water drips from a silk bandanna. Her legs enfold me in the wooden tub. Waves oversplash onto the tongue and groove floor. Lips are soft. *Futatsu koi o oyojimaste* are above white marble chips.

*Anata to nematai des.* She giggles. *Domo arigato, Leo san.*

Sybil and I rendezvous for lunch, drive the hot asphalt ribbon to the Oasis. We buy not; pluck peaches, grapes, figs, and dates. Homeward munching, I watch mirages shimmer in the heat. Sybil says, "It's hot. I feel sticky." Making an awful face she wiggles away moisture.

Back again on the cold steel grate, Silverbow says, "Write of mud:"

I write, I run laughing through cold waves. Diana's breasts bounce in their wisps of cloth. We walk the mud flats, she bikinied and I short shorted. Warm smoothness slides our feet. Over the warmth we lie in ooze, caressing, kissing. Like the tickle of an anemone's tentacles her tongue touches my lips. Naked we float in the mushy clay, glide through soft folds of powdered milk from glacial cows. The notochordal Amphioxus worm engorged to firmness glides the mud. Warmth dissipates in fading paroxysms; other creatures are cold, with blue blood, green blood, transparent blood flowing beneath bright sunlight. Look at the water, white like clam milt, fish milt, white on the dark smelly sulfurous tide flat. Rivers bifurcate, teratology, branching rivers, arteries, veins, blood rushes through our legs. Content constrictors slither full, unwanting more now of the crush suck inhalation of fat peccaries. Frog loins open, thighs white below, on top green and amber. Sunlight through green warm pond water, blossoms float in the glowing sun. Wonder sun gives life, gives a child. No. No. Away all mud. Warm tide deceiving tide pools. The sculpin bites with his back. Anemones fornicate my finger. Tiny arrows target keratin concentricities that laugh; the giant laughs looking through the microscope at the runaway thumbkins, run away, away to the mountains along a ridge. The soft mist enfolds a cave, waits. See Sybil? Avoid her lure lust arms; keep to the ridge, run over the ice slide, shooop. The marmots slide; dine on glacier lilies, chomp, chomp, chomp. Run, run, run. Avoid grizzly bears, they are too huge. Time for a check. Take flashlight. "Open wide please." Measure rear molars. If over two inches wide get the hell out quick, gently close bear's mouth, run. It's a grizzly fur sure. Not a black bear. Flyaway, flyaway, flyaway home. Run from your mother, run from your pa, run away, run away, boy man, away from your job, away from fears, run away.

That evening Stein read about the time his father had gotten angry with him for missing his violin lesson. His mother had protected him and said, "Don't be so hard on him. He's a good boy."

Dimpling his cute cheeks Karl Pearson asks, "Were you twelve or thirteen? Why was your father mean? Is the book autobiographical? What year was it published? How many copies have been sold?" Hands touching the pistol handle protruding from his belt holster Stein plays with his recently purchased Colt 45. His other hand fondles the ivory handled sharp bladed hunting knife. It looks as if he is contemplating sudden action.

In the morning Silverbow says, "Write I smell."

I write, Fe fi fo fum, I smell the blood of an Englishman. I know a man who says he can smell a woman having her period from across a room. He says that the smell of menstruating women triggers grizzly bear attacks. Dogs. Wild animals, delight in smelling one another; yet women and men take offense at this idea. They don't want to be like dogs, wolves, mink or wolverines. They want to be refined like pure cane sugar from Hawaii. That fat girl in grade school smelled of vaginal juices, smelled of urine. Poor girl. Why so much odor?

No wonder psst, psst sprays for under arms and asses and far up crotches. In France I danced to momentous stringed waltzes. I imagined great events happening during the waltz; the mob against the Bastille. Chewing garlic salami, gently nibbling *Camenbert, jambon sandwiche avec beurre, pain avec jambon.* Salads green red and crisp as cold autumnal Wisconsin nights, sprinkled with oil, vinegar and garlic, crunch, crunch, crunched by ladies, breathe deeply *mademoiselle.* Let me smell your breath, your sweat, dance giggle ladies, pink cheeked giggle girls, our hands whipped the air walking to the cinema past cows in the mud, your voices high splashing cascading over the rock that was I. I held you in my foreign arms. *Monsieur Leo* said, "*Voulez vous couchez avec moi?*" They laughed, said "*mais oui*," laughed. Ahead of us a woman stopped in the dirt road, peed from within cover of skirts. Then quickly walked. I tingled. The air was moist. Drizzling. Smells were intense. Even Channel number five, especially Channel Number Five as a gift from me would not open the gates of paradise. Was I too foreign? Perfume masks the smell of urine.

That old wall in Mexico. A *Parque National.* A wall of urine. Oh Paris smelled good. Shops smelled. Things not sterilized. Real cheese, not over killed in stainless steel death pots. Rene Dubois said a few germs are OK. Vaginas like mouths, soft to kiss. Some acrid, some sweet, some pleasant. The fishy ones gag the gobbler. Is it bad hygiene? Some women find few to kiss them there. Imagine a young man trying that for the first time. Would he ever try again if the first time he licked stench? He'd die in the fuzz. Meow. Poor first time at anything shrivels future resolve, kills ambition. Bad breath. I won't dance again with her. Does my breath stink? Now there is a coating like cotton cloth, a swelling between molars. Is pyorrhea pussing my body? Will my teeth push in like feet in swamp muck? Pretty jumping iridescent black and white feathered magpies pluck maggots from bulls. Sometimes a woman walks away, says "I'll be back," remains away forever. Perhaps my breath does smell. Tonight I shall use dental floss. Must be more conscientious.

That evening, after a vigorous flossing, I go drinking with sweet Sybil. She talks of her lover. I say, "He's an older man. No wonder your parents were furious. I can understand their feelings."

"I can't lead a life of my own," Sybil complains.

"Leave home," I advise thinking, "Does my breath smell good?"

"My parents are getting older. I don't want to hurt them. Dad might have a heart attack."

Later on the porch we embrace. She is firm, no flab. She feels my back, strong from hiking and canoeing. We kiss for three and a half seconds. Separating we enter the barracks by sexed doors. Pete still up smoking, drinking Rainier beer, offers me a can. I accept. Pete says, "In fiction, we learned how to set a scene in six words."

In the morning showering I watch images pass through the frosted warbled glass. I choose the second spigot in a ring of three. Soap remnants and wet paper lay on the slimy tiles beneath my feet.

Later clean, dressed, free of an overpopulation of germs, in class I listen to Stein's account of a gang war in New York City. I am glad I don't live in New York. Karl Pearson's clean boyish face opens like a telephone operator's larynx. "Why do they let young boys have switchblade knives? Aren't they illegal? Do People really like living in New York City? Are you a former gang member?"

Stein sitting on the table crossing and uncrossing his legs answers, "Switchblades are outlawed. I like New York. I hate idiots."

Pearson asks, "Did you ever cut anyone with a knife?"

Stein says, "I'm considering it." He discusses his method of writing. He starts early, at one A.M. and writes until seven. He eats breakfast while dressed in silk pajamas and a kimono. His wife wears a red nylon nightie to breakfast and supper. Still he writes all through the night. On the wall in back of his desk there is an oil painting of Aphrodite. The desktop is paper free, bearing only a typewriter and a Dictaphone. Some of his writing is composed orally. A typist comes in during the day while he sleeps. While writing he drinks vodka and orange juice. When he suffers from loose bowels he uses Pepto Bismo followed by crackers and cheese. He and his wife make love every night just before he starts to dictate. It gets his creative juices flowing. He asks, "I trust I've answered your questions Mr. Pearson?" and sits down without waiting for a reply.

That afternoon the Director drives Stein to the airport. During the drive he gulps Pepto Bismo and eats crackers and cheese. He never explains why he has shortened his visit.

While Stein was being strapped into his seat, Silverbow in the silo says, "Write what you can hear:"

I write, the motor scooter zanged, quieted after changing gears. Diesel snorting hungry lorries attempt to climb up the ass of the glowing rear lights of my light green Lambretta bought just before George O'Brien, always grinning curly haired eager Bostonian, my best friend, close associate in the skilled art of picking up girls, hit a Renault, flew over the hood, landed bruised on the pavement. Lucky George. No bones or teeth broken, he sat on the pavement smiling, chipmunk eyes bright and shiny; brain uncracked. The Commandant issued a directive; was he a general? Must have been, never had a beer with him or even met him. Once I marched before him. The order was succinct: MOTOR SCOOTERS AND MOTOR CYCLES BANNED UNTIL FURTHER NOTICE. I polished the light green fenders; my pretty scooter sat neatly by the barracks for months. Later weather bad, legal again, I was in the snorting belch line to Paris. Leaving the fumes, munching French bread with the hard crust, sweet butter, and *jambone*. Never again so delicious. Paris. *Vin rouge. Vin blanc. Monseur* Leo, *Je vous aime. Mon cherie.* Giggle. Giggle gaggle of girls. Duty done for God bless our country: sometimes on the sly, we walked in a weaving line, girls, boys, youths, me, to town, to a dance, together, I a man with a new country revealed by my green leather tight body jacket. I didn't know it at the time. I had bought a woman's jacket. None the wiser, tourists asked me in stunted French, "*ou est? ou est?*" I pulled off my impersonation, speaking French with *merci.*

Attention. Open your footlockers." He has found dirt. We can see the smudge on the tips of his white gloves. A howling devil jet takes off. I thought it has to crash. Crunch. *Pain. Beurre.* Tickle wine.

Many fine poems were written in that vast rocket echo chamber. In the afternoon, on some days, the teachers read their words. On other days students read. Some enjoyed what I had written, but said, "Leo this is not poetry." Regarding an 18-page poem of mine Silverbow said, "Put in the names of actual people. Don't harangue your reader. Use images, metaphors and you may have a poem. Half the class appreciated Skooby Woman written in honor of Sybil. I didn't tell them that. Half said it didn't make sense.

Our Poetry group wrote a collaborative poem, each person did several lines. All of the poems were typed and duplicated by Silverbow; they formed the *Prickly Pear Anthology*. Some of my lines were included.

Many of the techniques we learned had been used by Silverbow to teach children. The kids learned to write poetry without knowing they were writing poetry.

The first week ended with me feeling confident; my decision to abandon biology and become a writer had been a wise decision.

Friday night Sybil, the rest of the group, and I go to the Oasis to eat and drink. We mingle with coal mining men coughing up black stuff. My lungs twice globulated by pneumonia behave. I wish Sybil would go my way. It is a frustrating entanglement. She dances with a young coal miner, muscles tensing his shirt; the man could powder anthracite with his fingers. Unwilling to watch them dance, I walk to the pool table. I am furious with my muscle shortage. I think, when I kiss and hug her, do I remind her then of her father? Daddy spoiled her. I am a would be sugar daddy. I do not want to be her father. No incest in my genes. We return to the base more strangers than friends in a carload of laughter.

Saturday in the roasting afternoon, thirsty, hung over, we again go to town. Drinking all afternoon, boozy, we dance, her pelvis presses, my mind prances. I want to be a wild mustang.

We sit down, thighs touching. Sybil says, "I feel the same way I did when I was seduced in Duwamps."

My hardness rises. I want to get her away from the bar, yet we drink and talk until Sunday morning. The bartender, an intermittent friend, becomes stern. "Out. Sorry. It's the law." We leave hearing dumped beer splash the shiny steel drain.

In the car Sybil leans her head on my shoulder. At the dorm I follow her like a beagle pup. She invites me in. In the dimness I watch her face disappear behind the high-necked blouse. Delicate fingers softly unsnap the bra revealing narrow girl's back, smooth soft chamois skin. The skirt unsnapped falls on the painted boards. Flannel fog rushes under the long soft dark hair, covering her glimmering back and pink bikini panties.

She crawls into bed. I the beagle lave her calves, caress soft inner thighs, touch silk, and float my fingertips above pubic hair.

She says, "I'm tired. I want to sleep. Go to bed Leo."

The pup's tail sags. I think, rich man, poor man, beggar man, thief. I need your belly and breasts. Nurse me. Take pity. Her nipples stiffen? Hope flares in my Byronic breast. I'll still probe the folds of this glacial furrow. I'm not gelded. I want. I want. The hunchback cried, I want fuck suck. Not a hunchback. Not a monster, I'm a lover. Lover. Ho. Ho. Ho. Lover?

"I want to sleep!" Four short words. Obeying her command I open the door, whisper "Good night," As I remember other rejections.

Sunday depressed, unwilling to lay my sad trip on Pete, I brood, listen to other typewriters clack, stare at my machine silent on the table, and try to read. My mind is absent. Leaving the room I walk into the sunny heat. Caress tiny stiff tri-lobed leaves, seek the company of fence lizards, and seek healing in silence.

# Chapter 61.

## PROLIFERATING PLOTS

Acknowledging my passion, I switch to fiction. I am filled with wonder over the ICBM Silo. It seems alive. I squat on the steel grid one hundred feet above the concrete circle, listening to and watching occasional jets of water. Laughter flows down the stairs and bounces off the walls. The grid is made of narrow steel rectangles.

The originators of such good humor, Albert Siegfried, the author of *Guts* and Berthold Günter, author of *Broken Bones*, stand chuckling in front of our class. Resembling each other they display bristly pendant jowls. They squat like Sumo wrestlers, bellies quivering above finely tooled tan cowboy boots. Günter passes a fifth of bourbon to Siegfried. After gulping a mouthful he politely returns the jug. Seeing such cultured behavior, I thirst. Siegfried says, "we will teach as a team. We are a team. Hooray."

Günter says, "We will read what you write, drink your offerings and consider additional emollients, favors and gratuities."

Siegfried emphatically adds, "Nothing is finer than a good woman or a nickel Havana. Class say after me, all I want is a gooood five cent ceeegar."

We enthusiastically reply, "All I want is a gooood five cent ceeegar."

Knees cracking, Siegfried stands. Towering above me he takes a swig, passes the bottle to Günter who takes a swig and returns the jug. Siegfried portentously says, "Class, life is not all play. We have important business to do this morning, don't we Günter?" Günter rolls his eyes. Siegfried continues. "Please write a first hand account of," he resembles a banana tree in a gale, leans over the girls, exhales, "LUST."

Apparently struck by the same wind, several girls sway. Like a piglet sucking hind tit Karl Pearson sucks his lips, asks, "Would you please give us your definition of lust?"

Poking Günter in the ribs Siegfried assumes a very serious demeanor as he says, "Karl, if it pleases you, the assignment is to write about FUCKING." Reddening, Pearson stares at concrete walls.

While the class writes, Siegfried and Günter laugh and talk about New York women, Korean women, German women, getting drunk in Chicago, getting drunk in San Francisco, getting drunk in Duwamps. As they talk they look benignly at the girls.

I write of a past neighbor: "A long time ago Sandy Adams lived next door. One night in my room, standing in the darkness, I saw her light go on. Thoughtfully, as if reviewing *Catcher in the Rye*, she unzipped her skirt, it fell to her ankles, she stepped forth, bent, retrieved the garment and laid it on a chair. Her panties were a beacon to me as she rolled her sweater up and over wiggling arms. With a twist she revealed small pendant breasts. Pushing down panties she and I looked down. My stare focused on brown curley maidenhair., I thought of that girl who wouldn't let me touch or see her hidden silk.

I thrilled as she faced the window revolving like a music box ballerina. She walked to the closet, pulled on a pink nightie, returned to the window and looked at the sky. I dove behind my bed. When I dared peek again she was out of sight. I imagined her reading, braced against the bolster, Catcher propped on thighs.

The class writes like people possessed. Pencils racing over the paper almost causes smoke to rise from scorched carbon trails. When the assignment is completed students read their stories, basking in the approving smirks of their professors.

Billy Bow, a vagrant from Utah, writes of a man with an obsession for women's crotches. His hero, John Sluggins, stares at the lower folds of Mildred's jeans, perceiving the furrows. Sluggins wants to run his fingers over the softness and caress and explore the stickiness beneath the cotton. Brass buttons on female jeans had probably reminded Bow of his hero, who was like a bee. Bees follow honey guides on flowers, buzz eagerly and enter. In the sunshine of Sluggin's mind pudendums press cloth with stout fur pressure. Girls roll in green grass, buttons brass, red, white, blue and black, snaps, clasps, and brass and plastic zippers open as the band plays the college fight song; while the football team huddles Sluggins focuses on zippers cleaving to left and right, assisted by a multitude of hands pushing on the nylon seams, as she comes, and they all come and all are grateful to the astounding super stud, John Sluggins, who makes it all possible in the land where such things are possible to any guy.

Straight haired, laconic, Sally Broll writes of Clara Zap obsessed with the seduction of men in different environments. In the snow Clara says, "I'm cold. Give me warmth." She clutches her man, seeking, discovering the soft lining of his mouth. Pulling open his zipper, her hands slip between insulated underwear to his razzle-dazzle fur. Nylon ski pants whisper. She undulates above him partially hidden by her bright yellow jump suit. A basket star of arms and legs they roll over crusty snow. She feels the scratch of ice and pinkens as her butt scrapes, thrilling to his burrowing penis which rejoices in her inner warmth. Steam rises in the air and snow melts as skin tingling they buck, twist and orgasm at a depth of eight feet below the newly melted crust: Much of the snow has turned to slush, which goes slumphf in pretty lacey patterns.

Tall strong Deborah Wilberforce writes of lusting for the waiter in a transvestite Chinese restaurant. Aware of her admiration he/she with long firm thighs and flat belly, seven feet of majestic beauty, handsome from the tips of red polished toes shining through clear plastic slippers to her dolly red hair. Like the buttressed foundations of Chartres Cathedral, a black nylon garter belt girds gluteal muscles. Black cones of sharpened steel encase her/his breasts. A crepe paper crotch bears an artsy fartsy phallus that curves, twists and dangles like an elephant's trunk above pink and blue crushed crepe balls. Pulsing to Glenn Miller she and the waiter/waitress man/woman of her dreams dance cheek to cheek in the belly of the Red Dragon.

Other students write of lust for mothers, sisters, brothers, fathers, boys, girls, professors, doctors, nurses, grandmothers, Alsatians, zebras, elephants, rhinoceri, wildcats, grizzly bears and fossilized saber toothed tigers. During the readings tears flow from pleasure as the class enjoys lust. Later, in a paean of praise, Siegfried said, "I have never heard such good writing on the first day of class."

While the students bask in the praise, Günter pokes the empty bottle with his narrow tipped cowboy boot, the bottle rolls about a foot. I move quickly towards the stairs. He again pokes the bottle. I remember the explosion from the wrench. His third poke pushs the empty bottle over the edge. Cupping his hand behind one large florid ear he waits, waits for the splintering that seems to take at least a minute. I am already on the stairs seeking the evacuation shoot when I hear the echo of breaking glass, and the teacher announcing, "Class dismissed."

Pearson, who unfortunately had not read, asked in the tumult of leaving, "Do we have homework?"

Already on the lift, I barely hear Siegfried's heavy expulsion of voice and breath, say, "Yes, eat a beaver and save a tree." Everyone except Pearson laughs. I imagine Pearson Driving to town, going into a restaurant and asking the waitress, "Please miss, I'd like a beaver, well done."

At the next meeting Pearson shows up with a black eye. Siegfried and Günter start class by scratching their bellies slowly and methodically as if they are affectionately caressing ancient horse fly bites.

Twisting off the cap of a new bottle of Jack Daniels, looking like babes in Toyland, they listen, along with their students, as Jophat RamDamDam, bearded boy patriarch, reads sitting as a yoga in the basic meditation pose with his hands open over each knee. This made it hard for him to read. I hope Jophat will not fall over from lack of energy. Sitting at the edge of the iron ribs he gently rocks while he reads. Each time he sways towards the void I feel a weakness in the center of my body. This keeps things interesting while Jophat reads, *The Citrus Fish*.

Citrus Motors sold me a fish. This fish has given me trouble from the start. For years this has been a rotten fish. It has taken me three years and over three thousand lemons to get all the bones out.

On Good Friday, 1970, five men wearing crucifixes dragged and ripped tuna hooks over my fish that which was lying in the street. A crowd watched. Suddenly a humble carpenter appeared. He erected a giant cross feelingly fashioned from a once feisty wooden anchor.

An artist wearing Hippie rimless glasses smirked diabolically as he trotted over while munching a peanut butter sandwich smeared with burnt sienna and charred fish bones. Whipping out a paintbrush from his hollow cane he drank some abstract of abstinence from the hollow tip and painted the scene. Five crucifixes turned white and Ahab the wooden legged cat yowled and ran clumpa pip, pip, pip; clumpa pip, pip, pip; clumpa, pip, pip, pip.

Benedict Orange Seed, the head of Citrus Motors, blanched, spitting seeds as he entered his dealership. Three hours later the flies were as numerous as sand in the Sahara. At that time my fish was served on a temporary injunction. On January 31, 1971, the fish was hauled into court. The judge heard the case in absentia. Deciding quickly in my favor the jury awarded me 100 pounds of tarter sauce and 200 sprigs of parsley as garnishment for the damages caused by the five hook dragging fishermen. The judge refused to confiscate the hooks.

Günter belched. I consider nudging Jophat in the ribs then waiting to see if he can fly. Would he, will he? Well tutored in hygienics, Siegfried washes his mouth with bourbon and swallows the mouthwash. He says, "Excellent. That story is decidedly original." He swallows more bourbon, making a face like a butcher greeting a customer with a cleaver whack.

Slender Sandy Sleekslacks stridently stridulates her story while Siegfried scruffs his scrobiculated skull watching her crotch flex from hortatory zeal as she reads *The Brass Chandelier.*

While I perused the bookrack in the Salvation Army Thrift shop, a pigeon flew out of the glowing brass chandelier that was illuminating the books and manuscripts. Neatly piling many books on the floor (my parents had always taught me to be neat), I climbed the paper steps and peered into the chandelier to see if there were more pigeons. Triumphant at having attained my goal, I yelped as the stack fell. I was grabbed, actually hooked by my nose to a brass spike. Blood dripped over my lips. It tasted rather good. Quite salty. Impaled, I waited for rescue. I perceived that in falling I had kicked John Updike in the garbage can. No offence was intended.

Sandy sits down. Raising his eyes from where her crotch has been, Siegfried says, "I liked that." He was probably referring to her crotch but Sandy probably assumed he meant the story.

Long bearded Timothy Shapiro reads *Helicopter Pilot* while slouching against the wall.

One day while attempting to observe whales in the storm tossed Antarctic seas we reached the zone of mechanical reversement. Helpless, we were terrified as the horizon blurred and we became a gyroscope. The blades were motionless but we in the copter rotated at 360 revolutions per minute, whooshing like an over powdered fireworks whirler. It became cold. Gasping, short of oxygen, drooling from anxiety, my beard froze to the control stick. As the machine whirled I spun around the stick. Damn it hurt. My feet kicking booted teapots, lace doilies, pictures of grandchildren, china figurines, silver spoon collections and teeny teacups with narrow waists. Fortunately English ivy plants tangled my feet and stopped my twirl within the twirl. However I stayed stuck, stretched tight like a Buckingham Palace Guard while the cabin whirled and Ahab the cat's left glass eye fell wobbling entering my mouth to bounce over the roof ridges.

Timothy inhaled. The rest of us also breathe. While in his slouch Shapiro's beard becomes caught between the upright columns and the arm rest. The class is divided on how to proceed, so half hold the chair and the other half hold Shapiro and both sides pull. Shapiro screams and lands on the floor rubbing his chin, his brow wet with sweat. He is breathing heavily while back on the chair an object resembling a Brillo pad remains fastened to the armrest. Professor Siegfried, a healing physician, hands Shapiro the bourbon and his pain departs after drinking two shots of the bubbling fluid of mercy.

Leaving the silo, I walk in the late afternoon heat through the arroyo formed by the separation between two ridges of mine tailings. Reaching an old mining village I sit and write:

This is a strange oasis. Sweet timothy and grass. Seeds plucked by the wind. Queen Anne's Lace sprouts from an old red table. Beneath paint is wood. The paint hangs, wings casting shadows in the sun. A rusted stovepipe rattles in a nearby shed. A sparrow chirps high: keep, keep, keep, keep. Vigorous sin red roses perfume the arid air. The claws of a tree scratch away at paint. I shiver. The wind is relentless. I hear the prophecy of a tree. "Fires in the night, through grass, open throated devouring over the hill, through abandoned housing. Yelling evacuate, evacuate, battalions of ghosts fly shrieking in the glowing tumult. Incandescent embers will be taken away by the wind."

Someone has tied five hundred red ribbons to one small bush.

The sidewalk is cracked. Underneath the dirt has eroded. I sit on the firm concrete, my upraised knees framed by blackberry vines. The community converses in the wind. If this breeze were on the coast I would be breathing cool salt sea smells instead of choking tan dust.

The clock ticks back. Leaves blow past my ear beneath Wisconsin oaks. Rattlesnakes rustle in Utah. Charlie Edwardson mines poetry. I am also a miner. My throat is dry. Lilacs jerk impatiently. The seeds dry and brown are weed seeds. I am a writer is a statement not a question. The hardy survive be they plants or people. Though the houses are unoccupied, water may be nearby. In this desert the rivers of my senses flow while I lie in the weeds in the wind on an eroded slab of concrete observed by a giant furry fly with black legs and orange feet, orange face, black eyes and black mica wings. The fly tests surfaces with its tongue. I hear the wind, feel grass, smell dust and remember what I have never experienced. I struggle to catch a rose. Hips will soon ripen; will I be here long enough to taste the desert juice? Every day there is warmth. Dried seeds crunch like pine needles beneath my feet.

Nighttime, hungry, drunk, sprawled on a mattress. I write: I am a badger. I live in a burrow. This morning a woodpecker looked for beetles in my head. Crows caw. Caw, Caw, Caw. Sparrows chirp. Somewhere a typewriter eats insects. We live together in the barracks. I watch for fires. I forgot to tell you earlier. I am a fireguard. This pays my tuition. I have done my job well. So far the building has not burned. Not even once. No one has died or run screaming to roll in the dry grass to set a conflagration. We have always lived together. I want to sleep with a woman. To feel her hair. I cannot sleep with a woman because they live in another burrow.

At night, earlier this night, we six men held coins, said "nine, twelve, eighteen." Pirate Pete and I. He smiled through his beard, laughed. Tossing away the wreck of his ship he says "six." At that time I say nothing. We have three. He says "two." I say "four." We have nothing. I say "six." He says "four." We have two. My face is scrutinized for holes. His hand tightly holds no coins. We have a bottle of brandy that pushes forth like a crocus. A bottle of wine comes from the wall socket. Muscadet. Cask of Amontillado. Cream sherry. Sauterne. They combine. Whatever is provided is consumed. The white-crusted salami from the Canadian Okanogan will never leave this place. We shall devour it slice by smoky garlicky slice. Whatever is given is devoured. I eat words. I am that hungry.

Every morning I am hungry. There are no eggs, no bacon, only crusts of bread, peanut butter and jelly. A dry leaf jiggles in the wind from crow's wing beats. Sybil sleeps alone. I write in the cool morning breeze with one eye. Give me a telephone pole. Hello my sisters. Hello my brothers. Good morning America. You want me to sit? No. Badgers never sit with other badgers. We are solitary and crusty and full of fleas. My salami lies half devoured on the counter. My beans are eaten. Thieves are afoot. Caterpillars gnaw through tin to get to the beans. My lunch has been devoured. Don't mix metaphors. Be easy with the reader who is of limited means. Poor, poor, poor, pour a cup of coffee. Drink. Describe a character in one word. A woman in one sound. I will call to you this morning my Scooby woman. Love me. Love me. For I am all alone. You can do whatever you want. Yeah. Yeah. Yeah. The queen of Aragon rides over this grass her horse farting, hooves sparking rocks, her hair blows straight back sixteen miles to the land of giants where sits the goose that lays the golden eggs. I want to climb her hair and follow each strand, examining the color. Biting chewing, eating the hair and getting to know the Queen of Aragon. I have written only two good poems. This is one of them. Don't expect anything more. Grinning sarapied Sybil skips through the door, grabs my zither, pulls my hand like a yoyo. Rancor submerged I spritely walk my seraphim to the porch where we sit against the dim wall. She says, "Play."

I think, Angel, my Angel. You see my Autoharp and say play. Despite your small entreaty you unknow the music I can produce. Some sounds I cannot play, some sequences. I will not play *The Man Who Walked Down the Streets of Laredo*, because I am not that man. I have my own sounds. Each composition is different. There is no correct piece. I play not for you but to please myself.

Then I sing my version of grand opera, "La, La. Tra la la. Birkle, splunk, twunk. Think, define play? I will not define play. Defining play strangles play. Swinging heels go high and heels go low. I dance the grass on tippy toe. Define grass. Define swing. Define professor. I sing, Roll out the beetles, roll out the beetles. Tip tip torero."

Sybil shakes me. She is awake and full of life. "Leo you're stuck like a phonograph needle." We roll in laughter while the zither says thwunk. Tears on our faces. We taste salt.

"We are the third wave," I say. "The first were the soldiers. The second the bad boys and girls. The writers are the third.

"Sybil, people live secretly in these abandoned buildings. At night someone runs the printing press, after the printer has gone home."

"I believe you," says Sybil.

I yell, "Screaming his lungs out while dying of high blood pressure the parent was unable to listen to the babble wherein lays truth. Once you come here you will never leave. This world is so filled with meaning there is little meeting."

While I talk I think, Listen to me talk. Watch me talk. Watch Sybil's kneecap. Watch me gently chew Sybil's inner thigh.

Sybil has opened her book. She reads, "In 1747 a wagon and a man discovered the Oasis. The man walked back across the desert. The wagon remained."

Eyes sucking light Sybil reads in the dark night-light.

Looking over her shoulder I ask, "Does it tell about the emigrants starving?"

Sybil replies, "Tell them to stop flushing the toilets."

"It's the shower. I bet you never eat flowers."

"Yes I do. Clover, nasturtiums, and dandelions." She reads.

"Cook me some nettle stew."

"I'm reading. I don't want to listen to you." She reads a moment, asks, "Where is Petersbork?"

"You don't want to listen to me, and now you try to tap into my brain with Petersbork."

"Forget about Petersbork."

"Once you tap in, it's not easy to close the opening. Petersbork is wherever it is; it is, that's where it is, it is there, that's where it is, there it is, isn't it there?"

"You're mocking me. I resent that." She pouts, reads.

I begin to strum, to pluck the zither. After a couple of minutes she asks, "How many octaves?"

Tilting my head I ask, "What is an octave?"

"Do you know what notes you are playing?"

"Of course not."

"I don't know if I can believe you." Sybil educated in a cultivated home complete with music lessons and a piano could not believe a person would play a musical instrument and not know how to play a musical instrument while playing a musical instrument. She rotates the conversation by pointing, says, "This pole holds up the building?"

"No, it's for firemen. When there is a fire they slide down the pole."

"Where do they come from?"

"From above."

"How do they get down?"

"Through the ceiling."

Silently she tries to read. Unable to tolerate her indifference I say, "My parents spent eight hundred dollars to have me learn to play the clarinet. I learned to play *Twinkle, Twinkle, Little Star*. Since that time, for years, I thought I could never learn to play music. I changed my mind about two years ago. In an orgy of acquisitions, I bought a Native American drum, a love flute, banjo, guitar, Autoharp and tambourine, all of which I learned to play one spring day."

"I'm proud of you," Sybil takes my hand.

"Twenty three albatrosses," I reply.

"I saw one hundred and four albatrosses yesterday," brags Sybil.

"One hundred and four. I am impressed."

Sybil stands. "Good night Leo."

I stand. She enfolds me in her arms, gives me a quick kiss. Later I dream of her. About standing close. Of our kiss. Her soft lips. The time she pushed her tongue into my mouth.

Later this morning I read the framed placard in front of the organ of the Intercontinental Ballistic Command Missile Chapel.

INTERCONTINENTAL BALLISTIC COMMAND ORGAN.

Below in smaller letters it read: Specifications for a manual pipe organ with pedals. The case is to be constructed of heavy hardwood. The vertical shades will swing on metal pins, will be bushed with felt, to guarantee tight closing and soundless operation. The bellow will be of sufficient size to guarantee a great quantity of wind, adequate to meet every possible demand. The panels will be screwed on and quadruply leathered utilizing the finest alum tanned sheepskin.

I have gotten used to my daily passage down the long corridors, beneath the dozens of Millipede lines, past the heavy springs, though various blast doors, and through the Control Center. The softly hissing ICBM will now become part of my past.

For months after leaving the workshop I think about Sybil, Pete, the ICBM and the Organ. I also miss Silverbow, Günter, Siegfried, and Stein and plan to return to the former missile base in a year or two. I had hugged my friends on the last day and said, "Let's write to each other." And everyone had said, "Yes, Let's write."

# CHAPTER 62.

## SICKNESS AND BIRD BRAINS

I drive the boys to the mountains after returning from Binker Bonker. The small delicate leaves of the vine maples are red, the alders cinnamon and the late afternoon clouds cadmium red crimson. All of nature is glowing. Spirits soaring on the wings of ravens, we laugh, run and yell, "Yahoo."

Two days later Arthur starts sniffling and I incessantly sneeze. A day after that I go to bed with a cough and spit up great gobs of stringy white gunk with gray centers.

Arthur wanders in from time to time asking, "When is supper? I don't have anything to do." I look at him through glazed eyes, mumble, "I'm sick. Take care of yourself." Karl makes himself scarce by playing with friends. On Sunday I feel well enough to get out of bed, although I am weak. I see Arthur curled up on the couch coughing and immediately mix orange juice and plug in the vaporizer. I feel guilty for having neglected him. In the evening I give him nighttime cold medicine. He coughs worse in the nighttime. He sounds like a barrage from some horrible guns, "Bzup , Brup, Bzup , Brup." He seems to be almost choking.

In the mourning the cough seems like a normal cough. The night before I had been afraid my son would die. He had seemed so sick, so vulnerable. During this day he is so irritable. I am now worried that my son will live, for the boy has become a demon. Sweetness seems gone forever. We go to the doctor. The doctor prescribes medicine that Arthur, pressing his lips tight rejects, pushes away. It spills on his clothes. I yell, "TAKE YOUR MEDICINE."

At mealtimes Arthur plays and spills food. He throws peas onto Karl's plate. "God dammit. Settle down," I yell.

"Did you see what that fucking brat did?" yells Karl.

"Stop that swearing," I yell. By the end of two weeks of crying and screaming, my compassion is gone. At times I react to the crying by yelling, "SHUT UP!" or "Go to your room if you have to cry." Instead of cooperating Karl leaves toys, jackets, books, bowls and glasses all over the living room. He argues with me and fights with Arthur. If we had been in northern Wisconsin I would have left them with the bears at the Manitowish Waters Dump. The idyllic weekend seems never to have been. I again take Arthur to the doctor. "Can you give him an antibiotic?" I ask.

"I don't like to prescribe antibiotics," says the doctor. He takes X-Rays that show no pneumonia. He prescribes a thick yellow liquid, a pediatric antihistamatic suspension.

Arthur says "this tastes terrible." I also give him a dose of antibiotic (Note: The boy remained on the medications all fall, winter and spring). Because of the doctor's appointment, I miss my weekly visit to the unemployment compensation office. The next day, a day late, I wait in line to see a thin middle-aged woman. When I reach the window I say, "I'm sorry. I'm a day late. My child was sick. He's been sick for two weeks. I had to take him to the doctor."

"I'm sorry. That's too bad," she says. "Please sign this form."

"What's this for?"

"This states that you weren't available for work yesterday, and as a result you agree to the loss of one day's compensation. This will be one seventh of your check."

"You mean because my kid was sick I lose eleven dollars?"

"Yes. It's the law."

"That's soul less. On top of spending forty bucks for medicine, X-Rays, and the doctor, I'm supposed to lose my compensation?"

"Like I said, it's the law."

"Bullcrap the law. Our country doesn't give a damn about people. Hell, I'd just as soon go to Cuba or China. At least they take care of people when they're sick."

The manager walks over and stands in back of the woman. His eyes focus on me. I think, he looks like a cat ready to pounce. I shiver. Oh Christ. Now I've done it. These bastards will start watching me. If they catch me doing anything wrong I'll lose all of my compensation. Shit.

"You can appeal this if you want to," says the woman.

"Can I win?" I say my voice wilting.

"It's the regulation," she shrugs.

I sign the forms and leave the office. While walking to the car I think, it would be nice to swim with the laughing people of Cuba. It would be enjoyable to cut sugar cane with a group from different professions. Everyone would be equal. How wonderful to experience solidarity and escape hypocrisy.

The next day the urge to go to Cuba recedes. I think, what do I know about Cuba? I've never been there. Maybe it's better, maybe it's worse. Anyway, Cuba isn't my land. This is my soil. America.

We adjust to Arthur's chronic cough and sniffles. Arthur, while irritable, is not completely unreasonable. Karl eventually tires of baiting his brother and goes on to other amusements. Our sick bed sessions create a bond as nightly I adjust the vaporizer, bathe Arthur's forehead, read stories, and often sleep on the floor.

During the sickness I have bad dreams: In one I am in graduate school. The Departmental secretary asks me if I want to do an operation in a special class called retarded birdbrain surgery. We are supposed to operate through a square opening in the top of the skull. One operation has been done with much skill. Another seems to have been performed by swishing the brain around as if it was made of bananas. The surgeon scoops out the mush, while the rest of us watch. Everyone has left except the secretary, by the time I get my chance.

She says, "Next year come early. They left you holding the scalpel." The bird starts talking to me. "It doesn't make any difference if you operate," says the bird. The bird holds me. I feel breasts. The bird keeps getting up, wandering around, going out in the hallway. It gets later and later. I don't believe that the bird doesn't care and wonder, Is the bird retarded? I wanted to perform a skillful operation on the frontal lobes to correct the problem. I didn't want to cut indiscriminately like a drunken butcher. Yet I was sure I would be inept. During this, my first operation, I cut on theory and instinct. My classmates who had botched their brain operations had been exposed to the same instruction as I. I doubted that any of their patients had lived. Who could blame my bird for wandering the corridors? Who could blame her?

# CHAPTER 63.

## WANTED-JUST A LITTLE APPRECIATION?

I invite thirty of my Humaluh faculty friends to a beer party. Only five teachers and three wives come, despite the fact that Cleo and I had thrown one of the best parties ever, our first year at the college. Perhaps I have scheduled the party too near the end of the quarter.

I regard the flop as a personal rejection. Most of the beer will not be drunk and will be flat in the morning. I learn college news from my guests. Humaluh's students are getting smarter. The over all college grade point has increased half a point in five years.

"Once in a while, couldn't they say, we appreciate your work," says Romeo Thrigwhistle. "They act as if I'm not here. I want some appreciation."

"Lacking water, flowers wilt," says Mary Jamison.

"Do you want me to sprinkle you," I offer.

"Don't mock," says Magnum. "Romeo is one of our best teachers. When they did Shakespeare, the sets were so realistic a bird attempted to nest in the ivy."

Nolen Volens says, "Things have really improved for me. Now they have me teaching business English and tech writing."

"That's terrible," says Magnum. "Your students rave about you.

Some of them told me you were a great mad Ophelia drowning by the castle, though they said you weren't so hot as Wilkins Micawber. I was in the audience when people cried when you were imprisoned in the Bastille as Sidney Carton."

"The next time you become Tom Sawyer, Huckleberry Finn or Nigger Jim, I'd like to go on the raft with you. We could go down the Mississippi together. One happy family."

"No more rafting or acting. From now on it's business English for me." We hear a Steller's jay call in solidarity from outside.

The general attitude is summed up by Malander when he says, "It's dog eat dog. The place has become a cesspool."

Volen's wife admits that the threatening environment brings their family together; "We are like a ship's crew trying to survive a storm."

Volens says, "Don't be disturbed by the low turn out. The teachers, isolated from one another, don't even go to the faculty lounge. The unhappiness spreads like a plague to wives and children. We are all robbed of sleep and smiles. Waiting for better days, we sail through turbulent waters beneath evil skies."

"Once this great institution," says Maqnum, "was famous for parties. No one entertains any more."

I say, "Why do the student's still come?"

Malander says, "It's like the girl with loose morals, and lots of boyfriends. When the boys were asked, why do you go out with her? They answer, because she's easy,"

"A third of HUMALUH cars still carry the sign of the Twit," says Volens.

"If it's so bad, why do you all stay?" I say.

"It's a good place for my wife and kids and I like the valley," says Magnum.

"The job markets tight," says Malander.

"I'm too old to get a job teaching elsewhere, plus we're in a recession" says Volens.

"I would be just as miserable elsewhere," says Mary.

It seems to me that the faculty resemble my parents. They had enjoyed the carefree roaring twenties and suffered through the worried thirties.

Emboldened by the weeping and wailing I decide to visit the campus and gloat.

Halting on the quad where I once listened to mad Butler, I feel alienated. Students pass. I don't know them. Who is everyone? I want to walk up to people. I am unable to talk. On this day it seems as if I never will fit in, will never again meet people. I must force myself to move. If it is so hard for me, a part time extrovert, to meet people, how difficult it must be to be an introvert.

A girl stops near me. Her thin lips surreptitiously beckon. My eyes catch hers. She grins. I grin. She must be wondering, who is this strange creature in beard and corduroy slacks?

I walk into the Watson and Crick Building and stop for a moment outside the biology classroom. Pompa is at the podium. The words "do you like cats?" are on the blackboard. Pompa is telling the story of his friend, Robert T. Armstrong, finding a dead cat on the road. I leave without listening further.

Someone whose name I have forgotten says, "Hello. Good to see you. What are you doing now?"

"Oh, I've become a writer."

"Have you sold anything yet?"

"Not yet. It's a new profession for me. It takes time. I'm also a full time parent."

"Good for you. Well see you around."

In the cafeteria I get a bowl of chicken noodle soup and reflect. When I worked here people were always looking for an excuse to waste time. They would spend hours talking about unimportant stuff. Now when I am visiting it seems strange. Most of them seem to be busy. They can only talk long enough to discover that I haven't found another job. No one knows that I haven't even applied for another job.

What has happened to all of my former friends? Since leaving I've gotten just a few calls. I am abandoned. People who once listened to me have decided I have nothing of importance to say.

When Cleo and I threw parties we were popular with liberals and conservatives. When we got divorced people phoned and said, we're sorry. They seemed interested in the welfare of my children. Since the divorce I've been isolated. I haven't been invited to parties.

Mary Jamison visits me from time to time. I can't lump her with the others. She is a damn good speech teacher. Enunciates clearly. She was rash to date me. Her parents discouraged our relationship. It was as if we were back in high school. They must have disapproved of her dating a loser. She hasn't gone to bed with me, but she did come to the party. That was courageous of her.

A single man, I am a threat to marriages. To the employed I am a person who has fought the hierarchy and lost. I am *non grata*. My passport has been lifted. Oh those old friends of mine. Sometimes I run into them in a tavern. They are profuse in their welcome as I join them for a drink. Yet before I've taken five swallows they stand and say, "We were leaving when you came in. It was good to see you."

It must be the same with all people who lose their jobs. Former friends disappear in the fog of remembrance lost.

It's funny, when I visit people in the privacy of their homes they are friendly. They never stand and say, "we've got to go now. We were on our way out the door when you walked in."

No. They are kind. They offer me beer or a glass of wine. Never whiskey or brandy. We enjoy talking. They don't even look at their watches. Perhaps they feel protected in their homes. There is confidentiality there. If anyone saw me enter or leave the hosts could tell them later, He wasn't invited. He just showed up. It would be hard for the administration to consider that to be an act of subversion. Still, other than Mary, none of my former colleagues has visited me.

Feeling a hand on my shoulder I cover my journal, almost spill my coke, and look into the face of Bobby Pompa; smiling like a politician getting a present from a millionaire buddy.

"Hello Bobby."

"Hello Leo. How are things going? Have you found a job yet?" Pompa's voice sounds as if he really cares.

"No Bobby. Fortunately not." I grin. "I have no money but I've lots of time."

"Times a rare commodity," says Pompa.

"How are things with you Bobby?" Pompa lowers his voice, sits down and huddles with me. We must have looked like old friends exchanging confidences. "Keep this confidential. *Biology For You* is going great. We're working on a second edition. The other colleges are wild about it. This year we'll sell fifteen thousand copies. We get seventy nine cents a copy."

"You're going to be millionaires."

"Not quite."

"What are you going to do with all your money? Travel?"

"We're donating some to the bird beak research project. Thanks to us, Isawaddy now has a gas chromatograph and carbon arc furnace for chemical testing. He has other gadgets for physical tests, to measure feather strength under tension while frozen, at room temperature, and while boiling."

"Has he learned anything?"

"He's come up with a low cost glue that can be made from the beaks of robins, starlings, black birds and sparrows."

"How wonderful," I say.

"Some of the money's gone into scholarships to summer session for training teachers in the DNA Litany. We've got a National Science Foundation Grant."

"Congratulations."

"I'm recruiting. I've visited every high school in four counties. Why should students go to the university? We offer more individualized instruction. We've got new microscopes, and five percent of our royalties are being set aside for an electron microscope."

"Just like the big time. You've really arrived." I excuse myself and walk off.

I heard what happened next from Malander who joined Pompa. Pompa said, "It's too bad about Leo. We expected a lot from him, but he had too many problems. The students didn't like his classes. They weren't rigorous enough. Students can tell. Bauer was more of a dickey bird watcher than a serious scientist."

"Students liked him," said Malander.

"Sure. There are sycophants everywhere, especially among students. But Bauer set our program back. We tried to work with him, but he was hard to work with. He always wanted to do things his way, like Frank Sinatra."

"He didn't want to do things your way?"

Pompa leaned his face close to Malander. "You know, it really was dumb for him to oppose us."

"I agree. That was stupid of him," said Malander.

"Why we were the leaders. With a weak academic background, he had the audacity to try to change things."

Malander sat back, "Other than that, you liked Leo?"

"Oh certainly. He's a very nice person. It's just too bad he didn't have it together."

"Yes, it's very important to have it together."

The next weekend, while hiking in the mountains, I come face to face with Pompa. Sometimes I think he is haunting me. The terrors of the ghost of a still alive man. After exchanging amenities I ask, "See any wildlife?"

"All sorts of things," says Pompa smiling. "Eight deer, 9 marmots, and 23 species of birds. What about yourself?"

"I've also been lucky. I've spotted 36 chipmunks, 169, 263 bees, and 438, 000 gnats." Pompa gives me a sideways glance. Waving goodbye, he is soon out of sight around a bend.

The kids and I drive to the Pacific beaches. Sitting in the sand I write:

Fang is running on firm sand. Her paws squeak. Running to the sea, snapping she gulps water. I hear splashes. Sand cliffs are collapsing into the stream. If they were magnified ten thousand times they would be a national monument. Seeing the cliffs collapse, my children say, "Wow. Look at that."

When the cliff falls, Fang jumps back. The shattered fragments form islands that dissolve and wash away. As the channel changes the stream changes its song. Waves that were once high and loud are now smooth and almost inaudible. They will rise again, those waves that move in columns back and forth across the mouth of this tiny stream. The bottom is cloudy from a severe mini marine storm. My perch is threatened by fresh bank collapses that create white frothing waves where a short time before all was smooth. The stream moves towards me. "Catch me if you can," I say laughing. The white waves last for two glances.

DAD + MOM=TRUE LOVE

The beach carries sentiments until the next high tide.

Another big sign message: THERE IS NO GRAFFITI TILL EARTH SUCKS.

Ahead of me cars roar in tight circles. Arthur prances feinting at the spewing sand. The cars shift gears and race up the beach. In the tide pool universe green anemones spread tentacles. Fang is trapped below a rocky cliff in this closed cove. She yelps, refusing to make a big jump. I call. She stays. I walk away. Her yelps change to panic. I keep walking. She leaps and is soon by my side. She wouldn't last long as an Alaskan sled dog.

I whirl by the waves, Fang yelps, then decides to let me do my thing. She walks up the beach. I sing a waltz. Spin. The houses along the shore form a band of green, blue and yellow. Below are rocky cliffs and white breakers. The view while traveling this way is similar to that from an airplane going close to the sea; or that from a train clicking through the world at ninety miles per, the near buildings a blur: it is like being at the window of a car looking at the near bushes, grass and trees. It is a magnificent melted collage. My vision sweeps to infinity. At waves end the flash of light reflects, the sand streaks past, houses merge. I feel I am at the speed of sound. At Mach one, rushing over the land, zune, zune, zune, one environment alternates with another, zune, zune, zune. I slow. The trip is over. Passengers please watch your step. There's a tendency to wobble a bit after such a ride. A mother walks away pulling her child's hand. Probably she is saying, "watch out for that man. Beware of anyone who twirls and whirls. He must be high on something."

The waves roar in parallel rows. One in back of another in back of another. The houses are parallel to the shore. They are separate from one another. The front rank has the best ocean view. The second has a good hear of the waves. Sand dollar currency, recently devalued in the world money market, lies like broken white crockery on the tawny sand. There is more love in lyrical script. Some of the letters are three feet high. Sand snakes have crawled in this dried out river valley of an old slow sluggish stream. I want you to say after me, of an old slow sluggish stream, of an old slow sluggish stream. What's the matter? I heard you slurring your words? OK for you. Those of you with thick turgid tongues shall get no fresh sweet sea grape soft wine sauce sand. Say that after me ten times. Those with thick turgid tongues shall get no fresh sweet sea grape soft wine sauce sand.

A flag flies from the top of yonder castle. It is red and white and says Camel. A spiral road descends. Guns poke menacingly out of numerous dark openings. They are ready to blast their enemies. A bridge crosses a moat. Other canals separate the castle from the sea. A wall of strong stout sand will be the first obstacle when the waves attack tonight. Waves are sneaky in the dark. A barred gate closes off an inner chamber. Is it the gate to a dungeon for *les miserables* and other victims of the revolution? Perhaps this is the fabled castle of Zor. Or is it the castle of Camel? And where are the children? Are they in the dungeons?

A sea gull asks me, "To what do you owe your present success as a writer of journals?"

I answer, "the day, that very day, when I hit my teacher in the eye with a spitball. After that she never did have anything good to say about what I wrote. Other teachers, hearing the message of the spitball, also rejected me. This gave me something to write about."

While I was talking to the sea gull, a man yells to me, "Watch out for the birds."

"Why?"

"They'll crap on you."

"Did they get you?"

"Yeah."

"What a shame. What a shame. What a shame" How strange. My children just came out of the castle. They say it is ours. Karl and Arthur own the castle of Camel. There are no arguments on the drive home. My kids deserve knighthood.

# CHAPTER 64.

# FORMER STUDENTS

I drive our Nash Rambler to a garage run by former students. The car has been running poorly. Whenever it starts it soon stops. Whenever it accelerates it coughs. I suspect automotive tuberculosis.

I park on the incline leading to the garage. No one is working. I have forgotten, it is Friday afternoon. They are partying. Some smiling bearded youths walk towards me. They give me hugs and a beer. Sally McGuire walks over with a big plate of stir-fried vegetables and brown rice. "I hope you like it. You were one of my favorite professors. I don't want you to go hungry," she says.

After leaving the college, whenever I have gone out, I have bumped into former students. One young man had come up to me saying, "Hello. Remember me? I was in your biology class in sixty-seven. Since then I've been divorced."

Former students often call me Sir or Mr. Some ask, "How are your courses going?"

It feels awkward to say, "I'm no longer at the college."

The students would say something like, "Oh?" The Oh was loaded with innuendo, as if meaning, tell me what happened. I often say, "There was a political hassle."

"That often happens," said the former students.

Sometimes I made a sad woe be gone clown face.

A few said, "The best people have left." Comments like that made me feel super good. I thought, I couldn't have been bad if most of my former students come over and say hello.

One night in a bar a youth swaggered over and said, "Hello, Mr. Bauer. I just want to tell you, your class was terrible. I didn't learn anything. I'd sit in the back usually half asleep."

"I remember you," I said while feeling my guts tighten as if they were pulled by a winch. If I had been a Hemingway I would have punched the young asshole. Instead I said, "Excuse me," and walked away. I wanted to yell "Asshole," but remained silent.

Sometimes while walking downtown former students gave a judgment of silence with averted eyes. This caused my mind to race frantically back through time. Why? Were they bible students who condemned me because I taught evolution. I also told the class, "The world, all countries, need population control. We are destroying our planet." They must have guessed I was an agnostic, Buddhist or Unitarian. Were they critical Catholics because I had taught about birth control? Or were their parents John Birchers?

I was very happy the day a young man said, "Mr. Bauer. I remember the time you took us out in your canoe. We came within fifteen feet of the snow geese. There were thousands of them and we were right there listening and watching. We were almost close enough to touch their soft clean white feathers."

"I also remember that day," I said. "It is one of my eternal memories."

A few days after my visit to the garage, I navigate the Devil's Gateway in my canoe. I am on the edge of the whirlpools, along the rocky shore outside the main currents. I wave to some young people on shore.

They wave back, and yell, "Would you like a beer?"

Their words pull me to shore. There I meet bearded Daryl Kamuda, student body president elect of Pish Community College.

"I used-to teach at a community college," I say.

"Why did you stop teaching? You're too young to have retired?"

"I got fired. A political hassle."

"Those assholes."

"You are correct. They were assholes. Now I want to move somewhere where I can have lots of friends and not get hassled. Where the land is good and wild. I used to follow the land. I went to colleges where the land was wild. I've always lived by lakes and forests, mountains and streams."

"I'm the same. I go to a place I like and rent a house. Now I've got forty acres. My roommate is an ex army sergeant. We get along fine. Good people are wherever I go."

I pull up a stalk of grass, push the stem between my teeth. "I used to have confidence. In my twenties, I thought I could do anything. My grades were good. I had girl friends. Things flowed. Responsibilities came. My soul was damaged by administrators. Once I was just like you."

"I wonder if losing your soul is like losing an ounce of hash. As long as you have it you're high whenever you want to be high. When it's gone, it's all gone."

"You can always get more hash, can't you?"

"Our generation is looser than yours. Maybe it's because of drugs. It started with hippies, peyote, and acid. Our minds were changed. Now there aren't so many hippies. They peaked last year. Now we value doing things instead of always sitting around getting high. Though when there's a need, we smoke weed."

Our glasses empty. Ignoring my thirst, I say, "Perhaps your generation is together. My generation is an uptight loveless crowd. It obeys the dictum of conformity and the denial of their own wisdom. You seem more independent. You may change. To keep your job, to advance, to guarantee security for yourself and your children you may sell yourself in a process so slow you will be unaware what's happening until one day, perhaps in your thirties or forties, you will suddenly realize you are trapped."

"Look Mr. Bauer. Just because it has happened to you, doesn't mean it will happen to me. If I see my freedom denied, I will stop whatever I'm doing. I'll quit if I have to."

"What if you have a mortgage on your house and jobs are hard to get? You won't want to lose that house? What will you do if have a pregnant wife and three small children?"

"Nope. Won't happen. I believe in ZPG. If I get married we won't have any children. Excuse me. I'll get more beer. Don't worry. I'll be back. While alone I think of my psychiatrist, Dr. Eagleton. He had counseled me, "Go after your dream. If you keep looking you'll find that place where people listen to one another, love one another and live in harmony. If you don't find it, at least you'll know, you've tried."

After the return of the president elect we sit sipping watching the white rooster tails of a ski boat. He introduces me to Andrea, his girl, and walks away. "Have you read Job?" I ask Andrea.

"A long time ago. I went to the Baptist church. They said it was wrong to see movies and dance. I started having fun. Fun was doing all the things they said were wrong. I left the church. Before leaving I read the bible. We had bible study in Sunday School."

"Well, Andrea, I identify with Job. He went through a lot of suffering. To start, he had plenty of wives, children, crops and livestock. One afternoon when God and the devil were bored they decided to test Job. Actually it was the Devil's idea. He and God caused his wives, children and livestock to die, and his crops to wither. Though he suffered and had boils and warts, Job kept his faith in God."

"If I had been Job I would have told God to shove it. That wasn't very nice of God to join up with the devil just to relieve boredom."

"I think Job did tell God off. He said to God, 'Look at the rich man who is evil. He just gets richer and richer at the expense of people he exploits.' I think he was telling God, it's all a big rip off. No matter what we believe, some of us get clobbered. If we try too hard to be good, it's easier to get knocked around."

"No, Job always believed in God. It was a test. God was testing Job, and Job was testing God."

"I think I'm like Job. Like Job I've gotten clobbered. I've even tested the elements. A river almost killed me two weeks ago. A buddy and I capsized in the main spiral rapids of the Humaluh. He managed to crest a haystack wave, was inundated, reached shore and a second latter when I shot past he reached out his hand to me. I've given mountains a chance by crossing glaciers alone in fog and rain. While pursuing the phantom of academic freedom, I tested the administration. If the administration is God, I have tested God. If God is the river and the mountains, I have tested him. I don't really know who God is. I have never heard the voice of Yahweh thundering in my ears. I guess I'm an existentialist."

"I learned about existentialists in college. You accept responsibility for your own actions."

"Yup, we accept responsibility for our own fate. Maybe I better stop doing so much testing. It destroyed Job and has almost destroyed me."

"Why not practice moderation? Instead of risking your life working for assholes, just smoke a little dope every once in a while. Mellow out."

"That's a good idea. Not too much yin, not too much yang."

"You got it."

"Except sometimes the urge to excess seems so strong I can't control it. Perhaps when I discover a good woman I will pass the rest of my days in love and moderation. I will say, maybe you're the one. Will you run away with me? I'll share everything I have with you. My two children, my debts, the unemployment check, everything." I take her hand and look deeply into her eyes. "Will you join with me?"

She laughs. "That's a wonderful offer. Want another beer?"

I laugh and nod. She heads for the ice chest. I spend the rest of the afternoon seeking moderation.

During the return paddle, I am fortunate, for the tide easily carries me through the gateway back to my put in spot.

That night I dream: After the biology department rejects me, I stop reading biology textbooks and write plays. I hope that the drama teacher will be interested in my writing, but he walks by without speaking. The student body is selecting leaders. The weather is freezing and they have rigged up a slide leading to a pond with a thinly frozen surface. The student who can slide the most times into the pond will become the student body president. I think, this is risky, because the leader might become hypothermic and die. The state held elections at the same time. I am at the meeting where people are selected to run. A friend of mine has helped collect signatures on my petition. Because it is my petition and I have collected the most signatures he says, "You should be the candidate."

My analysis of the dream reveals I am afraid to try things because I have been hurt. I fear failure again. The drama teacher symbolizes all who reject me. Students still try things because they haven't failed.

The next day Rearden comes up to me in the grocery checkout line. He produces his famous greeting smile. Many times he has indicated friendship with that grin, yet his friendship is elusive. After saying "Hello, no time no see," he adds, "I've often seen you bicycling when I've been driving."

I say "yes, and you never slowed down and waved. Who threw those rocks?"

Rearden tries to laugh. When I leave the store I give him a half assed wave. I see him a few days later. He is petting his orange striped cat. I walk to his front stoop and pet the cat. The cat meows. "That's a fine cat," I say.

"Do you have a job yet?"

"Not yet. Do you plan to sign me up for the mid-management program?"

"Are there are no jobs for you?"

"Oh there's plenty of work for two dollars an hour. Many opportunities. I can sell refrigerators, proof read the paper, or work harvesting peas, broccoli and tulips."

"Take my advice. Go to the city. Make friends with someone on the school board. Before you go, shave your beard. Get your hair cut like mine." He runs his fingers over his short-cropped hair. "Get a job teaching. There's no better job in the world. You get your summers off."

"In case you forgot. I used to teach. I know all about the pastures of plenty."

"You were a good teacher. You always showed up. That's the first thing we teach in our program. The importance of showing up."

"The administrators are what counts. More important than showing up. Did you know the Guinness Book of records says, one man got struck seven times by lightning? That means I can lose teaching jobs seven times in a row."

"Leo, you were too honest. Next time don't tell them what you think. Sure their book is terrible. I read a few chapters. You shouldn't have told them. Next time when you want to say what you think, go off for a weekend far from where you are working. If you want to get drunk, vacation north, south or east. If you want to play around, go to the next town."

"Shit. I've got to find a job where I can be myself. Where everyone has a beard."

"Leo, How old are you?"

"Forty."

"You've got to think about retirement. Get a job. Grit your teeth. Put in your years. Make sure you get a good pension and have health insurance."

"I'm not interested in pension plans. I want to be fulfilled."

"Take my advice. Think of the future. You've got two boys to raise."

"I've got to go now. See you." I turn, quickly walk down the sidewalk. Think, God I hate getting advice.

Tonight's dream: On the street three nine year old boys surround and grab me. I feel sharp pain as a letter opener goes into my shoulder. The children run off shrilly chattering about their bravery. Holding my shoulder, I walk past a dance hall. A woman embraces me. Feeling the blood, she falls back and hits her head on a concrete wall. Blood spreads like thick red muddy water over her forehead. Her face elongates. Her eyes are pop eyed. Distorted, she flows over the stones. I run away.

I interpret the dream to mean I have much anxiety over not having a job. I decide to spend more energy and time on my job search. In the dream, the nine year old boys are all the people who have been asking me if I have a job yet. The knifing symbolizes the repeated agony I feel at being asked if I have gotten a job.

# CHAPTER 65.

## WE HATED TO LOSE ELMO

Seeking work I head to Duwamps. After four futile hours I stop at a bar across from the City Hall. A printed signed certificate above the bar reads, Sponsor Cascadian State Council of Police Officers-1972. An adjacent sign reads, Sea Charters Bring the Sea to the City.

A man laughs like a stone rolling down a saw. "These charter fishing boats sell escape, but the tickets are good for only one day."

The man on the other side orders a pitcher of beer. It seems like a lot of beer for one person. I am intrigued by the man drinking directly out of the pitcher. Quite coherent, he says, "My daughter is seventeen. Self reliant." The man holding the pitcher in both hands tilts the golden pitcher. I imagine a complete upright pitcher sitting in the man's stomach, the white head of foam upwelling into his esophagus. Putting the pitcher down heavily, he says, "I graduated from high school in 1940. In 1954, when I was thirty-two, I lost my job. It wasn't my fault. I've gone to court. Our attorney general ought to be shot. He doesn't care about the little man. Instead of helping me, the court advised a psychiatric examination. I'll beat them. Don't you worry."

"Why don't you get another job?"

"I liked my old job. I did my work. I made lots of money. I was an administrator in Cascadia state government."

"You were an administrator? I didn't know they ever lost Jobs."

"It doesn't happen often."

"I lost my job also."

"Why?"

"Because of the administrators. It was during a recession. I was laid off. If I would have been in good with the top people I'd still be working."

"So would I. You've got to have the right friends."

"I won't let my job loss hold me back. There are lots of careers out there."

"I can't forget or forgive."

"If we don't forget and move on, we stay stuck."

"I may be stuck, but I'm not going to forgive those bastards."

He tilts his pitcher. Empties it. Calls for another.

When he offers me a drink I say, "No thanks. I've got to drive to Duhkwuh. My kids are there."

"My daughters in California. I'd like to see her."

"My wife's there. Or ex wife. I'd like to forget her. A woman gets in your blood."

"When it goes to court, I'll get my job back."

"Good by. I wish you luck. I shake the man's hand.

Driving home I think, how dumb it is for him to devote nineteen years to a losing cause. Wonder why he never got another job? That night after the kids are asleep, I write: I wonder why that man in the bar never went back to work? Maybe he didn't want to be a clerk. I want to be a naturalist. I spent eight years studying how to be a naturalist. In our nation, for a short time, we praised the naturalists. Kids rushed to school yelling, I love nature. I like Smoky the Bear. The TV shows changed. Police fought with crooks. Cops were heroes. Now the pay is good for cops and crooks. Crime increases. Police are part of a growth industry.

Engineers level the land. Cops and crooks level people. People and the land die. There is little land alive. Buildings and pavement grow. Every year there is less need for biologists to shepherd the wildlife, because there are fewer living things. When I go downtown and ask for a job, I don't know what to say. The man doing the hiring will ask, what can you do? Should I be honest and say, I know the scientific names of lizards, snakes, fish, mammals, and birds. Will he give me a job? Shit. With my learning I can only teach in some other college or go to work for the government. I wish I could go anywhere in the world and hustle a job, live in any community the boys and I choose. Oh I must go where the wild goose goes. Tame goose, chocolate *mousse*, which is best? Perhaps a kingfisher? They fly over water while the rest of us waddle around in goose shit. Winter is the time of death in the Humaluh. Nature seems dead. Sometimes I yearn to lie with the rotting wet leaves, I want to watch the mushrooms grow?

Debts increasing and needing dental work I write to the Teacher's Annuity and Insurance Association asking how to cash in my retirement plan. I add, I realize there might be a small fee involved in this transaction.

The retirement fund informs me: the cashing in of a retirement plan is called repurchasing. The agency, which employed you, is entitled to retain some of the funds they have contributed to your policy.

After waiting six weeks I get more specific facts by mail. The letter includes: Because half of your retirement policy money was contributed by Humaluh Valley College, your retirement policy cannot be cashed in without the consent of the college. The college will only give its consent if every dollar they have contributed is returned to them. There will also be a service charge imposed by this association.

"Shit, shit, shit," I say, "I'll get less than half the money I expected." My gut tightens. I crawl into bed fully clothed. Repurchase is a mockery; a hollow privilege. To settle an old score or to save a few bucks the employer lays someone off. That is an option of the employer. The employee having few rights in the matter is suddenly thrown into financial crisis. The photographer gives the child a sucker, the child smiles, the picture is taken, the sucker is yanked away. My sucker was that retirement nest egg. It is closer to being a rotten egg. I think I detect an odor, a stench. I will not give them the pleasure of giving back their contribution. They can go to hell. I won't cash the damn thing in.

There was more good news today. Our fifty dollar dental bill is now fifty-five. The dentist added a five dollar late charge.

The bank won't loan me money because I'm unemployed. We might lose our home. All of the cards are stacked in favor of the big institutions. An individual is helpless.

After two more futile weeks of looking for work, I write: In eleven and one half weeks my unemployment compensation will run out. Then we will have no income. What shall we do then: Laugh or gnash teeth? Hell, my sons are not even aware we are in a crisis. Knowing myself, I an optimist expect to become employed before the time of my last unemployment check, before the time our food is gone and the car out of gasoline. I persist in expecting to be employed because in my mind I am employable. I am a very desirable person, aren't I? It is hard to grasp that no one wants me working for them. Hell. What do they know about me? Do their inquiries reveal that I am a drunkard? Do I smoke opium at night? Am I a snorter by day? Do I dance with blue crystals? Perhaps I am a security risk. When wearing my army uniform I did get thrown out of that bar in Wisconsin because I said Senator McCarthy was a drunkard and a liar. Do they now suspect me of being an agent of Russia or Cuba? I bet the connection was established when I was in Guatemala during a revolution. Perhaps the government has learned about that night I spoke with the communists. If they don't like it, they should have been in my shoes. I could have been killed, wandering around during a revolution. And the man I was talking to didn't have any shoes or wristwatch. Pointing to his bare feet and my shoes and watch he said, "This is why I am a communist?"

What does the college say about me? "This is the college speaking. Unfortunately we, ah hmmm, had to let him go. He wasn't amenable to taking orders. Always wanted to do things his own way. He was smart, we'll grant him that, but he used his intelligence to udercut the administration. He was disloyal to the college and to the government. Once he organized a group that coerced the teachers into saying they disliked the administration's priorities. And he fomented rebellion in his department. Refused to use a well written text coincidentally written by two of his colleagues. We could go on and on. And those beer drinking orgies with his fellow schemers. We're after them too. They'll be let go. Don't worry. We're on to them. No doubt about it, Bauer's a bad egg. If you want to hire him that's your business. We've tried to be honest about the matter."

In the termination meeting I had asked the president, the dean, and the division chairman, "Will you give me a good reference?"

Each of the administrators had answered, "We will not give you a bad reference." Because of this assurance, I had not opposed the layoff. I should have hired an attorney. My original plan had been rudimentary. Studying writing and emulating Thoreau. I had written the start of a novel, some poems and a journal. When my money ran low, I had intended to immediately get a good job. Now the money is low and there is a slight hitch. Despite nine years of college, no one will hire me. Suspecting a torpedo job by the college, I write to them for copies of references that they have sent to prospective employers.

The dean writes back, "I only send copies of references to the prospective employers."

During a phone conversation, the president tells me, "I tell them the truth. That you were a rotten teacher." When I hear that, I feel like throwing a rock through the president's window. Instead I softly say,

"Go fuck yourself Chrome Dome." That makes me feel better. Do you believe in the power of negative affirmations?

A letter from my division chairman saying such information is confidential makes the wall of silence word tight. It is as if there is a conspiracy against me.

The college must have a rubber stamp reading incompetent to use on replies to every request for information regarding Leo Bauer.

I read in the Duwamp Tribune that the unemployment rate for Cascadian ex convicts was 90%. I imagine that is close to the unemployment rate for ex teachers.

I feel solidarity with the ex convicts. I have compassion for them. All those rejected are my brothers and sisters. If they are in America, in Russia, anywhere in the world, they are my kin. For one or two mistakes their potential is ignored. Good accomplishments are discounted. A career record is like the evening news. The bad is emphasized.

Oh when I lost my job they were smooth as KY Jelly. They said, this is only a layoff. We are dropping your program. No wonder I agreed. They were soft and furry like the underbelly of a sleeping wolverine, *Gulo gulo luscus*. Now they show their teeth and claws. I expected them to go about their business and forget about me other than to make an occasional statement saying, "yes, he taught here for seven years. In addition he developed several new ecology courses."

It isn't fair. We disagreed. A conflict takes at least two parties. Don't I have the right to state my side? Why are those records one sided? Why are they confidential? Why can't I include in them testimony from my students and other supporters? How long will I have to pay the piper for the way they sing my tune?

Is there any way to purge the records of negative information? Will I be branded for the rest of my life because of a small philosophical disagreement? Whatever the charge I am labeled. Must I spend the rest of my life scurrying through the cracks and crevices of society, like a big cockroach hiding from light and living on crumbs?

Perhaps I will have to become a revolutionary. I feel a kinship with the softly speaking people in Moscow cafes, Managua churches, Duwamps bars, and Washington hallways. Will I plot instead of work? Where are there no oppressors?

If I become a revolutionary, who shall I follow? The situation is futile. How can I plot alone? Perhaps I can multiply myself by recording my voice and broadcasting from thousands of speakers, turning my voice into a voice for the multitudes.

If I am caught in the web I will be labeled again. Will I be called a revolutionist, or insane? Before my conflict I could not comprehend paranoia. Now I wonder why there are not more paranoids. It is a valid condition. It is more valid now than in the days of Machiavelli. Poison is more honest than the memories of the files. In the time before universal records, if you screwed up in one place you could go elsewhere.

I have the solution. It came as a vision. I shall start a firm. My company will generate new records, new information. For a handsome yet reasonable fee, based upon assets and income, our personnel department shall create new personal files. Our clients will tell us what job they had with us, including their income, their strong points, and a few weaknesses, just to make the whole record believable.

My main job or task as president will be to write glowing comments about my "former employees" and to say how much we miss, we sorely miss, Elmo Butts who was characterized for his reliability, enthusiasm, willingness to take orders, skill at groveling, and initiative. The 93 employees under him all hated to see Elmo leave.

Eventually our firm will have as former employees half of all people of working age. We shall establish branches in every city and belong to credit bureaus. We will be the real life equivalent of Dr. Seuss's star off and star on machine, which enabled belly stars to be in and out of style at the flick of a switch. By taking away whatever was bad in the past, we shall give true freedom to the people. Society will be transformed. There will be a massive infusion of new blood. People will become brothers and sisters. Through our subsidiaries in China and Russia and the Third World we will unite people. And I Leo Bauer shall be the judge of what is good and what is bad, for our clients cannot be allowed to have complete freedom to recreate their past. They might goof. In addition all people will be divided into two categories: Those who divide people into two categories and those who don't.

# CHAPTER 66.

## THE JOB HUNT

I apply for minimum wage jobs. After interviewing for a fiber glassing job at a boat works, that pays $3.00 an hour, I pull off the freeway at Wisdom. Sounds like a good place to get some answers. There is a carved sailing ship hanging from a post outside the Wisdom Bar. A little depressed I seek beer. Just inside the door the sign says happy hour, 25¢ a beer until six. Twenty five minutes to go. Time for three.

I stand next to a full bellied older man with plump cheeks and a ruddy face who immediately says, "You can't walk with your drinks in Cascadia."

"That's been changed. Have you been out of the state?"

"Some. I'm a boiler maker. Just got laid off, and today we're going on strike. I'll be able to collect unemployment."

"How much is that?"

"Eighty six a week. My buddy Jake is from Illinois." He turns to a black man sitting next to him. "He gets a hundred and thirty four a week."

"I thought it was the same in every state."

"No. Cascadia's one of the lowest. In Illinois you get more if you're married and have children."

"That's the way it ought to be. Here everyone gets the same. The young single man lives high on the hog, and those with dependents starve."

"It's not fair, that's for sure."

"I'm looking for a job. How much do boiler makers earn?"

"About twelve dollars an hour with fringe benefits. I get eight in take home pay."

"That seems high."

"We're at the bottom of the craft unions. The iron workers are higher. We used to be at the top. Would you like a beer?"

"Sure." He orders me three beers, after asking if that is OK, to take advantage of happy hour. Apparently boiler makers are frugal.

"Thanks. Does it take much skill to be a boiler maker?"

"Damn Yes. We're highly skilled."

"How long is the apprenticeship program?"

"Four years. How old are you?" He frowns at me"

"Forty. No. I wouldn't do it now. I'm a biologist."

"The son of our union leader is studying to be a biologist. He's a boilermaker in the summers. Goes to college the rest of the year."

"Well. I'm an out of work biologist. How much do apprentices get?"

"Six bucks an hour."

"What kind of raise are you guys asking for?"

"Two fifty an hour."

"That's what some jobs pay."

"We need it to keep up with inflation." Defensive for a moment, he gentles and then adds, "We want more per diem."

"What's that?"

"We get it if we have to work more than forty miles away. We're trying to cut that back to thirty miles."

I thought, the raise they are demanding is probably more than I'd get fiber glassing. The boilermaker says, "My son in law gets two thousand dollars a month in Illinois."

I think, in a month and a half he earns as much as an average first novelist earns on a novel he's taken three years to write. The boiler maker calls "Happy birthday" to the bartender.

"Thanks," she says. "Last call for happy hour."

I order a round of beers. Five minutes later the boiler maker asks for another round on happy hour. It is past six. The bartender grumbles, "I'll give them to you this time, but next time when I say last call, order immediately."

When our beer is gone the boiler makers and I leave. Driving home I feel low. I won't work for three dollars an hour. I'd sooner starve.

That evening I read, Humaluh College teachers may strike. Thomas Thaumaste is quoted, "we average only $13,700 and aren't keeping up with inflation."

The highest paying job available in the Cascadia Employment Office, pays $6,000 a year. Mushroom pickers start at $2.00 an hour. With two weeks work picking I could pay my rent. Working two more weeks for an additional $160.00 could I buy booze, food, electricity, clothes, oil, shoes, insurance, gas, medicine, books, meals out, and use the excess for the doctor, dentist and baby sitters?

Again in a bar, after a job interview, I sit next to a man in work clothes with grease on his forehead. The man buys a round of beer, turns to me and says, "Yup. Seven dollars an hour and look at this." He holds up a small bottle.

"When I get a prescription filled it never costs more than a buck. I waves a flag saying stop. I waves a flag saying go. I earns seven dollars an hour."

On the way home I stop and buy a can of tomatoes for 43¢ and a bottle of marmalade for 64¢. Not long ago it seems to me, a can of tomatoes cost 33¢ and marmalade 54¢.

The energy I expend in seeking jobs is most profound. Dozens of hours a week are sucked away. It deflates my ego. I know ahead of time I will get rejected. I have been a supplicant for weeks, for months. It is a subservient position to be unemployed. When linked with writing it becomes a powerful combination of negative affirmations. Each week I form two stacks. One of rejection slips from publishers and the other of rejection slips from employers. It is hard to write, to be organized, to be efficient, to look for work with a low ego. Yet this dilemma is of my own making. If I had not chosen to write, I would now probably be working at a good job and have money in the bank. By being in charge of my destiny for several months, I may have lost charge of my destiny forever. I hope not. I believe my journals will be published and make money. I will again get a job as a biologist. This I believe. This I have to believe. I must be patient.

I spent years giving advice to my students. Ha. I told them how to get a job. Ha. I am different than the young. The young have hope. The world is their oyster. They have strong legs and straight firm backs. They are hopeful. They are forgiven mistakes and excesses.

Once I was like an oyster catcher, my bill was red and strong. Now maybe I am a carp straining mud for nutrient. The waters are murky.

Though I am seeking I cannot find a new identity. What mockery. I went to college for nine years for what? For to be laid off, to become unemployed? Diplomas on the wall, I went west to seek my fortune. Should I go to Alabama with a diploma on my knee? Oh where is Susannah?

Will the government retrain me? I don't want to become an electronics technician. I do not want to bang clang car fenders. Perhaps I am a snob. The working man has calloused hands and hair on his balls. A teacher, member of local ABC, has hands as fine as a woman. I must make a speech about that. I shall cry out, yelling Give me my balls. A different version of give me liberty or give me death.

Perhaps I should become like an ostrich, head high, proclaiming, "I trained as a professional educator. Now America do you expect me to suddenly become a pipefitter?" Actually they wouldn't take me. I don't know how to stick pipes together. You see, I been to college for so long I don't know about those things. I got a lot of books though. How much an hour is my knowledge worth?

As a child I hated to be in crowds. Though I wanted good friends I cringed when face to face with someone or when I got jostled in crowds. I was like a mousetrap: Though set, I never snapped. When I started teaching I discovered that students sought my advice. I willingly wore the mantle of tribal elder without following the strictures and social morays of the community. I have survived by acting on impulse. I've never had a steady adviser who told me to think this over, consider all the options. I needed an uncle living down the block for consultation. Not dishonest, I believed myself when I told the students "Follow your passion. Whatever you do, never select a profession for money alone. If you can't enjoy your work, what good is it to you?"

When I worked as a naturalist I enjoyed people. The park visitors were pleasant and receptive to my ideas and my youthful enthusiasm. When they violated the law, I regarded them as gentle bears who try to get away with what ever they can get away with. Often while standing deep in the woods, I watched fathers studying signs that said, KEEP AWAY. Turning, while standing next to their son or daughter, the dads had looked into the forest and up the trails, not seeing me in my badge and uniform. I was skilled at standing still and at times was invisible. Well, those fathers led their children over the rails, over the fence and across the soft brown needled red chunky bark strewn soft ground to stand posing, hands on the massive trunk of a sequoia; standing on ground forbidden to them because thousands of walkers would compress the earth and be harmful to the tree.

I timed my approach so I appeared like magic the instant the wife clicked the camera, "You're not supposed to be on that side of the fence."

They always turned to face me like a family of doughnut fed bears caught raiding a campsite. "I'm sorry. I didn't see the sign," the dad would say. That may be also be a major problem with my life: Not reading the signs. When I'm in the city I often acknowledge my beardom by jay walking.

What are the signs of loneliness? I was never lonely until I lost my job and wife. I have my children. Yet as a single father often I have no adults to talk to. Restrained by children and the cost of baby sitters, I stopped most hiking and canoeing and now spend most of my free time seeking people. I like to go to the Shiptown Deli. We have a small group that includes a poet, a potter, an architect, and the Duchenes, the Frenchman and Frenchwoman who run the Deli. We sit at a big round community table, sip coffee, and talk. It is a major pleasure to sit and gab. Several of our group live in shacks in Salmon Town on the banks of the Humaluh. There they paint, do collage, write poetry, play flutes and beat drums.

To break the cycle of loneliness I walk city streets, feel pleasure as a young woman brushes by. I sniff her perfume like a hound scenting a rabbit. I delight when visiting Duwamps to see the variety of costumes and faces in the open air farmer's market. How wonderful are the hand crafted jewelry, small boxes, hand tooled belts, bronze buckles cast in the Shiptown foundry, and massive displays of fresh vegetables and red, orange and yellow ripe fruit and best of all, Wisconsin Brick Cheese. I love the strong pungeant smell. My eager nose sniffs garlic salami, tries to sniff Brie in the round, and bread baking. The best scents of all are the cinnamon rolls in Pioneer Bakery in the basement of Totem Square, original home of loggers, and stumble bums.

When in Duwamps, I brush past hundreds of strangers. I don't cringe when drunks lean against me asking for money. One sought only three cents. When I gave him the money, he became confused, tried to change the figure and ask for more. Unable to solve the problem, he gave up. I have bought canned goods from drunks. This is my philanthropy. My love for humanity increases when I see someone poorer than me.

I still need the mountains and lakes. My earlier fantasy of wanting to live alone as a hermit in a small Walden cabin, has been replaced with the urge to live in a cabin with a good woman and my children on a lake close to stimulating people, discussions, plays, and concerts. I need solitude and community. Where are they? In Duwamps there is community. In the forest, in the mountains, there is solitude. These are my options; are they my only options? What should I do? Where should I go?

# CHAPTER 67.

## THE CITY AND WORK

I have decided. We will move to Duwamps. There are one hell of a lot more jobs in a large city although rent will be higher. Of course, each of the boys said, "I don't want to leave my friends." I am scared to death. I will be without day care. I can't take Mrs. McGrudder with us. Finding a place to live seems impossible. One major problem is Fang. Landlords are opposed to having tenants with big dogs.

Fang gets ill. She lasts only a few weeks. Her last day is mystical. She is in the back yard, her body aligned with the passage of the sun. She watches the sun as it goes down. As the sky darkens I cradle her in my arms. She dies of liver cancer. I bury her in the woods near the sacred stump.

While grieving the loss, weepy eyed I drive to Duwamps. It is now easier to find an apartment. Our new place is in a building with 47 other apartments. There is a wall around the complex that blocks off the adjacent park. The wall transforms a short walk into a mile. Just down the block from the apartments is a big shopping mall. After we move in we learn a rapist has been attacking women.

My science background enables me to get a job within three weeks. Oh the irony of it. I become a biochemist. I don't want to become a biochemist, but I have to pay our bills and feed and shelter my children. Actually, I am not exactly a biochemist. I have become a chemical technician. My new specialty is polymer research. Actually I am happy when I get the job.

A few weeks have passed. I am surrounded by the sound of motors. I feel anxious; maybe from electromagnetism. I feel trapped. I want to escape. I seem to be aging rapidly, my body aches, and bending is difficult. I hurt.

Help me analyze my anxiety. My life is threatened at work. Poisons (phenols, formaldehyde, sodium hydroxide) are in the air and on the counters. My lungs may become destroyed. One dot of sodium hydroxide in my eye and that eye will immediately become forever blind.

Two months later I have solid reasons to worry. My job is threatened. I am not a good worker. Boredom is a factor. I do the same job every day. I don't earn enough money to get ahead on our bills, so creditors still threaten me. We need so much. Doctors, dentists, utilities. My sons are so unhappy. What should we do? Arthur says he wants to be a ghost. That sounds like a death wish. Karl seems to worship violence. It is his solution for every problem.

I want to run off, to escape. I am incarcerated like a criminal. What do I work for? Future happiness? Now there is misery upon misery.

Malander wrote me. He said the college is almost as bad as when I was there. He complains because he will only make $16,000 this year.

If I were still married and teaching, I would have an estate. I could walk my land and watch my desires come to fruition. My children would advance from grade to grade in the same school instead of hopping around like fleas. Students would boost my ego. I wouldn't have to spend my free evenings chasing skirts.

My opponents have won. They hold the stakes. I hold an empty sack. My back hurts. I am weary, aging fast in a life of little meaning. If I had it to do over again I would not fight them. I would say, Yes Sir.

There should be a course required for all high school and college students. It should be titled "YES SIR!" All students should learn to clearly enunciate those two words. Other important words are, "What is it you wish boss?" The students should say those words every day. They should learn to recognize that decisions that appear to be made jointly are really "Yes Boss" decisions.

I hate the sound of motors. I need the sound of water waves. My arteries are constricted with tension; they must be filling with cholesterol.

I am moving in small patterns, saying the same things, getting more linear, feeling hopeless, not OK, talking scatologically. My humor has become twisted and deviant. I do not radiate joy or confidence. My voice is a whisper. It would be good for my children to go away for a year to separate boarding schools. To break the pattern they need new identities. Perhaps there is a witness protection program for children. It would be good for me to be all alone for several months without responsibilities, to eat out, heat canned soup, be on a boat, float down the Mississippi. I must go away and get recharged. For several years my battery has been discharging. There is little energy left for others or myself. At night I curl, rotate, and try to sleep; slowly spinning memories are like rotating mirror/mosaic mobiles. I examine options, roads not taken, money spent.

I need air, new breath. I shall write a letter of resignation. Dear Boss: In the lab I am a fish out of water, a frog out of the bog. I am resigning. Regarding the reason. Gentlemen, Dear Sirs, I am a bird with no air for my feathers. As a fish my gills are covered with plastic wrap. As a mammal I'm held squirming beneath the water and the water is so murky I cannot breathe. If I'm a rabbit I jump at sounds. I live in a burrow of motors. I want to jump, but cannot. The ceiling is too low in this burrow. Only rarely can I go out to silflay. I am aware of the coming and going of the sun because of a distant glow. I can barely perceive the white incandescence.

One day later while trying to come out of depression I write: This morning melancholia seems gone, yet I hate to think of seeing the boss, of asking for more varied work. He may come down on me, criticize me.

I am merely trying to survive, yet I get much criticism. The message is, I am not OK. The motors thud at my skull. Outside our toxic smoke goes straight up and merges with the gray dirty sky. Some swirls back to re-enter our laboratory. Bells clang on a backing train. It is a funeral dirge.

I am like a child. I want to suck my thumb, hold onto a blanket. Is it wrong to seek warmth and nurturance? Shall I place a note in a bottle and toss it into the sea: HELP. I am a prisoner in the Phenol Colony. The steamy molecules are growing. They are coming to grab me: To inundate me in phenol. Help. I need rescue.


I am relaxed today, Monday, while coming to work. I cannot imagine why? Over the weekend Arthur refused to clean his room. Karl has been gone for over a week. Where is he? Roaming the streets. Is he now a member of a marauding gang? He is angry with me. My car now runs on two cylinders. This morning it crawled up a hill and a car tried to force me off the road. I hit the curb, gave him the finger.

A distant heavy motor throbs. It gives me anxiety. The steady noise makes me sleepy. I don't want to fall asleep. I might fall into the phenol. If I get splashed with phenol, I might die, unless I can wash it off in a few seconds. I am surrounded with poison.


A week later. Karl has returned. He has not joined a street gang of drug addicted muggers. We all drive North to Humaluh County to visit friends. My body begins relaxing. My backache eases when we see the Humaluh.

The weekend over, returning to Duwamps, at first driving is relaxing, then I notice my forehead tightening, my back rigid, as if I am being wound tightly on a spool.

I have never felt successful in a big city or in the suburbs. Life is meaningless. Perhaps I should bathe in a tub of phenol.


I am a file clerk. I got fired from mixing toxics. At first I was elated. Here there are no bad chemicals, but I feel isolated. I take breaks alone, eat meals alone, and get little human contact except with Cindy, another clerk who hates clerking. She is lucky. She's in the next office and gets to talk with the secretary. Sometimes they laugh.

I feel as if my workplace is a citadel of Calvinism. People keep their personal lives hidden. Cindy's supervisor seems like a nice lady. She talks with me when I pass her desk. My supervisor doesn't even say goodnight when she leaves. Maybe she is lost in her own hell. Sometimes I go for lunch in the Blue Bottle. While I wait for my soup I look at the tables and watch professional people eating lunch, talking, laughing. There are flowers on their tables. They are well dressed. They eat $3.00 lunches. I eat soup and a roll every day. That is OK.

I yearn for people contact. I am inefficient doing filing. It is as if my brain keeps stopping. I am following a path with unsure steps, unsure of the way, not eager to walk any way but back home to where there is friendship and warmth. My sons and I belong in Wisconsin.

It is fall. The young people are pairing for the winter. At singles parties the older people pair before eleven. After eleven and after October it will be too late. The moon is full. An old lady just got blown against the wall, but it was OK, she bounced back.

I no longer have usable field glasses. Today I looked in the leather case and they were gone. I wanted to look at some kinful birds, the English sparrows. Everyone hates those poor sparrows. Where are my binoculars? Has some child taken them? An adult would sneer at them. The black leather covering is mostly worn off the metal. The straps broke and are knotted. Last summer Karl borrowed them. He said later, "My friend broke the strap." Later I discovered that the metal clasp had broken. That's why the strap was knotted.

It isn't much fun to use field glasses when they hang awkwardly around your neck like a noose. Perhaps I am lucky they are gone, I won't have to be angry any more with Karl. His friend must have caught the strap on a branch and pulled open the metal fastener. Boys today lack patience. They never told me who broke it. I remember now. They said it was weak. The breaking wasn't their fault. Why is it that boys are never at fault?

I have just sold some of my books. Rent is due. They included the volumes on protozoans and coelenterates by Libby Hyman. I used to be enthused by protozoans. I told my students all kinds of special things about them. Of how exciting it is to have an organism simply divide. Instead of one, there are suddenly two. I sold my book on zoogeography for two dollars. That book told about how animals are distributed. Why some fish are found in rivers on both sides of a mountain range, because one watershed has stolen from the other side. That intrigued me. The stealing of water by rivers. I got thirty-five dollars cash and fifteen in trade. It's nice to get some new books. The biography of Thomas Wolfe was a real find. I've been reading other biographies. Lives seem so miserable. Filled with such striving that doesn't measure up to expectations. And when we're done with our great work, what do we get? Praise or condemnation. And what do we remember? The condemnation.

I am like Wolfe. Criticism makes me want to curl up. It is easy for someone to sit at a typewriter and criticize or mock, but the harm they do is lasting. No wonder decent writers drink. In honesty we reveal ourselves. Lesser people matter of factly, as if they are gods, announce to the world that someone else's work is poorly organized and a waste of time. May Bernard DeVoto roast in hell.

One honest book is worth more than one thousand lives spent plugged into a bureaucracy that gives a person weekends, holidays, and two or three weeks of vacation so the employee can do his or her own thing. They return to work and brag about the wonderful things they have done and the places they have visited. It is like watching a poor person sitting on a dock in Trinidad looking at the American tourist who thinks, I sure am glad I am not a poor jobless person in Trinidad. And when he returns to Duwamps he says, "God it was wonderful, sitting two weeks in Trinidad doing nothing." Is that picture mixed up or what? What do you think? Hell, isn't it better to live in misery on ones own terms than to graze in homogenized pastures of plenty?

I should give up trying to get a decent creative job. Less striving would free energy for writing. I must stop pimping my mind. My dignity vanishes when I imitate businessmen. In my new suit I am a mannequin, a listener not a participant. Why in the hell should I have to wear a suit and tie to sit at a desk as a clerk?

If I ever can brag again, it will be because of what I have produced. If I have a book published, it may occur because my hands have selected the type and locked it tight in the frame and pressed the switch to run the press, and fed the paper, collated the pages and bound the book. And if it is successful, it may well be because I have carried an armful to the campuses, and hawked it as if it was the greatest thing on earth.

Campuses won't be a good market. Most of the students, unless they are English majors, buy only textbooks.

Once my ex girl friend, out of love for me, typed my stories. This was one of the services provided prior to marriage. When we got married she stopped doing my work and I had the arrogance to become angry with her. I acted as if she had broken a written contract. Fulfilling my time in jerkdom I stayed angry about this for our entire marriage. I kept away from the final typing and mailing of manuscripts. When I taught, I waited for typists to type my tests and cursed delays. Sometimes I typed my own exams and made many mistakes. I rationalized, saying in my mind, because I'm not a typist, I don't have to have high standards.

Now I realize it's up to me. I've got to do it all myself. The whole damn job. My fingers and lips will get covered in ink. People will reject what I offer them. They will refuse what I sell. I don't care. I'll persist and keep trying and when I die, I may be unknown to most people, but others will say, "God damn it. Leo Bauer tried. The man wasn't a quitter. You've got to give him that much credit."

Some will remember me for my enthusiasm. And in addition to publishing my books, damn it all, I'm going to get another pair of field glasses. They'll be light, 7X35. And I'll lead hikes again and tell people how wonderful earth is.

I won't waste time waiting for someone to offer me a job, because I'll do my thing without money. Not because someone is paying me, but because it is important to me.

I've fallen enough. I've been rejected enough. Now you watch. I'll fly again. I'll soar above this earth above young people dancing their hearts to jelly while ignoring mother earth and above older folks chasing dollars.

And the meek shall not inherit the earth for the meek do not breathe as deeply as the swallows. Remember the angry chatter of the pine squirrel helps him survive. Oh the quiver of the meek is not worthy of respect, and I Leo Bauer must live from now only on my terms, not to inherit the earth but to interface, to merge with the living fabric of dirt, for this earth is a wonderful place exciting and alive with oxygen for all unless we screw up big time.

Let us give glorious exhalation in praise of our planet, our life, our children and our friends including those with two legs, those with four legs, those with many legs, those that spin, those that fly, those who swim, and those who crawl.

# CHAPTER 68.

## THE JOB INTERVIEW

Tired of being a clerk, I interviewed for other jobs. One interviewer says, "I see you lived in Humaluh County. Have you ever canoed the Humaluh?"

"I'll say I have. Rivers are part of me. While a student I wanted to follow in the footsteps of the early naturalists, like John Muir. While a teacher I wanted to be another Agassiz and inspire students to greatness. After losing my job I ate blackberries in the warm sun. When you ask me if I've canoed the Humaluh, there isn't enough I can say. When I went down the Humaluh a green heron ate a small fish while sitting on a branch above the shallows. I looked at the fish in his beak. He was very quiet. There were snapping sounds in the fields, a chewing by grasshoppers or leafhoppers. A wren quibbled with neighbors. In the tide flats the main indications of life were yellow legs in shallow water. The top of the dike was hard like cement. A hawk bobbed, white rump patch shining, gliding just above the cattails and grasses.

"I admit I am curious. A pill bug, hauled around like a turtle, always seems to be released, and the grasshoppers pass with impunity. Perhaps because the one spits tobacco and the other wears flashing orange armor; the tiger beetles leave them be. Tiger beetles glowing metallic green, moving in bursts on the hot dry earth. One followed a pill bug, rolled it over, and watched the legs scramble. Tiger beetles walk so fast, it is as if they slide over the soil. Another tiger beetle followed a small grasshopper. Bumping into the hopper, the beetle turned and quickly ran away. As a naturalist, I have been a herdsman of tiger beetles. Do you have any vacancies? The blue heron has a sweet lovely voice.

I withdraw my application for the first position. Do you have any other vacancies? An opening for a clerk you say. No thanks. I'm doing that now.

"The blue heron, as I was saying, has a lovely sweet voice; after a few squirts of throat spray. Unfortunately they rarely get to the pharmacy so their throats remain scratchy. Consider their neighbors. The greater yellowlegs are snooty birds as shown by a long upturned bill. As if to pay for such pomposity they must continually walk in mud all the while poking that proud beak into gunk.

"The marsh hawk glides, then flaps. Did you know that? I have much knowledge that may be of benefit to your firm.

"I was canoeing the Humaluh with my friend Sally. You'd like her. She is good with a paddle. Two red flapping dragonflies rode in tandem looking like tangled helicopters. We started with the current. When the tide came in we went upstream down river. It sounds confusing but you can do it. Small weathered fishermen's shacks were perched along the dike that was overgrown with blackberry, willow, and cottonwood. The shack town was a city with no name, electricity, or refrigerators. Logs, neatly lashed, were boomed to shore near slanted bleached towers and strange ramps holding chains and spikes. Bodies from some long ago revolution were nailed on the stumps in warning. They grinned. Their jaws were open. We pushed through overhanging brush. Saw no boats, heard no motors. A huge log with a thick moss hide floated while stuck to the shore. A man sat, fished alone. Nearby, on the bank, a father and two sons. A train came by hidden by the trees and brush. The wheels clicked. Upstream went the train to the mountains.

"We reached the saltwater and angled north through slough's edge with grassy flat even shores. Going for the open water we paddled in water warmed by the mud. Huge navy planes, landing lights on, flew over.

"An orange eye, the sun, sank behind a big island. The mountain, Kul Shan, glowed with it's molten eye. The full moon came up. The sun, the moon, and Kul Shan saw each other. Sally and I were part of it all. In the center was Kul Shan. I saw the sun, Kul Shan and the full moon. One hovered, one was anchored, one had vanished, and we sat in the canoe. We all revolved. Two were on regular cycles. I am irregular. Sometimes I set at night, sometimes at dawn, sometimes at dusk. Can your organization accommodate someone who has irregular setting times?

"Most often I rise close to the time the sun rises. When the sun urges me to wake, I usually wake. The full moon also affects me. The moon calls, come walk in the meadows. The meadows call, smell me, and I smell them.

"Do you know the Greeks have a word for the rising moon, the setting sun, and the reflecting mountain? It is a quiet word in strange letters. It was mentioned in The *Odyssey: a Modern Sequel* by Nikos Kazantzakis. He also wrote *Zorba the Greek*. Did you read Zorba or see the movie? It took place on Crete. I would love to go to Greece.

"That evening thousands of ducks and gulls were silhouetted against the orange horizon. They were quiet. Close flights of four and five gulls glided by without a sound. The earth was quiet. The sea was molten brass. The shore was ringed with glowing orange.

"We were in the middle of the sea. In back, far away, blue bright white town lights twinkled. To the west an island was dark, like a long ridge. To the north a mouse sat low on the water. Actually it was an island resembling a mouse.

"We paddled towards the mouse's nose. Of course he waited. Bare patches said cliffs. Never before was an island that small so big. We had the urge to paddle to the leeward side. We thought, there must be water there: A way through. Yet I already knew. The island was connected to land by cattails and sedges. We could not paddle over cattails and sedges.

"The big bay was ringed by the wide marsh. Half of the sea was a tide flat. No wonder the water was warm. Earlier the water flowing over hot mud shooed away the droning flies and bees. The lapping flood surrounded stumps while the water rested on the mud-covered reeds, weeds and asters. While we paddled offshore, cataracts plunged over the banks and the sea became warm. To the east ducks sparkled like pieces of wind tossed silver.

"Lacking a light we paddled the shallows and avoided open water. The night was growing. The moon though shrinking was still the source of a silvery trail. In the dark we heard waves chew the shore of the island and splashes as ducks leapt free. A blinking light marked the channel entrance. The light was blotted out by the island; like a ship passing. We were glad of the moon and the near by waves.

"Rounding the island, we saw a spotlight sweep the green water. Are they looking for corpses? I thought. Other lights were red and green. We worried. If a motorboat came it might hit us in the dark. We gave thanks for the moon. We almost ran aground. If stuck, could we have waded through the muck to solid land? We headed towards the open water. Again the current was strong. We headed upriver and the tide was going out full bore. With hard strokes we paddled towards the searchlight. A lamp glimmered yellow orange through sooty glass. Another light flickered. It was on a buoy marking the end of a net. A few fish sprawled on the net, which was inhaled over the spool at the end of the boat; the salmon were picked off and tossed in the bow. We heard them flop.

"'Is the opening of the breakwater near?" we asked.

"'Yes,' grunted the dark fisherman hauling in the net. 'Over there,' he pointed. We paddled along the towering black breakwater. The fisherman approached, his motor rough and loud. Parallel and twelve feet away he matched our pace, grunted, 'Where you from?'

"Duhkwuh, by way of the South Fork. It's been a long day."

"'Wanta tow?' he grunted.

"Sure," we said. We converged, touched. Got on board. I held the rope of the canoe. My feet were next to a large long plump silvery king salmon. Eight more were near by. My butt was on the fiberglass hull, which bent. I hoped it was stronger than it seemed.

"'Deer are on the island,' he smiled. The motor bumped along the sand. I worried, will the motor stop? Will we float all night? He swept the water with the spotlight. Turning the light off, he said, 'I can see better with the moon.'

"A while later his light again swept the mud flats now high above the water. A sailboat lay on its side at a sharp angle. It had been caught when the tide left. He offered us a beer and Indian cigarettes. Listening to the motor we smoked and drank. When we reached his village, he said, 'Good by.' We paddled across the canal to Shiptown, where we tied up and got a beer. We laughed at our good luck, and said how nice were Indians. And you asked me if I have ever canoed the Humaluh.

"Do you have a job for me?"

"No?"

"That's too bad. I've gotten so much out of our conversation. And you'll keep my resume on file? That's good. This is a good company. I'd like to work here. Goodbye. Thanks. Let me know when you want to go down the Humaluh."

# CHAPTER 69.

## THE STORM

Sometimes the life of a clerk is good. Today rainwater pours from evenly spaced troughs of the bank across the street. Hitting the concrete forty feet below it blows over the marble, dances like Peter Pan. The daffodils move frantically as if trying to escape. There is lightning. White flashes.

The girl standing by my side says, "I love it. Look, the trees bend like ballet dancers."

We look at the building next to the bank. A fan of water follows the walls from the top, forms a cross ripple curtain. The wind rushes through the portals of the bank's plaza, pushes waves the length of the 400 foot rain pool. Drops fall down and drops swirl up. A lady in a white hooded coat runs down the sidewalk and across the street. An older lady, laden with packages, runs with part of a clustered group to her bus. A lady carrying bright red flowers runs across the street. The city's people are speeded up. Four run in a pack across the street and one walks very fast. A man in a gray jacket takes big leaping steps for a full block; has to wait for the light.

"Looks like it blew all the daffodils away." Says another clerk who by chance is also a biologist. On the south side of the bank they are all gone, but they have been clipped, not blown away. No flowers are bent to the soil.

Now people walk. Only a few are runners, say one in ten. A few minutes earlier everyone ran except the halt and the lame. I walk to the opposite side of our building, look to the west. Far away, beyond the point, the ocean is silvery. The water closer to the docks is dark but back lit. I say, "Isn't it great?"

"It's OK if you like that sort of thing," says my fellow biologist who has followed me around the building. "I don't like the wind," he adds.

It is black to the south. There is blue sky to the north. The windows of a building looking south are silvery gray, creating the illusion that I can look through the building, as if it is burned out, for the gray of the glass matches the gray of the sky.

A few minutes later I am outside waiting for a bus. The small trees are bending; I feel the rain on my face.

"Exciting weather," I say to my neighbor, a bearded tall youth with a red jacket. "It reminds me of Wisconsin."

The young man turns to a lady next to him, says, "He likes this weather. Reminds him of Wisconsin."

"I wish we'd have April weather," she says.

"Yes, I like April showers," I say.

"The wind, the wind," she says. "I don't like the wind."

In Wisconsin the winds raced across the lake. You could watch their progress. The pines bent. The deciduous trees are leafless today in Wisconsin.

In the forest surrounding Duwamps the coniferous forest will be dark. As we wait for the bus, the wind sings through the cracks in the metal frame of the big solid bank doors. The closed sign rattles. The doors are an organ. The pitch changes, the bank screams, quiets, becoming almost inaudible, then loudens as if someone was driving a turbine engined car fast on the straight away and slow on the corners.

According to rumor, there is a very bad man in the building. He sets elevator door controls so that they will not stop closing after they start to close. If a person tries to hold the elevator by spearing his or her hand through the crack, they get a surprise when the door keeps closing. As proof, several one handed people work in the building.

I finally get a job close to biology. I accept a temporary position as a trash man at the Duwamps zoo. I hide behind a dumpster filled with zebra and monkey shit on the day the Humaluh College biology class comes on tour. My luck holds. They fail to see me.

My good luck continues. I am promoted to cashier at the aquarium with reduction in pay. In scanning the list of tour groups I notice Humaluh Valley College is scheduled. My they are on the move. I do not want to give Pompa the pleasure of seeing me cashiering. I get someone to relieve me before the group is due.

I am on the roof of the aquarium when the group comes through. Peering past cruising sharks I watch my former colleagues and students. Their faces are dull orbs, like furry shells. I recognize them by their shapes. Not expecting me, Pompa and Isawaddy see a nameless dark figure through the silvery surface beyond the kelp. My imagination loads the tank with piranha. I will go below and invite Pompa and Isawaddy for a behind the scenes tour of the aquarium. Once on top, above the tank, I will have them pose for a photograph. One shove will take care of both of them.

My car is a problem. Each evening when I get in to drive to my encounter group, the car refuses to start. What does my car have against my psychological development? Is this a revolt by a machine because I look with distain upon machines? Today, as usual, the car immediately starts because I am not in a hurry and it is daytime. However there is a ticking sound as if the fan is hitting the radiator. I check. It isn't. Does my car spray oil because it knows I hate oil that is worse than gold, because gold remains gold, but oil is devoured in Bachalanean orgies involving thousands of cars; all abreast racing down the roads through cities, over the deserts and through the forests spewing forth swirling fumes.

Threatening to choke us all. Cars destroy tranquility. We are in a competition to get where we're going; we will get there by and by, when we get there we may die.

When a car passes away there is drama in the oil fumes and smoke billowing from under the hood as if a smoky dragon lurks there. Perhaps it suffers from indigestion caused by too many additives including xylene, alcohol and STP. As an ecologist, I hate to see a cloud of pollution emerging from my car.

Today, trying to pull tons of auto body up a hill, my engine can't go all the way without resting. I pull over just as the power leaves; as the motor quits the smoke billows. I am lucky the damn thing doesn't explode. After a rest, just like an asthma patient or someone with COPD, barely running it makes it to the top.

Oh the indignity of having to call in a specialist in a last ditch attempt to keep the old car alive. The mechanic, who advertised his services as being cheap, adds a gas filter, new electric wires and rebuilds the carburetor. After estimating $40.00 he asks for $84.00. When I splutter in protest he denies making the estimate. Then he says, "Yes, I did say that." We have another squabble because the car is barely running. His work has made no difference. I am doubtful I can get the car home. He says, "I'm sorry. I forgot you said you were short of money and the car was dying. Often you have to tune up a car to find out what it needs."

How dumb I have been to ignore my gut feeling that the car is dying. If I would have taken it to a diagnostic center I would have learned that a valve or ring is gone. That diagnostic information would have cost only ten or fifteen dollars. Instead, like most of the time, I tried to save money by going to someone who advertises he could save me 40%. It was like giving a dying man a gold crown. We finally compromise on sixty dollars after one hell of an argument.

By coaxing and careful driving I manage to drive the car to a wrecking yard where I sell it for $40.00 complete with new wires, and filter.

Looking in the mirror I inspect my beard. The goatee is set off like a mountain. Moss hangs from the rock of my chin. Below my lips there is a bare place the size of a pack of paper matches. Turning my face causes the beard to obscure the bare place. The curved edge on one side seems different than on the other. The angle is slightly different. Actually from mirror view it comes abruptly down. The mirror right goes off at a gradual angle. A mountain climber could survive a fall on mirror right, but would plummet to death from mirror left, unless he or she caught hold of a branch.

Some of the hair is individualistic, long white threads curl into my nose from my mustache.

I look at our dishes. The pile that overflows the sinks onto the counters dismays me. Open jars of peanut butter and jam are lures for flies and mosquitoes. Clouds of fruit flies protect their chromosomes by having an over population.

I walk into the living room. A cyclone has hit. A set of World Book Encyclopedias lies across the floor like broken pieces of limestone at a quarry. The leaves of a table turned into a bookshelf, extend obliquely. A clear corridor gives access to the television set that is mainly watched by my children and their friends. Oh I am such a good dad. An antique brass vase holds bursts of tiny yellow straw flowers. I have modified the Dewey decimal system. Books are in piles by subject including history, natural history, novels, biographies and memoirs, art, music, crafts, and writing. Other objects scattered over the floor include an iron death bird I had fashioned in welding class. The assignment had been to weld two pieces of steel together. I changed the assignment to the construction of steel birds.

Near by is an embroidered pillow, towels, pajamas, T-shirts, camping packs, a cowboy boot sitting inside a leaky truck inner tube, a toy rocking horse, a wooden crane, scattered newspapers, an orange basketball, a faceplate for diving, and a snorkel. Phonograph records are piled against the phonograph. A folding chair faces the couch.

Looking at the mess I am dismayed with the realization: it is time to clean house. In addition to being used for reading and TV watching, the room is used by Arthur for dressing and Karl for dining. For some strange reason I find it difficult to use the space for meditation or writing.

Often the children hear me sing, *"Oh once I was a bachelor, I lived all alone, I worked at the weaver's trade, and the only only thing that I ever did that was wrong, was to woo the fair young maid."*

Regarding dishes. Most people buy dishes in sets. I bought our dishes in second hand stores. Our cups are white, brown, green, red, and blue. In addition to solid colors, some dishes carry maple leaves, cattails, roses, an American flag (to show our patriotism), and trees. One blue plastic cup bears the legend: For Restful Sleep-RX Pares (Methalqualone HCL) Parke-Davis. Consult accompanying labeling before prescribing.

That blue plastic cup is my least favorite. Each time I drop it I bitch, "The damn thing refuses to break." The ceramic cups break smartly the instant they hit the floor. These fortuitous accidents enable us to have a changing selection of cups.

# CHAPTER 70.

## BRAINS AND THE GOAT FARM

Tired of coping with my sons, I send them to Cleo for a few weeks. Next I call the temporary employment service. "I won't be available for a few weeks," I say.

Time is again mine. It seems important to sort out feelings. To help me I write and drink French brandy. I sniff the scent, look through the clear amber fluid and enjoy the subtle taste of good French brandy.

I become a raccoon. Wearing my shiny dark mask I begin my return to Wisconsin. On the way I pass fouled rivers, and gummy shorelines. To improve the environment I knock over a bunch of factory chimneys. Upon my arrival I watch crayfish. Their red eyes glow while they tickle my whiskers with their antennae. I don't eat them. Leaving the water I climb to the top of the old pine. The marshes are brown around Trout Lake. The water is low. After cutting the logs, I build my cabin, carefully notching the ends and fitting the logs together. I carry stones from the lake shore to construct the fireplace. No sooner have I moved in then fire sweeps the forest. Under a glowing sky, paws blackened, I return to Cascadia to a farm next to a marsh of rushes. Oh there are crayfish, blackbirds, and a porch. By my side is Sparkle Eyes my mate. Our whiskers tickling we curl in softness. She suckles our young. When their eyes open, they seek the breast of their mother. I dream by her side that I have walked all the shores of the earth until they are clean. I eat with smacking relish the clams, oysters and mussels. What pleasure it is to feel the soft white salty flesh with paws and tongue, to feel with my soft tactile fingers the anemone tentacles. Sparkly with millions of floating long antennaed Dinoflaggelate specks; the water is green.

PROCLAMATION: In the future to raise the standard of living the speed limit will be raised to 180 miles an hour. Freeways will be constructed 200 feet high with no curbs or railings. Tenements beneath the freeways will house the poorest families. Every ten years the land beneath the lanes will be mined for scrap metal.

In the forest east of Duwamps I write: I am like a baby. I can no more go out and provide for myself and my family than a child can provide for his parents. When there is little work available I am not a good scrounger. I cannot fix an engine. Although I can saw wood, I don't know how to nail it into a sturdy frame. I have only invented one tool. All I have is my mind. No one wants to rent such a complexity of tangled neurons. More often they would rend such a mess. I am worse than a baby, for a baby can cry and get sympathy. When a man whines he gathers no kindness.

Trillium wilt in the dusk. Robins chirp. Ravens sigh. Frogs join in the dirge. There is a far off motorbike. It is spring yet there is no joy. Flowers are not cheerful when the leaves fall, but now it is spring. Why is nature still sad?

A vine catches my foot. The trail is wide, muddy, dark. The snow is in the mountains. My nose is partially blocked. I smell no perfume. For odor I crush sniff cedar leaves. Water flows from the base of the hill. A grouse explodes from my shoetips. At the lake, the geese of challenge have gone for the night. All I hear are frogs.

More is needed to exorcize my depression. No job. No car. No date. No one to talk to or lie with. Gas pains. No one else to wash the pots. Spring. Why depression? Yesterday was bad. Two bomb scares at employment security. They gave me the wrong address for a job interview. I went by bus. Walked two miles to the wrong place. My aching feet. When I went to the right place it was wrong. Shit. The frogs croak. The bus smoked. Slow, slow, crawling, smoking uphill. Shit. I sold my car for forty bucks. A day later I saw it by the IGA. The man who bought it has it running. He did it himself. No sweat. If only I could have fixed it I'd have a car. Nothing goes right. Shit. The quarter moon is not clear. I fart. Even my guts are foul.

The next day, looking for a new home, I go to the market: A youth stares into my eyes. He sings, *"Old Man, look at my life. I'm a lot like you were."* I think, not yet, Christ, not yet. I hate that arrogant young bastard sitting on that gum specked black sidewalk. The gum looks like eroded coins. A red nailed levied laughing girl sits on his right and on his left a blonde in pink. His eyes above his wretched pimply beard try to see into me as he sings, *"Old man, I'm a lot like you."* A leather hat is for offerings. Pink pus bumps edge his hair. He shows no love for me. I stare at him as if he is a Gila monster. He is not like I was.

An evangelist talks, yells "God is wonderful." I pass. He pushes brochures in my face. I say "I'll believe in God when he gets good jobs for the unemployed." My words take me from the roll of observer to that of participant. How do I really enter the world of the living? Now, when I do live, it is not the life of a man. I do not like what I have become. My name stands for the wrong things.

Brandy is dandy. With brandy all things are possible: We have been brought here to a dream within a dream.

Is that you?

Yes. We are all here.

Good. I am not alone. I am alone. The moon is full. I shiver. The dew softens paper scraps. The yellow hall light shows through tiny rectangles. The moon sucks me to the sky.

I will fall away. I will fall away and leave you. You do not deserve me. Listen your lungs protest. I resent those storms of smoke. I need air. I resent shallow breaths, I will dry up like bird lungs drying in the sun. Say this. "This is my body, this is my flesh. Must I destroy my body and flesh?" The women and men are unwilling to listen to the screams that crash within the garbage can of life.

A wild raging dark hairy beast rips off chunks of meat from the belly, throat and asshole of a road killed antelope. The claws soften. The beast turns into a koala bear. The antelope comes alive. I repair, sculpt her body; trace her flanks with gentle hands? Sing a song to the antelope.

Goodby to the antelopes, petalopes, rattletraps and poodlelaps. Sing out to the dundermats. Ride the cone of light triumphantly into the sunset.

But your parents say no. NO. NO.

Apparently you are a problem.

You should not do that, you can not, you must not, we have said no, do what we say or we will not accept you. We have spoken.

We will not say this again. You are a problem. You? YOU or THEY? They are a problem. They were the problem. They gave the womb, they send the tomb. I must escape. Alone, sitting alone on a mattress in the middle of an empty room. Going across the universe at the speed of light. I can go back to the womb or forward to the tomb. Stop. Alone at the day of death. The hour of death. I must escape. This is not the time.

Eating slices of orange, slowly rotate the chunks, squeeze the cells. Drops of citrus fall on my tongue. Within the curl of tongue there is escape.

There is no escape. You will come to me. You will come to no good. I your parent prophecy your doom if you do not reform. You will not reform. How can you. Your doom is written in the stars by me your father almighty creator of my children on earth, one and indivisible. I am the spirit and the light, all is heaven, world without end, my children perpetuate me. Forever I will sit on their shoulders.

Priestly father why did you forsake me? Did you die on your rood in vain?

My son we are nailed together like old crates once filled with apples and oranges, books, plates, dust, silverfish, mould. We will be and forever will be a Dermestid feast. Life is a howling crate nailed together or ripped apart, loaded or empty, down at the station, cheerful or gloomy, early in the morning, waiting for the little huffer bellies all in a row.

Father says, "My son, in regard to excess weight, a question of exercise. Walk, talk, run, swim, play kissy kissy chomp chomp, run around the block, all around the town, bicycle and you will not grow fat. For stomach trouble take emulsions. Without proper medication the sea cuccumber throws up its stomach for all the world to see. Just needs some gut drops, that's all. The sedentary tube worm sends feathers into the current, stays slim without exercise. If you eat with feathers, you won't have to exercise either.

"Hold your head upon your shoulders, stand tall, bear your gutflab proudly, chin, belly will retreat into your redness. The belly sets on the sea of dreams. On a nearby ferry tourists oggle, say, Our sun is in good shape, doesn't look a millennia over thirty three and a third eons having gone from sea to paternity and maternity, let's watch our sun set while we wiggle our toes. I swim notwithstanding the glacial ice that slides below the waves. My goose bumps wait until the swim is over. I shiver violently. My arm hurts, the sun sets, the sun is always setting, somewhere someday the sun will set for you. A bright green flash is seen from the top of Mary's Peak in Oregon too far away to see the waves, the sea flat orange, the sun is gone, the flash is over, hidden waves crash against a rocky shore too far away to hear the sun, both sons are out of sight on this day of our lord's traverse, the travesty of change on this day the first day the one day the birthday the birthday the deathday the last day the only day for there is just one more sunset, watch the clouds tall crimson yellow azure amethyst argent purple violet look, look, ooh, ahh, ohh, ahh, ohh remember if you never lose sight of the sun when you die you will be just one day old even if your beard is tangled."

After a day of recovering from the brandy I dream: My former room-mate, Leonard Danton, now a professor, phones. "I've got you a job as a teaching assistant." Accepting the job, I arrive with my children and unpack. The building is being built. The stairs rickety and sparse dangle. Once up I'm not sure I will be able to climb down.

When I went to the college. people laughed Of course I climbed to the top of the specimen cases. While on all fours I heard a coed ask Leonard, "Where did you find such a weirdo?" I blushed, hiding. I didn't see anything wrong with where I was.

Using the metal door as a hand hold I climbed down and moved down the hall. Discovering that my pants were too long and were wearing through, I started ripping them off at the bottom. Although I thought this would make me look better I was wrong. It created more derision.

Leonard told me my second quarter classes had been canceled. There were too few students. My assistantship had been canceled. I asked if he would still teach and he smirked. I went back into the building, crawled under a table and cried. I thought of having to pack again and of moving, perhaps to Southeast Los Angeles where there was supposed to be work. I didn't want to go to that land of freeways and smog but there was no money. When I felt better I visited Arthur at his school and learned a simple dance where we chanted, one and one makes two.

I became a turtle: I cannot teach again. Who would risk hiring a failure? When they get older, my sons will ask, Father, why have you failed? I face a life of justifying myself, accounting for a sin that to me was no sin, yet I don't know if I was blameless. I am no more guilty than most men; no more innocent. I admit, once I thought I was pure. My snow was driven on.

I am Mock the turtle. Crawling, lumbering towards a goal I imagined I was running. Running? Why when the little children saw me they laughed, said, "Turtle, turtle," as they scratched my carapace and itched my nose. That was good. I can't reach my nose. The next thing I knew, those same children kicked me. Lifting my plates they pushed and tilted me over so I fell and lay on my back exposed to the hot sun. Adults were there. They should have cried, "Turtle, turtle, don't hurt the turtle."

Turtle that I was, turtle dove and turtle hawk, snapping, sea, tarrapin, tortoise, swimmer, crawler, wise, stupid, leaving a trail in the sand, I offended other turtles by my turtlenacity. Flipped over once, I was righted. Flipped over twice, righted again. Again and again, thrice, four times, my beak clacked hollowly.

"What does the turtle want to say? Poor, poor, poor turtle. How are you today turtle?"

"Do I look sick?"

"Well, you're on your back and I just thought I'd ask. Oh, by the way Mr. Turtle. To what do you owe your downfall?"

"Clack, clack, clack. I didn't realize I was a turtle. Despite my turtlenacity I didn't acknowledge my turtleness. You know the old saying, turtle see, turtle do? Well I watched a fox. I think it was a fox. Well turtle see turtle do: I raced with the fox. I was winning. The fox was sleeping. Suddenly they were aware of me. I was sort of running. They should have laughed. Instead taking offence, they ran after me with sticks. Who threw the first stone? I don't know. Does it make a difference? Once I was caught they roasted me on a spit of hot sand. Still they were polite. They asked, "How are you today turtle?"

"Rather Warm, thank you." I've always been polite. My back hurt and my flippers were weak. I was put in a shack on that dry sandy beach off Nicaragua. A woman moistened rags, squeezed water into my mouth. "What a fine turtle you are. You are a fine turtle," she said. Grateful was I for large favors.

Oh flat on my back I rock, remembering turtle heaven. Oh, oh, shiver my carapace, that diamond studded record of when the sun shone pleasantly and I floated. The water was gentle. Now I think turtlehood may be an illusion. I may be a clever fox.

Bless me fox mother for I have sinned.

Don't spin me. Don't make fun of a turtle. Don't hurt me, or I'll snap your leg like a toothpick.

Cleo telephones, says, "When can you meet the boys?"

"Don't ever make fun of a turtle or I'll snap your leg off like a toothpick," I say while hanging up.

Leaving California Cleo and the children drive to Cascadia. I heard later about their trip. They discover an empty apartment. I had moved our possessions into storage and disappeared. I had moved quickly like a fox and cautiously like a turtle. My disappearance was not complete because I saw Johnny Petrus, who had moved to Duwamps to work in a fish market. I ducked down so he did not see me hiding in an alley next to a gray striped tiger cat, drinking out of one of Cleo's mugs. Photographs of my sons were on my lap.

After he passed, I talked to passer bys as if they were students. I said to the tiger cat, "Once I used to skin cats. Sorry about that. It was part of my job description." Next I apologized to a gray cat who had wandered over. The cat meowed. I continued. "There are as many ways to skin cats as there are cats. Consider cats. There are big cats, little cats, pussy cats, tigers, lions, wild, tame, spitting, mewing, meowing, purring, friendly, hateful, angelic, diabolic, dyspeptic and dirty cats. Some are too big to be skinned. Some are too loveable. Cats willing to be skinned are the best ones for skinning. In the jungle, the quiet jungle, the Old Man of the Sea dreams of lions frolicking on warm sandy beaches. Let us grab a scrawny cantankerous caterwauling spit spitting cat. Reaching around to your back remove the claws implanted in trapezoidal and pectoral muscles. Put him in a Jug. Watch him grin on a museum shelf. If that is his destiny, so be it. We need skilled specialists to determine if occasionally twitching cats are alive or dead. When lions become old let them crawl into the bush. Though they may be toothless, let us not mock the KING OF THE BEASTS.

"One, two, three, four, who are we really for? Now's the time to celebrate, all lions good and great. Do you have trouble concentrating during lectures? If so, go to Africa and become lion food, that is; cat food.

"Once I was a lion. Running through the tall grass I leapt at my sister, Bompha. I clobbered her in the rear end, knocked her over and licked her face. Near by the secretary birds walked, disapproving of my foolishness. I purred at them. Linear creatures, they looked away. The warmth of the sun came through to my coat. I licked my fur."

During the previous twelve months I have applied for several professional jobs including: Exhibit management technician, water quality technician, college professor, water quality planner, environmental specialist, ecological analyst, community environmental liaison, environmental health specialist, newspaper reporter, landscaper, environmental consultant, park technician, park naturalist, environmental planner, zookeeper, planning assistant, wildlife biologist, fisheries biologist, natural resource technician, bioanalyst, and assistant in land inventory. Things seemed horrible. Therefore I put our possessions into storage. Friends knew I had no trouble getting jobs clerking, so they must have wondered, why did he vanish? My disappearance was just one of those strange things. Like that song, *One of Those Crazy Things, It Was Just One of Those Things.*

I chose an alley in downtown Duwamps as my new home. Nearby in the Farmer's Market I discovered Johnny Petrus throwing fish. He was tired from a hard day at the scales and disappointed because I did not acknowledge him, although the cats licked his boots. He told me later, before leaving, he heard me call out: "Brains for sale. Brains for sale," as I shook my head beneath my well oiled broad brimmed olive drab camping hat.

He heard one of the crowd ask, "Have the brains been marinated in brandy or Burgundy?"

"A young man while carefully examining my brow said, "Are they fresh?"

"Are they big?" Asked a third touching my forehead.

"I wonder if they're holy?" a woman whispered while crossing herself.

"Have they been baking in the sun?" a man asked.

"They have not been in the sun too long," I said.

After hitting bottom, I return to my possessions and pack for a road trip. Like millions of other Americans, I am receiving monthly unemployment checks so I have a little money. I think, I'll check out some communes. Could communal life be any worse than the lives of the rest of us?

Goats have always intrigued me. Therefore, when Johnny told me of a goat farm commune, the only class A goat diary in Cascadia, I resolved to visit. I was hoping I'd discover how to milk a goat. I knew of the goat's reputation for butting, and of their smallness. I wondered, how could a herd of small goats provide enough milk to make it worthwhile?

Hank, the commune leader, invited me for dinner. A tall muscular ex soldier, he had the same name as my uncle's black curly cocker spaniel. He said "Welcome Brother Bauer."

Our circle held hands. Hank said, "Let us break bread together."

I talked while the bowls of steaming vegetables and brown rice cooled.

I looked about for bread. Seeing none I assumed that was a figure of speech. The basmati rice smelled good. The vegetables were seasoned with garlic and lemons. I looked at the people. The men were all bearded. The women wore long flowing dresses. I was pleased. There were more women than men. Two kerosene lamps hanging from a beam above the table warmly lighted the room. After eating we moved to the floor of the large room adjacent to the dining area and sat in a meditation posture on the floor.

Hank told the story of the commune. "I inherited the land from grandfather. He was an inventor. As a child I had many pets. The 4H taught me responsibility. I became the owner of three goats. Milking was part of the project. Other boys tried to make fun of my smelly goats. The goats weren't smelly! They knocked this off real soon because I was bigger than the other boys. I was drafted to Nam. After discharge I wanted to create a society opposite to the regimentation of the military. The commune came into being. We started with the same three goats from the 4H days. In half a day I built a ramp to an elevated platform. They can defend them selves when they have the advantage of height. We acquired other goats to diversify the breeding stock. Goats live about twelve years. Visitors are welcome to stay, but only if they like goats."

After our group meeting I unroll my sleeping bag on the solid floor formed with thick heavy Douglas fir planks. It is a floor that can be used for heavy dancing. I think, this commune makes as much sense as anything. I will ask them tomorrow if I can stay. I can study goats. After all, I am a field biologist.

During the coming days I learn amazing things. During the middle of the day while looking into goat's eyes I see the pupils turn into dark rectangles. Imagine, peering into a woman's eyes and seeing long wide rectangles. That would be one hell of a surprise. I would think she was into satanic rituals. This may sound kinky to you, but I learned how to exchange my breathe with the breath of a goat. When inhaling I found their exhalation sweet.

Their reputation for stinkiness comes from male goats. We have a male goat visitor in for breeding. He smells like rank cheese. He is disgusting. I watch as he pees in his own face, rubs his face on his fur. Shakes his head. Looks up pleased. If the male goat had remained the milk would have tasted gamey.

They let me milk several, which have different sized teats. Some give forth strong squirts, others thin streams. I develop a rhythm and feel triumphant with my success, especially after my failure at milking Mormon cows. If we are late with the milking the goats get restless, are displeased at having full udders. Sometimes they bray like donkeys. The milk is like human milk. It does not settle out like cow's milk. It is already homogenized. It has a unique sweet taste and is loaded with good enzymes, which would be killed by pasteurization. "Nubian goats have good dispositions, and are fatter. Toggenburgs are different," says Hank. He adds, "We have to tie up the legs of some if they have bitchy dispositions."

We milk them twice a day after feeding. This mellows them.

Now, as I end this book I hope for the future. I wonder, will I be able to drink the milk? I am lactose intolerant and after drinking cows milk I get gas, stomach upset and diarrhea. Will goat's milk be any different? Will goat's milk from this farm commune be good for me? I have high hopes for the future. Soon I will get Karl and Arthur from Cleo and have them join me in the commune. Life is again good.

The facial hair of goats tickles me when I get close, muzzle-to-muzzle. When that happens, I wonder, does my long mustache tickle my favorites Mable and Mollie. While I am reading Cervantes I notice the animals are watching me. This includes the feral cats that would never sit on my lap; instead they sit on the floor with forepaws straight looking at me until I notice them and the watching cat runs off. Sometimes when I feel observed I slowly turn my head to discover Thomas the llama watching me until I look at Thomas and he looks away. The white nosed cat with a black love spot on his chin, the one who wouldn't approach sits by the side. Yellow eyes surrounded by vertical black pupils. Glistening eyes silently watching. So much of the lives of critters is silent including those of cats, llamas, and goats. Of course when there is disagreement the cats, usually at night, screech and the goats sound off; asserting primacy. I like going nose to nose with llamas. To feel that tickle of hairs against hairs. They seem spiritual to me. Their breath is sweet. Their hide smells of lanolin. Oh there is such tranquility on this farm.

I am making up for that time in Utah. My Mormon girlfriend, her family, mother, father, aunts, uncles, brothers, sisters, all watching, all laughing as my hand clutched the teats, squeezed a few drops, a few squirts from the full sacks of the irritated confused cow. Life is a chess game. You think up strategies. Then you goof, make a bad move, fail to successfully milk a cow, lose the game of the day or of your life. So I didn't get a Mormon wife, perhaps because I failed to learn to milk a cow.

Although I failed to milk a cow, I have learned to milk a goat. There will be no large Mormon families laughing at me. I will be supported by the loving energy of my fellow members of the goat diary commune. I will learn how to make goat milk cheese. I love goat milk cheese; feta on salad and in omelet's.

I hope my sons will love this life, their next life. I hope Cleo will go along with my firm decision. I must heal. Must heal in the country, on this farm in the bosom of my new loving friends. I see a carving of the Buddha. Hank said he would teach me to meditate. They also do yoga. I will do yoga and meditate. My life will be based on becoming centered by sitting on the floor in the prayer position, my thumb and index finger touching in a circle. I will have peace. Finally I will have peace. My children will become peaceful. If they learn yoga as children they will be able to stretch their legs way out to each side. They will be able to surpass me and that will be good. I can't wait until I will see my children peaceful and happy. We will become a loving family at one with the universe. Of this, I am sure.

# APPENDIX

# THE SUGARY BAUER IN THE
# PERSONNEL FILE

I discovered the Sugary Bauer Report in my personnel file. Undoubtedly it was written by a high administrative source. The libelous nature of the document is indicated by the refusal of the news media to print the account. Nevertheless, in order to give the reader a complete account of myself, this book includes the proven and the unproven, the scurrilous and the heroic.

The Report claims that Leo Bauer and a student machine gunned sugar and spice in high school cafeterias. Accounts that appeared in the newspapers stated that the marauders wore ski masks. How could someone identify anyone through a knitted woolen rainbow? On the day in question two unidentified people kicked open the twin steel doors of Duhkwuh Junior High, frightening the cooks out of their pots. The attackers ran through the barrage of kettles and skillets tossed by the cooks that clanged from them to the concrete. Twin blasts from gizzard guns spun the pots in circles of sparks and sent the cooks running out into the sunshine. The students, upon hearing the sound of gunfire, thinking the television had been turned on in the library, ran from math, speech, Engfish, and social studies so as to get good seats in the library.

Tracking down the sound, the students stood open mouthed watching the attackers remove forty-fives from M.P. holsters and blast bubbling red, green, blue and orange canisters of sweet drink right out of their ever loving chromium cradles.

As multi colored cataracts burbled to the shiny floor the hoodlums bowed. The students, though saddened at the loss of their sweet drinks were elated at the show and therefore clapped and whistled. Responding positively to youthful enthusiasm, the twisters of innocence laid down their guns and did somersaults and back flips. Still leaping and spinning they juggled gleaming metal cylinders while they danced their way to the candy, cake and pie machines. As if in a religious ritual, they carefully laid metal objects on top of each machine and connected each of them to a long cord. Cupping their hands, they lit sparklers; drew arabesques with the sparkles. They ran, then falling to their bellies skidded toward the students yelling, "Get down. The aliens are blowing up our ship." The students screamed, fell flat, covered their heads, hearing "Fizzzzzzzzzsplat;" they clapped at the fire fountains.

Their applause changed to sobs when the fire melted through rods, knobs, springs; coins fell in showers to the sticky floor, a stench filled the air from smoking melting chocolate, nuts, lemon merangue, pecan clusters and angel food that after flowing to the floor hardened into black charred mountains, buttes and canyons. Girls and boys in tantrums jumped sobbing, "They've ruined out candy. We have nothing to crunch and nothing to chew." Donning yellow polka dotted capes over backpacks containing cylinders connected to hoses the visitors pointed nozzles at bags of pure cane sugar from Hawaii and white bleached flour from Minneapolis. Fiery winds whirled fed by combusting dust. An ooze of flaming blackening magma flowed from shelves to floor. There were also a series of poofs. The smell got so bad, so horrible, the students ran back to class.

The guerillas ran out the side door onto the loading dock where they unplugged a small black electric car. A moment later they whizzed down the street to disappear around a corner lined with horse chestnut trees.

Advancing on other academia nuts, the fiends attacked the cafeteria of the Duhkwuh Senior High. Bashing through the exit door, they stopped to say, "Excuse me," as a bra less coed brushed past. Halting for a moment they watched her cross the street. Bashing through the exit door they ran into the cafeteria looking fearsome; bandoleers of machine gun bullets crisscrossing their chests. Unaware of the danger in their midst, the students continued playing cards and flipping matches and bottle caps.

"Clear out," shouted the gunmen. "Evacuate the cafeteria. We're going to blow it up." They were ignored. There was too much noise for anyone to hear.

Furious at being ignored, the masked raiders marched to the serving line and shot a poor boy sandwich through the heart.

Blanching, the cowardly cooks abandoned spoons and spatulas. The potential killers shot instant potatoes in the stomach, white rice in it's bleached soulless heads, and French fries in their greasy guts. Despite the din the cafeteria was becoming quieter. A few of the students heard one of the attackers sing an operatic aria, "Figaro, Figaro." The other laughed, as he or she exploded a coke machine in a shower of glass and syrup.

More students were breaking free of the intellectual concentration required playing thirteen in cards. Others were abandoning match flipping. With mild curiosity they watched the strange behavior of their guests who were gizzard gunning doors to splinters. White streams poured out of the ripped torsos of flour and sugar sacks.

The doughnut machine got it next. A short circuit sent an ominous cinnamon flash across the room. The students were finally alert. A boom halted the last card game before anyone reached thirteen. The raiders abused their newly acquired attention by tumbling head over heels on the trampoline like tender bellies of 99 loaves of white bread. This pleasure was interrupted when the doughnut machine exploded sending intruders, white bread fluff, chocolate and jelly doughnuts, and oil through the window. Abandoning their weapons, the criminals, who may have been injured with a minor degree of burns, ran to the loading platform, unplugged their electric car, and whirred off.

The principal, who always knew what was going on, correctly surmised that something was wrong. After hearing the explosion, he took only one more bite from a jelly filled doughnut. He was dining with a cop at the time. He had just said, "I agree. The instant soup machines will look good along the south wall." Adjourning the meeting he ran to the cafeteria and immediately concluded, the cookie, or rather the doughnut machine had split and the doughnuts had crumbled. This created a major problem for the principal who was fascinated by doughnuts.

Five policeman, led by a lieutenant, arrived ten minutes later. They became outraged at the loss of the doughnut machine. "Do you know who did it?" they asked the principal.

"Perhaps some students unhappy with low grades. We have very high standards in our high school. Do you know that our grade point has risen for the past five years?"

Much police work is routine. Culling out the names of students who had received low grades during the past ten years, and who had attended both schools, the police produced a list of 3,232 suspects. Reducing the list further by including only students who had shown some type of negative behavior towards teachers, the police had 3,231 names to work with.

Despite excellent police work they were unable to pin the crime on anyone, although they had gotten excited by a hot tip provided by President Davis, of Humaluh Valley College.

He said, "I bet Leo Bauer and Johnny Petrus did it."

"Why?" asked the police chief.

"Both are suspected of involvement in subversive activities, including ecology and the anti war movement." A short time later a sharp eyed college administrator noticed the perpetrator's capes hanging from the top of the DNA Helix.

A microscopic examination utilizing the high school microscopes proved definitively that the nose hairs were similar to the nose hairs of Bauer and Petrus. Some partially eaten doughnuts were discovered at the foot of the molecule. Tooth patterns in the doughnuts matched dental impressions that were in Bauer's personnel file and the student records of Petrus, and the files of the police chief and principal. Despite this overwhelming evidence no charges were ever placed against Bauer, Petrus, the principal or the police chief. When Davis asked the Chief, "Why no trial?" the chief shrugging his shoulders, said, "If only we could find the electric car, we might have a case."

The Humaluh County prosecutor, who had declined to prosecute, had attended one of my night ecology classes. This may have been a factor in his decision. I had given him an A.

The Roaring Tide, a hippie newspaper, took advantage of the incident. Their headline read: REVOLUTIONARY HEROES DESTROY SUGAR AND STARCH.

The article theorized that Che Gueverra had left South America and taken charge of the revolutionary struggle in Humaluh County. The raids were the first blow in a nationwide guerrilla campaign against junk food sold by bloated capitalist purveyors of nutritional rubbish.

The overly emotional account lacked footnotes and other evidence of objective scholarship. Nevertheless it appeared in underground newspapers throughout the United States and Europe. Additional articles said: The Duhkwuh raid was the greatest blow for the American consumer since the Great Minneapolis Corn Flake Conflagration of 1938 that had been responsible for the corn flake companies decision to add nutrients to the cereals before shooting them from guns.

Sensing a conspiracy, some advocates of law and order threw rocks through the windows of health food stores in Chicago, Duwamps, Los Angeles, New York and Duhkwuh. When a student asked me his opinion of the raid, I said, "The fools missed the chocolate, pineapple, and caramel syrup." I am not an easy man to please. A man of the times, I had incorporated the event into my classes.

I and my students also discussed other current happenings that included: NEWS FLASH-A Pawtucket Rhode Island woman, Mrs.

Diana Adlefitch and her two children died tragically yesterday evening. Mrs. Adlefitch, whistling and singing, had prepared the evening meal. The menu included synthetic pork chops, instant vegetables, soft as silk desert, immediate potatoes, synthetic sour cream, gravy like mother used to make on the day she died, reconstituted garden fresh potatoes, and fresh hydroponic salad with artificial bacon in the dressing. All of the foods were fresh and in addition were heavily fortified with essential fats, amino acids, iron, minerals and vitamins.

When the mixture reached their stomachs an unpredictable chemical reaction occurred. Because of an unusual rare synergistic response, the molecules polymerized, amid much heat, and the entire mass solidified.

A visiting neighbor said, "Mrs. Adlefitch and her children died in terrible agony. I can still see their contorted faces becoming silent in mid scream."

Medical researchers from the Bureau of Food Additives released the following statement: The unfortunate deaths of Mrs. Adlefitch and her children were quick. The chances of this happening are one in one and one half trillion. It has happened only once before and is covered scientifically in the bible. They went into great detail over the case of Lot's wife turning into a column of salt. There was scientific evidence proving the pillar was definitely made of salt..

The last supper of Mrs. Adelfitch was adequate, containing the essentials of modern nutrition including BRA, modified food starch, sodium phosphate, sodium nitrate, calcium phosphate, fumaric acid, artificial protein, synthetic color, hydrolyzed vegetable protein, autolyzed yeast, beef abstract, tartaric acid, synthetic cream, caramel color, monosodium glutamate, BHT, plus other medically proven ingredients.

Those wishing to view the statues of Mrs. Adelfitch and Lot's wife can see them in the Chicago Field Museum of Natural History located on Lake Shore Drive overlooking Lake Michigan.

The personnel file claimed I had forced students to view TV commercials that are here described: The announcer, Studly McMasters, frequently oils and twists his long dark mustache. Viewers hear cows moo and chickens crow. "You'll love Jack the Ribber's Steak House," McMasters says in a pleasant voice. "Our specially selected grain fattened herd has been castrated with human teeth for your dining pleasure." Panoramic shot shows bawling calves wiggling as men with buck teeth hold and snap sacks dangling in the rear of the calves.

"Our mountain oysters are slippery and super tasty." Close up of platters of heaps of mountain oysters. Extreme close up of seminiferous tubules. Microscopic view of pool of sperm.

"Our steaks, slashed from living steers, are fresh. These specially selected chunks are so fresh, they quiver on your plate." Close up of quivering steaks inserted in a panoramic view of men with knives ripping their way through the bawling herd. A bull charges in terror towards the screen. Saliva drools, splots on the lens.

"These next shots were taken by our new cameraman," says Studley laughing. "The steaks are cut right by your table, to insure freshness." The camera drops back. Diners wolf down red meat while other customers watch the cooks slice steaks from bawling steers.

The camera zeroes in on McMasters, as he sneaks a snack. He is lustily chewing. Blood dribbles down his chin. He wipes it off with a piece of French bread. Looking straight at the viewer, he says, "Don't forget. For dining pleasure, it's Jack the Ribbers."

"Mothers." His voice drops, gets serious. "Your children need fresh arteries, veins, sinew, gristle, fat and muscle. Feed your children good raw meat. It's good for them."

His voice takes on a medical tone. "Doctors agree. Your children's cute little polished white canine teeth were designed by Mother Nature to rip, tear, and shred. When this happens, the tongue cleverly pushes the mass to the molars that grind and smash the connective tissue, leaving only a few fibers trapped between the teeth. Don't worry about them, they'll naturally rot away in just a few days. Just look as these hungry tots devour their din din."

Close up of the mouths of children chewing on the side of a

restrained steer. The action speeds up. The children appear frantic to finish. The steer shakes in rage. Kicking, he narrowly misses a cute little girl in a pink polka dotted pinafore. Unfortunateley her once pristine dress gets spotted by mud and blood. This image is replaced by a view of a contented steer eating grass. A children's choir sings, "Meat is good for us." There is a close up of a smiling boy. His teeth resemble a line of brilliant white stakes. The boy sings, "Eat sugar. Stuff your mouth and fill your cheeks, with sweet, sweet, sugar." The camera pulls back. A circle of laughing children are eating candy bars. The action speeds up. Candy bar after candy bar disappears into their mouths. Wrappers fly in all directions. Their chocolate smeared faces are covered with pimples. Their teeth are chiseled and splotched with decay.

Apparently some of the commercials had been produced by an underground film company. This so called evidence was bearing false witness. I never used those films as teaching materials, for they are clearly subversive to the American way of life.

Some of the information in the file dealt with my activities before coming to Humaluh. The first incident was alleged to have taken place in Wisconsin. The sun had just sneaked over the white pines. The sky above the lake was purple. I was sitting on the shore meditating on a loon that was wildly screaming, "Ha, Ha, Ha, Ha, Ha." The loon's tranquil call echoed in the still air. Suddenly, seemingly out of nowhere, a thousand horsepower motor boat pulling two water skiers ran over the loon. The feathered corpse floated in the wake. Meditation broken, the film showed me turning; picking up a polished Winchester 30-30. Peering through the telescopic sight it showed me aiming at the driver and squeezing the trigger. The driverless boat circled, ran over the water skiers, who joined the loon in perpetual tranquility. The boat roared as it smashed into the rocky shore, there was a horrendous explosion.

Soon silence returned and the film showed me meditating.

When in Utah, I had resented the overpowering ever-present Mormons. I had especially disliked their telling me I was a sinner because I drank beer. I did not believe in the Mormon words of wisdom.

Because I was angry when a Mormon college friend had said I would go to hell; it was claimed by the authorities that I had rounded up my closest friends for a picnic. Sitting comfortably on the fresh green grass of the Mormon Temple in Logan, we enjoyed several martinis. In response to a jangling switchboard, the police dispatched thirty-eight squad cars to the temple. Meanwhile, my friends and I, having left the green temple grass, were climbing a nearby mountain lugging the martini shaker and a mortar. Watching the scene below, we laughed when several squad cars collided.

Raising our martini glasses in a toast, we were supposed to have said, "One for the temple," then lobbed a mortar shell into the imposing stone edifice and drank our martinis dry. A cloud of dust rolled across the west fields. With each additional toast they claimed we had lobbed another shell.

At first we were supposedly puzzled by a roaring sound on the slopes below. Suddenly we perceived a vast horde of saints clambering our way. They may have been left over from the Mormon Battalion of the Civil War. Worried that the approaching men would try to convert us we wedged a rock so that it happened to roll down the mountain, thus discouraging the saints who all fell down. Astutely recognizing we were in danger, my friends and I had one last martini. After eating the olives, we rolled the mortar down the hill. Clambering up a rocky draw, we reached a wooded level shelf that we traversed to a creek that we followed to a wooded grove suspended like a bright green amulet on the dry rocky slopes.

Putting our shoulders to a boulder, we opened a cave that served as our refuge (after we rolled the boulder back across the entrance). Later that evening we listened to the sounds of the searching saints and their officers calling, "To the right harch. To the right harch." Down to our last martini, which we shared like brothers, we were in a crisis. The remaining olives were our only source of food for the seven days we remained in the cave.

After this incident the Mormons banned the sale of alcoholic beverages in Utah.

The old testament refers to the destruction of a temple. Perhaps this incident occurred during a previous incarnation of yours truly, when I was a Roman soldier. In rebuttal I never learned how to use a mortar. The account of the passing away of the fun loving water skiers is doubtful because I never owned a 30-30. Additional information in the folder caused it to be over one foot thick. I could easily imagine a prospective employer forming a mildly negative impression of me after a perusal of the file. If so, that was their affair, for that's the way the cookie crumbles.

In an apparent attempt to discredit me in the eyes of my followers, the following account was slipped to the editors of the Roaring Tide. They rejected it because the man who brought it in wore a suit.

After leaving Humaluh, the account stated, Bauer lived among the goat farm people who raised and worshiped goats. These people attained great proficiency in the production of goat's milk and goat's milk cheese. Similar mountain meadows were visited by Homer, Theocritus and Moschus.

Moschus saw the goats munch plants that were just right. Not too dry, not too wet, but just right. And Pan, the half man half goat god symbolized sex and booze. He got the urge to drink from his man part and the urge to screw from his goat part.

I was supposed to have learned that goats can make it in a minute, and a hassled goat smashes his horns into competitors. I wondered why mankind hadn't imitated goats more. Goats, as part of their courtship ritual piss all over each other. The report said I had written that people doing that would be considered by their friends to be: A. Former friends. B. Perverted. C. Better friends and fellow perverts, D. Administrators.

After living among the goats and devoting many hours each day avoiding piles of goat shit scattered about like hay stacks, I apparently had decided, I was a bigot. How could I like goats and not like goats?

Throughout history they have gobbled up the vegetation and made the land dry and worthless. They have made some contributions. By cleaning away the forest, they have removed the source of much Oxygen. Thus creating natural pollution, and vapors. The grape is grateful however. The Arno once ran full with dancing fish. Now the fish are a historical footnote and muddy silt tickles the toes of marble Roman and Renaissance statues.

The file said my exact words at the time were, "Damn the goats. This land, receiving 180 inches of rain a year, cannot tolerate goats. Slash, kill, down with goats."

It was claimed I had visited the goat farm because goats were worshiped, and no goats were killed. They were allowed to live out their lives and die a natural death. Besides people became addicted into looking into their horizontal pupils. I was supposed to have stopped being nice to the goats. This meant my life was in danger. One night, eyes dancing in the light of a full moon, they said I brought a surplus military MP club; crashing it down upon the skull of the biggest billy. It was as if he was one of the links in ten thousand generations of trolls.

Removing my knife from the scabbard, after encircling each hoof, they said, I slid the knife up each leg and up the belly to the chest. Separating the hide, I nailed it to the wall of the goat nursery causing deep psychological harm to all of the bleating hearts within. Rejoining the meat, I sliced off a bunch of chunks tossing them into a pot containing olive oil, tarragon, rosemary, and vinegar. While the meat soaked I built a fire; while the new moon watched I sautéed, shish kabobbed, and devoured the best of all goats. Bloody deed completed, before the milkers connected udders to stainless steel suckers, I ran past the watching eyes of the mice, reached my car, and hit the road sure I would be shunned by the Goaters. I stopped along the way at a little cafe for coffee. Pleased at the taste of real cream free of goat smell I smiled at the waitress who had a pumpkin full belly and ran a flea circus. They said the waitress heard me ask her if she thought folk singers would sing about the clubbing of the biggest and best goat at the All American Goat Farm. I was supposed to have said, that the goat people would follow my example and start having weekly goat sacrifices; following biblical precepts. I was supposed to have preached that this would cause the herds to stabilize. This cursory look at the contents of my personnel file is mostly apocryphal. For one thing, I like goats. Look in their eyes and you will be intrigued.

Such a mish mash of charges. How could I ever kill a goat? I ask you. If I had cooked goat meat I would have stuck cubes of Picorino cheese in the saucy dish. I would have supervised the digging of pits, built the fire, put the meat on the fire, seasoned it with black pepper, sea salt and lots of fresh garlic sprinkled with olive oil and wrapped with parchment paper. After the coverage I would have let it cook for 24 hours, then dug it up. This would have been using young goats, not the prized oldest goat of the flock. Oh that would have been good eating. I will not even deign to answer the charges of sacrificing on some altar as if I'm some crazy sort of biblical prophet.

# LEO BAUER'S WISDOM REGARDING MAIL AND POSSESSIONS

I am sorting mail and other beloved possessions late at night. A strong west wind is blowing. Occasionally I check the banging door. Nobody is there. I return to my work. Dented brown cardboard boxes contain a scatteration of mailings from publishers, scientific supply firms and amalgamated multi-national junk mail corporations.

For over twenty years I have received annual gifts from a Catholic boys home. I examine the craftsmanship of a well made plastic red head of an Indian chief, and a white plastic Jesus before dumping the icons into the wastebasket, to be followed by samples of cloth from a pants by mail firm, an offer of a months supply of sanitary napkins, and a ditto from the dean saying: Save paper, don't waste dittoes.

The mailings include wildlife stamps and Xmas Seals. Teacher's Union mail follows Jesus into the wastebasket, including pension plan, insurance and retirement options, tire and battery discounts, and other similar professional information including union newspapers lavish with fine portraits of black and white union leaders standing together in solidarity.

I am momentarily attracted to a sample copy of *Believe*, a glossy magazine that contains colored pictures of trees, meadows and churches. The pictures of churches were cleverly taken so as to preclude identification as to creed, so as not to offend the delicate sensibilities of the subscribers who include nuns, ministers, and inspired believers. I rejected having Believe in the bathroom because the paper lacked the moisture absorbing qualities of paper towels and the softness of the toilet tissue prefered by King Farouk who had tender rectal tissue.

By merely spending only one day a month sorting mail, I manage to keep the paper from overwhelming the floor and spilling out through doors and windows. Unfortunately however, although keeping up, I am not gaining. Much of the problem dates back to my years of graduate research spending my time with Swirlopeds, when I had accumulated departmental handouts and professional mail. By the time the Swirlopeds were all corked up and identified, I had accumulated thirtyeight beer cases of assorted paper and other artifacts that are stored next to my desk on book shelves and under tables.

Research memorabilia including scientific publications, abstracts of articles, vials of specimens, my inventions, and other trash occupied seventeen additional boxes.

As a teacher I receive free books from publishers. These tomes join books I have purchased and borrowed. This collection includes two boxes of lab manuals, twenty -seven boxes of textbooks marked-DULL, two boxes of foreign language books marked-UNREADABLE, and eight boxes of magazines including *Ecola Monthly, Ramparts, Animal Behavior, Audubon Magazine, Playboy, Scientific American, the Nation, Psychology Today, New Republic, Time,* and *Evergreen Review.* Additional containers have chess sets, college notes, old files, term papers and examinations.

My complete collection of professional information comes to two hundred and ninety-three boxes.

Less you are assuming I am an amateur in the sorting of mail, while a soldier I worked in a message center sorting and distributing battalion mail into square wooden cubbyholes. When I was a park ranger I spent many productive hours reading and initialing memos, magazines and reports. And during the previous two summers I have spent big chunks of my vacation sorting the husks from the seeds. I have accomplished much, and one day, with great relief, I acknowledged to Cleo, while we were still together, and myself while I was trying to hold it together, in two more years barring dengue fever, malaria, or an accidental fall from a horse, or a head on car accident I'll be caught up.

Like most Americans, I have paid bills, handled stock market transactions and read financial balance sheets, for in addition to other duties I have been a part time financier and accountant. You probably thought I was a pauper, however I owned ten shares of A T & T, and twenty-two shares of General Dynamics (purchased at sixty-on this day it is down to twenty), and five shares of General Motors.

Resting, I cogitate. I admit I am a prisoner of my possessions. I resemble that mythical man Sisyphus who for eternity was required to push on a boulder that wanted to run down the mountain. He was engaging in self-defense. What am I doing? Is this what I am all about? Am I just a scrap of flesh floating down the river of life bumping into the flotsam and jetsam of my career and life? If I was illiterate I would be free of all this nonsense. How I envy prehistoric man. His days were spent in living instead of paper processing.

Look at that box, the one over there by the file cabinet. It contains 195 copies of my Swirloped paper. I sent five copies to scientists in the United States, one to a professor in Germany, and the others to fellow Americans loving natural history. One was Canadian; British Columbian, but to me he's American. Perhaps through the years other scientists will request copies. Eventually I may be down to only 190 copies. At my death my heirs can fight over who gets them.

Walking to a small stiff rectangular cardboard box I pull open the flaps and stare, thinking, the glass caskets, so like astronaut capsules, preserve their contents. So like Sleeping Beauty, my Swirlopeds wait out eternity in alcohol and glycerin. If they were frozen they could be maintained by that cryogenics guy preserving people after death in freezers, waiting for a time when advances in science will enable eager scientists to bring them back to life. They could follow in the *Sleeper* freezer nose steps of Woody Allen. None of these Swirlopeds will be kissed into wakefulness, though by the hundreds they stand at attention tied into groups with rubber bands, waiting for that time once each year when they will be fed, say topped off, with alcohol and glycerin, to continue to be nursed for my life span, much the same as the Atomic Energy Commission must nurse for millennia those seething canisters that repose in concrete sepulchers on the other side of the mountains. When my vials and the AEC's radioactive canisters crack open, will that be Armageddon? The time of the Rapture?

My Cerberus has only one head. With eyes as big and dark as pecans, he guards purple crystals of amethyst and orange crab backs as delicate as babies. Those crystals, lugged on my back from 10,500 feet elevation. Straining that day, I emulated miners returning to civilization, vertebrae compressed; they could have crumbled with broken backs. Like a man packed with gold or diamonds I could have fallen into a fast crystal clear stream like Icicle Crick and swirled to my doom over some far off waterfall.

Cities at my feet consist of skyscraper towers of Kodachrome slide trays, each rotundity holds eighty slides taken to amuse, stimulate and inspire thousands. Oh where are those audiences? The city has a dump, with piles of unsorted slides, rejects, and the effluvia from shattered fibrous boxes orange, green, blue and yellow. It is important to me that this dump not eat my slides. Instead I shall invite people over. Come see my slide show of only eight thousand or is it eighty thousand slides. Come over to my house, I'm going to show you slides for a long, long, time, for days and weeks. To guarantee faithful attendance, I shall chain you audience members to the floor. I know that even while chained you will keep asking, are you almost through? Ah fickle audience. How quickly you get satiated with my life's work. When a choice portrait comes on the screen, instead of praising me you ask, are you almost through?

I will not be easily defeated, plugging my ears with cotton, I insert another tray and brighten the beam. While hating the audience, grinding my teeth, hating myself, I will hear the slides go click a chat, click a chat.

Ideally I don't want to chain my audience. I want the room filled with those like Andy Warholites now Leo Bauerites. Clever worshipful people, hour after hour shall watch my slides while recalling previous pleasure watching films of people sleeping. After an hour things get exciting, because the sleeper rolls over. The camera moves in on a baldhead and a massive rump of a man smoking a cigar. The ash gets long. When the man waves his hand, the audience leans forward, expectant. It is the high point of the film. Will the ash fall? Will the ash fall? My God, will the ash fall? When will the ash fall? Some of the audience is distracted. Medics are called. A man has died of a heart attack. The excitement was too much for him. The film continues. The actor returns the cigar to his mouth. The ash is intact. Everyone relaxes. The drama continues. The smoke floats.

I tell my students, it is easier getting bored looking at ten thousand rocks, than at one rock. They laugh and think I've got a screw loose.

My film, what remains of it, is in brown steel tins. Frequently in the past, the film, approaching the light beam has been grabbed by the automatic pickup and directed sideways into sprocket teeth to be ripped and torn. On the screen my audience sees a flowing bubbling universe form and disappear in the flash of bright light before darkness. The next boxes are eager to talk. Behind cardboard walls the sea roars, each individual wave submerged in the electronic roar. Nearby in a small cove the waves sound like waves should sound, and water drips from a mossy overhang. In that box there is laughter. Maniacs scream. There are the tears of a lost people. An angelic choir fills the air with beauty, unless those sounds recorded in a cave are played at a different speed and witches chanting obscenities shock the audience. There is a way to satisfy every censor. Dirty words at one speed become transformed into Donald Duck when speeded up and everyone will laugh.

Tiring of some words, which are tangled like spaghetti, I toss them into the garbage, never to be heard again.

My plant collection. How carefully I placed green on newspapers and arranged the flowers and leaves between layers of blotting paper.

With exertion I cinched the straps tightly over the wooden slatted lids. The foot high plant sandwich slowly dried. When dry, carefully, I separated the layers I had pressed. I worried about the most succulent strands turning black; they passed with flying colors. Carefully I slid them to a piece of shiny white cardboard. When centered, dabs of white glue anchored the flattened flowers. While I worked bouquets of flowers perfumed the air. Neatly I printed labels with the necessary information required by the plant in its passage through the halls of science.

More delicate than the plants are the insects housed in redwood box containers, smelling of aromatic oils, with fancy joints and close fitting tops. I inspect the collection. The scent of mountains of shiny dull opaque moth crystals pushes against my nose. The piles need replenishing to ward off Dermisted beetles.

Most of the insects are speared through the thorax. The three legs on the one side are neatly parallel to the three legs on the other. The butterfly wings are spread open, in death as in life, though not beating.

Neatly I printed labels giving obituary notices to the creatures with all the important data. The Insects are grouped into order, family and genus. Other white tags give information such as: collected in Humaluh County, Cascadia, July 6, 1969 underneath a rotten mattress at the abandoned Happiness Gold Mine. This information will enable future collectors to return to the Happiness Gold Mine and uncover unusual life. I am proud of my collection but worry about the insects. One jolt to the box and the wings might break and the thoraxes fall. The pins might tilt and the legs touch. If the nearby mountains crumble the beetles will break apart. When I uncover the lid, if I am still alive, I shall see ebony exoskeletal fragments, wing scraps and heaps of wing scales and insect dust.

Loose cover slips are delicate. The pressure of my tongue could smash them. Microscope slides preserve Swirloped parts. They are stained to show the digestive, nervous and reproductive systems, each of which resembles a coat of arms for a family of Angora goats.

An old Red Wing shoebox is filled with dissection tools both tiny and large. There are scalpels, scissors, probes, brain scoops, and tweezers of many shapes. Some are made by and designed by me; tools fashioned of sliced rubber tubing, some cracked and turned yellow with age though not many years have passed. Now I pick up and examine the drawing board I invented. It can tilt at any angle. I used it for drawing through a camera lucida attached to the microscope eyepiece. I thought, I should publish details of my invention. It would keep other scientists from making false drawings. Before using it, I drew creatures fat on one side and thin on the other. A copepod became a monster with a huge head and a tiny tail or a huge tail and a tiny head.

I am in a predicament with my books. At some future time I may again teach biology and zoology. Therefore I must keep the old textbooks and anatomy manuals. I have the cat, frog, pig and pigeon manuals but lack the snark, snipe, python, gorilla and Orca. This encyclopedia of Science is easier to use than the dictionaries of French, German, Spanish and Russian. I bought them to help pass the language exam and to understand articles in foreign journals. This will come in the future. So far I have not completely read any such articles. Some of my extra textbooks are also encyclopedias. I like to read books, and am frustrated because most of my books are for reference and are not to be read. Most of the time when I want to know something I go to my reference collection and cannot find the answer. I remain miserable until I forget what I was so desperate to know.

My college notes have gone unread since the time of taking. I cannot get rid of them because I may need them some day. In addition, if each year of college cost me three thousand dollars, my notes are worth a total of $21,000. If each year of college cost me six thousand dollars, the notes are worth $42,000. I can't throw away that much money. Project this all into the future when tuition and room and board might reach $30,000 a year. Seven years of notes at that time will be worth $210,000. Ask yourself, How much is each page worth?

Some things are more usable including the power saw and drill, other saws, wrenches, hammers, nails, loose screws, and assorted bits of toolish matter including washers and wires. I envy the carpenter who builds and sells the products of his hand's creation. The collector is like a caged coyote on a frozen mound of gnawed bones and feces. The coyote is nervous and would like to escape. If someone accidentally leaves the latch unbolted, the coyote will leap off his pile, jump out the door, and be gone. The collector bolts his own cage and can never escape.

It's all about words. I will call myself a curator. That sounds better. People are paid to be curators. Instead of being a curator of the Orchidaceae wing of the *Smithsonian Botanical Museum* I will be the curator of the *Leo Bauer Natural History Museum,* which bears more than a passing resemblance to the museums maintained by Victorian Gentlemen.

As a curator I am maintaining vases, statues (of wood, ceramics, metal, enamel both ancient and modern original, and Japanese) delicate as eggs or tough as cannon balls, paintings and all manner of fine things. As a curator of art I am also caged, but my floors are covered with fine rugs. From the walls hang tapestries and paintings.

Be I curator or be I collector, I look out over the covered floor and say why? There is no answer. There is the Kodak illusion. Mr. Kodak said, go forth and take pictures and multiply thy pictures and they shall be things of great beauty. My parents said, my what beautiful pictures. You are talented. My professors said, what a fine collection, and I was happy.

Spurred on by praise coming in from many people I knew including lovers, I collected with a vengeance until today I sit surrounded by assorted fragments, scraps of paper, wings, bones, fecal fragments, needles, statues of little old kindly men and women and a pretty green mermaid from the harbor entrance to Copenhagen. By now they may have discovered its absence.

With so much work to do, I hope you can forgive me for falling asleep on the job. Jerking my head to stay awake, I finally give in and sleep cradled by a stack of solicitations from book clubs and magazines. I have a dream. In the dream I sit at a table covered to overflowing with paper. Fluorescent ceiling lights flicker. The light barely reaches the edges of the room. Boxes are labeled: Books to Buy, Conservation Causes, Business, Personnal, Miscellaneous, and Throw Out. I tear open envelopes, rattle jewels to stay awake, extract the contents and scan the appeals for action. I have to decide what to discard or keep. If the decision is to keep, I have to decide where to file it. When I complete action on one box of mail I commence working on another box. When the discard box is full I take it to the garbage can. A custodian in waiting quickly trundles the paper to the incinerator. This keeps the building warm enough to maintain the dexterity needed by me to sort the mail. Though my fingers are warm, my head nods. The college runner, groaning under the weight, dumps a new box of correspondence at my feet and leaves without a salutation. I realize, I have to continue to process the mail. If I refuse, the steady arrival of new correspondence will block the exit and I will be trapped. Nevertheless my head again sags to the desk and I dream.

I was dozy, the room is warm, and I might also have been high on moth crystals and leaking vial alcohol.

**THE POSSESSION VOW**

From this day on my space shall be for living. As I have spent forty years collecting, now I shall spend the next forty years getting rid of what I have gathered. I shall discard the insignificant. I shall examine and retain the best. Unused books, especially reference, shall be sold. I may allow myself two or three magazine subscriptions. The insects shall go to a museum. Also the Swirlopeds shall go to museums. I shall acquire new possessions, only after I have discarded or use up what I now possess. The new acquisitions will be finely crafted and functional or be of high aesthetic value. Never again shall I become a captive of possessions. I shall free myself from the incubus.

In the memory of Gandhi's satchel and sandals.

Leo Bauer

It is the next day. I am reading an ad in a magazine I have just purchased. There is an offer I cannot refuse. I will get fifty dollars in free books for joining a book club. Unfortunately for me, I have forgotten to include I shall not take advantage of bargains in my vow.

# THE CURRICULUM OF DEATH

President Davis, perceiving a common thread, combined diverse elements into a core curriculum for all students. His most brilliant achievement was The Curriculum of Death. It was designed initially as a pilot program to produce soldiers and policemen. A few years later, because of pressure from a small group of influential Sicilians, carrying a lot of weight because of their ownership of casinos, taverns, soda, and tobacco distributorships, prospective criminals were admitted to the program. Prudes among the alumni objected to opening the curriculum to crooks, but accepted the idea after studying evidence showing that in some towns, cities, counties and states many cops became crooks and many crooks became cops.

The laboratories were fantastic. Students were taken to the morgue to view corpses of people who had died violently. After touching the firmly embracing cold bodies, the students crawled onto adjacent slabs to compete in their imitations of rigor mortis. The police and marines assuming rigid straight positions lacked the flair of the criminals who curled as if they had been stuffed into the trunks of cars (already dead or soon to be asphyxiated).

The most popular part of the curriculum were the car chases where the scholars while driving at high speeds shot the tires of their classmates causing them to crash amidst flames and explosions.

The military part of the program introduced exciting battles involving automatic weapons, mortars and hand grenades.

For their final exam the pupils stood at attention watching a man and woman copulate. They got demerits if they made any simple gestures such as licking their lips.

Later, the Curriculum of Death was broadened when civil servants and politicians were admitted in the realization that it was also important for them to learn how to conceal true feelings and emotions.

"Join me in my tour of the Curriculum of Death. The scarred and pitted face of the instructor, Milan Astray, intrigues me.

"Doesn't the man's thin emaciated body make you want to take him to a homeless shelter to get him fattened up and restored to health?"

This urge quickly leaves me as Milan looks into my face. It is as if the instructor knows everything bad I have ever done. I hope he won't tell the administration my secrets. He steps close, I feel like I am a rodent attracted to a snake; a murderer who says hello to the detective; an arsonist who warms his hands on the flames. I remember playing panzers in Utah. The house-to-house fighting was fun. I enjoyed shooting classmates in the gut. I am eager for Milan to begin.

"I hope you are enjoying yourself. Look at the walls before we join Astray and his students. Aren't you impressed? Listen to Astray."

"One entire wall is covered with a fine reproduction of *The Triumph of Death* by Pieter Brueghel. Another wall has a version of *Death's Triumph* by Francesco Traini, featuring reproductions of his fresco showing decomposing bodies in open coffins plus including an exquisite skeleton. These works of art were in honor of the bubonic plague that wiped out half of Europe's population and the *One Hundred Years War* that killed off half of the French from fighting, sickness, starvation and plagues. The war transformed feudal armies by introducing new weapons and tactics. God entered the war by telling Joan of Arc to drive out the English. The English won and Joan was burned at the stake. The French could not withstand the English longbow.

"Illustrations from the *Danse Macabre* are used for festive decorations during the *Curriculum of Death* graduation. During spring break we take our students on a field trip to Guanajuato Mexico for a viewing of the mummies? We ask them to bring cameras. Some students switch majors just to go on the field trip, for where else can a person have so much close contact with dead people? Our pupils get to smell corpses. I bet you envy them, don't you? In Guanajuato, in the old days, if your family could no longer pay the cemetery fees, the workers dug you up and into the museum you went. Some of the people had died of cholera. Some were buried while alive, which provides the viewer with dramatic facial expressions such as when at the time of death they were gnawing their fingers. Perhaps they wanted to get out of their coffins. Unfortunately they stopped adding new mummies in 1958.

"Regarding our writing program; one person can error. However, when many people do the work of one person sequentially all mistakes are eliminated. Joint labor eliminates the prosaic disfigurement caused by individual idiosyncrasies. In most places, the prima donna authors of such garbage, stand up the minute they put words on paper and crow and strut as if they were new fathers or the husbands of many hens.

"In our writing program students learn how to get away from egocentric behavior. Within three months all documents will read and sound exactly the same. Isn't that grand? Homogenized writing. Think of it. Exactly the same, day in and day out, freed forever from those inefficient highs and lows so prized by *prima donna* creative writers.

"I confess. We are not the first. Years ago Federal, state and corporate bureaucracies became aware of the harm caused by super egos. Within a few decades they developed techniques to cut down the superior person and lift up the inferior worker.

"Our pre-civil service students take letter rewriting, report simplification, plus three courses in how to plagiarize; all good solid meaty courses. Extra credit is awarded for themes that are not distinctive, and can never be traced back to the author. By merely copying, without wasting time to think, consider how much money will be saved in government and industry.

"Courses for policemen and criminals include humanity concealment, enemy identification, and simple solutions. Soldiers take The Joy of Killing, War is Holy, and Your Weapon is Your Wife So Sleep With Her. As a side benefit the students form close friendships for future networking.

"Come. Join me. We shall visit the classrooms.

"Leo. You are grinning. Do you think this is a joke? You'll learn something today." Earlier while shaking Astray's hand, I got confused, for the instant our palms touched, his hand retracted like a pocketknife before chopping to his brow.

Astray says, "Listen. *The Star Spangled Banner*. Salute!"

We salute.

The music ends. When will Astray's hand come down? My arm is tired. We remain at attention, hearing *From the Halls of Montezuma*. Astray's mouth opens. His teeth resemble a row of gravestones. I hear marching feet. "Jump you fool. That tank is heading straight for us. Jump." I suck in my belly, lean into the wall. The tank is passing. I feel the vibrations. Listen to the treads.

We can smell gunpowder, grease, oil, and exhaust. The tank passes. "Thank God, we can relax."

Astray's teeth become bullets. Strings of cartridges move to the chatter chamber, tracers glow arcing through the night. While appreciating the beauty I feel warm stickiness run down my leg. "I've been hit. Isn't this supposed to be a tour?" A hear a chopper. Feel the concussion from Mortars. "Did you feel that?"

Falling to earth I feel heat. Flames are devouring buildings. Flaming roof tar drops in blithiting orange globules. A Vietnamese girl runs, flames blossom from her billowing gown, brown hair flares. Mouth open she collapses, burning drops fall into her eye sockets. Briefly I doze. I wake by a stream. "Where are you? Have you been killed?"

People are singing on their way to work. We are in the rice fields of the Plain of Jars. Birds are singing. It is the kind of rural beauty I have always loved. I listen to the propellers of a slow flying bird dog, an

L-19, making lazy circles in the sky. I wave to the pilot. He is friendly. The wings waggle. I listen to the river. People stop and talk. I share chewing gum with a mother and her child. She speaks to us. Says, "We are happy people."

I say, "if I lived in this paradise, I would also be happy."

Bowing and smiling she says, "Excuse me, I have to go home and fix dinner for my husband." The mother and son leave. They are waving as an explosion knocks them down.

Checking myself, I find I am OK. Down the road the mother and child lay next to a dead buffalo. The mother's leg is gone. The boy has lost an arm. I make tourniquets from my sleeves. Villagers arrive from the burning hamlet. They carry the family to a clinic.

I return to the stream, and look at the sky with fear. I will no longer wave at L-19's.

I hear Astray say, "We are fortunate. War is efficient and effective. We can destroy villages or large cities while sipping our coffee."

Rebelling against Astray, I decide to oppose the war with passive resistance. True to my word, for the rest of the tour, I refrain from drinking coffee.

"Again you are by my side. Where have you been?" Astray's teeth are landing lights. F-105's and Convair B 58 Hustlers are landing. Damn it's noisy. I hope this won't damage my hearing.

Astray says, "We are the friends of freedom loving people all over the world. Welcome home boys." He adds, "Think of earlier wars, when it wasn't so easy."

I hear propeller driven planes. A wing, bearing a swastika, breaks away and falls like a maple samara. A searchlight pins the aviator as if he is an insect on a pin. Through the sound of sirens and explosions I hear Edward R. Morrow say, "London is burning."

"Listen to that explosion. The bomber has crashed. I see the flames." My teeth grind grit while we cower under a doorway.

Astray is shouting, "People can sleep because patriots give their lives. An eye for an eye. A tooth for a tooth. Death for death. Kill, wound, maim. Destroy our enemies. Don't take any crap. Kill the bastards. Stand up for America."

The lights come on. The war is over. We feel our legs, stomachs. I am OK. "How are you doing?" I touch my pants. "Shit. I peed in my pants." The air stinks from my urine.

Astray is studying a print out. He says, "Leo. Your breathing was minimal, pulse faint, muscles rigid, posture twisted, emotions fluctuating, and compassion maximum. After six months in our program you would have normal breathing, strong pulse, rigid muscles, straight posture and minimal compassion. Congratulations." Astray extends his hand; his face cracks into a smile.

I hear my own voice trying to be husky, "Thank you Mr. Astray. Thank you." After shaking Ashtray's hand, an act that makes me wince, I watch you shake his hand. Then we leave *The Curriculum Of Death*. We say goodbye to each other and go our separate ways.

I have poignant memories of Astray for the next few days, like flashbacks. My hand hurts. I wonder if it has been injured. Perhaps I have a broken phalange? I hope I don't have to wear a cast.

Astray's strongest supporter is President Davis, an old military man himself. It flattered him when Astray appeared on national television. The entire nation heard his voice, yelling, LONG LIVE DEATH."

"Did you watch him? Did you hear his voice?"

According to some psychologists this is a healthy way to view our destiny. Most Americans and Europeans fear death. When viewing the dead or dying they often say "how great he looks." When Astray sees someone mortally ill, I have heard, he grins and congratulates the person, saying, "I'm jealous of you. I can't wait until I also get to shake hands with the grim reaper. Tell him hello for me, won't you?"

# THE BOEUF AU JUS CURRICULUM

The Schnitzel Haus Gang, during frequent gatherings around the bathtub fire, while gently quaffing beer, happily anticipate the eagerness with which their leaders will acknowledge, accept, adapt and incorporate their suggestions into the college program. Therefore they apply themselves to devising additions to the curricula while devouring *Boeuf au jus.*

Because these men are modest and seek no individual credit, their suggestions are presented unchanged as they came forth while dining off the slab of beef or slowly roasting hog.

THE BOEUF AU JUS CURRICULUM

GENDER STUDIES

All male students are required to take Machismo Maintenance including the growth, cultivation, combing, cropping and curling of chest and nose hair.

All female students are required to take Fuck House Work.

ACADEMIC CURRICULUM

Art: Coping with Rejection, Ear Removal, Sandal Adjusting, How to Live on Pennies a Day, How to Make Big Bucks Doing Tibetan Sand Mandalas.

Accounting: Juggling, Dodging, Laundering, Weaseling.

Chemistry: Alchemy and Incantations, Easy Chemical Experiments including: Lye on the skin or student soap production, how to safely toss sodium on water or ice, how to smoke around ether, fart collection and ignition, and how to generate and collect hydrogen near sparks, Sink Cleaning with Household Lye including: Eyeball washing; care, feeding and utilization of seeing eye dogs, Phenol Spill Control Technology, includes: Instant showering if clothed: Instructions are given on how to keep your nose above water after you collapse, and if naked how to scrub all over while keeping privates covered, Fail Safe Hydrocarbon Combustion Management, includes door jam, and window leaping, fire fighting and damage control technology, shrapnel evasion, personnel identification by the use of belt buckles, shoe lace tips, eye glass frames, and teeth, Hearing Loss Technology. Chemistry students shall in addition each year honor the patron saint of Fireworks San Juan de Dios.

Education: Perambulating Technology (teaching babies to walk utilizing the lecture method), How to Wee Wee (by demonstration), Chalk Board Stance, How to Painlessly Handcuff and jail Twelve Year Olds (low stress method).

Fantasy Studies: How to Make Government Flexible, How to Make Friends with Sharks at Sea and Grizzly Bears in the Wilderness, How to Play with Lions and Tigers, How to Get Extremists to Consider Alternative Points of View.

Literature: How to Replace Reading with Television or/and Listening to Audiotapes.

Mathematics: Toe Counting, Finger Counting, Toe and Finger Counting, Sand Scratching; Clay Tablet Stamping (Sumerian text required), Math of the Pill, Rhythm and Blues, Abacus Technology, Tip Calculating.

Music: Metronome Maintenance, Guitar Smashing, Foot Tapping, Sound Amplification, Hearing Aid Operation, How to be Faithful on the Road While Surrounded by Groupies, and How to Make Accordion Students go to Lessons Without Having to Handcuff or Shoot Them. Music will include an ethnic element including hambone, *Someone's in the Kitchen with Dinah, She'll be Coming Around the Mountain,* and How to Play the Gamelan in One Hour. Another course to be completed within one hour will be how to do Double Breathing; students will be requested to bring instruments including shakuhachis, Tibetan trumpets (zangs dung) and Australian didgeridoos. Percussion, in which students will make and learn to use bullroarers, gum leaves and clapsticks. As part of the class students will take their zang dungs, blowing them into townspeople's ears alerting local spirits and community members to their performances. Classical Native American courting flute music will be performed with full symphony orchestra in the round. Voice instruction will include the always-popular *How to Yodel* textbook.

Twentieth Century Philosophy: La, La, La, La, La.

Poly Sci: I Feel Your Pain, How to Destroy Featherbeds, Belt Tightening, Fat Removal, Earmark Rationalization, The Theory of Transparency.

Physics: Elementary $E=MC_2$, Home Atomic Bomb Construction for Minorities and Cults, Angel Recognition.

Prelaw: Truth twisting, Badgering, Drama, Sincerity, Subpoena Envy, Sheria Law.

Pre-Theology: God Identification, Angel Recognition, Non Believer Identification, Devil Identification, Ostracism, Inquisition (includes the rack, the smack and the torch), Exorcism, Suffering, How to Shake Hands With God, Adulterer Identification includes Stoning of Adulterers and How to Reject, Maim, and Kill Daughters and Sisters who are Rape Victims and How to Convert Moslems and Jews to Christianity. Field Advice for the Ministry: In Oklahoma and Kansas make sure there are no bulls in the pasture of the wedding: pre-requisite: Bull Recognition. Have awnings stuck to steel posts to prevent loss of awnings to wind, Bride Retention: instruction on fabrication of velvet lined diamond decorated collar and leash to keep bride from running off, bungee cord inclusion into leash to snap bride back to altar in case she runs off, Wedding Dress Modification: How to sew one pound lead weights in the seam of the dress to keep the gown from blowing up in the wind, Veil Pinning (to hair to keep veil from blowing off in the wind), Equipage of Bridegrooms and Bridesmaids (with fire extinguishers to put out any fires caused by candles during the candle light transfer ceremony, be especially alert when bride leans over to light candle, important not to lose any brides in sudden conflagrations), Training of Wedding Party in Breath Holding (in case extinguishers used are filled with water, sodium bicarbonate and sulfuric acid; a traditional theological extinguisher from the 19th century). Special Funeral Training: Have members of immediate family entrusted with transport of corpse read *As I Lay Dying* by Faulkner, especially if they live in Mississippi and heavy rains are predicted. In case members of wedding party fall into grave have trampoline awaiting them from within the grave. Dirt Tamping 101 (to eliminate holes under carpet so folding chairs don't tip party goers into grave), Special preacher awards if during career no caskets fall on preacher or preacher doesn't fall into grave and if no corpses are left out too long in the sun. Note: In desert areas corpses need less preservation because they will effortlessly turn into mummies. For further information see *Terry's Guide to Mexico*: 1947 edition which states: *regarding Guanajuato: certain mummified bodies are placed in standing rows along the rows of the vault covered with a sheet from chin to the ankles... The sight is so gruesome that one scarcely ever succeeds in effacing it from the mind. Ladies will not enjoy it and persons with "nerves" are recommended to devote the time to more inspiring sights*: Note: During *Day of the Dead Celebration* in Mexican cities it is customary for bands to play and people to respectfully party: During this event make sure you don't trip and fall into a grave or you may remain in Mexico longer than intended.

Teaching: How to Identify Criminal Behavior Including Evidence Identification such as Tracking Traces of the Writing on Desks, Whacking Without Scarring, How to Lock Children in Closets, How to Subdue Children While Minimizing Screaming.

WRITING: How to Write a Novel in Thirty Days, How to Write Short Stories of Eighty Words or Less, How to Write What Other People Want to Read, How to Pick Your Genera While Picking Your Nose.

## MEDICAL ARTS CURRICULUM

Nursing: Servicing and Manipulation of Physicians, Orifice Identification, Gas Control Technology, Suppository Stuffing, Administration (of enemas), Bed Pan Cooling, Bottom Wiping, Sex Identification, Incontinence Control, Body Cart Wheeling, Food Chilling, TV Tuning, Blip Identification, Shrouding, Wheeling and Disposal.

Pre-Mortuary: Insurance Policy Precognition, Stabbing and Slabbing, Solicitude and Demeanor Mastering, Perpetual Condolence Mask Creation.

Pre-Medicine: Sleep Avoidance, Patriarchal Beneficence, Medicare Form Completion, Bill Collecting, Tax Sheltering and Avoidance (taught by Greek Immigrants), Mansion Acquisition, How to get Elected to the School Board (by running), Suicide Avoidance (includes Golfing, Hasselblad Camera Operation, Flying, Yachting, Safaris (lion pacification, tree climbing), How to Meet Young Women (money flashing), Divorce Negotiating.

Pre-Dentistry: Photography, Sculpting, Mercury and Religion, Injecting; Drilling, Chilling, Filling, Pain Recognition, Clamped Teeth Opening, Finger Reattachment, Smiling, Bank Account Precognition, Depression Management, Suicide Prevention.

Gerontology: Nutrient Extraction, Vitamin Removal From Grains, Vitamin Addition to Grains, Home Freezing of Single Portions, Gourmet Cooking Using Micro Wave Ovens, How to Cook the way Grandma used to after she Developed Alzheimer's, How to Live in Isolation.

Pre-Pharmacy: Telephone Answering, Subservience, Pill Counting With Spatula (by groups of 3 and 2 to 100), Pill Counting (in groups of 5 to 100), Pill counting (in groups of 10 to 100), Label Centering, Plastic Novelty Identification, Perfume and Cosmetic Guidance.

Veterinary Medicine: Bloat relief, Rectal Thermometer Insertion, and How to Get The Arm All The Way Up.

## VOCATIONAL CURRICULUM

Agriculture: Beekeeping includes Bee Identification and Pacification, Broken Field Running, Jumping and Swatting, Creative Panic Management, Underwater Submergence Technology, Wound Balming, Swelling Control Technology Including Butt Identification, Epinephrine and Benadryl Administration, Bee Hive Marketing.

Auto Repair: How to Talk to Customers includes: Do you Need Your Car Soon? Come Back Tomorrow, Sorry, I Can't Find Anything Wrong, I Need More Money.

Ceramics and Carnival Glass Sales and Manufacture: Gift Wrapping and Bow Tying, Cash Register Operation, Counterfeit Bill Identification, Bankruptcy.

Electronics: How to Read Japanese, How to Dress like a Geek, How to Invest Millions.

Furnace Sales: Furnace Kicking (how to Produce and Identify Broken Furnaces).

Landscaping: How to Kill Wildflowers With Sprays, Garden Forks, Dandelion Diggers, and Napalm; How to Transform Natural Gardens Full of Life Into Barren Lands Inhabited by Occasional Shrubs Separated and Surrounded by Gravel, or Bark, Leaf Blower Operation, Night Neighbor Pacification, How to Remove Leaves the Instant They Strike the Earth so as to Prevent the Formation of Soil or Humus, How to Blow Dust and Leaf Fragments into the Atmosphere. This is one of the most successful programs at the college; it is cost effective because it can award certificates of training after a mere forty-five minutes of study.

Locomotive Engineer Training: Supervisory training includes standing on hills with telescopes to keep engineers under constant surveillance, Hobo Stomping, Choo Choo Train Compartment Control Operation, How to Weld Shut Doors on Cabooses so Conductors, and Brakemen Don't Slack off Sitting Inside by a Nice Warm Fire, Recognition of Tie Damage and Smoking Ties While Looking Ahead From Caboose Rear Platform in Winter, How to Pour Oil on Wadding and Brass Bearings, How to get Assigned to Cushy Routes with Automatic Sensors Alongside Tracks to Pick up Heat, Note: If 482 Axles are on train, signal might indicate problem on 200th axle right side, Training of Conductors and Brakemen so as to Punish Negative Whiny Behavior, Methodology: Set brakes on every car; open throttle while engine is pulling, kick off brakes. Causes huge jerk along entire train, brakeman calls up, what happened? Engineer says, nothing. Smooth up here. This trains the brakeman to have a pleasant disposition, The Carrying and Reading of Rule Book the Size of a Zane Grey Novel. There are binders for the rules. Each employee has to read the rules each day including: Air Brake Rules, Operating Rules, and Safety Rules. As long as you don't break a rule you are O.K. However during the daily classes disputes break out over rules. One point of view: it is impossible to go from point A to point B and not break a rule. The teach when asked, is this true? walks away without answering. How to Defy Authority and Break Rules: Come down steps face forwards and avoid three point contact, fix safety goggles so they are low on nose so you can see over them, walk on rails. Note: when caught breaking rules expect to be fired for 5-10 days or longer. One rule frowned on is peeing on tracks, especially on the third rail. Whatever you do, don't pee on the third rail. Example of a goof: On going from A to B to C if the rules state stop at point B and if the train goes to point C, all three crew members can expect to get fired because they are all expected to have read the rule. This would be a Federal offence. All rules are Federal. Hazardous Duty Training: if train is heading for a problem situation such as when the bridge is out, know how to wipe your ass (in case you shit in your pants), fight past co-workers so you are first to jump, Bramble Identification, so you can spot a soft landing place. By regulation all crew members must wear swimming suits under those bib overalls milkman pants so after rapid stripping you are ready to leap away, leap away, timing leaps so as to land away from the nose diving engine while simultaneously recognizing deep diving pools. Rewards of being an engineer: Expect to receive a Ceramic wall plate for every year with a perfect record. Each plate has a different choo choo on it.

Outdoor Recreation: Blow Gun Acquisition, Operation and Maintenance, Puckering, Inhalation Inhibition, Bow and Arrow Hunting Technology, Cow Recognition, Farmer Pacification, Buckshot Removal, Bungee Jumping, Splat Avoidance, Paint Ball Targeting, Skate Boarding, Field Splinting.

Police and Fire Fighters: Fire Hydrant Recognition, Hand Strengthening by Hand Milking Cows, Fire Hose Holding and Manipulation, Fire Recognition Test for Determining how Close you can get to a Fire, Rapid Turning and Panic Running (indicates a failure. Obviously you got too close). Smell test to make sure fire is real, How to Make Down Wind Approach to Fires, Portable Radio Operation so when too close you can get somebody else to fight the fire, Mind Bending class on overcoming fear of fire, How to Run into Fires, How to Perform the Last Rites, Hernia Acquisition, Keeping up With Modern Crimes Including Recluse Reckless Driving, How to Become Disabled and Retire by the Age of Forty, Double Dipping, Dream Vacations in the Bahamas.

Radio announcing: Time Travel, How to Speak Three Times Faster Than Normal, Learning New Vocabulary including We've got to wrap it up, We've got Breaking News, Thanks for a Great Report. You Talked About That? Is That Right? Did You Have Sex? Have You Ever Had Sex?

Investigative Reporting: Are you Willing to Reveal? It's Good to be on This Show. You've done a Stellar Job. We will be on Top of This. Facing a Barrage of Questions, Do They Have a Handle on this? Below us on the Freeway is a White Ford.

Radio Listening: How to Listen to and Understand Someone Speaking Three Times Faster than Normal.

Welding: Chastity Belt Fabrication, Installation and Adjustment, Lock Picking, Sword Fighting, Spear Removal, Commercial Welding For Philosophy and Art Students.

All students shall take a Survey Course of Opportunities for College Graduates including: ditch digging, carpentry, encyclopedia selling door to door, Time Life book selling by telephone, cold call real estate selling, and job finding and career switching.

While my colleagues develop the curriculum I daydream about my pet theory: You turn into your specialty. As an example, the engineers, and scientists who do lots of measuring and analyzing and the accountants who add up figures all day long will become more and more like calculators. The artist will turn into a rainbow or a dab of magenta or turquoise. A pop artist will turn into a bottle of catsup. The pianist will turn into a metronome.

Each teacher will turn into the essence of his course. The welder becomes a pool of swirling molten iron. The pizzazz auto man becomes a 1000 horsepower wheeled bolt of lightning and the nostalgic repairman becomes a model T jerking its lonely way over the washboard surface of a country road. In Future Studies one electronics teacher becomes a pulsing pulsating printed circuit, the other the flashing lights on a digital clock. The registrar becomes a whirring machine spewing out punched cards reading don't fold, staple or mutilate.

In the front office secretaries tell students, "Print your name. Fill out triplicate copies." Other secretaries fill out forms in pentacate, sextacate and octacate. As they work each becomes more and more like the copies (some are more smeared with ink than others). The sameness of their work spills over into conversations, the answering of phones, the lunchroom laugh.

The teacher of secretaries teaching smiling is a real pro. A natural smile would shatter the keyboard, her teeth would go whizzing off into space. History professors have lots of options: One can be the Pope, another FDR, a third Churchill, a fourth debates Darrow. Yelling,

"Back to the bible," his stomach shakes with rage. The herpetologist crawls on his belly, tongue flicking, eyes moving from side to side. The missing link teaches evolution. His arms reach the floor.

Basking in the flames of my fireplace I daydream: Davis has taken the ultimate step of proclaiming: From now on biologists will teach literature and English teachers will teach biology. Once every seven years the dean of students will become a full time student, nurses will become bedridden, zoologists will bathe in formaldehyde and be connected by the vagus nerve to wires for a wiggle-ability inspection, engineers will be planted, heads waving, among the cattails, to observe first hand the bulldozing and filling in of a marsh with landfill and garbage.

Each professor, locked in a windowless room, will have to listen to his or her taped lectures for 168 hours. At the end of that time he will be given blank paper and told to write. This abstract from memory will become his new lectures.

Each student will be given a journal, in which to write down the significant knowledge they have learned outside of school. The summary of this knowledge will be added to the curriculum.

Happy people will be recruited from nearby offices, farms, houses and asylums so as to instruct students and staff on what is significant.

Each of the wealthiest people in the community will be injected with truth serum and asked to explain their value system and how they acquired their wealth. Each minister will be injected and asked to tell his or her sins.

After injection, parents will be asked what he or she really wanted to do in life and why they didn't do it.

Each teacher and each administrator will be required to show proof that they have at least five student friends and at least five teacher friends who are not subject to their intimidation. Those without ten friends will be fired.

Clean sanitary cubicles for laboratory rats will be placed above each food in the lunchroom serving line. The rats will be fed the adjacent food, hardtack and water. The coffee rat will be a nervous creature envious of the Coca Cola rat, Seven Up rat, orange juice rat, and milk rat. There will be a mashed potato rat and an overcooked spinach rat, a cinnamon roll rat, a catsup rat, a Jell-O rat, a green salad rat and a sprouted rat. If a rat passes away, the vital statistics and cause of death will be noted on the cubicle.

Coaches with potbellies and coaches who do not toe the mark will be required to run in tight circles until they fall over. For each student a coach has turned off to a sport, the coach will have to do forty-eight push ups.

Biology teachers will have to eat a pithed frog for each student turned off to biology. English teachers will have to copy Shakespeare's plays on the green board, mathematicians will have to eat isosceles triangles, and drama teachers will have to chew greasepaint. Each administrator will have to listen to ten thousand words of his or her speeches lauding the arts for each play, concert or visiting art exhibit they missed.

Each student will have to listen to ten thousand minutes of lectures for each area of knowledge he or she has rejected.

Each teacher and each administrator will have to apply for a job away from the college once every seven years. Those who do not receive job offers will be fired.

The college ecologist will have to analyze his relationship with the environment including energy consumed and miles travelled.

The sociologist will spin a pointer to determine if he or she will have a new life as a bum or wino, a pothead picked up for possession, an escaped con, or a welfare family parent.

The police science teacher will be arrested during a robbery and get to experience prison and the pleasures of having an affectionate cellmate. Upon his release, he will have to apply for work stating on the applications that he is a felon. If he can't get a decent job outside of the college he won't be able to teach again.

Psychologists will be committed as schizoid paranoids. At the end of a month he or she shall be given the opportunity to try to talk his or her way out of the institution. If they fail they shall remain in commitment.

Faculty hating police shall take jobs as police people. People hating hippies shall join a commune. Teachers of business will devote six months to reading great books of poetry, looking at butterflies and collecting unemployment insurance.

While I strenuously pursue my day-dreams my friends, fueled by beer, and bathtub heat are going ahead full bore.

New math courses included: Don't put Descartes in Front of the Horse, Which Way am I Coming From (Norbert Weiner once asked some friends, which way am I coming from? When told, he said, Good. Then I've already had lunch.), Key Trying (The same mathematician tried his keys on many cars to see, which one was his), Manhole Avoidance Technology (Einstein fell into an open manhole), Earthquake Recognition Skills (a group of mathematicians talking about earthquakes failed to notice a major quake shaking the ground beneath their feet).

Politicians and stewardesses will take Sphincter Control Technology. In addition politicians will take Decision Avoidance, and two years of Jargon Studies. They will be taught how to compose speeches and press releases in a simple way by picking out numbers at random keyed to a list of prewritten impressive phrases. Speeches composed in this manner will save energy because the speaker will no longer have to waste time thinking about what he or she wants to get across to people. These speeches will undoubtedly have as much meaning and will be listened to just as intently as any other speeches. Additional speechifying methods will include writing notes on the palm in pen.

Politics for Every Day Joes and Janes. Textbooks include: *How to be President With a High School Education, How to Use Ignorance to Get Elected, How to Attack Your Opponent, How to Mock the Well Educated, How to Run a Modern State Without Taxation, How to Give People Benefits Without Having to Pay, How to Run Just Wars Without Having to Give up Steaks and Luxuries.*

Christianity Revised for Modern Living. Text: *If Christ Were Alive Today he Would be a Capitalist.*

Radio: teachers will have their own radio shows. Course will emphasize mockery, extremism, and mobilization of the listening audience. Constitutional Law will be explained by ten easy steps.

Economics and Business Management will teach Money Management for the Unemployed, and There is no Free Lunch plus Tax Loopholes.

In Philosophy for Numbskulls students will learn how to generate scholarly work by turning a crank. Individual words will drop from the basket and swirl like snow, the student's task will be to catch the words and paste them into meaningful combinations. Other projects will include looking up words in the dictionary including mother, apple pie, flag, country and freedom. By shaking dice they can objectively determine what to retain. At the end of each quarter they will publish their conclusions in a group essay titled *America*.

Malander swore on his stein that Rearden was teaching a business course in the gym where students, like vertical greyhounds, chased bundles of dollars tied to the tails of mechanical rabbits. The students never caught on: they could never catch the rabbit until after leaving college.

Alfo suggested giving history students more innovative information. He said, "Humaluh can lead the way in elevating Theodore Boz and acknowledging his brilliance." When none of the company admitted knowing about Boz, Alfo explained the Popsicle Theory of How the South American Indians ran on the Inca Roads to Tierra Del Fuego Carrying Flasks of Orchid Nectar Collected in the Jungle by trained moths: Reaching the ocean, flasks balanced on their heads, they plunged into the cold water. Swimming to the penguins, then arranging transportation they were carried to Antarctica, staying long enough to freeze the nectar into popsicles. Upon their return, after paying off the birds with sweets, they exchanged the rest for gold, which became the fabled treasure of the Incas. Other Indians, obeying that old adage, waste not want not, gathered up the old popsicle sticks and fabricated huge rafts with popsicle stick sails, popsicle stick masts, and popsicle stick rudders that they used to sail to the shimmery islands of Polynesia. The Asian islands were populated as the result of this voyage. Boz, former U.S. Counsel to the peaceful Falkland Islands created his fortune in the spoon tip trade. A nervous man with bloody fingertips, he had decapitated numerous spoons while dining in restaurants and cafeterias. This was before he became counsel. Deciding to travel for his nerves, he stuffed years of spoon tips into a duffel bag and awkwardly tugged them clanking and banging up the gangplank. The sailors said, "That guy's nuts."

Once in Brazil Boz traded spoon tips for boa constrictor hides and piranha bellies that are valuable items of commerce. The natives in turn used the tips to make arrowheads, necklaces, amulets, wind chimes and broaches. After selling the snake skins and piranha bellies and becoming wealthy, Boz lost his nervousness. One day while visiting Hong Kong he ate a Popsicle. In mid bite he instinctively knew how the Incas had sailed to Polynesia.

The *Boeuf Au Jus Curriculum* contained a modicum of research. Although not a scientist, Malander claimed that by frequently urinating off his back porch onto his garden he had produced man high basil and oregano and fourteen foot tall tomato plants. He apparently received many compliments for the strong piquant flavor of his salads, spaghetti, and meatballs. In emulation of Malander, some of his students managed to grow and disguise eighteen foot tall marijuana plants that they cleverly turned into sunflowers by wiring yellow plastic flowers to the branch joints. One stimulating research project was focused on showing students how to find sweat glands in pigs.

Magnum said the faculty should fund a roller skate research project. Student nose nerves would be connected by orange glowing Lucite tubes to chest computers. Finger suckers would enable the students to control their speed, because some students get rattled when they have to go too fast. Their fingers stuck to lollipops would remain sweet as long as the student learned correctly. When attention wavered or the scholar misinterpreted information, the lollipop would turn rancid or foul and the input wires would transmit the smell of burning hair, burning rubber and other nasty aromas. Students were taught to say blat for true and blot for false. Teachers looked forward to observing a room full of skate clicking students occasionally banging each other, faces changing from joy to dismay, agony to ecstasy, the whole accompanied by the sounds of learning: blat, blat, blot, blat, blot, blot, blat, blat.

Girodias recommended a course for more mature students. Each candidate would be given 472 pounds of books and 472 pounds of pencils and blank paper. They would be instructed to copy the contents of the books onto the blank pages. After the project was completed they could turn in all 944 pounds to a clerk who, would award them with a college diploma. Perfect work would reward them with a Magna Cum Blat Blot.

Malander mentioned how the administration was already quite progressive in that it measured pedagogical achievement by giving points for abstruseness, hours of courses taken, and numbers of degrees held by faculty. By merely adding up the points they determined the brilliance of a teacher. The curriculum of the college leads the student, after two, four, seven, eight, or nine years, to graduation.

**GRADUATION**

At the end of the school year students and faculty attend commencement. Looking like a huge gathering of shaggy mane mushrooms they march into the gym accompanied by golden triumphant notes from the organ. On this sacred occasion, I along with the other professors sit in the front of the room near the organist who wears a very short skirt. Watching her, I have learned to appreciate music especially when her dress slides up her vigorously thumping thighs. At such times my colleagues and I lean forward so as not to miss anything of the commencement exercises.

The fortunate graduates get to hear Davis and other great people, giants so to speak, assure each of them, that they personally will fulfill the American Dream and become even more successful than their fathers and their father's fathers. And Davis will assure each student that he or she can return at any time to learn more skills and knowledge. They will never have to worry about becoming obsolete because they can always come back through the open door.

Meanwhile as the organist thumps away her skirt sneaks up her glorious thighs while the graduates march out into the world to triumph and gloriously succeed and in eventual humility accept the honors, wealth, emoluments and prestige accruing to those who make it big, and they will have cause to rejoice for they will be fully trained to operate the cash registers, program the machines, insert the tapes, oil the levers, ink the spools, solder the connections, and record voices, until it is time for them to return for post graduate study at Humaluh Valley College.

# ROSTER OF FACULTY AND ADMINISTRATION

President Elmore Davis
Ben Coolsam, Business Manager, Associate Dean of Business
Gary Pantagruel, Vice President
J.M.Keene, Director of Continuing Studies, Director of roving studies
G.O. Telomyup, Director of Counseling
William Atoruk, Director of Minority Affairs
John Jennison Drew, Registrar
Dietrich Eckart, Director of Planning
Rodney Mann, Dean of Directed Instruction
Milan Astray, Director Curriculum of Death

BIOLOGY
John Isawaddy, Chairman Biology
Dr. Bobby Pompa, DNA Litany
Dr. Robert Jackson, invertebrate zoology, vertebrate zoology
Leo Bauer, invertebrate zoology, natural history

PHYSICAL SCIENCES
Alfo Narf, Physics, behavior of gases
Thomas Seabeck, electronicss
Dr. Ollie Ivar Sharp, physics
Bev Frazier, chemistry

HUMANITIES DIVISION
Joseph Apfelboeck Head of Humanities Division. Theology, sociology
Mary Jamison, philosophy
Tom Magnum, history, leader of Crunch and Munch Chorus and Band
Henry B. Olmsby, history
Tom Mun, economics
FINE ARTS
Barnaby Thomas, chairman of fine arts
Joseph Malander, art

MUSIC
Dr. Peabody, head of music department. Violinist
Francis Butler, music, chorus leader
Paul Dallapicolla, music, President of Humaluh Valley College Teachers Association

DRAMA
Romeo Canterberry, acting
Thomas Thaumaste, speech
Mary Jamison, speech

LITERATURE, LIBRARY STUDIES, CREATIVE WRITING, DISSIDENT STUDIES.
Nolen Volens, creative writing, actor
Phoebe White, literature, business English and English for auto mechanics
Silas Thrigwhistle, literature. Threw out Waste Basket Papers
Maurie Girodias, head librarian
Silas Thrigwhistle, literature

HEALTH SCIENCES DIVISION
Ed Bellerophon, Head of Health Sciences Division, President of Humaluh Valley College Teachers Association

VOCATIONAL TECHNICAL DIVISION:
electronics, auto mechanics, welding
Walter Simons, Vocational Technical Chairman, electronics, auto mechanics, welding

BUSINESS
Henry Rearden, business mid-management

Mrs. Helena Johnson, president's secretary
Bob Pyle, President Valley Manufacturing, Chairman of the Board
Mr. Fleisch, Member of college board
Otus Tyton, Janitor, edited and published *Wastebasket Papers*